The Grant Conspiracy

The Grant Conspiracy

WAKE OF THE CIVIL WAR

Lee Martin

ISBN: 1516941160
ISBN 13: 9781516941162
Library of Congress Control Number: 2015913647
CreateSpace Independent Publishing Platform
North Charleston, South Carolina

Dedication

To my lovely sister, Arlene, with whom I have shared a lifetime of joy mixed with hardship and adversity, yet blessed with laughter, and to our wonderful brother, Don, who has always been our hero.

Prologue

In early summer of 1880, near the midnight hour, Matt Tyler left a carriage some distance from the White House. Icy wind and driving rain, tearing through the trees in his path, chilled him to the bone, whipping his long coat and yanking at his Stetson as he held it down.

Matt leaned into the wind. He favored his right leg, as he followed a uniformed army major, their boots sucking mud. A gnarled branch wrenched from a tree. It jumped in front of him as he dodged it and dodged it again.

The sweet, wet scent of red roses led them toward the side of the illuminated building.

At thirty-three, Matt, a veteran of the War between the States, the Chisholm Trail, and a few wild years before practicing law, had gained great self-confidence that now dwindled. Nothing prepared him for the apprehension he felt about this meeting.

Matt stood six feet tall. Husky more than handsome, with a cleft in his strong chin, he had unruly dark-brown hair with a cowlick never quite contained. His dark-brown eyes glistened with a penetrating gaze.

Tough and resilient, and always spirited, he had been in control of his life and work until this night. The roaring wind and rain slammed into his face. He longed to turn back.

The White House intimidated him.

Matt caught up with the sour, gray-haired officer. "Where are we going?"

The major didn't answer and continued around the back to a door marked for servants.

The major knocked on the door. A young, pink-faced lieutenant in full uniform opened the door to let them inside and led the way through back, barely lit, but shining corridors.

Matt's annoyance faded as they entered the president's private office.

Lamplight gleamed in a room simply decorated with gold and dark wood.

Matt saw a grand painting of George Washington on the wall. Crossed swords glistened on the wall behind the desk. The Star-Spangled Banner gracefully draped a walnut pole in the corner. Paintings by Remington and others of the western frontier hung on walls in gold frames.

A pitcher of lemonade and a dozen glasses waited on a walnut side table.

Standing behind his desk, President Rutherford B. Hayes, fifty-eight, wore an ill-fitting but favorite blue suit. He was strongly built, of average height, with deep-set blue eyes, graying auburn hair, and a full beard. He was a religious man, lawyer, and Republican, and though he appeared no more impressive than a street merchant, his very presence intimidated even Matt.

Near the desk, the president's aide, Colonel Harriman, now gray and sixty, a civilian with a cane and nervous tic, stood stiff with a poker face. Harriman had put on weight, as his tight vest and black pinstripe suit revealed. His skimpy beard, near white, added to his mystery.

The major and lieutenant left the room, closing the door behind them.

"Now, Mr. Tyler," Hayes said, "I assume the colonel has advised you of our problem."

"No, sir."

"Mr. President," Harriman said, "I thought it safer not to send word."

The president sat down. Harriman remained standing.

Matt, nervous in the office surroundings, held his hat in his hands. He knew a lot about Hayes from the daily paper and reports during the war. The president had been a major general with the Ohio volunteers. He had fathered a daughter and seven sons. A Methodist, he had a wife who served only lemonade and kept the White House pure and Christian.

"I notice you're still favoring your right leg," the president said.

Matt shrugged, surprised, so uneasy he wanted to turn and run.

President Hayes finally got to the point.

"We're told you're going to decline that offer from Colorado."

Matt wondered how they knew so much about him. He took a moment to come up with a respectful response. "Yes, sir."

"We also understand you had wanted very much to go to the Rockies," Hayes added. "You're a hunter and a fisherman, and you would have been in your element."

"Yes, sir."

"Instead, you're staying here to get married," Hayes said, "to the judge's daughter."

"This fall—yes, sir," Matt said, further surprised.

"But their offer of three hundred a month is a lot of money for a young lawyer," Hayes said.

"Who told you, sir?"

No response, so Matt continued.

"Sir, they only wanted me because I won with that writ on property rights. Before the Supreme Court."

Hayes leaned back in his big leather chair, fingertips together.

"Yes, you're a fine young lawyer," the president said, "but that's not why that firm in Mountain Springs wants you out there."

"Sir?"

Matt, still intimidated by the office, looked from the president to Colonel Harriman, then back to Hayes.

The president leaned forward. "They know you saved Grant's life during the war, and Grant would seek you out."

Matt shrugged. "He never has, sir."

Colonel Harriman clarified. "He would if you were in Colorado. And they know that. You see, Mr. Tyler, Grant is touring Colorado with his family, but we have word he's also making plans to travel the Rockies on his own, which will make him an easy target. We think they want you as a draw for Grant, so they can lay a trap for an assassination."

Matt squirmed. "How do you know this, sir?"

"We received a letter," Colonel Harriman said, "from a law clerk at that same firm in Mountain Springs. Leander Pocket. He was convinced Grant would be murdered, but he gave no details except that the law firm was behind it. When we sent an agent to talk to him, we learned he had disappeared. The agent reported unrest but could not put his finger on anything certain. He had an earful from the local newspaper, but it was all speculation."

Matt worried where this might be going.

Colonel Harriman continued. "The mines at nearby Silver Gulch are run by Red Ferman, a suspicious character, and a lot of Southerners. He's also the biggest client for the law firm."

Hayes clasped his hands. "We want you to work for us, Mr. Tyler. Take the job, do your own investigation. And yes, you could be putting your life on the line. Would you do that again for Ulysses Simpson Grant?"

Matt had only one answer for that. He nodded.

"But my going could do just what they want, get him in their trap," Matt said.

"Without you," Colonel Harriman said, "they'd just find some other way. With you there, maybe you could do something about it."

Colonel Harriman handed him the letter from Pocket, written on the law firm's stationary.

Matt stared at the letter and read it aloud.

"Dear Mr. President, this law firm plans to murder General Grant when he comes to Colorado. Leander Pocket, law clerk." Matt frowned. "Not much to it."

Matt returned it.

Colonel Harriman folded the letter. "So will you go?"

Matt could do nothing less than nod his head.

Harriman smiled. "You can still get married and have your bride join you when it's safe."

The next morning, in the plush parlor of a fine house in Washington, Laura Millican, blonde and pretty, stood with her back to Matt. Her blue dressing gown, decorated in silks and lace, fell in folds around her. Twenty-five, spoiled, and pampered, she knew how to get her way.

Laura smelled of fine perfume. Her every movement held grace and polish.

Rosewood furniture, red velvet drapes, and a lush, blue rug made it feel warmer than the fire in the hearth.

Matt, standing numb with hat in hand, had misgivings.

Not the type of bride his folks were hoping he would find she would never live on the farm. Just the same, he loved her.

Her sweet voice suddenly turned cold and nasty, her back to him.

"That's why you're here at this horrible hour?" she demanded.

"It's good pay," Matt said, lamely. "A great opportunity."

He came up behind her, his hand on her shoulder. He turned her to face him. What he saw in her face and gaze startled him. The affection she had professed had been replaced with stubborn selfishness and a snobbery hidden until now.

Shattered, he withdrew his hand.

"Laura, don't you want to see the Rocky Mountains?"

"Absolutely not."

"But you led me to believe you would be my wife."

"I said the same things to Robert Finch."

Matt, stunned, stepped back, as she continued.

"And to Douglas Nolte."

Matt could only stare, as he backed farther away.

"You think yours was the only proposal?" she asked, nose in the air. "It amused me to think I could make a gentleman out of you. I was wrong. You'll always be nothing but a cowboy."

Matt stood speechless.

"You must have known I was only teasing," she said.

He kept backing away, hurt and bewildered, then angry as he put on his wide-brimmed Stetson. He felt as if a hammer had struck his heart. Sweat formed on his brow.

Matt knew if he stayed a minute longer, he'd be telling her exactly what he thought of her, and how she had led him on, all the while with others in tow. She had toyed with him as if his heart and affection were of no real matter.

Nothing in his life had hurt him as much as this. Not even a bullet. He could barely muster a painful farewell.

"Good-bye, Laura."

She offered her hand to be kissed, but he ignored it.

He turned, spun on his heel, and headed for the door.

"You're no gentleman," she called after him.

Matt left, closing the door behind him.

Never again, he told himself.

CHAPTER 1

At the family farm in Illinois on a starry night one week later, Matt and his father, Nate Tyler, sat on the porch swing. They wore heavy coats that barely kept out the icy wind. Yet Matt enjoyed every minute of it.

Lamplight glowed through the white curtains on the window behind them.

They looked across the dark plowed field to their right, and then to their far left at a herd of cattle, horns gleaming in the pale light. Father and son, always close, understood each other.

"You know, Pa, we never got around to just raising horses."

"Maybe someday."

Nate Tyler, in his sixties, had a hard, lean body with wiry hands from years of working the land. His handsome face had deep wrinkles from the sun. Weary, Nate had never known an easy day and had never wanted that for his son. Now that Matt was practicing law, Nate had also hoped Matt would have an easier life. Now he could see the dark change in his son.

"There's one thing you have to remember, Matt. Just as it takes a lot of manure to grow a good crop, everything that happens along the way just makes you a better man."

"I sure hope you're right, Pa."

"And you'll find the love of your life when you least expect it."

"Never again."

"I had my heart broken twice before I met your ma. Trust me, she was worth the wait."

"The only thing on my mind right now is Colorado."

"Don't worry, son. We'll forward any letters to Washington, and we get any back, we'll send 'em to you hidden in a box of cookies."

"I'll be sending a test letter direct, but there won't be any secrets in it. Just a phony thanks to Colonel Harriman for arranging a friend to take over my practice."

"Just remember we're here and ready to help."

"Thanks, Pa. I can't let anything happen to the general."

His mother, Janet, pretty and gray in blue calico with a white apron, came out the door with a tray of milk and cookies. Chubby and jolly, she had dimples.

"Ma," Matt said, chiding her, "I'm not a kid anymore."

"Yes, you are," she said, "and so is your father."

They looked fondly at her bright, sweet smile and had to laugh.

A freezing Friday night in early summer of 1880 in a lush green valley, deep in the Colorado Rockies, greeted Matt on his stage ride west. The silver moon escaped the clouds now and then, casting eerie light on the snowcapped mountains that seemed to crowd the valley even more.

The gilded stage hit every rock and dipped in every rut on the road.

Riding up front with the driver, Matt wore his tan, wide-brimmed Stetson, new black boots, and a tan duster over his dark-blue, store-bought suit. Under his coat, his gun belt hung out of sight.

Matt felt every bump on the road, as the stage bounced and swayed.

At the same time, he enjoyed sitting next to Greyson, the old driver, a bearded man with floppy hat who reminded him of his father.

Greyson, a lonely man, enjoying his time with Matt, slapped the lines as the six bay horses trotted ahead of them. He let them walk across a low water creek, splashing water that sprayed back at them.

Nearby in the pale light, to their left, a loose rope dangled from the barren hanging tree.

"Yup," Greyson said as he followed Matt's gaze.

The stage bucked across the green, wet meadow as it headed for the distant, flickering lights of Mountain Springs. As they approached, Matt's mind filled with thoughts of his mission, but his excitement at being in the Rockies could scarcely be contained.

Greyson gestured to distant meadows. "Son, you'll find elk, mule deer, grizzly bear, and just about every kind of critter you might want. And as for fishing, you ain't seen trout like we got. Big, fat, and juicy. They jump right up and grab your hook."

"Great country," Matt said with a grin.

"You ain't seen nothing yet, son."

Greyson soon turned west into the main street with its bushy trees and window boxes of red-and-white flowers. It looked peaceful and quiet with occasional lanterns in front of buildings.

Matt saw a small but prosperous town. No drunks lying around. The street muddy but clear of debris. The boardwalks seemed in good repair and well swept.

An empty wagon and team stood down from the hotel. At the rail farther west, near saloons, a few horses seemed resigned to a long wait.

Greyson pulled up the team in front of the stage depot, just before the Grand Hotel, on the south side of the street. He set the brake, secured the lines, and climbed down.

Matt stepped down with his briefcase.

Two elderly couples, shaken from the ride, left the stage as Greyson assisted them on the steps. He directed them to the hotel entrance. Their luggage would follow later.

Greyson went to the rear of the stage to open the boot.

Matt recovered his carpetbag. His duster opened enough to reveal his gun belt, strapped under his suit jacket. He grimaced, for his new shiny black boots hurt his feet.

He pushed his Stetson back from his brow. He felt more in place on the frontier than in Washington. He didn't miss the capital or its fast pace. He felt at home in a new land so spectacular, he knew he could look forward to a great view come sunup.

Two handlers came to take remaining luggage to the hotel.

A stout, bearded man from the stage line came to board the coach and drive it to the livery.

Greyson watched it drive away, and then he gave Matt directions to the boardinghouse, pointing along the south side of the street to the east.

Matt began walking down the boardwalk, favoring his right leg.

He noted the one-story, silent courthouse on his left. Across the street, he saw the brick building with the gilded sign that read FROST, HANCOCK, and EBERLEY—LAW OFFICES. A lamp burning near the front door cast a glow on the sign. He would be working there in a few days. Reluctantly.

Matt had always been a sole practitioner, but now he had a mission of great importance. He must let nothing distract him. Nothing must happen to the general.

He already knew, from Colonel Harriman, that Frost and Hancock were the partners who were Southerners. Eberley, a Union veteran, mostly retired, had been the partner with the money.

Wimpy clouds partially covered the moon. The night shivered in damp and cold.

His boots seemed louder on the boardwalk.

As he walked farther down the street, Matt approached an alley. The next building beyond the alley had a sign on the corner reading Pop's Café. Lights showed in its windows.

At the alley entrance, before he could cross, he heard an animallike noise, a deep plaintive wail to his left. Something dying, he thought, his defenses rising.

Matt turned to see a man on the ground, crawling toward him between the courthouse and the next building.

A corner lantern spread pale light on the young man with bloody fingers grabbing frantically at the dirt, pulling himself along on his belly. The back of his head showed heaps of blood that had spread to the back of his gray suit. His legs dragged behind him like useless sticks. His pale-blue eyes, round and glazed over, looked crazy and wild. He smelled of ugly death. His gaze suddenly fixed on Matt's boots.

Matt's stomach reeled with memories of the War between the States that ended just fifteen years ago—the dead and dying, pieces of men trying to survive. The memories came rushing back like a flood, engulfing him. He pushed his Stetson back from his forehead. This was not the welcome he had expected.

Breath tight, Matt scanned the alley without moving. He saw nothing, only the far end of the alley and distant houses spread through the aspens. All remained silent, except for snorting horses at the hitching rails farther down the street.

He turned and called to Greyson, who stood in front of the hotel. The old man hurried over. They knelt by the dying youth and turned him on his side.

The driver shook his head. "Well, I swear. It's Pete Banner. One of the law clerks at your outfit. Sure looks like he's a goner. I'll get the doctor and send for the sheriff."

"I'll have a look out back."

Greyson stood and hurried away.

Pete, the wounded youth, barely able to lift his head, stared up at Matt with glassy eyes. His parched lips kept moving, but only agonized groans came forth. Matt, his stomach reeling, tried to remain calm for Banner's sake.

"Who did this?"

Pete's mouth opened with a gasp, his fingers involuntarily clawing the dirt as he went silent, still on his side, with his life gone. Matt gently closed Pete's eyes.

Sickened, Matt stood up, drawing his army Colt and walking down the narrow alley between the courthouse and the next building. Very slowly, he limped alongside the death trail in the pale moonlight. Sweat trickled down his neck.

He wondered if a bullet would stop that kind of mad killer.

But there were no signs of anyone to be seen.

At the back end of the alley, he found kicked-up dirt and blood next to the rear of the courthouse. He knelt, checking the bloody scene in the now rising moon. Any boot prints had been brushed over. He could not tell how long Banner had been lying there before crawling toward the street.

The moon slid behind the drifting clouds again, leaving the night even darker. Rows of houses spread before him, most with little white fences, but no one stirred. Curtains remained drawn across the windows with some showing light from inside. He saw smoke from some of the chimneys.

He stood a long moment, drinking in the cold night as if hoping to grasp a sound. The dark held only stillness and the fragrance of white roses and fluffy lilacs. He holstered his weapon and moved back up the alley to where Banner lay near the boardwalk.

The elderly doctor, hatless, wearing spectacles and a coat over his gray nightshirt, came hustling over in his slippers and knelt beside the body. Greyson and Matt stood nearby, watching as the doctor checked Banner.

Matt hated the sight of a dead man. In his memory, he saw the black cannonballs bouncing through the bright green grass like some child's toy, and then the ones that had the range, blowing men apart. It echoed in his ears, darkened his vision, haunting him like a bad dream.

"This is your second law clerk," Greyson said. "The first one, a fellow named Pocket, he up and disappeared. Probably dead. Now Banner gets it."

Matt recognized Pocket's name, the one who had written to Washington.

Grant's life had to be in danger.

The doctor, his bald head gleaming damp in the glancing moonlight, stood up with the driver's help. "He's gone. You can send for the undertaker."

Greyson adjusted his sweat-streaked, floppy hat and scratched his head as the doctor left, and he turned to Matt.

"Well, son, ain't much of a welcome for you."

"Why is someone killing law clerks?"

"And both from where you're gonna work. Makes you think, don't it?"

Matt swallowed hard, his mouth bitter dry. He could smell trouble. It smelled like death.

"Look, son," Greyson said, "this is the end of my run, and I don't go back till morning. The passengers are in the hotel, and the sheriff's coming. The coach and horses are being taken care of, so why don't we have supper at Pop's?"

"I'm supposed to check in with Mrs. Ledbetter's rooming house, and I'm late."

"You won't get nothing to eat past seven, so you may as well chow down with me."

"I've kind of lost my appetite."

"Wait'll you taste Pop's berry pie."

They paused as the lean sheriff, about fifty and wearing a thick gray, handlebar moustache, came walking across the street in his shirtsleeves, star on his black leather vest, and carrying a shotgun. His worn tan Stetson, back from his forehead, revealed the lines so deep in his ageing but otherwise handsome face. He looked like a man weary of his job.

Greyson greeted Hicks with obvious respect.

"Sheriff Hicks, this here's Matthew Tyler, a lawyer from back east. He's come to work for Frost, Hancock, and Eberley. And he's the one found Banner."

Hicks shook Matt's hand. "Banner say anything?"

"He tried to, but nothing came out." Matt gestured down the alley. "There's sign of a struggle and a lot of blood. No tracks to follow."

The sheriff went over to the dead man as the skinny undertaker, wearing black and carrying a tarp, joined him.

The sheriff and undertaker remained in the alley between the courthouse and Pop's Café.

Greayson turned Matt away from the scene.

Matt could only think of the general.

Late that Friday night, leaving the sheriff and undertaker with the dead body in the alley, Greyson, the coach driver, and Matt entered Pop's café on the adjacent corner.

Matt liked the small, very clean restaurant, which had a half dozen tables with checkered red and white cloths and a bakery out back. They were the only customers. They took a back table against the wall with no window behind them.

Pop, a stooped, grumpy, and gnarled old man in his shirt sleeves, wore a clean white apron. Matt liked him right away. Pop had baggy pants, heavy gray brows and a beard, but no hair on his head. Matt leaned back as he took their orders for steak and beans.

Pop and Greyson bantered back and forth. Pop laughed and returned to the kitchen.

Greyson sought to cheer Matt, who welcomed the change of conversation.

"You married, son?"

Matt shook his head. He had shut that painful door and had no further interest in tying the knot with anyone. Never again could he trust a pretty woman.

"You born in Washington?" Greyson asked.

"Illinois. My folks have a farm. Wheat. And cattle."

"You sound homesick."

"Ma's a peach. But it's Pa I miss."

"Look up to him, I expect?"

"If I'm ever half the man he is, I'll be happy."

"So I can't figure why you come all this way just to work for a couple of Rebs. Oh, one partner's a Yank and mostly retired, but he's not the problem."

"Meaning?"

"Reckon you'll find out soon enough."

"Many lawyers in town?"

"Besides your outfit? A half dozen. And we got us a county prosecutor, a real Southern gentleman and right snooty."

"You don't like lawyers."

Greyson chuckled. "Does anyone?"

"But for a small town, it sounds like a lot of litigation."

"Well, it's the county seat. We're halfway between Poncho Junction up a ways and Alamosa, down south of here. And Frost's been bragging how your being here is gonna get Grant to come visit. And he claims all the to-do will get us a railroad."

Matt couldn't help but be annoyed with not being hired for his skills.

They were busy with their meal.

Matt liked the old man and wanted to change the subject.

"What's there to do around here?"

"Well," Greyson said, "you mean besides hunting and fishing?"

Matt leaned back and nodded.

Greyson had to grin. "We got us a church. But on the west end of town, there's the Red Light Saloon where they got two women, except sometimes they don't smell too good. There's a couple other places. But the worst is Bittner's gambling hall. You can lose your poke at faro, chuck-a-luck, or whatever. He's a nasty one, so don't cross him."

Pop came to refill their cups and take their plates.

"Listen, son," Pop said, "ole Greyson here will talk your ear off."

Greyson made a comic face, as Pop shuffled away.

"You have Indian trouble around here?" Matt asked.

Greyson paused to down some more coffee, and then he answered.

"Mescaleros some time back, but lately they been raiding south to Mexico. As for the Utes, the miners and the government keep crowding 'em west across the mountains on account of all that gold and silver. Last year, that Indian agent Meeker was killed. You can only push the Utes so far, and they're real good when it comes to fighting."

"What they need is a good lawyer."

"You?" Greyson grinned. "Cock sure of yourself, ain't you?"

"You have to be, if you want to win."

"Well, son, when I was your age, I was just as big a fool."

Matt nodded with a grin. He leaned back as Pop served them hot steak and beans. He refilled their coffee cups. They both ate hungrily and fell silent until they were stuffed.

Pop again refilled their cups before taking away the empty plates.

Matt felt calmer now. "Town seems right peaceful, except..."

"You mean except for a murder?" Greyson grunted. "Well, some bad fellahs come and go. We had some what used to run with the Youngers and James boys, but they didn't stay long. On account of Sheriff Hicks."

Matt sipped his coffee. "They're afraid of him?"

"Hicks has a reputation."

Matt listened intently as Greyson continued.

"But we still got Red Ferman and all his Southerners over at the Silver Gulch mines, while this here town is mostly Union. Most of 'em on both sides just want to put the war behind 'em. But there's always some crank. And when somebody starts killing law clerks, you got to think about all them claims your firm is winning for Ferman."

"I don't see a connection."

"You will, son. If you don't, our newspaper lady will set you straight."

"You mean, a woman runs it?"

"Yeah, just wait and see. She's not very big, but she's real tough and right crabby."

"I can handle little old ladies."

Greyson laughed, leaned back. "Yeah, sure."

Later that night at lawyer and partner Jared Frost's magnificent mansion on a hill north of town, his wife Morna, a thirty-year-old, exceptionally beautiful and sensuous woman, primped in her bedroom on the second floor. The room looked plush with gilded trim and rich, maroon velvet drapes.

White and yellow roses smelled sweet from the vase on a chest of drawers.

She perched in front of her dressing table and gold-trimmed mirror, combing her long, wavy blond hair. Her blue, shiny silk nightgown barely hid her full figure.

Eyes as dark blue as a mountain lake added to her glory.

Morna smiled to cover her sadness. She felt she had lost her way, but here she waited, still trying to find love and romance, something that had eluded her in her marriage. In her looking glass, she saw a very lonely woman. Beauty and wealth could never fill her heart.

In the reflection, she could also see Red Ferman, leader of the Rebel miners and her husband's biggest client, as he sat on the huge bed in his long, red underwear. A clean-shaven, husky, burly man with a ruddy face, red hair, and a romantic figure at fifty, Ferman made her feel admired and wanted.

Morna had no friends and needed affection. This big man seemed to love her, but being terribly sure of himself, he never paid much heed to her feelings, only his own.

She could see that he had holes in the socks still on his big feet.

Nervous, his voice cracking, Ferman scratched his chest. "Are you sure Frost won't be back until tomorrow night?"

"Yes, but he may stay in Denver even longer."

"If you were my wife, I'd never leave. And you'd have live-in servants."

"Jared doesn't like them lurking around the house. But we do have a cleaning lady who comes twice a week. We have a visiting cook, as he calls her. And I get so lonely."

"You have friends."

"The ladies in town are very polite, and they will come to tea, but I stopped inviting them, because they never invited me in return. I found out later that their husbands objected because of Jared. And Jared didn't like it either. I think he was always worried I'd say something he didn't want heard in town. And so here I sit in my castle, all by myself."

"Yeah, so why don't you leave him?"

"I'm afraid of him, Red."

He didn't pay heed to her serious posture.

"And I have nowhere to go," she added. "No family left in Kansas."

"I know how that feels," he said.

"Have you seen her?" Morna asked. "His woman in Denver?"

"I don't think anyone has."

Jared, though discreet, caused her pain with his actions.

Ferman watched as she fluffed her hair.

"Morna, you're so blasted beautiful."

She turned to smile her thanks.

Both Red Ferman and her husband, Jared, had twenty more years than she.

She paused to stare up at the new cobwebs in the gold-laced corner of the high ceiling. The strands gleamed silver in the lamplight and stretched to the green velvet drapes. The frontier came into the house whenever it chose.

Sometimes she had the urge to run away from here, but without Jared Frost, she'd have no money for so much as food. He had a very tight rein. And without this redheaded scoundrel, she'd have no love and affection, only Jared's lust.

With no family and no close friends, she remained alone except for these passionate encounters.

She stood up from her dressing table.

"Jared's been acting so strange."

Ferman didn't answer as his gaze followed her every curve.

"He's covering up something that makes him very unpleasant," she said. "And sometimes in his sleep, he shouts and fusses about the 'colonel.' Do you know any colonels?"

"Any fool can claim he was a colonel in the war."

She moved toward him. "And why does that newspaper woman write all those nasty editorials about the firm, and about you?"

"Morna, I leave all that outside the front door."

He smiled and reached for her, as she moved closer.

Suddenly, the loud barking of a large dog echoed from the night and slammed against the window like a hammer. With a grunt, Ferman sat up.

"It's just some old mule deer," she said. "That dog barks at anything. And he doesn't like being tied up."

"I hear a wagon."

"It can't be."

Frantic, he tried to swing off the bed while tangled with a blanket. He lost his balance, tumbling to the floor with a complete roll and crashing down on his rump with a loud grunt.

He scrambled to his feet while she giggled, then sobered at his glare.

"It's not Jared. Besides, you're bigger than him."

"He's a good shot."

"Oh, those duels. They don't mean anything."

"The men are dead, and he ain't. Besides, killing him doesn't fit in my plans. I need him right now."

"For what?"

As he hurriedly gathered his clothes, she walked to the tall window. Peering between the velvet drapes into the moonlight, her dark-bluc eyes went round.

She covered her giggle. "My God, it is him."

"Has he gone past the window?"

"Yes, but it's too late to go down the stairs. And if you try to jump, you'll get hurt."

"Morna, I stay here, somebody will really get hurt."

They could still hear the dog barking at the end of its long chain. The barking appeared to follow the wagon out of sight around the house, then abruptly fell silent. They could hear no further sounds, except Ferman's heavy breathing.

Ferman pulled on his black felt hat, buckled his gun belt over his red underwear, carried his clothes and boots, and then hurried over, as she fought to lift the windowpane. He grabbed it and slammed it upward, nearly shattering the glass, leaving a big crack down the middle of a side pane.

They heard a door slam downstairs, inside the mansion.

He charged through the open window like a cannon, falling outward and grabbing wildly for the nearby aspen. He missed and went sailing down like an overturned frog, arms flailing as he rolled over in space.

He landed on his rump in the wet grass with a loud grunt.

He jumped up with boots in one hand and clothes in the other. Limping the first few steps on the damp grass in his stockings, he frantically watched for the big German shepherd in the moonlight, but there was no sign of it.

Morna giggled, her hand over her mouth, watching from above with delight. He crazily ran north up the wooded hillside, hopping and jumping like a lost rabbit, his house waiting on the next hill beyond.

She could not help herself. It really struck her as terribly funny.

Still giggling, she closed the window and drew the drapes tight. She checked the room. She sprayed musty French perfume in the air, especially over the bed.

She dabbed rose-scented powder on herself. With a towel wet from the pitcher on the wall table, she wiped her face and throat.

Jared would have seen the lamplight from the road, so she left it burning on the wall by the cherrywood table and rechecked the room. She paused to view herself in the large looking glass next to her dresser. She removed her negligee to reveal her blue, satin gown. It flowed about her generous form and draped down to her bare toes.

She climbed into bed and drew the covers up to her chin, lying back with her eyes closed and lips parted. Breathless, she heard the bedroom door open. She could hear his limp, for his right leg had never healed from the War between the States. His boots and clothes soon hit the floor.

"Wake up, Morna."

Morna knew Red Ferman's life and perhaps her own could well depend on her response. About to turn fifty, Jared constantly needed reassurance of his power over her.

The next minute, the bed was giving way to Jared's weight.

She opened her eyes and smiled. "I expected you tomorrow, Jared."

"Came back with the mule train over the mountains. Why'd you tie up my dog?"

"Someone said there was a rabid skunk found in the hills. Is he still tied up?"

"Yes, but I'll get him later."

"Did you bring me a present?"

"I always do, but right now, I'm busy."

"But, Jared, can't we talk first?"

He silenced her with his hungry mouth.

Later when he lay sound asleep, she would lie beside him with tears in her eyes and on her cheeks. Tears that would last into the late night.

Morna saw no escape from her unhappy life.

While Morna and Jared Frost were together, Red Ferman ran uphill in his stocking feet, through the scattered pines in the moonlight, cussing when he stepped on wet grass, sharp rocks, and thorns. Carrying his clothes and boots, he ran down into a wash and then back up the slope.

On the next hillside, his big white house stood across the road and alone to the left. On the right stood lawyer Hancock's and then lawyer Eberley's, followed by four other mansions.

He paused to gaze back down the first hill overlooking the town, a wooded rise occupied only by lawyer Frost's home. He saw the lamps still burning in the master bedroom. His big feet were freezing on the wet grass, but Jared could put the dog on him.

Trying to pull on his britches as he ran, he stumbled, hit the ground, and rolled, cussing.

"Dad blast it!"

He got up, pulled on the other pants leg, realized his gun belt hung over his underwear, hiked it up to draw up his pants, and readjusted it. Before he could pull on his boots, he thought he heard something. He started running again, grimacing every time he stepped on a stone or bramble. Any minute, that big dog could be after him.

He left the trees, went through the hollow, and up onto the rough road near his house, only to find himself standing face-to-face in the moonlight with Brandon Wills Eberley, the older partner and only Yank in Frost's law firm.

"Well, Mr. Ferman."

The amused Eberley looked his seventy years. Balding, lean with a little round potbelly, he wore a heavy coat and white muffler, his black small-brimmed hat pulled down tight in the chill. Clean-shaven with dusty gray hair, still a handsome man, he had few wrinkles. He had little in life to enjoy, but this moment put a smile on his face.

Eberley's little black-and-white dog tugged at the end of a long leather leash that Eberley extended as the animal ran around him and barked at Ferman.

Eberley quieted the animal. It came over to sniff Red's stockings, and then recoiled.

Ferman tried to appear normal. It was difficult with his boots in one hand, his coat and shirt in the other, and his big jaw dripping with sweat. Being humiliated made him angry. Who did this blasted Yank lawyer think he was anyhow?

Eberley could not stop smiling. "Aren't you going to catch your death of cold?"

"Just get out of here."

"Public road, Mr. Ferman."

Ferman, over six feet tall, squared his big shoulders. Lawyer Eberley barely reached five feet five inches. Yet Ferman had no ready answers. His face burned hot.

"Either way," Eberley said, "I suspect your life expectancy is getting shorter by the minute."

"Whatever you're thinking, you're wrong. And if you go shooting off your mouth, I'll blow your tiny little Yankee brains out."

"Your eloquence is matched only by your attire."

Eberley stifled a laugh and walked away, east along the road, heading past Hancock's and toward his own house, his dog sprinting about him. The lawyer did not look back.

Ferman muttered to himself, "Yankee bastard."

Ferman prided himself on his record as a top sergeant with the Confederacy. He also thought of himself as ten steps above these stuffed-shirt lawyers who had been officers.

He had been just as rich as any of them before Black Friday, when he lost his fortune, same as they. Even now, controlling the mines, he felt he could buy and sell Frost or Hancock.

Best of all, he had Frost's wife.

He pulled on his coat and turned toward his own house, a two-story mansion just as fine as the others, but all the more empty.

CHAPTER 2

Early Saturday morning, the *Mountain Springs Recorder* had set up the next Monday paper. The whitewashed building stood alone and apart from other structures on the south side of the street.

Jennifer White had perfect features, except for a slightly turned-up nose and a few freckles. Gorgeous with large shining green eyes like jewels under dark lashes, she had long chestnut hair. Now twenty-seven, she looked younger. She sat at her cluttered desk behind the front counter and railing that kept inquisitive customers at bay.

She fingered the white, satin ribbon holding her hair away from her neck and the collar of her faded blue dress. Her full lips tightened in a stubborn frown.

She had made this her life, her journey, but it had no joy.

Many lonely nights would haunt her with no end in sight.

With no ability to retreat, she had to keep her crusade at full speed. Like her father, she had never learned when enough was enough. Stubborn, she could never let the bad guys win.

She made a face. The new ready print still smelled of heavy ink and crackled in her slim hands. She glanced from the blank side, which she would fill, to the side with news supplied from Chicago.

"Jennifer," said Frank, her printer, in his gravelly voice, "this is a mistake. You could end up dead like your father."

A stooped and bespectacled, balding man in his sixties, Frank Choper looked unhappy and worried about the blistering editorial he had just set in a tray at the shelves on the back wall. He sat on a tall stool, his apron smudged with black ink. He had tried to replace her father His efforts had been to no avail. He could see nothing but trouble ahead.

As usual, they worked alone in the crowded one-room, single-story newspaper office. Large boxes took a lot of space at the right of the three-legged Washington hand press. There were stools, a table, and chairs. Behind her desk, a gray coffee pot steamed on the round and flat-topped iron stove with its chimney angled to the ceiling. Away from the stove stood the hand-operated job press.

Jennifer, ever fond of Frank, knew he was trying to take care of her. It pleased her that he tried to fill the loss in her life. She loved to argue with him.

"An editor has a right to an opinion, Frank."

"But you make it sound like they did away with witnesses."

"Well, I'm sure they did."

"You're letting Ruben Smythe push you into this. You know, it could be sour grapes on his part. We don't know how legitimate his clients' claims are."

"What about when a mine owner disappears and Red Ferman shows up with a transfer deed?"

"But the deeds were found to be legal."

"And signed before they were murdered?"

"You don't know that."

"All I do is ask questions. Let the readers figure it out for themselves."

Frank lifted the heavy tray of type. He sidestepped the papers stacked all over the floor.

He set the heavy, arranged tray on the arms of the hand press, which reached forward from the rear. Above a large, square lid, two uprights lined up near an extended handle and crank. Across the top on the frame, gold imprinted letters read Washington Press.

In front of the counter and railing, the only windows faced the street, both large with fluffy white curtains and on each side of the solid door. A little bell dangled above the entrance.

Frank gripped the two-handed ink brayer, the roller.

Jennifer continued reading the ready print.

She stared at an ad for a new-style, glove-fitting corset. Right next to it were offered braided-wire dress forms to crunch a woman's breasts into shape.

"Always something to make women more miserable." She made a face. "And look here, Frank, the United States has nearly fifty million people now. Where are they going to put them?"

"I know why you're doing this."

Weary, she set the paper down and turned to listen.

"You're fighting to catch every liar, thief, and murderer, because you're trying to be your father, Jennifer. So you won't have to face living your own life."

She leaned back in her chair, as she smiled up at him. "You're a good friend, Frank, but I'm doing what I have to do."

"Your father wanted you to get hitched."

"You mean like with Richard, the man I was going to marry down in New Mexico Territory? The man who saw what they were doing to my father and ran inside a store to pretend he hadn't seen? Even as they knocked me down and murdered my father, right there on the street?"

"There was nothing anyone could do."

"Richard was the best of the lot, so that can't say much for anyone else, Frank. They're all gutless sheep in a real pinch."

"Now, Jennifer, you don't know that."

"Yes, I do. Besides, marriage is only a bargain for men. They get a field hand, barn cleaner, milkmaid, housekeeper, cook, washerwoman, seamstress, and someone to bear and rear their children."

Frank grinned. "So you're going to be a spinster."

"You're absolutely right."

"Meanwhile, you're making a lot of enemies. I worry about you."

"Well, let me ask you this, Frank. All three partners went to that Harvard Law School, and if you listen to Hancock and Frost, only the rich and elite should be lawyers. Yet they have a new lawyer coming who learned his trade in a law office."

Frank just shook his head and didn't respond.

"It's all politics. They want Grant to come here and see his hero. Just to get a railroad."

Frank shrugged. "What's wrong with that?"

"There's something fishy going on. Look how Pocket went missing, and Banner was murdered right here in town."

"They say they were both mixed up with gamblers down at Bittner's."

"I don't believe it. And when I get a smell of something, I've got to follow through."

"Maybe so." Frank wearily removed his heavy apron to stand near her desk. "But there's one thing for sure. You're playing with fire, Jennifer."

He turned and went to the stove for coffee.

She returned to reading the ready print.

News included the Lincoln County War in New Mexico. Billy the Kid had killed the sheriff in Lincoln just one year ago, and he was becoming a legend.

"Now I know what to write," she said, taking up her pencil.

Jennifer wrote for a long while in her tablet, then held it up to read aloud.

"Four years ago, Wild Bill Hickok was murdered in Deadwood, Dakota Territory. Three years ago, John Wesley Hardin, the most feared killer in Texas with twenty-one victims by his gun, and who had then killed a sheriff in Comanche, Texas, was arrested in Pensacola, Florida.

"Two years ago, bandits robbed a bank in New York City of over three million. Shortly after last Christmas, two alleged murderers were taken from the jail at Golden, Colorado, and lynched. Last year, Jesse James robbed the Alton Express near Glendale.

"Perhaps Mountain Springs is not that unusual. The frontier, after all, is still a frontier, no matter how many trains arrive or how many farmers plant or fence. The Mescaleros are still crossing back and forth to Mexico with a frustrated army in pursuit. Law and order is only beginning to take hold, and not every sheriff is as honest as Will Hicks.

"Mexicans are still being shot or hanged in New Mexico Territory as certain whites, some who still remember the war with Mexico and lost brothers, try to humiliate or suppress them."

Frank nodded approval.

She put down her pencil and went for more coffee.

At midmorning, Jennifer knelt behind a stack of boxes in the newspaper office, disgusted as she picked up lead type that had scattered all over the floor. Faster at setting type than Frank, she had yet undone a whole frame.

Now tired and hungry, her apron and faded blue dress marked with ink smears, she paused to reflect. Here she was on her knees. No life for a woman, and yet she couldn't help herself. Driven to succeed, she no longer thought of children and a home, a need destroyed by Richard.

The hard floor hurt her knees. She smelled of ink, not perfume. Being a radical woman in a man's world really wasn't that much fun.

Frank sat quietly at the table, mixing ink, his fingertips black as usual.

Behind the boxes, Jennifer grabbed at more type.

When the front door opened, the little bell jingled like a spoon on tin.

Jennifer, still kneeling, peered between the boxes.

Matt Tyler, a man she had never met, wearing a dark-blue, store-bought suit, gun belt, and big Stetson had entered. She squinted for a better look at his carefree smile, the cleft in his chin, and the shine in his dark eyes. She saw him as a little too handsome and obviously sure of himself, and yet so masculine, he could sweep a woman off her feet.

Jennifer felt a surge of infatuation that startled her. She stayed hidden because of it.

"Hi," Matt said to Frank. He fingered the stack of outdated newspapers on the counter. "I'm Matt Tyler. When does the paper come out?"

Frank grunted and turned. "Frank Choper. And the paper comes out on Mondays."

"What's that you're mixing?"

"Lampblack and oil."

"Bet it's hard to get off your hands."

"You be that new lawyer in town."

Matt grinned. "You don't like lawyers?"

"Ain't got much use for 'em. The boss was over to the rooming house to ask you some questions about the murder, but Mrs. Ledbetter put a stop to it, sent her packing."

"Didn't you talk to the sheriff?"

"Yeah, but it seems like you was the only one there when Banner died. Did he say anything?"

"No, he didn't."

"I find that hard to believe," Jennifer snapped from her hiding place.

Matt looked startled as she stood up and appeared from around the boxes. He removed his hat, running his fingers over his dark, collar-length hair as she came to the counter.

She took his breath away.

"You're the little old lady editor?" he asked with a big grin.

She gazed at him a long moment, her interest and curiosity rising. He looked so cocky, so innocent and lovable, she felt almost reluctant to throw reality at him.

Matt saw her to be as pretty as morning sunshine. But Laura had been just as pretty and had been a liar, a cheat, and a selfish woman. Matt remained skittish.

"I'm Jennifer White, and I can't believe a man as strong as Banner could crawl the length of that alley and not be able to say something."

Matt leaned on the counter, his gaze all over her, from her soft hands to her chestnut hair and somewhere in between, causing her to blush. Yet she was still attacking him.

"You realize this is the second law clerk from that firm to disappear or be murdered? What do you think of that?"

Matt just grinned. "I thought I'd buy myself a newspaper."

"It'll cost you ten cents when it's ready, but there's some old ones on the counter for free. Maybe you'll have a better picture of what you're getting into. Or have you already talked to your new employers?"

"No, I'm a couple days early."

"I hope you haven't signed a contract."

"You have something against lawyers?"

Despite his irresistible grin, she kept her frown, even as the unruly cowlick dangled over his brow, a thin strand of his dark hair that tickled her.

"Mr. Tyler, your law firm defends that thieving Red Ferman, one of the biggest mine owners at Silver Gulch. Men have died up there, and their families got nothing for it."

"Didn't they have a lawyer?"

"Sure, but your firm knows all the tricks. Although I can't see why they sent for the likes of you. You look like a cowboy in a store-bought suit."

Matt, still grinning, did not respond as he pulled on his Stetson.

"And that gun belt you're wearing. Judge Waller won't let you in the courtroom with it."

"Thanks for the advice."

Nothing she could say riled him. It miffed her. He kept grinning as he chose a few of the past newspapers. He tipped his hat, and left, the tin bell jingling his departure.

Staring at the closed door, Jennifer put her hands on her hips and blew a strand of hair from her hot cheek. "Did you see that, Frank?"

Frank nodded. "Yeah, he sure didn't miss a thing. And I don't think you did, either. This is the first time I seen you turn color."

"You're out of your mind. Besides, with his innocence, he won't be around long. He's a little fish in a sea of sharks."

Frank grinned and wiped ink from his fingers. "Well, get yourself a net."

Jennifer sat down at her desk and felt wobbly. Frank was right about one thing. Matt Tyler had unsettled her.

The door opened again with a jingle.

In walked Travis McComb, the county attorney, a tall, lanky man in a dark-gray pinstripe suit with vest and a starched white collar. In his late forties, he had deep-set, dark eyes and a wide smile. Although clean-shaven, he had thick, long sideburns. Decidedly handsome with a Southern drawl, smelling of musk cologne, he wore his charm as if he still lived in the Old South.

McComb, ever sure of himself, knew he looked impressive.

"Jennifer, have you forgotten our drive this morning? I have the new rig outside."

"Mr. McComb, you're early."

"Have to be at a meeting this afternoon at two, so I thought we'd go now. And when are you going to call me Travis?"

"I have to keep my distance, remember? How can I complain about you being the county attorney if you're holding my hand?"

"Are you going to let me hold your hand?"

"No."

"So you're going to blast me in your next editorial?"

"I'm afraid so."

"Well, I'll just suffer. Shall we go?"

She smiled and turned to Frank, who looked sour. She knew her printer and longtime friend did not like or trust the county attorney.

However, she learned a lot from McComb, who liked to talk about his trials and helped her understand legal terminology. She also liked being treated as if she were a queen without being touched. He never failed to be a gentleman.

"See you later, Frank," she said.

Jennifer pulled on her blue cape and a simple, brimmed hat, sliding a hatpin through it and her thick chestnut hair. She and McComb walked into the sunlight.

McComb's rig, a surrey, new and polished with gold trim, had two rows of padded, black leather seats under a fringed top. A black gelding stood in harness. The outfit looked right fancy. She had to admit she would enjoy herself.

As they drove across the green, rolling hills dotted with yellow flowers, the sunlight warm and friendly, skinny red wheels bouncing on the rough ground, she glanced at his solemn demeanor and began to probe.

"Have you met Matt Tyler?" she asked.

"The new lawyer? No, why?"

"He's very sure of himself."

McComb smiled. "All lawyers start out that way. You have to show a lot of bravado to prop yourself up and bluff out the opposition. A lawyer's only happy when he wins."

"What about you?"

"I've sobered a lot over the years. You learn there are a lot of things you cannot accomplish. A little like being in the army."

"You never talk about the War between the States."

"That was a long time ago."

"But you were in the Confederate army?"

"Are you interviewing me again?"

"I'm sorry," she said. "It's a bad habit, I know."

"Just relax, Jennifer, and be a woman. That's what I like about you the best."

"Like a Southern belle who thinks only of flirting?"

"No, that would fit Mrs. Frost, not you. There's a lot more to you than any woman I've ever met. And that's why I like to be with you. Now, is that all settled?"

She smiled and held on to her hat.

That same Saturday, Matt had taken the outdated newspapers back up the street to Pop's Café, across the alley from the courthouse. The same alley where he had found Banner.

The small café smelled like fresh baked bread as he entered. He wet his lips. One thing a man always remembered—his mother's fresh baked bread. He suddenly felt a little homesick, thinking of his father in the open fields, his mother taking his noon meal to him, and the house smelling of delicious everything.

Matt, the only customer, took a table against the wall where he had a view of the street.

Pop served him coffee and cinnamon bread, while Matt skimmed the papers. The tables had fresh, new checkered tablecloths. White lace curtains, tied back, were on the front windows.

Matt tasted the coffee and bread, and he smiled. “It’s good.”

“So’s that newspaper. But she’s gonna be shot one of these days. I can’t see to read hardly any at all, but they tell me she’s real pushy.”

“Is she married?”

“Nope, but every young hoot in town is after her.”

Matt told himself he would not join the crowd at her doorstep. She may well be beautiful, provocative, and defiant, but he would never trust a woman, not ever again. They knew how to manipulate and be coquettes at the same time they were lying through their teeth.

He leaned back to study the papers.

“Have a seat, Pop. I’ll read some of it.”

Delighted, the old man brought coffee and sat down.

“Well,” Matt said as he scanned a paper, “there’s advertisements for stage routes, lady’s hats, cattle, iron stoves, corsets, and indoor facilities, all on the back of the pages where they get the news from the East.”

Pop leaned closer to enjoy the larger drawings.

Matt grinned. “Here’s Dr. Pareira’s Great Italian Remedy for diseases of a private nature. And here’s liver pills and cures for an opium habit.”

“Opium, yeah. Not much of that around here though.”

Matt continued to scan the ready print. “Building of the canal across the Isthmus of Panama will start next year. And Sarah Bernhardt’s coming to New York City. ‘The Divine Sarah,’ it says. ‘Her American debut.’”

“You ever see any of them there shows?”

“A few. I think the actors would make great trial lawyers.”

On the back sides, Jennifer had printed local news, including firewood and stock for sale, and reports on the fight for women’s suffrage.

Her sarcastic editorial reported a recent trial where Frost had successfully defended Red Ferman’s mine syndicate against an alleged prior claim to very rich ore.

Matt frowned. “She writes, ‘Missing Witnesses, Again.’”

"She has a hot tongue all right," Pop said.

Matt noted searing editorials about the balance in law and order. Jennifer White had a scathing way with words. She blamed his firm for tempering justice, which Matt read aloud.

"'When justice is ruled by the eloquence of a lawyer's oration instead of the facts and evidence, something is vitally wrong. Convincing a jury with valid argument is one thing. Swaying them with twisted words, trumped-up facts, and without conscience is another.'"

Pop grunted. "She's asking for trouble."

"I doubt they'd hurt a woman."

"Don't count on it." Pop grinned. "But you like her."

Matt had to chuckle. "I like her turned-up nose."

"She's out buggy riding with the county attorney."

Matt suddenly stiffened. "It says here, 'General Grant, former president of the United States, is again touring Colorado, and is presently in Central City and Leadville. He is traveling with Mrs. Grant, their son, and various officials, and will soon return to Denver.'"

"Hey, now that's one fellah I'd like to see."

"Doesn't sound like he's coming here."

Matt continued to stare at the words. Finally, he folded the paper.

Now two fat merchants came inside, and Pop had to take care of them.

With a twinge, Matt remembered the first time he had seen Grant, a colonel with the Twenty-First Illinois Infantry. Matt had lied about his age and joined up at fifteen. When Grant became brigadier general, Matt became his messenger.

He had even taken a bullet for Grant and earned a citation, along with an unforgiving right leg, but the general's thanks had been worth it.

"Son," the general had said, "you're bigger than you look."

Since then, Matt had shot up from a skinny five feet six to a full six feet with wide shoulders. Grant would never recognize him now, not after all these years. Maybe Grant wouldn't even remember him. After all, Grant had gone from the War between the States to the presidency and on to a world traveler. A lot had happened to both of them.

But Matt would never forget the man who loved cucumbers for breakfast, snacked on fried apples, and carried a battered copy of *Ivanhoe*. A man who had been fatherly to Matt, looking after him even before Matt's saving him from a bullet.

He stared into his cup, remembering. A deep sadness suddenly charged through him. The past was gone. Here he sat, a young lawyer in a new world. Yet he felt as if he had left something behind, something he needed.

"Mr. Tyler, I presume?"

The voice, feminine and sugary sweet, seemed to echo.

He leaned back to stare up at Morna Frost.

She looked gorgeous in a green silk dress with lace at the collar, black velvet trim, and a moving bustle that swayed with her hips. Her blond hair glistened in long curls under her feathered green hat. She had a pretty face with devilish, dark-blue eyes. She held a parasol in her gloved hand.

. Overwhelmed, Matt froze for a long minute, and then took a deep breath.

He struggled to his feet and removed his hat. "Yes, ma'am."

"I'm Morna Frost."

"Yes, ma'am."

"May I sit down?"

Quickly, he came around to move her chair under her as she sat down with a sweep of full skirts. She smelled of rich, flowery perfume, and more, she smelled like a woman. She could stir any man's blood, and she made him really nervous.

"I heard you were in town."

"I came early, yes, ma'am."

"My husband is still sleeping from a long journey. Perhaps you will join us at church services tomorrow. Ten o'clock?"

"Yes, ma'am, if I can."

"I see that you're catching up on our local gossip. Miss White does have a sharp voice, does she not?"

"She writes very well."

"And she'll be writing about poor Mr. Banner. But these law clerks are young and foolish. They gamble too much and mix in with the wrong type of people."

"Do we have any left?"

"Oh, dear, yes. My husband believes in slave labor, but don't tell him I said so."

"I guess they have to earn their stripes, ma'am."

"Yes, perhaps. But tell me about yourself, Mr. Tyler. No women in your life?"

"No, ma'am."

"I shall have to do something about that. You're a war hero, after all. Back in Kansas, my father said if you hadn't saved Grant's life, the war could have lasted a lot longer. He said Grant was the driving force. Lincoln and Grant were his heroes."

"You still have your folks, ma'am?"

"No."

"Sorry to hear that."

She looked strange and twirled her parasol.

"But you'll soon learn that my husband, Jared and Mr. Hancock were Confederate officers. Their partner, Mr. Eberley, was Union, but he's mostly retired."

Matt had trouble meeting her gaze. She really unsettled a man.

"I want you to succeed, Matt, so I'll give you a few hints to keep you out of trouble."

Matt knew he had to watch his step, so he just listened.

"You must never talk about the gold market or the War between the States."

Matt sat quietly as she continued.

She twirled her parasol. "Mr. Ferman is your most important client. He runs Silver Gulch where the mines are, but he is a gentleman. He owned a small plantation, but he lost it in the war."

"And now?"

"Please, I've already said too much. I just wanted to help you last longer than some of the others who tried to work here."

"Thank you, ma'am."

"You're quite welcome, Mr. Tyler."

She stood up with graceful movement.

He scrambled to his feet, nearly losing his balance, for she sure did rattle him. His face burned hot as fire.

If she touched him, he would shrivel up.

She smiled sweetly, then turned with a whirl of skirts and left the café, her perfume lingering. Matt drew a deep breath and sat back down.

One thing for sure, he had to keep a lot of distance between himself and the boss's wife.

CHAPTER 3

Saturday evening, Matt walked to the main street. Lanterns on posts cast eerie, smoky lights on the rough surface of the midtown street and barely lit the lonely boardwalks. To the west, he could see the bright lights of the saloons and gambling hall where a lot of horses and mules waited at the hitching rail, but he wanted to see the sheriff.

There wasn't much of a moon. Stars twinkled so close, he felt he could lasso one. Oh, yes, he gave up his practice to come out here on a mission, but despite the intrigue and the murder, he truly liked this mountain valley. He had never felt air so fresh and clean.

At the same time, he had to think of Grant and protect him.

Matt, favoring his right leg, walked toward the east, past the courthouse and Grand Hotel, pausing in front of the stage depot. Across the street, a light burned in the jail, barely visible through the shutters.

Matt thought of the sheriff's professional manner the previous night, and he missed his own father all the time. The lawman felt like a good substitute. Matt crossed over and knocked on the door. Windows, shuttered, gave a pinch of light.

Sheriff Will Hicks seemed glad to see him.

He let Matt inside and barred the door again.

Hicks, his gray handlebar moustache neatly trimmed, gave the appearance of a clean, orderly man. An orderly man with a fast draw that kept rowdies out of town.

"Sure is quiet out there," Matt said.

"Yeah, because folks lock up early on Saturday night on this side of town. Some of the rowdies from the west side will wander up this way if they see any stores open."

Wooden chairs sat by a table next to the hot iron stove. Checkers waited on the table.

The open door to the two empty cells in the back allowed a smell from the latrine buckets. The sheriff walked over and closed the door.

"Sorry about that."

His office, some twenty feet square, had two shuttered windows hung on each side of the front door. Rifle slots marked the walls. His desk to the right of the door looked heavy and old with scratches. The thick floor and walls smelled of pine.

Hicks poured two cups of thick coffee and brought them to the table.

They sat down and stared at the checkerboard.

Matt's curiosity prompted a question.

"I hear there are some vigilantes around here."

"Yeah, you saw the hanging tree? You can forget about them having anything to do with Banner. Most of it's the miners' courts, and they always hang 'em. Last one was a sluice box robber. I haven't been able to catch 'em at it."

"I'll remember to stay away from sluice boxes."

"They don't discriminate, I'll tell you that. Yank or Southerner, you'll hang."

"Well, the war is over."

"Most of 'em want it to be. Out at the mines, there's a few like Ferman and his cohorts what still have an ax to grind. But most of the men out there—and they're from the South—they want to put it behind them. In town, it's pretty much the same."

"There's hope, then."

Hicks nodded. "I went up to see one of your new bosses today. Jared Frost. He got back from Denver late last night. He claims Banner was gambling too much. Figures somebody he owed got mad. He says Pocket was the same way."

Matt jumped two of his checkers. "I met Frost's wife today."

"Morna Frost? Now that's a lot of woman, busting at the seams. And I figure, real miserable being hitched to a man like Frost." Blue eyes twinkling, Hicks jumped Matt's last three checkers and snorted as he laughed. "For a lawyer, you ain't too smart."

"For a sheriff, you're right sneaky."

Hicks brought them more coffee and settled back in his chair. "Not sneaky enough. So far, I ain't figured out Pocket or who got Banner. Of course, there are some bad ones around."

"Such as?"

"Anybody who works for Bittner at the gambling hall. Crazy Albert, out at Silver Gulch. And Bo Raddigan, Ferman's hired killer. Raddigan ain't the type to use anything but his six-shooter. He's too arrogant."

"This Raddigan, he ever challenge you?"

Hicks shook his head. "He mostly stays in Silver Gulch."

"Anybody else I should know about?"

"You'll like Gentry, the barber. He's colored. Ferman and his Southerners would love find an excuse to string him up." Hicks fingered a checker. "Gentry lost his right leg below the knee fighting for the Union. Hobbles around on a wooden leg. He's an inventor of sorts."

"What about the lawyers?"

"You mean outside your office? Mostly a good bunch. Sometimes I wonder about McComb, the county attorney. He's a little too dignified for my liking. Probably wants to be governor."

"How about sheriffs?"

"I take a lot of abuse, and I ain't sure it's worth a hundred a month."

Hicks set up the checkers for another game. He then leaned back, running his hand over his nearly bald head, pausing to scratch his left ear. His moustache twitched.

Matt sipped his coffee. "How is it you don't have any deputies around?"

"Got two. Little's the lover, always after the women. Right now, he's down the valley checking on rustlers. Lacey's home. His wife is having a baby."

"You got a wife?"

"Nope, but I have my eye on a nice widow woman. Makes great apple pie." Hicks studied the board. "Man gets older, he gets lonelier by the minute. What about you?"

"No, sir. A man alone can do what he wants."

"Yeah, all by himself."

Matt jumped the rest of Hicks's checkers.

Hicks grimaced, pushing his hat back.

"It seems to me a young fellow like you, brand new in town, would be seeing the sights instead of sitting here playing checkers like an old man."

"The best place to learn anything is from the sheriff."

Hicks reached for his hat. "Well, maybe I should take you on a tour. It's early for lockup, but let's go. We'll work our way to the west side of town where the saloons are."

Outside in the chill of night with a pale moon, they walked along the north side of the street, boot heels thumping on the boardwalk, passing the dark town hall and a woman's clothing store with a seamstress advertised. Hicks checked the door. When they paused in front of the law firm's office, he checked that lock also.

The brick building's strong design and embossed window glass impressed Matt.

Hicks continued to check doors as they walked, first the clothing and dry goods store, then the Miners & Merchants Bank with its stone front.

"Ever had a bank robbery here?" Matt asked.

"No, but a few dead bodies now and then with empty pockets."

Matt looked at the dark street and nearby alleys, as he thought of Banner.

Everything he saw and felt told Matt this was no place for Grant.

Hicks led the way to the post office, where the upstairs housed a doctor. Next door, the saddlery occupied the downstairs, but a sign indicated the second floor had two lawyers named Ralph and Ruben Smythe.

"Smythe brothers," Hicks said. "They take any case against your law firm. They also defend thieves and murderers."

"Someone has to."

"You work for that big firm, you'll be defending more thieves and murderers than you can count, but they'll be wearing tailored suits, solid gold watches, and diamond studs."

As they crossed back over to the south side of the street, they saw a light in the newspaper office. The isolated building looked silent and lonely.

"Now I told her to close them curtains at night," Hicks growled.

At the same time Matt and Sheriff Hicks walked the street that Saturday night, Jennifer White left her little white house, which stood some distance behind the newspaper office. She carried a tray of hot food for Frank as she headed back to the office.

In the cold moonlight, she shivered despite a heavy coat over her blue dress and apron.

Weary and tired, she held on, because Frank had insisted on finishing his work on the job press. There were times when she wanted to slow down. As long as Frank kept pushing so hard, she couldn't rest, but they sure put out a good paper.

She kicked at the back door of the newspaper office.

"Frank?"

Annoyed that he didn't answer, she balanced the tray in her left hand and put her right hand on the latch. To her surprise, the door slowly swung open. Her back to the door as she grabbed the tray again with both hands, she pushed her way inside.

Moving to the lamplight, she let the door slam on its own, behind her.

"Darn you, Frank, why didn't you have the door locked?"

She paused, staring at Matt Tyler and the sheriff, both standing behind the front railing with weapons drawn. She set the tray on the table and walked around the Washington Press. She started to question them. She lost her voice when she saw Frank Choper seated at the desk, his head down on his arms as if asleep.

The back of Frank's head oozed with blood, so dark-red and gory, she gasped and looked away. Her insides wanted to come charging up her throat. She couldn't breathe. She wanted to scream so bad it hurt.

She reeled against the press, her left hand resting on sticky molasses that had been poured over gears and toggle joints, lever and rack. She gasped, pulled her hand free, and put her right hand over her breast.

"My God," she whispered.

Hicks holstered his six-shooter and came through the gate to take her elbows, escorting her to the table and chairs. She sat down clumsily. Matt took Choper's coat from the wall hook and covered the body. Then he drew the curtains and latched the front and back doors.

Hicks poured coffee for her and sat at her side. Matt stood at the back wall, his hand on his holster.

Jennifer's tears were flowing down her hot face. Hicks reached out to take her wrists, trying to calm her as best he could. She trembled down to her shoes. She felt ready to vomit.

Jennifer stared down at the curling steam, as she held the cup in both hands.

She couldn't stop her tears. Her eyes burned. Chills ran through her.

The sheriff's voice brought her back.

"Now, think, Miss White. Did you put out a paper today?"

"We ran it off for Monday. It's stacked on the counter with the old ones."

"There are no papers there."

Pressing her handkerchief to her face, she choked on a sob.

"Anyone come in here today, at any time?" Hicks asked.

"Matt Tyler this morning. Mr. McComb. Mrs. Jeffrey on her store posters. No one else. Saturdays are slow, so we get more work out. An hour ago, I went to my house to get supper for us. Frank wanted to finish next week's work for Mrs. Jeffrey. On the job press."

"When you went to supper, was the front door locked?"

"I asked Frank to lock both doors when I left."

"Seems like he didn't have the chance," Hicks said.

Matt sat down opposite her, his hands on the table, leaning toward her. "What was your editorial?"

Tears unheeded, she stared at her cup. "I didn't like the results of that trial last week."

"You can't believe the firm had anything to do with this."

"Then why are the papers with my editorial gone?"

Hicks got to his feet. "Miss White, you haven't spared a soul in town or at Silver Gulch, so it's hard to pin this on anyone. Matt, help me get Frank outside. I'll get the undertaker. Frank have any kinfolk, Miss White?"

"A brother back East."

"His effects will be at the office. Matt, you keep an eye on things. They may come back."

When the body and Hicks were gone, Matt locked the front door and rechecked the back.

She continued to cry as she stood by the printing press, trying to turn the lever. The molasses had seeped into the type tray, toggle joints, and gears.

She had to lash out at someone.

"Are you a deputy now?" she snapped.

"No, but why are you all alone? Where's your family?"

She sat down at the table. He bravely sat near her. Her tears dribbled into her coffee cup, as she tried to sip the hot liquid. Her hands were shaking. She leaned back in her chair, fighting for calm. Finding it difficult to breathe, she had to force herself to speak.

"My father was a newspaperman in Tucson. A little over two years ago, some ranchers didn't like his editorials about their shooting Mexicans for sport, and they murdered him. Oh, they put a gun in his hand and called it a fair fight, but it was murder."

"I'm sorry."

"Afterward, Frank and I left town and moved everything up here to start over."

"And your mother?"

"She died when I was small. I had an older brother, but Johnny was killed in the war. He was with Grant."

"So was I, but I didn't know your brother."

She glanced at the desk where the blood had been covered up with a sheet of newsprint streaked with it. She wiped at her eyes and sipped the coffee, holding the cup in both hands. She had never felt so alone. Still grieving for her father, she knew Frank would also be haunting her.

"What will you do now?" he asked.

"Clean up the press. Do the printing myself. There's a young man named Henry who delivers the papers, and he's helped set type now and then. I'll ask him to work for me in the daytime. It wouldn't be fair to ask him to work at night, not after this."

"You shouldn't either. They may come back to finish the job."

Her chin went up. "I can shoot, Mr. Tyler, and I'll be armed."

Suddenly shivering, she wrapped her arms about herself.

Matt's worry showed in his face. "You can't do this alone."

"I have no choice. I haven't found anyone man enough to stand up to what goes on around here."

"If you did, would you carry him off into the sunset?"

She glowered at him. "You're making me angry."

"That's the idea."

A flickering smile crossed her lips, as she understood his effort to bring her into focus. She had the urge to slide into his arms for comfort, but she couldn't move.

A knock on the door startled her. Matt got up. He silenced the bell in his grasp. He let the sheriff back inside.

Hicks convinced her to close up. Both men walked her home, waiting for her to collapse, but she held herself together. Her little white house stood some distance behind her office and just west of Mrs. Ledbetter's boardinghouse.

"Wait until we look inside," Hicks said.

They lit the kerosene lamps and checked the front room, bedroom, water closet, and kitchen. Neatly but sparsely furnished with heavy blue drapes on the windows, it appeared very comfortable. A cast iron-stove, stacked wood beside it, stood in the kitchen.

In the front room, newsprint crowded one wall by a treadle sewing machine. Furniture included a worn blue circular sofa, a stuffed blue chair, and a wood rocker. A Currier and Ives print on the wall depicted a battle of the War of Independence. The one rug lay green and thick.

"Maybe you ought to have another woman come and stay with you," Hicks said. "At least for tonight. I reckon Mrs. Ledbetter would oblige."

Jennifer refused at first but finally relented. Matt went for the chubby blond woman, who gladly came with her knitting, gave Jennifer a hug on the porch, and went inside.

Hicks frowned with worry. "Jennifer, you have to promise me you won't leave the house tonight. Keep all the doors and windows locked, and don't let anyone in."

"Yes, and thank you both."

They stood outside, listening as she locked the door.

"My window looks down on her place," Matt said, nodding toward the nearby rooming house. "But I think they'll be all right. Whoever did it was trying to stop the press, and they accomplished that. Right now, I'd like to have a look at the other side of town. Maybe we'll make someone nervous."

"Why are you mixing in on this?"

"I don't like seeing a woman in trouble."

"She makes her own trouble, Matt. Just like you're doing right now. You're a lawyer, not a gun hand, and this is my job, not yours."

"I've been here two days and seen two dead men. I don't want to see any dead women around here."

Matt also worried about Grant riding into this kind of danger.

CHAPTER 4

On the west side of town, the Miners' Saloon quietly sat on the south side of the street between the noisy gambling hall and a hardware store. On the opposite, north side of the street, the Red Light Saloon, the only two-story building in that area, beckoned with more than whiskey. Next to the Red Light sat the Wagon Wheel Saloon. Smoky lanterns burned on posts in front of each, casting strange shadows in all directions.

Horses and mules lined the railings in front of the saloons and gambling hall.

Matt walked along with Sheriff Hicks in the night.

"Keep your eyes open," Hicks said. "And watch out. The Red Light is the only one with women. Two of them."

Matt could see through the dirty windows. The Red Light's smoke-filled room faced a very long walnut bar. It had six tables, where rowdy cowhands and bearded miners filled the chairs and tried to outdo one another at cards. The bartender, tall and skinny, had large ears and a curious gaze.

Hicks and Matt entered. Saturday night's crowd filled the room.

The place reeked of sweat, warm beer, bitter rye whiskey, and tobacco.

Matt could see right away the women were less than appetizing.

One of them, Minnie, a bit hefty, had a large nose, ruby lips, and an ample bosom. She looked lazy. The other, Lupe, had dark hair and large eyes, looking skinny but warm all over. Both wore red-feathered dresses with puffed-up sleeves and very low necklines. Their skirts bared their ankles. They smelled of more than pungent cologne.

Minnie hovered at a table crowded by miners.

Hicks murmured, "Watch your step."

Lupe had had too much to drink. She swayed between two miners at the bar, one on each side of her. Rough, sweaty men with big arms, large shoulders, and thick necks. They had crude faces and thick black beards. No one else came near the bar.

Lupe giggled. "I don't believe a word of it."

Everyone turned to watch Matt and Hicks move to the bar. The bearded miners on either side of Lupe watched them in the streaked mirror.

Matt leaned on the bar five feet away from the larger of the two miners. The sheriff stood between Matt and the wall. They could sense the hostility.

"You seen Crazy Albert lately?" the sheriff asked the barkeep. "Or Bo Raddigan?"

"Nope. What'll you have, Sheriff?"

"I'll have a beer."

Matt shook his head. "Just give me some of that cider."

Matt knew the women would drink cider to pretend they were drinking. He also knew he could stir up some trouble with his request. Maybe that's what he wanted.

The biggest miner turned and leaned on the bar with his left elbow, his right hand near his holster. Bearded and grizzly, he looked huge. His deep and raspy voice twisted his mouth as he snorted.

"This is a man's bar."

"Is that so?" Matt asked.

"I said it, didn't I?"

"Then why are you in here?"

"Maybe you don't know who I am. They call me Moose. I can break you in two with both hands. Or blow you away with one snort. And my friend here, they call him Grizzly. He'll chew your ear off while he wrings your neck."

"Well, you sound pretty tough, but I got more brains than both of you put together. That's why I practice law and you dig in the dirt."

Moose straightened, his dark eyes wild. For a long moment he looked ready to jump all over Matt, whose mouth felt dry as bone. The room fell silent with everyone afraid to move. Moose's face slowly turned color.

Hicks held his breath.

Matt had both hands on the bar, his coat drawn back over his holster. He had a hunch he could draw his Colt before the man cleared leather, but if Moose got his hands on him, Matt knew he'd be dead for sure.

Sweat trickled down Matt's neck. A sorry spot for a lawyer to be in, because he didn't know how to back down. A good offense had to be better than any defense.

The bartender backed away for safety.

Moose's fury steamed in his face. Matt stood his ground.

Suddenly, Moose threw his head back and laughed, a loud roar that shook the room like an earthquake. "Here's me hand. I'll buy your blasted cider. You got more gall than any fool I ever met."

Moose's grip nearly broke Matt's fingers. Lupe wandered off. The four men ended up at a side table that had just been cleared. Matt and the sheriff made sure their backs were to the wall.

Moose and Grizzly acted congenial.

The onlookers, disappointed, having been hungry to see a good fight, turned back to their cards.

The sheriff kept shaking his head over Matt's foolishness, but it had worked. Matt sweated with relief.

Moose and Grizzly were big talkers.

"I've sailed around the horn," Moose said. "And most every one of the seven seas. But it's these here mountains I belong to now. Grizzly, he's a real mole. He digs right into that wall of dirt like he knows where he's going."

"We're so high up," Grizzly said, "we can look down on everybody, including Silver Gulch. We got a plateau up there with plenty of feed for the mules, and we got springs. It's a big mountain, it is. Even has a cave full of bats, but we never go in there. We get a little dust now and then, enough for a good Saturday night and some grub."

"You got to come up," Moose said. "Real steep but you can make it."

After the two men had bragged awhile, the sheriff turned to them.

"Any strangers in town?"

Moose grunted and shook his head. "Nope. And we got here afore sundown and lost ten dollars at poker already."

"You see anything suspicious?" Hicks persisted.

"No," Moose said. "Why, what happened?"

The sheriff told them about Banner and the printer.

"Blast," Moose said, shaking his head. "I didn't know that Banner fellow much, but I sure knew ole Frank Choper. Now there was a good man."

Hicks sipped his beer. "You ever see Banner or Pocket over in the gambling hall?"

"Oh, sure," Grizzly said. "Every young hoot in town goes in there."

"You was asking about Crazy Albert," Moose said. "Well, I seen him over in Silver Gulch a few days ago, talking to himself like he always does. He's crazy as a loon."

"And Bo Raddigan?" Hicks asked.

"He's real creepy, I can tell you that, with them eyes near white," Moose added.

"I don't trust anyone works for Ferman," Grizzly said, "but they ain't bothered our Maverick Mine yet, count a we're so high up. There's only two sides of the mountain they can climb to get at us. From the front by way of Needle Rock—and there ain't no cover—or from the real narrow canyon on the north side. The rest is all cliffs, straight down."

Learning nothing more, Matt and the sheriff left the Red Light. Hicks had to pause in the moonlight with a grin.

"That Moose could have killed you."

"You're right about that."

Hicks laughed with a snort. They walked next door to the Wagon Wheel with its long, smoky room. The crowded bar had all sizes and shapes of men, including some farmers. No women. Everyone said they had neither seen nor heard anything. Half a dozen looked as if they would slit your throat for a dime.

Hicks and Matt came back and stood outside the batwing doors. They moved across the street toward the noisy gambling hall on the south side. Smoke filtered out into the night.

Hicks spoke in a whisper. "You won't like Bittner. They say you can still smell the blood of slaves on him. He was a trader and he didn't care how he done it." Hicks adjusted his gun belt. "I figure his hands are still dirty."

Matt didn't like the smell as they entered the gambling hall. Smoke and sweat mingled. The big rectangular room had a small bar, two roulette wheels, faro tables, and games of twenty-one being dealt, with the house constantly winning. Most of the customers were miners, some still covered with red dust, others having had their baths and haircuts. A large chandelier of oil lamps hung from the ceiling.

In the back, behind a cage with the gold scale, stood a plump man in his fifties. He wore a fancy red vest and diamond stickpin. Hair blond and thinning, he had a round face above at least three double chins. His beady eyes gleamed like hot black marbles. No one could trust a man with his demeanor.

Hicks muttered. "That's Bittner. I'd sure like to catch him at something."

Hicks led the way to the window of the cage, leaning on the counter. "Mr. Bittner, I'd like you to meet Matt Tyler."

Bittner didn't offer his hand. He had a marked Southern drawl. He smelled of sweet cologne, which didn't divert the image of him offering slaves on the auction block. That stuck in Matt's mind, so that nothing this man said would carry any weight with him.

"Did that law clerk Banner ever come in here and gamble?" Hicks asked.

"Sure did. I gave him too much credit, and now I'm out the money."

"What about Pocket?"

Bittner frowned. "Pocket, oh, yeah. He left town without paying his dues. All them law clerks keep asking for credit. I guess I'm a softie."

"Yeah," Hicks said. "I bet. You mean all the clerks? MacCready and Loring, and Lucifer Rawlins—they all gambled?"

Bittner made a face and tapped his fingers. "All but Lucifer Rawlins. Yeah, they came in late at night when the good folks couldn't see what they was doing. I saw 'em borrowing money from other gamblers, and that's a bad way to go. I figure one of them got Banner."

"You hear anything," Hicks said, "you let us know."

Outside in the moonlight, Matt breathed in the clean night air with relief.

Matt grimaced. "Under that toilet water, he has the smell of death."

"You're right," Hicks said.

They paused in front of the Miners' Saloon. They looked over the batwing doors to see a crowd of grubby miners. Anyone walking in there would have to squeeze between men who looked mean as sin. Hicks shook his head, signaling he would not enter.

"Sure looks like a den of thieves," Matt said.

They decided to head on back to the east side of town.

"Let's have a look at Jennifer White's," Hicks said.

They walked between the newspaper office and the drugstore, slowing down as they neared the path to her little house. They could see that she had lamps burning in every room, disproving her bravado.

"Looks quiet," the sheriff said.

"I'm going to turn in."

"You act like an old man."

Matt had to grin. "Well, I spent half of last night on a stage that broke every bone in my rump. I'm ready to call it a day."

"What about the Red Light?"

"Those two women? I'd have to find something a little cleaner than that."

"Lawyers don't have much fun, do they?"

"Maybe we just pull down the shades."

Hicks laughed with a snort. "All right, Matt, but keep your eyes open."

While Matt and the sheriff went their separate ways to turn in for the night, law partners Hancock and Frost conferred at Frost's mansion in Frost's large, ornate office on the first floor. Morna would be upstairs, or so they thought.

They could not see the stairs leading up from the parlor, nor the curious Morna listening just around the corner. She wore a blue velvet wrapper over her white gown. Her husband had been acting strangely of late. She wanted to know why.

She leaned on the wall and paid attention.

In his office around the corner, Jared Frost settled comfortably in his padded leather chair. Paintings of the frontier, dueling pistols, and a saber decorated the walls. The open door to the parlor allowed heat from the fireplace to enter the office

Frost scratched his goatee and gestured upward.

"Morna sleeps a lot," Frost said. "Maybe that's why she's so beautiful."

Hancock, standing, nodded, looked around. Restless, he kept pacing.

"So why are you messing around in Denver?" Hancock asked.

Frost gave him such a glare, Hancock backed off.

Both men had another glass of brandy.

"Still cold in here," Hancock complained. The scar on his left cheek gleamed white in the lamplight. He often touched it without thinking.

Frost cautioned. "Just be careful. Voices carry from the parlor."

"Our business is done, so I should leave as soon as I finish this brandy."

Milton Scott Hancock, a husky, balding man in his midfifties, had graduated from Harvard in 1855 with Frost. He looked older than his years, had a scar on his left cheek from the war, his eyes pale blue in a thin face with a wide mouth. He had a thin nose and very thin moustache, a smelly pipe clenched in his teeth. He had his own practiced arrogance.

Hancock could muster bravado when needed, but he had a secret. He had let himself be captured to get out of the fighting. The Yankee prison had left him with recurring lung fever.

Scratching his graying goatee, again, Frost adjusted his right leg, which still pained him. His nasty brown eyes and his rather round shape took away from his handsome face. He stared into his glass, and after a long while, he spoke.

"Last night, I dreamed about the old days. A hot afternoon in the shade. A mint julep. A colored playing a banjo down by the creek. Gospel singing out at the shacks. Best of all, my first wife, Julianne, fussing in the house. Watching the cook make hoecake, collard greens, and bacon."

Hancock nodded. "And sweet potato pie."

"Our wives were the Old South, Milt. Oh, we were gentlemen, but it was the women who were gracious and above reproach."

"Julianne gave you two sons. I envy you."

"Yes, but I get lonely for her."

"And I miss my wife," Hancock said. "But at least you have Morna."

"She's from Kansas. It's not the same."

The two men gazed into space a long moment. Hancock could bear the memories no longer and changed the subject.

"You had a defense verdict in Denver, and that should make Red Ferman happy. Now if those mine claimants file a writ, are you going to turn it over to Matt Tyler?"

Frost shrugged. "He has the experience."

"So if he's in town, why hasn't he presented his card?"

"He's a young man. Probably wants to see the sights."

Hancock nodded. "But he's not smart enough to know why he's here."

"Not all of it."

"Meanwhile, we're trusting the scum of the earth," Hancock said.

"You want to tell the colonel you're backing out?"

Hancock shrugged. "Not me, but think about it, Jared. First the war, then Fisk and Black Friday. If Fisk hadn't been killed over that woman, I might have done it myself."

As the men talked, Morna stood out of sight by the bannister, listening intently but not catching every word because she could not hear them very well.

Who was this mysterious colonel?

Yes, she heard Jared praise her as beautiful. She also heard Jared say he set more store by his first wife than by her. And he admitted to a woman in Denver.

Suddenly, she heard her husband cough on his brandy. Startled by the sound, she became frightened. Turning, she hurried in her bare feet to the stairs and scurried up to the landing. Out of breath, she paused where she could no longer hear.

Another night with Jared's demanding passion.

Another night to cry herself to sleep.

On Sunday morning, Mrs. Ledbetter had left Jennifer's at sunup to prepare breakfast for her several roomers.

In the cold brisk morning, Jennifer headed for the office. Hatless but wearing a cape over her faded blue dress and heavy apron, she appeared angry and in a hurry.

Carrying two buckets with scrub brushes and a scraper, she looked down at her white hands. Frank had always mixed the ink and used the roller. Maybe Henry would now, but if not, it would soon be all over her.

Chilled to the bone, she had never felt so weary or so alone. She had to force herself to walk, to move, to carry the weight of her load. It would be difficult to continue, to drive herself without Frank at her side.

"Miss White, wait up."

She paused, turning to squint at Matt Tyler in the sunlight. She moved into the shade and waited in the alley, watching him approach from the direction of the rooming house.

As much as she tried, she could not dislike him. He seemed so full of himself, it plain tickled her. Right now, she really needed something to cheer her.

He joined her, tipping his hat. "Are you all right?"

"I'm just mad, Mr. Tyler."

"Matt."

"As long as you work for that firm, you're Mr. Tyler to me. Now if you'll excuse me, I'm going to spend all day scraping molasses off the press."

"You're not going to church?"

"With all those hypocrites?"

Her chestnut hair, still tied back with a ribbon, fascinated him. "Can't you get anyone to help you?" he asked.

"Maybe Henry, later on. Right now, I have to do something. I can't just sit still, Mr. Tyler."

"When is the funeral?"

"This afternoon at three o'clock. The cemetery behind the church. But you don't have to go. You didn't know Frank that well."

"But I knew Banner."

"He was buried yesterday at sunup."

Matt frowned. "That was kind of fast."

"Now you're getting the picture. Good day, Mr. Tyler."

He followed her up the alley to the boardwalk. They paused to look west up the street. A parade of men and women, all in their Sunday outfits, were leaving their buggies and walking up the slope through an aspen-shaded lane. They moved toward the church, the view rising above the general store, which stood just beyond her office.

"That's Frost," she said. "The man with the goatee. See how he limps with his right leg. He claims that Robert E. Lee gave him that cane. And he has a missing earlobe from the war. His left ear. That's why he wears those heavy sideburns."

"What about the others?"

"That's Hancock there. The husky man with the little moustache and receding hair. He's a widower."

"Which one's Eberley?"

"That's him, following Hancock. The older man with the moustache and beard and bow legs. He's a Yank, but he had all the money, so they tolerate him."

"Who's that tall man following them?"

"Travis McComb, the county attorney. He rides a circuit."

"Are you sure you won't take off that apron and go to church?"

"I would never go to church with a man. They'd have us married on sight."

Matt admired how truly lovely she looked in the sunlight, but his defenses rallied.

"Well, you can rest easy. I'm not looking for a wife."

"And I do not intend to marry."

Matt had to grin as he studied her.

"You're going to be an old maid?"

She drew herself up. "Now run along and catch up with your new bosses. Be sure to bow and scrape. That's what they like."

He grinned. "You're tough."

"I have to be, Mr. Tyler."

She walked to the office front door with her key, hesitated, then firmly shoved it in the lock.

Matt understood why she avoided the rear entrance. He knew the trauma of finding Frank murdered had left her badly shaken.

Matt followed her inside. She nearly caved in when she had another look at the office and the molasses-covered equipment. The image of Frank remained like a ghost.

"Are you going to be all right?" he asked.

She turned, chin up. "Run along, Mr. Tyler."

"Well, at least lock the door."

"I know how to do that."

"I'd like to be friends."

She flushed. "So would I."

He reached out and put his right fingers under her chin, startling her. "I don't want you hurt."

Her eyes brimmed with tears as he withdrew his hand. She turned her back. He put his hand on her shoulder. She knew he could feel her tremble.

"It's OK to be tough," he said, "as long as you're careful."

Matt hesitated, not knowing how to comfort her.

She stood stiff, her back to him.

Finally, he stroked her shoulder gently and turned away.

Matt left her, but outside, he had to pause and tell himself to hold back.

A pretty face had devastated him in DC. No other woman would have a chance to rule his life and break his already shattered heart.

Yet something about Jennifer gnawed at him.

Any other woman, he could admire from a distance, but her grip on his senses grew every time he saw her. He knew keeping his distance would not be an easy task, but he also knew his heart had too many bruises.

At the same time, he reminded himself, his mission here revolved around Grant, not romance.

CHAPTER 5

The white church, a rectangular building with a steeple, bell, and cross, rested on a high slope above the schoolhouse. The ringing of the bell had a musical tone on that sunny morning, echoing in the slight breeze.

Sweet-smelling yellow flowers lined the stone walk.

Matt wore his suit, Stetson, and boots. He neared the well-dressed crowd already funneling into the church. He paused, looking back down at the spread of Mountain Springs, a little pretty town on its face.

Beyond the cemetery to the south, he saw green rolling hills dotted with dark-green pines, grazing cattle and horses. Matt thought back to his youth, when he and his father had thought to raise horses instead of wheat and cattle. It had never happened.

"Mr. Tyler," a sweet voice called from near the foot of the steps.

He turned to see Morna beckoning to him. He removed his hat.

Smelling of violets and wearing a soft violet gown with white lace, she introduced him to her husband and his law partners, Hancock and Eberley. Matt shook their hands. He walked inside to sit with them.

The minister, a short, young, curly-haired, vibrant man, had a loud, husky voice, calling for purity and justice, and decrying the violence.

After church and outside, as others passed them by, Matt visited with the Frosts, Hancock, and Eberley. The lawyers seemed glad that Matt had arrived, all making him feel welcome with a lot of empty small talk.

"Would you come for tea?" Morna asked Matt.

"Thank you, but I'm going to the funeral."

"Oh, dear, but Mr. Banner was buried yesterday."

"This is for Frank Choper, the printer."

Morna stared at him. "Oh, no, I'm so sorry."

"He was murdered last night, just like Banner."

Eberley looked surprised.

Matt couldn't tell from the sober expressions of Frost and Hancock whether they were equally astonished. So far, Matt had no answers, but he knew something really smelled.

Morna twirled her parasol, looking distressed.

"Poor Miss White," Morna said.

Frost cleared his throat and ignored her. "Mr. Tyler, I assume we will see you in the morning at eight o'clock sharp."

"Yes, sir."

"You'll soon meet the other lawyers in town," Eberley said to Matt. "There's Judge Waller, the short one going down the hill over there with McComb, the county attorney."

When Morna and the partners were finally walking down the lane and away from Matt, he stood watching them leave. Frost and Hancock, distinguished looking, could have passed for congressmen or senators.

Eberley, less impressive, seemed more of an intellectual.

Matt continued downhill alone as the others turned the corner and out of sight on their way back to their mansions in the northern hills overlooking town.

He reached the main street and stood aside as remaining churchgoers filed past.

Now alone in the warm sun, he paused to gather his thoughts.

A husky voice startled him.

"You're that new lawyer."

Matt turned as a tall, chunky black man in a gray coat and white shirt approached him. The man hobbled over to Matt. Hidden by his pantaloons, his lower right leg seemed troubled.

"My name's Gentry. I'm the barber. And you need a trim, Mr. Tyler."

Matt grinned at him. "Well, unless you open before eight tomorrow, I'm afraid—"

"I'll take care of you now, before the funeral."

"Why?"

"I want to talk to you."

As they moved slowly down the boardwalk, Gentry hesitated now and then.

"This here leg I built, I think it needs more work."

"You did it yourself?" Matt asked.

"Sure I did. Carved it out of wood, foot and all. No peg leg for me."

"That's quite an accomplishment."

"I made some in the war for our men. And I make stuff for people, like cabinets. They got a sash and door factory over behind the furniture store, but there's no real good carpenters there."

"I ever build a house, I'll call on you."

They went into the sparkling clean barbershop on the north side of the street and just west of the newspaper office, which was on the south side. The small shop, well organized with three waiting chairs, sparkled clean with white and blue walls. Gentry locked the door and had the shades partway down.

Matt removed his coat and settled into the barber's chair. He watched in a wall mirror while Gentry covered him with a towel up to his chin.

Gentry argued with the strand of hair that kept falling on Matt's forehead. "Now about this cowlick..."

"Leave it," Matt said, "or my mother will have your hide."

Gentry chuckled. He settled Matt farther down, as the chair reclined.

"Just relax, Mr. Tyler."

"It's Matt. And you?"

"I never had a first name till I joined up with the Union. Now I'm Ulysses Simpson Gentry, but everybody just calls me Gentry."

"You know Grant's real name was Hiram Ulysses Grant."

"Yeah, so where'd the Simpson come from?"

"His mother. West Point made a mistake and used Simpson instead of Hiram in the middle. Did you ever meet him?"

"No, but I remember you saved his life. I was with the Fifty-Fourth Massachusetts Colored Infantry, Company C. General Ullman told us about it."

"The Fifty-Fourth. Didn't you take Fort Wagner? And your sergeant won the Medal of Honor."

"Yeah, Sergeant Carney."

Matt held the mirror up higher. "You said you wanted to talk to me."

"Yeah, I did. As soon as I finish, we'll have some coffee."

After Matt praised his haircut, they went into the back, where Gentry lived in a single room with a bed and dresser, iron stove, table and chairs, and a water closet, which Gentry said he'd built himself.

"Too cold in the winter to be traipsing outside to some little house," Gentry said. "And chamber pots, they never get clean. Now Moose, he knew ships, and he helped me with sealing the wood and all. And the blacksmith helped with the plumbing. As soon as I built it, we got all kinds of orders to fit 'em in people's houses. Of course, if you have a lot of money, you can order some fancy ones from back East. Porcelain and such. Like your lawyers done."

They sat at the table and enjoyed the hot coffee.

Gentry fondled his cup. "Matt, I thought you should know what's going on."

"You mean the murders?"

"I figure it's a lot more'n that. On Friday, Banner was in here for a haircut. Fellah gets in my chair and nobody else in the room, he starts talking."

"What did he say?"

"He was going on about the law firm, saying as how there were some strange happenings. He kept saying how Pocket had overheard something at the office a few months back, when Hancock and Frost were in the library, but Pocket wouldn't say what it was."

"Maybe they were going to fire him."

"Maybe, but Pocket's nowhere to be found, and now Banner's dead. I figure the firm just got rid of them."

Matt frowned. "That's a pretty strong accusation."

"I told the sheriff, but I didn't have no proof. Jennifer White said I should tell you about it. She said you were a good man, and I could trust you."

"She said that?"

"She also said you were like a little rooster."

Matt grinned. "Now that sounds more like her."

Matt sipped his coffee. He liked Gentry. It seemed mutual.

"But, "Gentry said, "I'm wondering why you come to Mountain Springs to work for some Rebs when you had your own practice back in DC."

Matt leaned back. "I'm here for the money, to help my folks. So they don't lose their farm."

Gentry sobered. "Good for you."

Matt suddenly grinned. "And to sow my wild oats."

Gentry chuckled, poured more coffee.

"Also, back East, we have nothing like the Rockies. I'm looking forward to some hunting. And fishing."

"You done any hunting since the war?"

"No."

Gentry sipped his coffee. "Ever stop to think why?"

They both considered Gentry's remark. Matt knew what Gentry meant.

"So I'll go fishing," Matt said, disgruntled.

"I'll join you up the creek for some trout. Anytime you say."

Matt smiled and relaxed. "Sure thing."

He resisted the urge to talk more with Gentry about the law clerks and about Grant's safety, even though he sensed Gentry would be loyal to Grant.

For now, Matt could trust no one.

That Sunday noon in her office, Jennifer worked on cleaning the press of the molasses. The harder she worked, the angrier she became. The sticky mass held like glue.

Through the front window, she saw Matt Tyler crossing the street from the barbershop. She wiped her eyes with the back of her hand, wondering how terrible she looked.

Matt came inside, willing to help. He pulled off his coat and hat, and with an ink-stained apron over his clothes, sleeves rolled up, he set about scraping the press with her.

"I saw you go into the barbershop, Mr. Tyler. What did you think about Mr. Gentry's tale?"

"A lot of hearsay." He worked harder. "But the less you discuss it with anyone else, the safer you'll be."

She shook her head. "I'm not afraid."

"You ought to be."

"Because I'm just a woman?"

"Until the world changes, yes." Matt paused to grin. "You're not muscle-bound, and you're just a little girl."

Jennifer's chin went up. "I haven't been a little girl for a long time."

"Yeah, OK, I think I noticed."

His big grin annoyed her. She found him so darn likeable.

She turned to gaze through the front window to the street. "Here comes Ruben Smythe. He and his brother are lawyers. They're convinced your outfit lets Red Ferman get away with murder."

Ruben Smythe, a tall slim lawyer with sharp but handsome features, wearing rough clothes and in his shirtsleeves, had come to help. Ruben had a slick look to him. His chin jutted out. His hair greased down, he had his own arrogant manner.

Ruben's stuffy attitude, immediately combative, filled the room.

Ruben paused to study the mess being cleared.

Most of the molasses now oozed in one of the buckets because of Matt's help.

Ruben pitched right in after a polite introduction to Matt.

The two men worked from opposite sides of the press.

Jennifer wearily sank in a chair. "Ruben, I really appreciate your help. And Mr. Tyler's. My arms are falling off."

Ruben frowned. "You've got to ease off on these editorials. They shoot editors, you know."

"I couldn't let that trial just fade away," she said. "Witnesses disappearing again. Especially if some Yank filed the claim."

"What about their depositions?" Matt asked.

Ruben grunted. "What depositions? We try, but witnesses disappear. They never want a record, Mr. Tyler. You won't find a single interrogatory in your files."

Jennifer nodded. "You see, Matt?"

Ruben frowned at Jennifer. "At least you have balance. You also blasted McComb, and he's the prosecutor."

"He's too aggressive in court," she said. "He's a nice polite Southern gentleman when you meet him on the street, but in the courtroom, he's vicious. And what about those strange dying confessions?"

Ruben came to stand near her. She liked him very much. A man so serious about the law, he made her wonder if he could ever settle down to a normal life. He always came across as ready for a fight.

"Jennifer, you take too many chances. And I'll say it again. Running a newspaper is no life for a woman."

Jennifer looked away, no longer amused by anything.

Ruben's attentions to her annoyed Matt, who grunted. "How about helping me clean these gears?"

Ruben returned to help, even while sarcastic.

"Matt, I haven't won a case against the firm for months. Why do they need you?"

Jennifer turned to the clock. "You can stop arguing now. It's time for the funeral."

Later that Sunday, at the little church cemetery, some fifty people, including merchants and miners, who had liked Frank, came to pay their respects. Ruben, the only other lawyer, Gentry, and the sheriff attended. Many had brought flowers, the sweet scents hanging in the stillness of the afternoon sun.

The minister gave a fine speech. The small crowd sang "Amazing Grace" with Jennifer's pure soprano rising above the others.

Back at the newspaper office, Jennifer wiped away her tears. She sat down while Matt and Ruben finished cleaning the press.

When they were done, they rested at the table with her.

Jennifer turned to Matt. "Ruben invited me to supper. Why don't you join us?"

Matt accepted readily, which annoyed Ruben.

Jennifer liked to keep distance between her and the men who called on her. Besides, she enjoyed Matt's cocky stance, her only entertainment.

At her request, they ate at Pop's Café by the alley next to the courthouse. Only two other couples dined in the small restaurant. The trio took a table by the wall. The elderly Pop waited on them. All three ordered steak and potatoes with cornbread. Supper was cordial.

Jennifer tried not to stare at Matt too much. She liked the cleft in his chin and his clear, striking brown eyes. His dark hair always looked in need of a comb. She had the constant urge to do something about it, especially that cowlick.

"Where were you born, Mr. Tyler?" she asked over coffee.

"Illinois."

"And your family?"

"My folks have a farm and some cattle. Grasshoppers hit them pretty bad in '74. The swarm was a mile wide and blocked out the sun. Lost all their wheat crop. They're still trying to pay off their debts."

"What about that new farmers' alliance?" she asked.

Matt shrugged. "They still have falling prices and high freight charges. I did what I could for them by pushing some legislation. But right now, they're all hurting."

"They chose that kind of life," Ruben said. "No one forced them into it."

Matt's face darkened with anger.

"They work for themselves and ask nothing of anyone," Matt said. "Working the land and cattle is probably the last honest way to make a living."

Ruben flushed. "Yes, you're right, of course."

Matt still looked angry. Ruben shrugged.

"My family were farmers," Ruben said. "They died with nothing left. I decided that would not happen to me."

Matt sipped his coffee to calm down.

Jennifer studied Matt. "I understand you have a brilliant record. Why don't you tell me about it so I can write it up?"

"No, thanks."

"What about you and Grant?" she persisted.

"Especially that."

"You're too modest," Ruben said. "Are you that way in court?"

"You'll find out soon enough," Matt said with a forced smile.

Jennifer glanced from one to the other. "There's something you should know, Mr. Tyler. Ruben and his brother, Ralph, work long hours for their clients. The law is their whole life, and they don't like it when it's abused."

"Neither do I."

Ruben made a face. "Then listen to this. Red Ferman is nothing but a claim jumper and buries anyone who gets in his way. Let's see how your conscience holds up."

Matt refused to engage in further argument.

"So you see, Jennifer," Ruben said, "advocacy has its drawbacks."

"And it's mistakes," she added, beaming as she planned her next editorial.

Ruben, obviously in love, smiled at her.

Matt admired her, but not enough to fall into any more webs.

His agenda had room only for his dedication to Grant.

That's what he told himself.

CHAPTER 6

THAT SAME SUNDAY NIGHT, FROST and Hancock stood outside the Frost mansion in the cold moonlight.

Both men wore heavy coats that barely cut the chill.

Frost's big German shepherd leaned on his left leg and growled at Hancock.

Hancock's buggy stood waiting with the black mare's head hanging as if it were asleep.

"The job may be already done," Frost said.

"I'm not sure it's worth it."

"You agreed from the start."

"I didn't realize..."

Hancock's voice faded. Nervous under Frost's gaze, he looked around at the starry sky and the distant snowcapped mountains.

Frost watched him carefully. "I want you to start thinking about how good you're going to feel when this is over."

"I also think of the consequences."

"If everyone does his part, there will be no consequences," Frost said. "No one would think we'd hire Tyler and drag him out here for nothing. And they'd never believe we'd give up a chance for a railroad. Especially since we've made such a big to-do about it. No, Milt, it's a good plan. We'll be in the clear."

"And you trust Shockley?" Hancock asked.

Frost shrugged. "The colonel does. So far, Shockley's arranged everything. But as for your question, I don't trust anyone. Not even you."

Hancock climbed into his buggy, slapped the lines, and drove away.

Frost watched him into the night. He wasn't so sure Hancock was going to hold together.

Frost said good night to his dog, which whined, as he was left outside.

Inside the mansion, Frost paused, as Morna came down the stairs in her nightgown and a green silk wrapper. Every time he saw her, she took his breath away, like that first time in Kansas.

Maybe she wasn't all that bright and spent too much money, but she belonged to him. Every inch of her, the dark-blue eyes and golden hair were his and his alone.

Frost had a great deal of love for Morna. So much, it frightened him. Maybe he needed Denver.

She moved gracefully into his arms. "Who were you talking to out there, Jared?"

"Hancock."

"He takes so much of your time."

"He misses his wife."

"Do you?"

"That was a long time ago."

"Are you happy with me, Jared?"

"You bet I am."

"I get so bored when you're away. At least I can plan a reception for Mr. Tyler. But I would so like some of that new white soap. You know you like my hands to be soft."

He kissed her passionately.

"You can have anything you want, Morna."

Except, she thought, the truth about what you and Hancock, and maybe Red Ferman, are planning with some mysterious colonel.

But perhaps, she told herself, it would be safer for her if she didn't know.

On Monday morning, Matt Tyler showed up at the law firm at eight o'clock sharp. He wore his one tailored blue suit with the fine vest and collar. He had always been a sole practitioner, making his own decisions. It would not be easy being part of a team with someone else calling the shots.

But the job only covered his true reason for being here.

The door opened for a greeting by Lucifer Rawlins, a young law clerk with small eyes, a large nose and pointed ears. In his white shirtsleeves, a pencil on his left ear, he looked very self-important. He also smelled of pungent cologne.

Matt disliked him instantly and knew by instinct that he could never trust him.

Lucifer could not have been a better name for the man.

"The partners, they're not here yet. I'll show you to your office."

"Are you the only clerk?"

"No, we still have MacCready and Loring, but they're sick with some kind of fever. Lots of folks been having it."

Matt looked around the plush waiting room. On the left was the clerk's small desk. Red velvet dressed walnut furniture in a circle on the right. Lace curtains centered in the middle of red velvet drapes at the front and side windows. A deep, thick rug lay in a champagne color. The wall trimmings had gold etching.

Lucifer, seeing himself as more than a law clerk, took Matt down the hallway past several ornate offices, showed him the vast library to the left and then his smaller office to the right.

Matt looked around his office. "Smells of tobacco in here."

"Banner was using your desk. He smoked, yes. Little cigars."

The clerk quickly exited.

Matt liked the office. He had a back window with a view of the distant trees, creek, and bridge. He settled in, reviewing the code books in his office.

Then he checked out the library, just down the hall, where he found the Twelfth Edition of Commentaries on American Law, edited by Oliver Wendell Holmes, and one of his favorites. The library, smaller than he had expected, had a disappointing shortage of books.

He did find that the Territorial Legislature had ratified the systems set up by the miners' courts and other informal courts, including actions of trespass, ejectment, and forcible detainer, long before Colorado had become a state.

Later, he helped himself to some coffee in a small kitchen area and returned to his office. An hour passed before he looked up from his desk and saw Eberley standing there.

"Are you all right in here, Matt?"

"Yes, sir."

Frost or Hancock would have invited Matt to their office to retain control, but not Eberley. The man just sat himself down at Matt's desk with his own cup of coffee and yawned. As Eberley stretched, Matt could see the shoulder holster with the Smith & Wesson revolver.

Eberley smiled. "We were very impressed with your successful appeals and writs, especially the Rothwell case. Frost was the first to insist we hire you as soon as your name appeared in the Supreme Court reports."

"I appreciate that."

"And I appreciate your saving Grant's life."

Matt tensed. "How did you find out?"

"We read it in a Denver newspaper when we first came here."

Matt frowned, embarrassed. "Any soldier would have done what I did."

Matt sipped his coffee. As Eberley continued to talk, Matt noticed a certain grief hanging over the man. It loomed in his dark eyes, the way his beard and moustache often twitched.

"Your family must be proud of you, Matt."

"I hope so. And yours, sir?"

"All three of us lost our wives during the war. Frost is the only one who remarried. I guess Hancock and me, we just can't let go of what we had."

Matt liked this man and wished he could confide in him.

"I'm pretty much retired," Eberley said. "Just a few local cases that usually settle."

"I haven't been told about court appearances."

"They want you to have some time first," Eberley said, turning serious. "But tell me, Matt, why did you leave Washington to come out here in the middle of nowhere?"

"Needed the money for my folks. So they won't lose their farm."

"I see."

Matt leaned back and grinned to lighten things up. "I always wanted to see the Rockies. Great hunting and fishing, I'm told."

"I felt the same, but my hunting days are over. Fishing, I can do. Anytime you say."

"Gentry told me the same thing."

Matt waited for Eberley's response to his mention of the black barber.

Eberley nodded. "I like Mr. Gentry."

Matt felt relief and continued to talk about the Rockies.

Eberley soon left him. The office felt empty, drab.

Matt downed his coffee. Still right nervous, despite his bravado, Matt felt intimidated by these highly educated men. He worried how his knowledge and experience would compare with theirs. His mission to protect Grant conflicted with his own need for respect.

He had already gone through his desk, but he looked again. Banner had left some research and notes on several cases. None of it meant anything to Matt.

Finally sick of the smell of smoke, he opened the window, letting in the fresh air.

Later, when Frost and Hancock came to work, they took Matt into Frost's office, outlined the firm's intentions, and gave him the royal treatment. They pandered to him, propped him up a little beyond what a new lawyer could expect. It made him all the more suspicious.

All three partners took him to lunch at the fancy restaurant in the Grand Hotel. Frost did most of the talking, as they sat at the table with their coffee.

"Property rights are an important issue for this firm, as are mineral rights. We're counting on you."

Matt studied them. In the various discussions, he realized from their comments that although they had gone to law school, he knew just as much, if not more, about the practice of law.

In fact, some of Frost's and Hancock's remarks made him wonder just what they had learned in school beyond the philosophy of the law. It gave him renewed confidence.

They were talkers. He was a fighter. He felt he could win against them in court, if it ever came to that. Except he admired Eberley, who had a deep understanding of the law and the Constitution, enough to serve on the Supreme Court.

Back at the office, later in the afternoon, Frost brought him a file.

Matt stood behind his desk, reached out to take it.

"This was a dispute over mineral rights involving Ferman's land grant and the claims of a small miner. They poach on his land and pretend they had been there before. It's already been researched and is off calendar, pending Smythe's locating his witnesses."

Matt frowned as he thought of Ruben's and Jennifer's accusations.

That evening, exhaustion from the tension he himself had created left him drained. And so it went for the next few days. One file on his desk. Codes to review. No court appearances.

On Friday, he received a file to answer an appeal, but it had already been researched. It was on one issue only. It didn't take him long to draft it. Again, very little discovery had been accomplished.

He worried about not being on calendar for anything.

"We don't want to load you down at first," Frost told him. "We want you to be well oriented."

The firm obviously only wanted him to draw Grant.

They didn't know he planned to protect the general with his life.

A planned reception in his honor on Saturday night would be at the Frost home. They said he could bring a guest and would send a buggy for him at seven o'clock on Saturday.

Matt didn't want to go alone.

On Friday evening, Jennifer worked at her desk, her heavy apron over a calico dress with the sleeves rolled up. A towheaded, short, skinny teenager named Henry had been helping her. He waved good-bye, as he left for the day.

Weary and discouraged, she knew her editorials could end her life. Yet she could not help herself. There seemed no way out of the job she had chosen. She felt grimy, dirty, and tired.

She looked up and smiled, as Matt Tyler entered from the front door. He always looked so ready to take on the world with a grin, she couldn't help but want to be around him. He contrasted her somber misery and frustration. She stood up and met him at the counter.

"Your door wasn't locked," Matt said.

"I knew you were coming," she fibbed.

She kept smiling, her green eyes shining.

The press worked fine now. She had a stack of papers on the counter. He stood there looking at the top one. He flipped through to her editorial. It was about Washington, DC, this time.

"Oh, I'm not backing off on Mountain Springs," she said. "I'm just furious with what's going on at the Hill. The Southerners are continually trying to stop funding for federal marshals to police their polls, and you know if they're not policed, the Negroes won't be able to freely vote."

"I've heard it's pretty bloody down there."

"And in Congress. The Democrats keep attaching restrictive riders to appropriation bills. President Hayes keeps vetoing them. I can't do anything about the Ku Klux Klan, but I can embarrass Congress, at least. I make sure they get copies."

Matt leaned on the counter and grinned. "You can't fight the whole world, you know."

"My father did. I was very proud of him, Mr. Tyler."

"I'll let you call me Matt, if you'll go with me to my reception tomorrow night. Up at the Frosts'."

Startled, she hesitated. "I don't know."

"As friends, nothing more. Agreed?"

She stared at him a long moment. "But I hate those people up there."

"Are you afraid to beard the lion in his den?"

"I'm not afraid of anyone."

"Then I'll pick you up tomorrow night at seven. Wear something prettier than that apron."

She gazed at him curiously. She managed a smile.

"All right, Matt. But I'm rather outspoken, and I can't promise I won't embarrass you."

The door opened, as Sheriff Hicks walked in. "There you are, Matt. I want to talk to you."

"Something I should know?" she asked.

Hicks nodded. "They found Pocket's body out in the hills. He's over at the undertaker's."

Jennifer took off her apron. "How did he die?"

"Same as the others. It wasn't a pretty sight." Hicks turned to Matt. "I want to chew it over with you, but over a game of checkers. After supper. I think better if I have a pea brain to bounce things off of."

After the sheriff left, Matt waited for Jennifer to lock up.

He walked with her to her house in the cold moonlight. He stood on her small porch, gazing down at her. Being close to him made her nervous, because she could not deny her attraction to him. He seemed so sure of himself, she would never let him know.

"The sheriff seems to like you," she said.

"He's a grumpy old man. He needs someone to like."

He put his hand at her chin, lifting it slightly, his dark eyes gleaming.

"You're a pretty woman, Jennifer White."

Color flushed through her cheeks. She drew back, her hand on the door latch. "Thank you, Matt."

Inside, she locked the door and turned up the lamp. Her little house felt terribly empty. She turned to look at her father's tintype in a gold frame on the mantel. A grim-looking man with a handlebar moustache and a lot of black hair, he seemed to be looking straight at her and asking, "Where are my grandchildren?"

Lifting the frame, she held it close.

"Well, Father," she said, "what do you think of that young rooster?"

Later that evening, Matt moved down the dark street with occasional lanterns lighting his way to the jailhouse. Moonlight came and went. Icy cold went through his coat.

Inside the jail, heat from the stove welcomed him.

Once again, the cells out back were empty. Alone with Hicks over checkers next to the hot wood stove, he and the sheriff drank the same thick, heavy coffee.

"That's going to rot my gut," Matt said. "Used to get that on the Chisholm Trail."

"Is that where you learned to handle a six-shooter?"

Matt jumped two of his checkers. "Yeah, I met some Texans after the war and ended up on the trail with them. They taught me a fast draw and how to hit what I aimed at."

Hicks studied the board, didn't answer.

"I was a brush popper for a while." Matt leaned back. "Those ten-year-old moss horns were a handful. Horns sometimes nine feet across, and if they ever got you, man, you knew it. And in a stampede, you had to get out of the way and let 'em run. I miss the trail."

"You ever kill a man, I mean besides the war?"

"A few rustlers. Maybe. Not sure."

"No duels? No gunfights?"

"I'm a lawyer, remember?"

Hicks chuckled with a snort. "They're the worst, you know. Frost has a real reputation. Killed a couple men in duels down South. I wonder how good he really is."

Matt jumped another checker. "He's still alive."

"So how was it this week at the firm?"

"They haven't given me much to do yet. I'm basically a trial lawyer, and sitting around an office is not my style." Matt studied the board. "I have Banner's old office. Nothing there but research and notes on files."

"Sure is a coincidence. Two law clerks getting killed the same way as Choper. And none of them robbed. Even Pocket still had his wallet. With money in it. That gambling story doesn't hold up."

"Who do you think done it?"

Hicks shrugged. "Could have been Crazy Albert, although he's kind of clumsy and likely noisy. Nobody heard anything when Banner got it. Must have happened fast. Like with Choper."

Matt jumped the sheriff's last four checkers in one swoop and leaned back to enjoy his coffee. The sheriff made a face and went about resetting the board as he talked.

"You know, Matt, there's a good chance you could be a target."

"Why is that?"

"Just got a feeling."

"Yeah, me too."

"Hear you got a reception tomorrow night at Frost's. I suppose Red Ferman's going to be there. Have you met him yet?"

"No, I haven't, but he's the firm's major client."

"Have you met the other lawyers in town?"

"Just Ruben Smythe. He's a sore loser."

Hicks jumped two of Matt's checkers. "Don't jump to conclusions, Matt."

"Well, you sure aren't letting me have peace of mind."

"What you need is a visit to the Red Light."

"And get my throat cut while I'm trying to have a roll in the hay? No, thanks. Besides, those women didn't look that clean to me. Maybe I'm a little too particular, but they don't smell too good."

Hicks laughed with a snort. "You got that right."

Matt yearned to tell him what he knew about Grant and a possible conspiracy.

Much as he admired Hicks, he kept it to himself for now.

Later that night, when Matt stretched out on his bed at the boarding-house, he stared at the silver cobwebs on the ceiling and thought about the dead law clerks. He and Hicks had talked for a long while about the possibilities, but they had no real answers.

And with the newspaper still operating, what would happen to Jennifer?

Worse, what would happen if Grant came out of the mountains?

The law clerks didn't die for just any reason.

CHAPTER 7

When Matt went to Jennifer's door at seven o'clock on Saturday evening, the sky darkened with fast-moving clouds and occasional moon. He carried a long, black umbrella Mrs. Ledbetter had insisted he take. He wore a heavy, black frock coat over his tailored blue suit. His white, starched collar itched. He felt damp under his new linen shirt.

Fear of his great attraction for this woman made him hesitate a long moment at her door. He stared at the solid wood with the metal knocker. He swallowed hard.

His Stetson in hand, he forced himself to knock.

When Jennifer came out and onto the porch, she looked amazing in a green silk dress with green lace at the throat and wrists, full skirts whirling about her. She wore a small bustle that lifted up in back with a lot of frills.

Her bright eyes shone like emeralds under long lashes.

So, he thought, she's breathtaking. No woman could be trusted with a man's fragile heart. Always unpredictable, even in their own hearts, they represented nothing but danger to him.

He helped her with her forest-green, soft velvet cape that matched her feathered hat. Her glistening chestnut hair, tied back with a ribbon and held by a jeweled comb, she beamed with beauty unmatched by anyone he'd ever seen. She smelled of lilacs.

"You look gorgeous," he heard himself saying.

"So do you. But are you sure you're brave enough to take me?"

"Your chariot awaits."

She took his arm. She could see that he was nervous.

"Be careful tonight, Matt. Two years ago, right after I came to town, they had a reception for another lawyer they had hired. He behaved badly and was fired the next day."

"Behaved badly?" Matt asked.

"I heard he'd had a little too much to drink and was dancing with Morna. He was getting a little too friendly and not getting much resistance. When Frost caught sight of it, he threw the man out of the house."

"He lets her get away with that?"

"You think he should beat her?"

Matt grinned. "No, but he ought to make her so happy she doesn't care about anyone else."

"I don't think anything would change Morna. She's a coquette. A flirt. But everyone sort of accepts her as she is. I don't think she can help it."

"Why do you say that?"

"She's a born actress, but she's missing something, and she keeps looking for it in every man she meets. Even when she knows Frost would kill anyone who got too close to her."

"See how helpless we men are? Women can flirt, but we're the ones who get shot."

"You're the ones who deserve it."

Matt laughed. She smiled to herself, enjoying the sparring. Yet in the back of her mind, she still thought of New Mexico Territory and Richard, her "wonderful" man who had hidden from the attack on her father.

How could she trust any man after that?

They moved through the alley and onto the boardwalk as twilight engulfed them. A buggy driven by Frost's handyman, a glum old man in heavy clothes and a felt hat, picked them up.

Sitting under the buggy canopy in the backseat with Matt, Jennifer felt comfortable and content for the moment but apprehensive about the reception.

Matt looked up at the fast-moving clouds. "It's going to rain before we get back."

"I'm the girl. I get the umbrella."

He grinned. "We can share."

The buggy took them north out of town and up to the first big hill where Frost's mansion stood alone. A dozen buggies waited near a row of saddle horses. A huge German shepherd, watching every movement with yellow eyes, lay tied up away from the large front porch.

Jennifer took Matt's arm. "Matt, I promise not to embarrass you."

He just grinned and walked her to the entrance.

A part-time maid in a white apron, her frilly gray hair under a cap, let them inside. The air smelled of liquor and delicious snacks that sat on a table in the parlor. The maid took Jennifer's hat, her cape, and Matt's coat and Stetson, along with the umbrella.

Jennifer felt ill at ease, for she had often chastised these people.

She counted fifty guests. They all wore their finery, especially the few women. She could see there were no lawyers other than the partners. It seemed obvious they only invited clients and a few of the merchants. No shady characters, except Red Ferman.

Jennifer and Matt faced Morna in her yellow silk dress. She maneuvered him away from Jennifer, who was stuck with a talkative merchant, and introduced him to Judge Waller, the mayor, various townspeople, and two doctors. And Ferman.

Jennifer watched from a distance. She could tell that Matt took an instant dislike to Red Ferman with his thick red hair. Both men stood six feet, looking at each other as if ready to fight.

She took little of the food and none of the wine and liquor being served all evening.

Matt spent as much time with Jennifer as he could.

The partners kept calling him away to join in one conversation or another. She didn't mind staying back and observing. The wives made sure their men did not approach her.

Eberley, the Yank partner, had no such restraint. He came to visit with her. He made her feel comfortable. A real gentleman, he seemed out of place.

Across the room, Morna seized Matt's arm when a fiddler started playing the traditional "Red River Valley" as a waltz in the back ballroom. Guests moved toward the dance floor.

"You're the guest of honor, Matt, so you have to dance with the hostess."

Morna ushered the flushed Matt toward the music.

Eberley took Jennifer inside to dance with her.

"Don't worry," Eberley said, as he gracefully whirled Jennifer about. "You're the prettiest woman here. Your green eyes could win a war."

She smiled her thanks.

Eberley continued to whirl her about, but she often glanced toward Matt.

"Don't worry about Matt," Eberley said. "He can take care of himself."

"He's too trusting."

"You underestimate him. He's survived a war, politics, and the courts."

"But he doesn't understand women," she said.

At the same time, Matt tried to keep Morna, smelling of French perfume, at arm's length as much as the dance allowed. She smiled up at him with her bright but dark-blue eyes.

"Matt, you look grand tonight, but I'm really surprised you brought that woman."

"That woman?"

"You know, Jennifer White. She's so liberated. She even wants women to vote, you know."

"Don't you?"

"Matt, I let the men worry about politics."

"I think you're smarter than that."

"You mean you think I may have something in my pretty little head?"

He grinned. "I think you're too careful to let anyone know what's there."

She laughed. "I think you're right."

The music stopped, and then restarted.

Matt glanced over her head to see Jennifer dancing with Red Ferman. He gritted his teeth. As he whirled Morna, she spotted Jennifer with Ferman.

Morna's mouth went tight. Matt watched Morna's face turn to flushed pink. It made him wonder.

Red Ferman kept busy trying to charm Jennifer as they danced. "I'll bet that if you found the right man, you'd be a lot happier."

"Then who would print the news?" Jennifer asked.

"You could hire someone."

"Someone who didn't make any trouble?"

Ferman just smiled and swung her about.

When the music stopped, Jennifer and Red Ferman were right next to Matt and Morna. Matt managed to change partners, drawing Jennifer into his arms. She felt mighty fine.

As they swayed about the floor in another graceful waltz, Matt saw a fire in Jennifer's emerald eyes. Her face a dark pink, she showed her annoyance.

"She was certainly dancing close to you, Matt. I was beginning to think you would be thrown out the same way as the last lawyer."

"Well, I wasn't pawing her."

"I was glad to see that."

He grinned down at her. Graceful and careful not to be too close to him, she remained elusive. He could see the conflicts between her being a lady and the way her spirit was driven to be bold. He liked it. All the more reason to keep his distance.

Across the floor, Red Ferman held Morna a little too close as he whirled her about, and she chided him. "My husband will throw you out."

"Without my business, he'd have to close up."

"Then he'll take it out on me."

Ferman relaxed his grip. "All right. When can I see you again?"

"I don't know."

"You were sure flirting with that Matt Tyler."

"What about you and Jennifer White?"

"Just trying to get her married so she'd stop being a nuisance."

"Married? You mean to Matt Tyler?"

"No, I don't want her to be a widow so quick."

Red Ferman regretted his words and laughed them away.

"Just kidding," he said.

Morna became nervous just the same and drew away from him.

The music stopped. Frost, visibly annoyed, remained cordial to Red Ferman as Frost recovered his wife.

The doors to the back garden stood open. Matt walked out into the night with Jennifer on his arm. The damp air chilled them under a cloudy sky. The moon only occasionally cast its light. Flowers lined the path and smelled sweet as chocolate.

The only light came from the open doors and a few small lamps in the garden.

Rain threatened.

Two other couples smiled as they went back inside. Matt and Jennifer stood alone. She put her free hand on his arm.

"We're going to get wet, Matt."

"I don't care. I've spent half my life in the rain."

"Back in Washington?"

He nodded. "Illinois, Missouri, Texas. The Chisholm Trail."

"That's why you wear that Stetson and your boots, instead of shoes? And that revolver?"

"Sort of became a trademark. And lets me hold on to what's really important."

"More important than the law?"

"The law is a means to an end. I had a lot more fun on the trail."

"Fun?"

"Seeing the country. Long days in the saddle, fighting rustlers, racing like crazy to turn a stampede. We moved some twenty-five hundred head on every drive."

"Sounds more like a lot of hard work. And dangerous."

"Well, sure but the men all look out for one another. Like brothers. Some nights we sat around the campfire, listening to a harmonica—that was right peaceful. Hearing the cattle bellow as the night riders sang to them."

Jennifer felt envious and cheated of a man's adventure.

"So how did you get into law?" she asked.

"There was a lawyer on one of the drives. I argued with him, and the next thing I knew, I was studying in his office back in Illinois. I was in court right away and learning on the job."

He stood gazing down at her, because right now in the moonlight with the shine in her hair and the delicious smell of roses circling her, the last thing on his mind was the law.

"What about you?" he asked. "Anyone get nasty in there?"

"No, they were very polite. And careful what they said."

Rain began to drizzle down on them. She turned to hurry inside. Matt followed as the maid closed the doors behind them and drew the green drapes. They moved back among the crowd as Frost caught up to him.

"Matt, can you join us in my office?"

Leaving Jennifer, Matt followed Frost, Eberley, and Hancock to the office for a business meeting with Red Ferman. They discussed mineral rights and land grants. He could tell the meeting took place so Ferman could take his measure.

Matt had taken an intense dislike to Ferman, but he had to remain pleasant.

While the men talked in Frost's office, Jennifer stopped at the punch bowl to help herself as Morna joined her.

"My dear Miss White, you look ravishing tonight."

"You always do, Mrs. Frost."

"Thank you." Morna became sweeter. "Do you have designs on Mr. Tyler?"

"Should I?"

Morna's lips twisted in a forced smile. "Jared plans to make him a partner in another six months."

Jennifer hesitated, biting her words. She didn't want to ruin Matt's evening, but she could not stand this woman's coy and slippery manners. She sipped her punch, trying to calm herself. Morna continued to talk as if they were old friends.

"Yes," Morna was saying, "I would love to live in the East, wouldn't you? Just think of the strawberries and ice cream and fantastic supper houses. And the fashions up to date. The opera and theaters, social events, such grand families to meet, all back there."

"There's opera in Denver."

"Yes, I know, but we're here in the middle of nowhere. With no culture."

"I think you should work on that, Mrs. Frost. Why don't you start a theater? You could play Lady Godiva."

Morna frowned, and then smiled. "Oh, you're teasing me."

"Well, you have the figure for it."

"And I'm pleased about that, Miss White. There's only one thing on a man's mind, and that gives us the only power we have."

"If we get the vote, that could change."

"Miss White, you are dreaming. They will never give us the vote. Men are actually afraid of us. That's why they need to be in control. And I promise you, if by some miracle we did get the vote, it would only be because they think they'll control what we do with it."

Jennifer smiled at how surprising Morna could be.

In fact, Jennifer found herself looking past the coquette and at a very wise woman.

The mayor's chatty wife came to join them. Soon, Jennifer wandered off.

When the evening ended, it began to rain heavily.

Frost's handyman drove Matt and Jennifer down the hillside in the downpour. The buggy top sagged but protected them until they pulled up in front of the newspaper office.

Matt took out his long umbrella and helped her step down. "Your shoes will turn to paste in that mud," he said.

Jennifer didn't resist as he lifted her in his arms, his right hand behind her waist, his left under her knees. She felt heavier than he had expected Her left arm went around his neck. She held the umbrella over them in her right hand.

Despite himself, he loved having her in his arms.

Beyond the umbrella, rain soaked her gown, cape, and soft shoes.

He thought of Laura, who would never consider getting wet for any reason.

Sloshing through the rain and mud, he walked slowly to savor every minute. As they entered the alley, she rested her head on his shoulder. A new warmth passed between them.

Until they saw the fire.

Flames licked at the front window of her house.

"Matt," she gasped.

He ran with her in his arms and set her on the porch out of the rain. "Stand back."

The roof, soaked by rain, held its own. Fire ate away at the interior. He knew if he opened the door, the flames would rush out. He had no choice, taking her key and unlocking it.

"You got water in there?"

"At the wash basin, over on the right. There's a pump."

"Run to Mrs. Ledbetter's and get help."

She turned into the rain with the umbrella and ran toward the boardinghouse, her soft shoes splashing the pools and mud, her gown dragging in the slop.

He pulled off his coat and put it over his head. He opened the door as the hot flames shot at him. He darted around them. The fire had started by the broken window from some kind of bomb thrown through the glass. He could smell the kerosene.

By the light of the fire, he saw the pitcher and a bucket of water at the basin. The windows to his right still had their heavy drapes intact. He grabbed them, jerking them off their rods, even as he coughed with the heavy smoke, his eyes burning.

He turned and threw the drapes in a great sweep over the burning stuffed chair, floor, and burning drapes. He stomped on them, smothering as much as he could. Then he grabbed the bucket of water and tossed it on the wall where the flames yet burned.

In through the doorway came four male boarders with buckets of water. Soon, the flames were under control, and then out as smoke dwindled.

With the boarders now gone, Jennifer stood just inside, staring at the broken window and the scorched wall and floor. Matt turned up the lamp on the table, opened all the windows, and came to stand at her side.

"They could come back. Maybe I should sleep on your couch."

She turned and gazed up at him with tears in her eyes but her lips set in a twisted smile. "Go home, Matt. I'll be all right. There's no fire or smoke in the bedroom. There's a lock on the door. And I have my revolver."

"I can see your house from my window. I'll keep watch."

"Thank you, Matt."

He wanted to hold her, give her comfort. Instead, he gave her something she could look forward to, something a little happier than this.

"Look," he said, "in a few days, they want me to take a ride to Silver Gulch with Eberley for orientation. They say you can go and come back in the same day. Why don't you come along?"

"As friends?"

"That's our deal." He moved closer to her. "He'll be our chaperone. So, how about it—will you go with us?"

"Yes, I will, because I've never had a chance to visit Silver Gulch and see Red Ferman in his den. No one else would take me."

"Why is that?"

"Because I'm a woman."

"I'll let you know when it's set." His heart pounded at her nearness as he put his hands on her shoulders. "Have I earned a kiss good night?"

"Not for taking me to that dreadful party, but for the fire, perhaps. As friends."

"OK, I'll give you a friendly smack."

She smiled and tilted her head back. Matt leaned down to press his lips on her velvet ones. A wild sensation shot down to his boots, up his back and to the nape of his neck, where it remained in a tickle. She smelled wonderful.

He fought his infatuation. This woman, intelligent and brave, had deep compassion. A man could fall in love with her really easily. Any other man, that is.

These thoughts charged through his mind, as she returned his kiss. Her response set his defenses in motion.

He drew back, his eyes wide open, but hers were closed a moment longer, her long lashes fluttering. Then she looked up at him with the sweetest smile he'd ever seen.

"Good night, Matt. And please be careful. They're killing off law clerks. What makes you think they won't start on the lawyers?"

He stepped back, knowing her words rang true.

Yet he would give his life for Grant.

CHAPTER 8

On Monday morning in Mountain Springs, rain continued to fall. At the law firm, Frost and Hancock talked privately in Frost's big, ornate office, both nursing a cup of hot, steaming coffee that smelled as strong as charcoal. Hancock looked sleepy in his chair, facing the grand walnut desk.

Frost leaned back in his soft leather chair, his cane hooked on its arm. He loosened his collar.

"Lousy coffee."

"I don't think the pot was washed," Hancock said.

"Maybe we ought to hire a woman."

Hancock laughed. "In a law office?"

"Well, I wasn't talking about a woman lawyer. I know they have a couple back East, which is a terrible mistake."

"You're right. Women are just too softhearted."

"Which makes us hard-hearted?" Frost asked.

"Last year, they won the right to argue before the Supreme Court."

"Doesn't mean a thing," Frost said. "They don't have the vote. I don't think they can cause any damage."

"So you're talking about a woman clerk?"

"They have a couple in Denver taking dictation. And as for those typewriter machines, you know the women were so good on them, they had to scramble the letters so they couldn't type so fast and jam the keys. I think a woman clerk would be an asset."

"Well, what about your wife?"

Frost laughed, figuring Morna didn't have a brain in her gorgeous body. He didn't want to say that to Hancock.

Hancock sobered, sipped his coffee. "We've got to give Matt Tyler more to do, or he's going to get suspicious."

"Give him some dormant files to work on possible motions for dismissal."

"You know," Hancock said, "the colonel was impressed with Matt's good manners, but Ferman took a real dislike to him."

Frost grunted. "Don't worry about Ferman."

After a knock on the door, Eberley entered, coffee in hand. "What's going on?"

"Just talking about Matt Tyler," Frost said. "We're going to give him some of the old files, see if he can get the cases dismissed. That way he can see how we operate from start to finish, get him better oriented."

Eberley sat near the desk, balanced his cup.

"Good idea," Eberley said. "I like that boy. He learned his trade in a law office. He's proof a man can be a good lawyer without going to law school."

"Poor people should not be lawyers," Frost said, agitated. "They have no fortunes to worry about, and they could do a lot of harm. I think background and family position is better preparation."

"I disagree," Eberley said.

Hancock quickly changed the subject. "I understand you're taking Matt out to Silver Gulch," Hancock said.

After further discussion about Silver Gulch, Eberley left them.

Frost grimaced. "He's too liberal."

"And common," Hancock said.

"He's bound to fully retire before long. And when my sons finish Harvard, they'll be joining us."

Hancock shrugged. "What about Lucifer?"

"He's slime, Milt."

"He's slime that knows too much."

"If he lives to tell it," Frost said.

Frowning, Hancock stared into his cup.

While Frost and the worried Hancock talked quietly, Eberley visited Matt, who had just finished answering the appeal. Matt nursed a cup of coffee in his small office.

Eberley closed the door and sat in front of the desk, crossing one leg over the other knee. Matt liked him. In some other place, they could have been great friends.

"Now then, Matt, they're going to give you some more files to work on. See if you can get some cases dismissed."

"I'm ready to do a lot more than that."

"I know, but my partners move real slow."

"When I was on my own, I had more cases a month than this whole firm has in the office. I covered a lot more territory, and I never lost a good case. But they seem afraid to let me cross over to the courthouse."

"They're a bit stuffy, but they built up this firm from nothing to a big success. They don't want to lose its reputation."

"According to Jennifer, its reputation's not that good."

"Is that what's bothering you?"

"That, and all these murders, one right after the other. And last night, someone threw a firebomb through the window of Miss White's house."

Eberley frowned. "So I heard. I don't know who's doing this to her."

"From what I saw of Ferman, I wouldn't put it past him."

Eberley shrugged. "I offered to pay for a body guard. She refused."

"Just the same, it's no business for a woman."

"Times are changing, Matt."

"I've asked her to ride with us to Silver Gulch when the rain stops. If you'll still lend me the bay until I can find a horse to buy."

A knock hit the door. Lucifer stuck his head inside. He had an armful of old files. Eberley continued talking as if they had been discussing cases.

"But Judge Waller, he's a fair man, Matt. I think you'll find that out. If you have the evidence on your side, you're bound to win."

Lucifer walked in with the files.

That evening when leaving the law firm, Matt pulled on a slicker and walked into the rain and down the boardwalk, water dripping from the brim of his Stetson. The newspaper office had no lights, but her house did. The jailhouse also looked dark.

Restless, Matt wandered down the street. He worried about Jennifer.

The firm made him nervous. He had a lot of unanswered questions.

More and more, he worried about Grant.

He found himself in front of the barbershop, but it was also closed. He walked on and over to the Red Light Saloon, also on the north side of the street, but not because of the women. His mind cluttered with worry; he needed a change.

Inside, he found only six men and the same two women, all seated at tables in the back. Miners with dirty clothes and grimy hands, they looked right unfriendly. Two of them smoked cigars. The women looked as weary and worn as before.

"Well, if it isn't the lawyer," Lupe said.

Matt ordered some cider from the tall, skinny bartender with the big ears. He sat alone at a table, his back to the wall, his slicker hanging on one of the hooks behind him. Minnie came over to smile down at him.

"Real men don't drink cider," she teased.

He looked up at her, still finding her appearance to be unclean.

"Have you seen Grizzly or Moose tonight?" he asked.

"Sure, they went over to the gambling hall. As soon as they lose everything, they'll be back."

"Thanks."

She leaned over to tickle his ear. "How about going upstairs with me?"

"Not right now."

She played with his neck. "Oh, come on."

He caught another whiff of her, became nauseated and reached up, grabbed her hand, and tossed it aside.

Angered, she went back over to the men. Matt could see her telling them something terrible. All of a sudden, a big man with shoulders like a bull and a clean-shaven face, wrinkled and scarred, eyes wild, charged over to him.

"Hey, lawyer, we don't like our women insulted."

Matt leaned back in his chair, balancing it. He pushed his Stetson back from his forehead and looked up at him. He had to show a lot of bravado in a hurry, or he would be pounded into mush. It had worked with Moose and Grizzly, but this brute looked right dangerous.

Matt swallowed hard and forced a smile.

"She's no lady."

"You only hump ladies, do you?"

Matt's face went dark. "Get away from me."

"They call me Bulldog because when I fight, I don't let go of a man for nothing. And I'm inviting you right now to get up and show me how tough you are."

"You got a face like a bulldog."

Matt didn't move. Bulldog kicked at his chair, sending it over backward.

Matt crashed on his back, legs in the air, his head barely missing the wall. He threw himself to the side, away from the big man, rolling from the chair.

He got to one knee, catching his breath. There was no way he could run from this fight. The laughter would follow him into the courtroom. Besides, he had never learned how to run away from anything.

Yet he knew he faced a real pounding.

Bulldog picked up the table in both hands and threw it across the room. It crashed on top of another table, stood on end, and dropped with a clatter to the floor. He kicked the other chairs aside, leaving nothing between him and Matt.

"Get up now, or you'll never get up again."

Matt dripped with new sweat. He got to his feet. They both wore gun belts and Colts, but Bulldog wanted a physical fight, possibly to the death. He snarled at Matt, lips curling back.

"First I'm gonna bite off your ears. Then I'm going to stomp your gut, so everything comes out a your mouth. Then I'm gonna pound your pretty face, so nobody'd ever know who you was."

"And what will I be doing all that time?"

"Not much."

Bulldog began to move toward him. Matt stepped to his right, keeping his eye on the other five men, who seemed to be enjoying the prospects and exchanging bets at their table in the back.

Pulling off his coat, Bulldog revealed great arm muscles bulging through his shirt. Matt peeled off his suit coat, right sorry he hadn't gone home to change. He removed his Stetson and hung it and his coat on a wall hook.

Bulldog unbuckled his gun belt, dropping it to the floor behind him. Matt did the same but hung his on a wall hook next to his coat and hat.

"I'm going to mash you to a pulp," Bulldog growled.

Matt moved away from the wall, his heart pounding in his chest like a hammer. He could hear it in his ears, thumping loudly. Sweat dribbled down his rear.

Bulldog sneered, arms akimbo. "No woman's gonna want you when I get done."

"You talk big."

Bulldog threw out his chest. "Get ready to die."

The big man charged like a locomotive at full steam. Matt leaped aside, slamming his fist into a belly so tight it nearly cracked his fingers. Bulldog crashed headfirst against the wall, causing the building to shake.

Bulldog staggered backward. He recovered and turned with a roar.

Matt he knew he had to hammer at that ugly, wrinkled face, make his nose bleed and eyes close and teeth crackle. If he lived long enough.

Bulldog charged again. Matt leaped aside once more. This time, he slammed his fist in the man's face, flattening the large nose with a loud crack.

With a yelp, Bulldog stumbled to a halt and grabbed his bleeding nose.

Bulldog whined, "You broke my nose!"

Sweat ran down Matt's face. He wiped his eyes with the back of his hand. If Bulldog got hold of him, he'd never get loose. He'd have to do a lot of dancing.

He jumped around every time Bulldog tried to grab him. Every chance he had, he hammered the man's face and head. Bulldog yelped when his nose got in the way.

Dazed, Bulldog roared and charged again. Matt jumped aside.

Matt shoved his right boot in the man's rear with all his weight.

Bulldog's head hit the wall so hard, the building rattled. He dropped to his knees, shaking his head. There was no stopping him. He roared, got back up, and turned around, big hands extended like claws.

"Stand still, you yellowbelly."

Matt maneuvered quickly in all directions, until he tripped on Bulldog's gun belt and crashed back against the bar. In that moment, Bulldog grabbed him, big arms around Matt like a vise, pinning his arms down, fists deep in Matt's back.

Matt could smell the man's horselike sweat.

Bulldog, nose bleeding, lifted Matt up in the air like a child and spun him around with a growl.

Matt felt his bones being crushed. His face inches from that of the snarling brute's bloody nose, Matt tried to stay conscious.

Matt slammed his head into Bulldog's face, hammering at his nose and mouth and one of his eyes so hard that Bulldog cried out with a yell that nearly busted Matt's eardrums. The big man threw Matt against the bar and grabbed his own face in horror.

"You bastard! I can't see!"

Matt, hurt even worse when the bar struck his back, stumbled out of the way and to the side. Bulldog spun around and around, clawing his face.

Minnie came hurrying to the big man's side. "Bulldog, let me help you, honey."

Bulldog whined and moaned. She put her arm around him, and then turned to glare at Matt.

"You meanie!"

Matt stared at her, his head spinning.

She led the whimpering Bulldog past where the other miners just sat staring at the whole scene. She took Bulldog into a back room, closing the door behind them.

Matt drew a deep breath and staggered over to where his chair had fallen. He lifted it and sank down in a daze, his back to the wall. He hurt so badly, he could hardly move.

He then realized Moose and Grizzly stood in the doorway. The two big men came over with amazed looks on their bearded faces. They moved a table in front of Matt and pulled up chairs to sit with him, one on either side. Moose handed him his Stetson and grinned.

"I didn't think anyone could take Bulldog, except maybe Crocker, but he hardly ever gets into town."

The bartender, trying to hide a grin, brought a glass of cider and two beers on a round tray. He went back to the bar as a miner came over to pay off a bet with him.

Matt wiped his brow. Out of breath, he managed to sip some cider.

"Bulldog works for Ferman," Grizzly said.

"What started it?" Moose asked.

"I turned Minnie away."

Moose laughed. "Yeah, she does take that personal."

Matt gasped at the pain in his chest and back and legs and knees and arms and head and neck and all over his body, knowing how he'd feel by morning.

"This is the only place in town with women," Moose said. "Otherwise, you got to go to Silver Gulch. They got a cathouse."

Matt made a face. "I was going to have Miss White ride over there with me, but it don't sound like a place to take her."

"She's tough," Moose said. "She'll be all right."

"Yeah," said Grizzly, "she's one of the few real ladies in town. How some ever, there a few others ain't so proper."

"Yeah," said Moose, lowering his voice to a whisper. "Like Morna Frost. Every time her man's away, Red Ferman slips in the back door."

Matt frowned. "I wouldn't say that to anyone else, if I were you."

"Oh, I know about Frost and his duels down South," Moose said quietly, "but Ferman would blow his guts out before he could clear leather."

"Just the same," Matt said, "as far as I know, Mrs. Frost is a lady."

Moose and Grizzly could only grin at Matt.

"You ever leave that firm and want to take on clients like us," Grizzly said, "you let us know. We'd be mighty proud to have you as a lawyer."

Matt leaned back in his chair. "That's a real compliment, Grizzly. Thanks."

"You got Bulldog's blood on your fancy shirt," Moose said.

"I won't be able to move come morning."

The men laughed. They watched Matt sip his cider.

"Hey, how come you drink apple juice instead of rotgut?" Moose asked.

"You just answered your own question."

"No, seriously," Moose said.

"My father used his strap across my rump every time I had a hankering. On the cattle trail, no liquor was allowed. Then I saw how it clouded the minds of other lawyers. After a while, I just had no taste for it. Made my folks real happy."

"What about Grant?" Grizzly asked. "I hear he did a lot of drinking."

"Not when the chips were down."

They paused as the sheriff came into the saloon. His handlebar moustache twitched as he walked over to Matt. Rain dripped from his slicker and hat.

"So there you are, Matt. I was hoping for a game of checkers."

"He's a little tired," Grizzly said with a chuckle. "He just beat the heck out of Bulldog."

Hicks look stunned. "What?"

"Yeah," said Moose, "it was a sight for sore eyes."

Hicks sat down, pulled up a chair.

While the men talked about Matt's fight in the Red Light, Jennifer visited Mrs. MacCready, an elderly lady in her nineties with gray hair and dimples.

Mrs. MacCready's law clerk son lay sick with the fever in a back bedroom.

Rain pounded the roof and rattled windows. The neat little home, the second house back behind Pop's Café, had frilly lace everywhere, on tables, windows, and chairs. It smelled sweet from yellow flowers in vases. The fat iron stove had the room very warm. They sat on the sofa some distance from the heat.

Lamps burned low and smoky.

Jennifer wore another faded blue dress. Mrs. MacCready had a white lace shawl over her calico and white lace around her head. Jennifer had always enjoyed the lady's stories and history, but tonight, all she could think of was the woman's law clerk son.

"Now, Jennifer," the woman said. "It's really late. And it's dark out."

"It's a short walk to my house. And I carry a revolver in my purse." Jennifer stood up. "Are you sure you won't let me stay the night?"

"No, dear, you go on home. You'll just catch his fever."

"Well, you lock up good," Jennifer said, drawing on her gray cape and pulling up the hood to cover her chestnut hair.

Mrs. MacCready walked her to the front door. "Thank you for the cake. And don't you worry about me."

They said good night with hugs.

Jennifer waited to hear the door being locked before turning away.

Still worried, Jennifer walked out into the darkness as moonlight broke through the clouds. Rain continued to fall. She looked around. No lamps burned in front of the houses here.

` She felt suddenly frightened.

She had only to walk behind the McCready house, then past the boardinghouse, which would be on her left, to reach her own home. It seemed like miles to go.

She drew the revolver from her purse and cocked it, then walked a little farther.

She paused, listening.

What had she heard?

CHAPTER 9

IN THE COLD, RAINY NIGHT, Jennifer moved against the side of the MacCready house. Revolver in hand, she listened intently, her heart wild in her breast. Certain she had heard movement behind the house, she shivered, cold with fear. Her green eyes round and searching, she saw nothing in the dark rain.

A bit of moonlight broke through but quickly vanished in the night.

Jennifer felt certain someone lurked out there.

If she ran now, that someone might follow.

She had to get back in the MacCready house.

About to turn the corner to reach the porch, she stopped.

As the moon briefly reappeared, she saw a shadow behind the house. The moon quickly moved behind the clouds as rain grew heavier.

Holding the revolver in both hands, she slid sideways.

Suddenly, she heard breaking glass behind the house.

A shout and a man's scream. Then a woman's shrill cry.

Rain in her face, Jennifer caught her breath, wanting to rush around the house, onto the porch and inside. Instead, she found herself stuck against the wall in a fit of horror.

She saw someone running from behind the house, into the dark rain. A small man in a floppy hat and slicker, hunched over, a dark moving figure, trying to get away.

"Stop!" she shrieked.

Her voice startled her. She fired at him. The loud crack of the bullet hurt her ears. She fought to pull back the hammer as the shot echoed.

The dark figure turned and fired back, the bullet careening off the edge of the house, inches from her head. Another bullet whistled past her ear.

She frantically cocked the pistol and fired at him.

She missed in the dark rain. She shriveled down against the house as she drew back the hammer. The man had gone.

She heard a horse's hooves, as he headed into the night. She realized she had been holding her breath. She gasped for air.

Now she heard running feet in the alley behind her, coming from the main street.

She spun, holding her weapon in both hands, ready to fire as Hicks and Matt, in slickers, charged into view with six-shooters in hand.

"Hold it," Hicks shouted.

She gasped and pointed the pistol in the air, afraid it would go off as she released the hammer. Then slowly she lowered it.

Matt came running toward her. Shaken, she could hardly stand.

The wind howled, rattled the house, and whipped the rain.

"We heard shots," Hicks said. "What were you shooting at?"

"A man. I think he broke into the house. I heard a scream."

Matt took her arm, steadying her.

"I heard him riding away," Jennifer added, knees buckling.

Matt kept her walking as they moved around to the porch.

The door front threw open.

Mrs. MacCready came out with a shattering cry. Sobbing, she dropped to her knees by the porch swing. Hicks ran onto the porch and knelt to take her hands.

"My grandson! They killed my grandson!"

Jennifer grabbed the porch railing.

Matt ran into the house, followed by Hicks.

Trying to breathe calmly, Jennifer climbed onto the porch, out of the rain, revolver still in hand. She helped Mrs. MacCready to the porch swing and sat with her, holding the sobbing woman against her as tears came to her own eyes.

After a moment, Hicks came outside. He shook his head.

"Did you get a look at him?" Hicks asked Jennifer.

"No, but he was a small man. I heard him ride away."

"Do you think you hit him?"

Jennifer wiped at her eyes. "I'm not sure."

"Ma'am," the sheriff said to Mrs. MacCready. "You can't stay here tonight."

"You can come with me," Jennifer said to her.

"No, take me to Mrs. Jeffrey. She knows how to look after my miseries."

Hicks nodded, taking the old woman's arm and pulling her to her feet. "You get your things, and I'll take you. Matt, you walk Jennifer home. Then get back here. I'll need your help."

Jennifer, still badly shaken, took Matt's arm as she stood.

Two men came charging from the street with guns drawn. They hurried to talk to Hicks on the porch.

As Matt walked with Jennifer in the heavy rain, his arm around her shoulders, he tried to keep her steady. Matt shook his head in frustration. His boots sucked mud as rain continued. He knew her soft shoes were useless.

Matt scooped her up in his arms. She pressed her face to his chest.

"You shouldn't have been out so late," Matt said.

"I was worried about Mrs. MacCready. And her grandson."

They fell silent as he carried her, both thinking about the danger she had faced. He liked holding her. She drew from his strength. When they reached her porch, he set her down out of the rain and joined her.

"Do you think the killer recognized you?" he asked.

"No, I don't."

"I'd better have a look inside."

After checking out the house and turning up the lamps brightly, Matt came onto the porch. He paused, gazing down at her as the light caressed her face.

"Thank you, Matt."

She moved into his arms and hugged him. His hands slowly went around her. He held her tight, her face at his chest, one hand on her lustrous hair.

He could feel her tremble. He hated how she had faced danger alone. He felt somehow that he had failed her. Then he wondered why he should be the only one to protect her. He felt confused and yet worried.

She drew back and went into the house, closing the door.

Matt swallowed hard, hurting for her.

He hurried back to the MacCready house. He saw men carrying the law clerk's body away. Hicks came out on the porch, closing the door behind him. Heavier rain splattered off the railing and pelted the earth and grass.

Rain dribbling off his hat brim, Matt joined Hicks on the porch.

Hicks looked grim. "There's one more law clerk down with the fever, Ted Loring, and I've warned his father to watch out. And that just leaves Lucifer Rawlins at your office."

"None of this makes sense, Sheriff."

"There's something real fishy about your outfit."

"Or someone's out to close 'em down."

"Maybe, but let's check on Loring," Hicks said.

Matt ached to tell Hicks all he knew.

They moved through the rain, their boots sloshing in the mud, each lost in his own thoughts.

They reached the little house with its broken picket fence. Hicks banged on the door.

Pa Loring, bald and in his late sixties, looked bent and damaged from years of hard work. He greeted them at the door. A man who had seen most everything in his life, he took it one day at a time. Nothing surprised him anymore.

Inside the small but neat house, Pa Loring welcomed them with a cough and apology for it. The old man cleared his throat.

"The MacCready boy is dead," Hicks told him.

The old man, startled, bit his lip. "My son's asleep. I've been sitting with him."

Matt removed his hat. "If you want to keep him alive, you'd better let us talk to him."

"But my son doesn't know anything."

"Just the same," the sheriff said. "It's time he talked to us."

Loring shrugged and led them to the back bedroom.

Ted Loring, in his late twenties and red with fever from his high cheekbones to his square chin, shivered in near delirium. "I don't remember hearing anything at the office, but Pocket and Banner were plenty upset about something. They wouldn't talk to me about it. Maybe because I was so much older. They were pals with MacCready though."

"What about Lucifer?"

"He never liked any of us, wanted us out, so he'd be the one they kept on as a lawyer."

Hicks fingered his wet hat in his hands. "Well, even if you don't know anything, the killers may think you do. So you keep that window locked, and don't be alone tonight."

"Don't worry," Pa Loring said. "I've got a shotgun, and I'm gonna be right in here with Ted. You can bet on it."

Outside again in the rain, which was pouring off their hats and slickers, Matt frowned. "Somebody could get in there and kill them both."

"Not with Pa Loring around. He's a tough old bird. Besides, I figure Jennifer scared the killer bad enough, he won't be around for a while."

Matt made a face in sudden back pain. "Right now, I hurt bad, so I'm turning in."

"I can't believe you took on old Bulldog. He's crippled a lot of men around here."

"Well, come morning, I may feel like he did it again."

"He's a foreman in one of the mines for Red Ferman."

Matt grimaced. "I heard."

"You think he singled you out?"

"No, it was over Minnie. I turned her down."

Hicks had to grin. "You know, Matt, I'm going to like having you around. You're reminding me I got a sense of humor."

"Thanks a lot."

In the morning in Mountain Springs, the rain had stopped, and the sky cleared slowly. The air brightened, fresh and clean. Mud lurked everywhere.

When Matt went to the office, wearing his suit, boots, and Stetson, he felt stiff and sore from the fight. Determined to put on a happy face, he found law clerk Lucifer at the front desk. Two clients, men with short beards in greatcoats and small bowler hats, sat in the chairs to his right.

Matt nodded to them, paused to look at Lucifer, ever stiff and properly dressed in a dark suit.

"The other lawyers here?" Matt asked.

"Not yet, sir."

"Come with me."

Matt led the way into his office and sat behind his desk.

Lucifer closed the door behind him. "Yes, sir?"

"Sit down, Lucifer. We have to talk."

"But I have clients up front. Two of Ferman's associates. I have to take their statements for Mr. Frost."

"Sit down, Lucifer."

Reluctant, the clerk sat down, rubbing his large nose and tugging at one of his ears.

"Something wrong?" Lucifer asked.

"Did you hear about young MacCready?"

"What about him?"

"He was murdered last night."

Lucifer didn't react. "I didn't know."

"Three law clerks from this office have been murdered. Banner, Pocket, and MacCready. Aren't you worried about yourself?"

"No, why should I be?"

"You don't think the clerks were killed because they all worked here?"

"Of course not. They were in debt to gamblers. They even tried to borrow money from me, but I didn't have any to spare. I knew, sooner or later, they'd have to pay up. I just didn't know how it was going to end. I know they were plenty scared."

"You know who the gamblers were?"

"No, but I told Mr. Frost about it."

"Why would you do that?"

"I thought he might want to help them."

"And did he?"

"I don't know. Look, I'd better get back up front."

Matt allowed him to leave his office. He leaned back in his chair, pondering the man's words. What did Lucifer, the uppity clerk, really know? Why wasn't he worried about himself?

He tried to concentrate on the old files, looking for grounds for dismissal on claims with poor discovery, missing information, and missing witnesses. His thoughts kept going back to his conversation with Lucifer, the law clerk with the big ego.

And ever on Matt's mind was his mission.

Too many dead men and too much mystery, when Grant could show up at any time.

After work at twilight under a cloudy sky, Matt walked down to the newspaper office and entered. Jennifer, wearing her apron over her pale-blue dress, stood at the back wall, setting type. The youth Henry worked the press in rolled-up shirtsleeves. The place smelled of ink and kerosene fumes.

She turned and came to the counter where Matt stood.

Being around her made a man feel good. Maybe too good.

"Are you all right here?" he asked.

"Yes, I was just getting ready to lock up."

"Henry going to walk you home?"

"Yes."

She reached over to place her soft hand on his. He felt his skin vibrate.

"Please be careful, Matt."

"And you'd better not be taking any more chances."

She smiled. "Women have been fighting Indians and every other kind of lowlife, ever since families moved west. A lot of us are pretty good shots, you know."

"Well, I'm a busy man. I don't have time to keep you out of trouble."

She laughed. "Just worry about yourself."

But he worried about her, knowing she could be a little too foolhardy. He looked down at her hand on his. He turned it into his grip, squeezing it. Then he released her hand quickly.

He left to go back outside. He returned to the rooming house.

He still hurt all over and could hardly wait to retire. Mrs. Ledbetter caught him in the hallway, her chubby face set with a sweet smile. She wore a full apron over her green print dress.

"Matt, you have a visitor. Up in your room."

"Why did you let him in there?"

"He paid me."

Her simple answer frustrated him. He went up the stairs, leery of what he might find.

When he entered his small room with six-shooter in hand, he saw a man sitting on one of the two beds. A man in his fifties with a short black goatee and moustache, long sideburns, and jet-black hair, a very stiff-looking military man.

His visitor looked familiar, but his rough civilian clothes against the campaign hat did not jog Matt's memory. The man wore a gun belt with a cavalry holster. Matt holstered his revolver and closed the door.

"Hello, Matt."

"I know you from somewhere."

"Captain Witherspoon."

"My God," Matt said, removing his hat.

The two men shook hands. Matt pulled up a chair to sit near him. They grinned at each other. Matt's thoughts whirled back to the war and the splendid figure of this man on a horse.

"Matt, you're a foot taller, and you look like a lawyer."

"Sometimes I wonder. Did you muster out?"

"Yes, I did, but I'm here with a message, and it can't go any further than this room."

"Just like the old days."

Witherspoon nodded. "Yes, but this time, there's only one life I'm concerned about. And he wants to see you."

Matt tensed. "Who does?"

Captain Witherspoon whispered, "Grant."

They both paused to look at the door. Matt got up, went over, looked out, closed and locked it, and returned to his chair. They spoke in low voices, often whispers.

"General Grant?"

"General and former president."

"I thought he was way up north at Leadville."

"He got tired of the handshaking and crowds. A fellow named Shockley at South Arkansas, arranged for the general to rent a wagon and get away from everyone after taking his family to Denver to wait for him."

"And then?"

"Grant and former governor Routt, they went off to sight-see the mountains on their own. Grant insisted on doing the driving himself."

Matt grinned. "Sounds like him."

"He fired the driver, who was real mad. Sent him back on a pack mule."

"Grant's getting cranky."

"You're right. Anyhow, Reis Williams and I caught up with them. Grant dotes on Williams, but Routt doesn't, so Routt got off at one of the stops and hired a rig to go back. Now it's just Grant and Williams, and myself."

"I remember seeing Williams, but I never knew him."

"Major Williams is the loneliest man I know. He never had any family, except the army. But he was Grant's tutor at West Point, because Grant was having problems with military tactics."

Matt had to grin. "Military tactics?"

"Just as well he didn't take it serious."

Matt shifted his weight. Stiff and sore, he had pain in his back. "Why does the general want to see me?"

"There's no way he could come to Colorado and not see you."

"But how did he know I was here?"

"He received a visit from a lawyer named Frost while we were in Denver. Frost told him how proud he was to hire the man who had saved Grant's life. I think he was trying to get Grant to come here. Something about a railroad."

Matt grimaced. "Three law clerks from my firm have been murdered. And the printer at the *Mountain Springs Recorder*. They're blaming gamblers."

"What's that got to do with Grant?"

"I don't know for sure," Matt said. "But one of the murdered clerks had written to the president before he died, warning there was an assassination plot by the firm itself. That's why I took the job, to look out for Grant. So where is he now?"

"I don't know. When I left, he was headed for Irwin, then Scofield. I was to find you, then wait for him and Williams in Silver Gulch."

Matt frowned. "There's a couple hundred Southerners in Silver Gulch."

"The war's been over fifteen years, Matt."

"I'd still keep him away from there." Matt leaned back. "Anyone know you're here?"

"Mrs. Ledbetter's the only one, and I paid her well."

"I don't know if we should even trust her."

"She doesn't know my name or who I am."

Witherspoon pulled out a gold watch and chain, flipping up the lid and gazing at the time.

"You'd better go to supper, Matt. I'm laying low. But bring me something, if you can."

"That's a fine watch."

"Gift from Grant. See here? 'To Captain Witherspoon from U. S. Grant. Let's go home.' He gave me this after the war was over."

When Matt went to supper, he had a better look at Mrs. Ledbetter. The chubby blond woman had a twinkle in her eye as she served him his meal along with five other men.

After supper, she prepared a tray for his visitor.

"I'll take it up," she said. "He may want more of something."

Matt took the tray. "This is just fine, ma'am."

"Is your friend comfortable?"

He nodded, trying to appear casual, and leaned over and kissed her on the cheek.

"What's that for, Matt?"

"Taking care of my friend."

She flushed but was beaming.

Back in Matt's room, Witherspoon welcomed the hot food.

Matt and Witherspoon talked long into the night, reminiscing about everything from Shiloh to Appomattox. They shared memories of Grant's eccentricities, along with their mutual admiration for the man.

Witherspoon began to yawn and, still fully clothed, took one of the two beds, and stretched out in sudden silence.

Later that night, as Witherspoon slept, Matt lay staring at the ceiling.

He couldn't help worry about Frost's telling Grant he was here.

It continued to add up to a conspiracy.

And what about this Shockley, who arranged Grant's wagon and drew a map for him?

CHAPTER 10

On Wednesday night, sitting in an abandoned cabin on Eagle Mountain with his friend, former major Reis Williams, Grant warmed his hands at the crackling fire in the hearth.

Ulysses Simpson Grant, former president of the United States, had a slight but muscular build. He stood five feet seven, had soft blue eyes, a Roman nose, some false teeth, long slim fingers, a nagging cough from his cigars, and frequent migraine headaches. He had a neatly trimmed beard and moustache, and he wore rumpled clothes.

Grant had not changed much over the years. A little more tired. Regrets over the corruption discovered in his administration. Feeling betrayed by men he had trusted. Deep, painful memories of the War between the States. Never feeling the hero he had been proclaimed. A humble man all his life. Lost now with nowhere to go. Nothing really important to do, except work on his memoirs, still churning in his thoughts.

At the same time, Grant loved the mountains, the clean cold air.

"I guess Routt's back in Denver by now," Grant said.

Reis nodded. "Good thing. If he kept trying to order me around, I would have had to do something about it."

Grant nodded with a chuckle. "And the driver's probably still cussing."

"This is better."

Venison steaks sizzled in an iron pan on the hot fire. Grant waited for his to be well done, as he could not stand to see animal blood. He chewed on his cigar and leaned back.

Williams, six feet tall, had a very straight body with strong shoulders. He had long arms and fingers, a long nose, a thin dark-brown moustache, and well-trimmed dark hair.

A lonely man all his life, Williams felt a brotherly connection to Grant.

As usual, Grant fell back to discussing the war, but this time, it was about Matt.

Grant leaned forward. "I can see the battle at Pittsburgh Landing as if it was right in front of us. I still can't believe how the Confederates kept rushing us. They were taking such heavy losses."

"And Matt Tyler saved your life."

"I've got to see that boy."

"Dammit, Ulysses, it's a setup."

Grant frowned at him. "Watch your language."

"Sorry, but I don't think you ought to go to Silver Gulch or Mountain Springs. Look how some cranks tried to assassinate you at Irwin. If that woman's horse hadn't shied in that canyon, she would have shot you dead."

"Reis, I think the meat is done."

"You're a stubborn man. Don't you have second thoughts about why that fellow Shockley insisted on drawing a map? And he bragged about the mines at Irwin. Said you shouldn't miss the Ruby Chief Mine."

"Well, he was right."

"He sure was. Sent you right into a trap. And another one's waiting at Silver Gulch. We should turn around and go back to Denver."

"You know I never retrace my steps," Grant said. "And Witherspoon will be waiting at Silver Gulch."

Reis threw up his hands. "Well, I'm going to protect you, whether you like it or not."

"You're a good friend, Reis."

Reis grumbled and checked the meat. "Somebody's got to keep you out of trouble."

"My wife does that. No smoking in the parlor or bedroom. No drinking after seven. No going around the house half-dressed. I have to sit up straight when I eat. Use those little napkins. Use a finger bowl. She's always trying to make me perfect. Got to have Brooks Brothers suits. And getting me baptized is one she nags about all the time."

"But you're crazy about her."

Grant nodded, smiled, and paused to reflect.

Reis sobered as he spoke. "I can't help but remember. She saved your life that night. If she hadn't been angry with Mrs. Lincoln, you'd have been at Ford's."

"Yes, and even then we were followed, but I made that buggy fly through town."

They fell quiet a moment. Reis decided to change the sudden gloom.

"She must have enjoyed your trip. Especially seeing your daughter in England."

Grant was suddenly grumpy. "I don't know what Nellie sees in that Englishman. I can't even understand what he says."

They looked at each other, and both suddenly laughed.

Early the next morning, Jennifer joined Matt, Eberley, and Sheriff Hicks at the livery stable. She sat sidesaddle on a nervous sorrel mare. She wore a blue outfit with velvet trim and velvet bonnet, her hair in a bun. Excited about getting out of town, she looked impatient.

Hicks wore a heavy wool coat, as he sat astride his blue roan. Grouchy, he looked as if he hadn't slept. His weathered Stetson shaded his face as he tried to stay awake.

Eberley looked fine on a high-stepping black gelding. In his rough riding clothes with a frock coat, he still looked like a lawyer. He sat straight in the saddle like a circuit judge.

Matt wore a heavy wool shirt and a leather jacket, Stetson pulled down tight. He rode a bay gelding Eberley had supplied. He sat easy in the saddle. It felt much better than sitting in an office.

They left town as the sun rose above the Rockies in the east.

It did annoy Matt that Jennifer tagged along, even though he had invited her. He worried about her, knowing she could aggravate people and get into trouble. He had to admit she could ride. He even admitted he may well be falling for her.

Just being around her made him turn to mush.

Even as the sun rose, they felt the chill as they crossed the green valley. Wet grass often lays flat. Elk could be seen in the far distance to the south. The country lay splendid in every direction. The magnificent Rockies rose all around with snow gleaming like crystal.

"We'll have our noon meal at Ferman's office and try to get back by dark," Eberley said.

Jennifer turned to him. "I saw Mr. Frost leave yesterday. Where was he going?"

"It's no secret. He went down to Alamosa to see about a spur. He'll be back on Monday."

"We have enough trouble," Hicks said, "without turning Mountain Springs into a rail town."

Jennifer disagreed. "Progress can be a good thing, Sheriff."

"Or not."

By midmorning, they still rode through the hills.

Now, a few hundred yards to their left, they saw a sorrel saddle horse lying on its side. Over it, three buzzards circled lower and lower.

Matt spun his bay around and headed for the scene at a lope, Hicks and Eberley right behind him. Hicks shouted for Jennifer to stay put. She hesitated only a moment, then followed.

The buzzards scattered and drifted in the distant sky.

They came on a grisly scene in a wash. A man lay face down in a pool of blood. Near him lay a campaign hat. Matt could see it was Witherspoon. His head had not been struck.

Matt, sick to his stomach, held his breath a moment. He had liked and respected Witherspoon, a man who had survived the war to end up like this. Sweat on his face, Matt drew on his inner strength to face this ordeal.

The men dismounted and went down the bank.

Jennifer stepped down from her mount and skidded down the slope, even as Hicks waved her to stay back. She stopped near him as he caught her.

Matt knelt to turn the man's face into view. Dead for days, Witherspoon had been shot between the eyes, leaving a purple hole in his forehead. Matt swallowed hard. Less brutal than the bloody hatchet murders, it was senseless killing, just the same.

Hicks knelt at his side. "Do you know him, Matt?"

"It's Captain Witherspoon."

Jennifer stared, then turned away. She looked sick and sat on the grass, against the bank. Eberley sat down to her left. She covered her face with her hands. Eberley reached over to touch her arm. She straightened, and then slid her hand into his.

Hicks searched the area and found boot prints in the wet grass. Up on the other side of the gully, they saw marks where a horse had been. It had headed northwest to the dirt trail, mingling with other prints toward Silver Gulch. They found nothing unusual to trace the killer.

All of Witherspoon's effects were gone, including the gold watch, except for his pistol, which was half-out of his unflapped holster. Matt covered the dead man's face with the campaign hat, then sat on the grass near Jennifer. Hicks paced around.

"They took everything but his six-shooter," Hicks said. "Don't make sense."

"It does, if you want to prove you were a lot faster," Matt said.

Eberley gestured. "We can take him to Silver Gulch. It's closer."

"No," Matt said. "We'll bury him here."

"That's not right," Eberley said.

"Not talking right," Matt said. "It's how it has to be."

"You got a good reason?" Hicks asked.

Matt nodded and went back to his horse.

Hicks and Eberley hesitated only a moment. They trusted Matt.

Matt roped and dragged the dead horse a good mile away.

Hicks and Matt then dug a grave in the soft dirt in the gully with hunting knives and their bare hands. Matt kept Witherspoon's campaign hat but buried everything else with him.

They covered the grave with rocks and made a wooden cross without a name.

"I'll come back when it's safe," Matt said.

Matt stood over the grave and said words of admiration.

"He's with you now, Lord. I hope you have a good horse for him to ride."

Later, after Matt, Hicks, Jennifer, and Eberley had ridden some distance, they found shade in the pines and a creek to water the horses.

Eberley and Jennifer sat on rocks. Matt remained standing.

Hicks paced around. They all waited on Matt's story.

It was a long while before Matt could organize his thoughts. Then he cleared his throat and turned to the sheriff.

"Let me ask you something first. What side were you on during the War between the States?"

Hicks frowned, annoyed. "I was in the Union army out West, fighting Sioux and Cheyenne. Why?"

"Where were your sympathies?"

"With the Union. What are you getting at?"

Matt looked at Eberley. "You were in the Union army."

"That's right."

"What about you, Jennifer?" Matt asked.

"My brother died for the Union. What's going on, Matt?"

"Well, the fat's in the fire now."

Hicks adjusted his hat. "Let's have it."

Matt looked from one to the other. They had trusted him enough to bury Witherspoon and wait for his story. Now he had to trust them.

"This can't go any further. President Hayes sent me here to stop Grant from riding into an assassination. He had a letter from Pocket, accusing the firm of planning one. That's why I took the job."

Jennifer turned to Eberley. "The firm wanted Matt as a draw for General Grant, didn't they?"

Eberley nodded. "For the publicity."

"What about the dead law clerks?" she persisted.

Eberley shrugged. "That had nothing to do with Grant. At least, I hope to God it didn't."

"And Frank?" she asked.

"That was to shut you down to keep the lid on their plans," Matt replied.

Eberley scratched his chin. "What would anyone have to gain by trying to harm Grant now?"

"For some the war's never over," Hicks said.

Eberley looked conflicted. "Well, yes, but my partners were much angrier about Black Friday back in '69. They were tied in with Fisk and trying to control the gold market. Grant threw government gold on the market. They lost everything they had, and so did Ferman. But it's more likely they'd be mad at the president's brother-in-law, who somehow let their conspiracy out of the bag."

"That's a motive," Matt said.

"Matt," Hicks asked, "who knew about Witherspoon coming to see you?"

"Only one person in town. Mrs. Ledbetter."

With a frown and a long, deep breath, Eberley shook his head. "I guess you didn't know she was a Confederate spy during the war."

The others turned to stare at Eberley, who continued.

"She was in Washington. We knew about her and fed her harmless information. All along, she'd been secretly married to a Confederate officer, but we knew that as well."

Matt grimaced. "Why didn't I know about it?"

"It would have served no purpose to make her a target."

"What's she doing here?" Matt asked.

"They came out a couple years ago, because of his consumption, like a lot of people. She was bitter, because bullet wounds had made his lungs worse. After he died, she turned their home into a boardinghouse. But you can bet she hasn't forgotten."

"Did she know Witherspoon?" Matt asked. "He was stationed in Washington for a short time during the war."

"I'm sure she knew who he was," Eberley said. "She never missed a thing."

Matt, angry, remembered how sweet Mrs. Ledbetter had pretended to be.

Jennifer hugged herself. "What can I do?"

"Stay out of it," Matt said, "and don't tell anyone what you've heard or seen here today."

"I won't, and I'll not write about it," she promised.

"The less they know, the safer you are."

Hicks nodded. "He's right, Jennifer."

Matt turned to his horse, tightened the cinch.

Once Hicks, Matt, Eberley, and Jennifer were again mounted, they turned to look at the Shining Mountains, the Rockies with their snowcaps circling the valley and reaching to the sky. Only an eagle could find Grant on all those trails.

"Now what?" Hicks asked.

Matt turned to Eberley. "Why don't you take Jennifer back to town."

"I'm staying," she said, chin up.

Eberley nodded. "It would look suspicious if anyone turned back now. This was to be your orientation, Matt. And a lot of people knew we're all riding together."

"So it's settled," Jennifer said firmly.

Matt looked at her and shrugged, too weary to argue.

Too much information weighed him down.

Now for sure, Matt must never let Grant reach the valley.

CHAPTER 11

At midday, Matt, Hicks, Eberley, and Jennifer rode toward the diggings at Silver Gulch.

The town nestled deep in the foothills, where pines mingled with heavy brush. Silver Mountain, with its shafts, rose like a beehive against the surrounding ridges and mountains.

As they rode in, they saw dozens of log buildings tucked in every level spot or corner down at the base of the mountain. In town, fourteen saloons crowded three stores on a crooked street. Rows of tents sagged behind the buildings on either side. Two smelters smoked away to the north.

Excited at the scene, Jennifer rode on ahead, out of earshot. Eberley rode on to keep up with her. Matt and Hicks hung farther back.

"That big building there to the south," Hicks said quietly to Matt, "that's the cathouse."

"No, thanks. You go ahead."

Hicks shook his head. They grinned at each other, then sobered.

Matt knew that Hicks thought only of the widow he was courting, while Matt had more than a casual interest in Jennifer. Except that right now, they had to think of Grant. As they rode into town, Matt studied every inch of it.

He could see Ferman's headquarters to their right on the main street. The log building had only one story. Jennifer and Eberley dismounted as Hicks and Matt caught up with them. Matt and Hicks swung down from the saddle to join them.

Matt looked around, watching two rough-looking men with heavy beards, big arms, and beady eyes, coming out of another building. Carrying new shovels, they gave Matt and Hicks a dirty look, studied Jennifer and Eberley, and then continued toward the mines.

Hicks watched after them. "A lot of men come here to hide from something. If I got no handbills on 'em, I leave 'em alone."

Jennifer's smile reflected her excitement at seeing the dreaded Silver Gulch for the first time. When she turned around, she saw Matt watching her with a grin.

"Don't worry about me," she said.

"Somebody has to."

Matt could not help himself. Being around her made a man feel good. Worried and annoyed, but with a good feeling just the same.

Inside, hot coffee steamed on an iron stove, along with beans, and hot biscuits with jam. They helped themselves. As they sat on benches at the long table, Eberley introduced the two men in the office.

Boner, the bookkeeper, in his sixties, tall and skinny, had thinning hair and a little moustache. He wore a rumpled, store-bought suit of clothes. Boner looked like he lived for his work.

Matt studied Boner, decided he was harmless.

Matt didn't like the other man, Carruth, a foreman at one of the mines. A short but husky man in his fifties, with a beard and gleaming eyes, Carruth had been Ferman's former slave enforcer and had an air of death about him.

Matt remained silent as Carruth calmly explained the operations in Silver Gulch.

All the while, Matt took Carruth's measure as a man who could kill without hesitation. Matt couldn't look at him without seeing a whip in his hand.

Jennifer enjoyed herself, as she made mental notes.

"Ferman in town?" Matt asked.

"Nope," Carruth said, picking his teeth.

While they all sat at the table with their coffee, another man came in. Tall and thin, wearing black, with conches on his gun belt and hatband, he had a narrow face with a long, thin nose and a black moustache. His dark eyes burned sinister, but his lips curved into a smile.

Matt knew on sight that the man was a hired gun and a cold-blooded killer.

Jennifer, nervous, moved closer on the bench to Matt.

"Bo Raddigan," Eberley said and gestured. "Matt Tyler, our new lawyer. And you know the sheriff."

Raddigan had come for his heavy coat, which hung on a wall hook near the door. He didn't miss Eberley's failure to mention Jennifer White. He looked them over with disdain.

"Well, Mr. Tyler, you look like a real dude. Can you do anything with that Colt?"

Matt smiled. "I'll let you figure it out."

"I already have."

"Then you know I'm a dangerous man."

Raddigan hesitated, irritated by Matt's easy smile. His lips curved into a sneer.

They had taken an instant dislike to each other. Raddigan knew Matt, as a lawyer, would not fight without being pushed.

Raddigan looked at Jennifer, his eyes roaming her so long it made her shiver. Then he turned on his heels and left with his coat, closing the door behind him. Carruth suddenly decided to follow and went outside as well.

Boner drew a deep breath with relief.

"Raddigan's right mean," Boner said. "He'll shoot a man down without blinking an eye. But he won't kill a fly or step on an ant. And he never kills birds."

"Yeah, he's a sweetheart," Hicks said.

"Not much better than Carruth," Matt said.

Boner nodded, equally leery of Carruth.

"You seen Crazy Albert out here?" Hicks asked.

"Yeah, sure," Boner said. "Talks to himself all the time. He comes and goes."

"And Bulldog?" Matt asked, curious.

"He's a foreman," Boner replied with a slippery smile. "No one talks back to him." "I'll bet," Matt said. "Are Moose and Grizzly around?"

"Nah," Boner said, "they're on top of Needle Mountain just south of town. They ain't hit a strike as yet. Just a few handfuls of dust, but they won't give up."

Outside, later, Matt and Hicks stood on the boardwalk and looked south toward Needle Mountain, its height rising boldly against the afternoon sky. Covered with pines and brush, it sported a great boulder with a sharp point on top, about halfway up, facing east.

Eberley and Jennifer stood in the doorway, talking to Boner, who then went back inside.

Matt and Hicks walked over to the horses.

Matt looked around at the empty street and then the beehive mountain rising from back of the town. He knew Ferman had a grip on Silver Gulch. It was no place for Grant.

Eberley and Jennifer joined them as Matt nodded south toward Needle Mountain.

"I'm going up," Matt said. "Jennifer, you go on back with Mr. Eberley and the sheriff."

"I want to see the mountain."

"It's no place for a woman," Matt said.

"I'm going with you," she insisted.

Hicks shrugged. "Yeah, well, if Jennifer's going, I'll ride along."

Eberley hesitated. "Then I'd better chaperone."

Jennifer smiled with satisfaction and rode out ahead.

As they rode south toward Needle Mountain, they had a better view of the sluice boxes and ditches and suspicious miners all over Silver Mountain to their right. Everywhere they looked, they saw a medley of shacks, entrances to dugouts and deep mine shafts, along with stacks of ore in iron carts on little rails.

Farther south, the mostly barren main trail up Needle Mountain wound its way almost straight up in places. They rode up through occasional boulders, junipers, and brush. Often they had to walk their horses. The pine scent hung heavy around them.

Matt reined up to gaze straight up the mountain.

"No wonder Ferman leaves them alone," Matt said.

It took a good hour to reach the nearly black, pointed boulder, which rose some fifty feet above the pines and brush. Near its tip, there was an open slice, just like a needle. The air grew thinner and colder now.

They rested their horses, loosened the cinches, and sat down on rocks.

From where they were, they could see far down into the little mining town, which was situated to the north at the foot of Silver Mountain. The smelters, even farther north of town, puffed smoke.

Beyond, in all directions, rose the splendid snow-crested Rockies.

Matt could see that Moose and Grizzly had a view of every approach from the Rockies down to Silver Gulch. That might come in handy.

Below, the rolling land spread toward the distant Mountain Springs. Green meadows, dotted with pine and aspen, creeks lined with willows, cottonwoods, and chokecherry, added to the glory of the valley. Birds flew across the landscape. Elk and a handful of mule deer could be seen in the far distance.

Jennifer stared in awe. "It's beautiful."

"We're not making it back before dark," Hicks warned.

No one seemed to care.

Eberley looked happy to be with them.

They tightened the cinches and mounted. They rode on up the open trail, which wound in loops up the side of the mountain. Away from the trail, yellow pine and blue spruce smelled sweet. They could hear a woodpecker hammering off to the left. A noisy magpie chirped to the right. Deer tracks crossed their trail several times.

After another hour, they came through a rim of rocks and onto a grassy plateau. The open space ran a half mile north to south, and slightly less from west to east, surrounded by rocks and pines. To their left, they saw the shack with smoke curling from its chimney. It nestled against a rise of boulders with only the sky beyond.

Matt looked around at the safety of the mountain. Anyone charging the cabin would have to come out in the open.

Now they saw Moose out front with an ax, cutting wood with great swings, shirtless, his big muscles and potbelly straining and covered with sweat. When he saw them, he waved and stopped to pull on his shirt, embarrassed that Jennifer should have seen him half-dressed.

"Hey, am I glad to see you folks."

The visitors dismounted and loosened the cinches, then tethered their horses near the cabin.

"Where's Grizzly?" Matt asked.

"He's in the house making fresh coffee. Come on. We got spring water, and this is gonna be the best coffee you ever tasted."

At the far end of the plateau, they could see the mine entrance up among the boulders, surrounded by heavy brush and shadowed by stunted pines.

Grizzly greeted them at the door, shaking their hands and nearly breaking their fingers.

"Sure glad to see you folks. And, Miss White, you get our good chair, over there, with the arms on it."

Sheriff Hicks, Eberley, and Matt sat at the hand-hewn table on stumps and barrels. The front room cabin had gear piled on bunks with saddles and harnesses in a corner. The small iron stove burned red hot. Ropes hung on the walls, along with bridles, halters, and two rifles. Doors were open to two back bedrooms. No liquor in sight.

The place smelled of coffee, leather, and pine.

They ate bread and cheese. The thick coffee, strong but delicious, warmed them. Jennifer's face, still flushed with excitement from the journey, showed how much she enjoyed the miners and being so high above the valley.

"Matt needs your help," Hicks told the miners.

"Hey," Grizzly said, "just ask."

Matt pushed his hat back. "First, I was wondering where your sympathies were during the War between the States."

Moose didn't hesitate. "I was with the Union navy, on account of I was already a sailor. I was there when we took Fort Clark and Fort Hatteras. And when we took Port Royal."

"You didn't do nothing but pull sail," Grizzly said.

"I was the bravest sailor they had, on account of I couldn't swim a lick."

Grizzly folded his arms. "Me, I was with Stonewall Jackson, until he was killed accidental. Then I ended up with Lee. I made a good account of myself."

Matt looked from one to the other. "You were on opposite sides?"

"After the war," Moose said, "Grizzly pulled me out from under a dozen Rebs. We got to be pardners."

Matt studied Grizzly. "How do you feel about General Grant?"

Grizzly shrugged. "He was a Yank, but he let us keep our horses and mules. I'd have to say ole Grant was all right."

Reluctant at first, Matt then spent some time telling the miners about Captain Witherspoon. They stared at him with round eyes, as he told them Grant would be coming to Silver Gulch and why.

"From up here," Matt said, "you could spot a wagon up in the Rockies and on any of those trails into town. Be two men, Grant and Major Reis Williams. If you could signal us with smoke, we'd come running. And in the meantime, you could try to get them up here before anyone sees them. They must stay out of Silver Gulch."

"Why would Grant trust us?" Moose asked.

"I've got Witherspoon's campaign hat. His initials are on the hatband. You show that to Grant, and tell him I said the captain's dead. He'll get the message."

Grizzly downed his coffee. "We'll take turns on watch."

"Could be any day. Or weeks."

"You can count on us," Moose said.

The visitors shook their hands again and went out to the horses. Matt gave the campaign hat to Moose. After tightening the cinches once more, he helped Jennifer up onto her sidesaddle. She had a little trouble hooking her right leg over the horn, her skirts catching.

"How can you sit on that thing?" he asked.

"It's not easy. You can bet a man invented it."

Matt grinned. "We have to get even with women somehow."

Going down the mountain, Hicks grumbled about it being dark before they got home.

Eberley just smiled, having the most fun he'd had in years.

That same night, Matt and Hicks delivered a weary Jennifer to her house. Eberley returned to his mansion. Matt and Hicks went to Pop's Café, where Gentry, the only customer, ate at a side table. They joined him.

They ordered supper. Gentry looked at Matt with a grin.

"You need a trim."

"Why me? Why not Hicks?"

"He's hopeless."

Hicks grunted. "Yeah, well, I save money by cutting what hair I got left by myself. You charge too much, Gentry."

"Two bits for a shave and a haircut?" Gentry asked.

Pop delivered more food and fresh coffee.

"You fellahs trying to cheat this hard-working barber?"

"He's a thief," Hicks said with a grin and looked around. "So are you. Beef don't cost you anywhere near what you charge."

"Who says it's beef?" Pop snickered.

They watched him go back to the kitchen. They laughed.

Their conversation could not be heard by anyone.

Matt sipped his coffee. "Gentry, you named yourself after Grant. Why is that?"

"I didn't have a first name when I joined up." Gentry leaned back, his cup in both hands. "Some of us had shoes worn down to nothing. We got sick on the food. But Grant had faith in us. We wanted him to be proud."

"What would you do if someone wanted to harm Grant?"

Gentry frowned. "I'd stop 'em."

"Then we need your help."

Gentry listened in dismay to Matt's story. For a long time, Gentry just stared at them. Then he sat up straight, his face grim.

"What do you want me to do?" Gentry asked.

"I need you in town to back up the sheriff," Matt said, "in case I need to head out there."

"You can count on me, Matt."

They fell silent as Pop served their meal.

When the elderly man had walked away, Matt leaned forward. "Sheriff, what about your deputies?"

"They're young," Hicks said. "And from Minnesota. Their fathers fought for the Union. They'll do the right thing if Grant shows, but I won't tell 'em yet. That'll keep 'em from shooting off their mouths accidental like."

"They're OK," Gentry agreed. "But, Matt, what makes you think Grant won't bypass the mines and come straight here?"

Matt shrugged, uneasy. "He's following a map some fellah named Shockley gave him, and then he was to meet Witherspoon in Silver Gulch."

They fell silent as Pop came to serve more coffee.

Hicks grinned, poked at Pop. "Another Yank."

Pop grunted. "Yeah, you wanta make something of it?"

They just laughed.

CHAPTER 12

Sitting by the smoky campfire late at night near the ridge trail, Ulysses S. Grant had a blanket around him. He leaned forward, warmed his hands. "One thing about this country, you sure know it's cold."

"Maybe you'd better get in the tent," Reis said.

Grant looked around at the night beyond the fire, shook his head.

"I'm hoping it's too cold for bear. Those tracks we saw, and that scratched-up tree, and where some had been rooting the ground. It's not too promising."

"We've been real careful with the food. They can't smell anything but us, and they hate fire," Reis said. "But I think we ought to move on, come morning. Witherspoon will be in Silver Gulch by now."

They paused to listen, as a lone timber wolf howled somewhere on a ridge.

They waited. Another wolf howled like an echo. The eerie sound hung in the night.

They waited a little longer. No more echoes.

"Gives me a chill," Reis said.

It only made Grant more content.

"I like it out here, Reis. No crowds, no newspapers, no one asking me the same questions, over and over."

"Yes, well—wait a minute."

Both men fell silent. Reis moved away from the firelight, picking up his Winchester repeater, working the lever to slam a shell in the chamber. He stood quiet, listening.

Coming up the trail, a small horse stumbled noisily out of the dark. A little man in a heavy wool coat and sloppy Stetson led the horse. Both moved into the firelight.

"That's far enough," Reis said, suspicious.

The little visitor had wild eyes and a little mouth, straggly white hair, and a round nose. He smelled like he hadn't bathed in a year. He held up his right hand in a sign of peace.

"Hey, there," he said in a small squeaky voice. "I seen your campfire, and I was mighty cold."

"It's all right," Grant said, his pistol handy under his coat. "Sit down, stranger."

The little man got down on his knees to warm his hands and take of the coffee in a tin cup. "My name's Albert."

Reis lowered his rifle slowly. "I'm Jim Brown, and this is Reverend Johnson."

Albert cackled. "Do tell. I could use a little of the word, Reverend."

Grant managed a smile. "Where are you from, Albert?"

"Down in the valley, yeah. I was working in the mines."

"What are you doing up here?"

"Got in a little trouble, so I took off."

Grant studied him. "What kind of trouble?"

"Nothing you'd want to know about. I got friends up in Irwin, if I can find it. Got any idea where we are?"

Reis shook his head. "No, we're lost."

"That's easy to do up here. Everything looks the same, eh? Well, I sure am hungry."

They gave him beef jerky and beans. Albert gulped it down. "Can you spare any? I didn't have time to stock up afore I left."

"We can give you jerky," Reis said. "We're running low on everything else."

"Can you give me some coffee?"

"A little bit."

Albert looked from one to the other. "You dudes shouldn't be up here wandering around. There's grizzly up here. You run into one of them sows, you'll be in trouble."

"We keep a fire going," Reis said. "You can sleep here if you want."

Albert kept on eating, shoving the food in his mouth. He seemed to forget they were there. Soon he started mumbling to himself with words they couldn't make out.

Reis, impatient, interrupted. "You got family?"

Albert set his empty plate down. "Nope."

"How long have you been in Colorado?"

"Don't be asking stuff ain't none of your business, or I'll get to thinking you're lawmen or something."

"You on the dodge?" Reis asked.

"Ain't none of your business. You keep asking questions, I'm moving on."

"No, we'd rather have you right here," Reis said. "You have blankets?"

"Yeah, I got blankets."

And soon the little man curled up by the hot, crackling fire, snorting and mumbling in his sleep with his back to them.

Reis turned to Grant. "I'll take the first watch. You get some shuteye."

Grant looked around as he stood up. "You think he's alone?"

"Who'd want to be with him?"

With a smile, Grant nodded and went to his tent.

Nearby, the wagon stood under the trees with the horses staked near it. Reis fingered his Winchester. Uneasy, he put two blankets around him and sat under the wagon, waiting and watching, a soldier's instinct keeping him wide-awake. Once, he got up to stoke the fire.

In the cold morning under a cloudy sky, Albert sat up, winced, and got on his knees, reaching for the coffee. Grant and Reis already sat across from him. Reis still had his Winchester across his knees.

"You know, I don't think you fellers trust me."

"We don't know you," Reis said.

"Hah. Nobody knows Albert. They just think they does. Ain't none of 'em really know what I'm thinking."

"Who are you talking about?" Reis asked.

"You never mind. I know how to keep my mouth shut, yeah, I sure do. And I got paid plenty, you can bet on it."

"Paid for what?"

"None of your business."

Albert helped himself to some beans and more coffee. He stood up, stretching. They could see a revolver in his belt, under his coat.

"Well, I'm heading for Irwin."

"I think it's northwest of here," Reis said with a gesture in that direction.

"I thought you was lost."

"We are now."

Albert squinted at them. "Can't figure out why you dudes are up here, but that's the trouble with dudes. Crazy in the head. Don't got no sense."

They watched him saddle his horse, mumbling to himself the whole time, shaking his fist now and then at some imaginary foe. Then he swung astride. He remained standing in the stirrups.

"Watch out for them bears."

"You too," Reis said.

They watched him ride on up the trail and out of sight.

Grant sighed. "Well, that's over."

"I'm still going to watch out for him. He's loony."

"You think he'll come back?"

Reis made a face. "Maybe not, because he didn't recognize you, but you know there's a few people out here would like to get rid of Ulysses Grant."

"Well, we'll go down to Silver Gulch, see Matt, and head back to Denver before my wife sends somebody after us."

"Maybe we'll go to Silver Gulch. Maybe not."

"What now?"

"I may go on in by myself and see what's happening."

"You're a worrier, Reis."

On Sunday morning in Mountain Springs, Matt sat in the sheriff's office, playing checkers by the hot stove and winning. Rain and wind drenched the outside. They could hear it on the roof like dragging branches. The shutters rattled.

Lacey, one of the deputies, a young, peach-faced, blue-eyed youth, who had fluffy brown hair and a skinny frame, sat in a chair next to the table, watching the game.

"I tell you," Deputy Lacey said, "my son is so darned handsome, the women are going to go wild over him."

"Lacey," Hicks said, "you've been talking about that kid for an hour. Ain't you going to church?"

"Holy cow, what time is it?"

"Nine forty-five," Matt said, looking at his watch.

"My wife will kill me."

They watched Lacey pull on his coat and head outside into drizzling rain. When the door slammed behind him, both men laughed, but each was envious.

"You ever have any kids?" Matt asked.

Tugging at his handlebar moustache, Hicks shook his head and leaned back. "Never was married."

"Ever want to be?"

"When I was younger. She was a Cherokee, down in the Nations. She was the prettiest thing you ever saw. I was crazy about her."

"What stopped you?"

"Her pa didn't think I was good enough for her. I was a buck private with no money, and he figured I'd never amount to anything."

Matt grinned. "So he ran you off?"

"Sure did. Indians can be right smart."

"I've seen some pretty smart Comanche."

Hicks nodded. "You want to talk about smart Indians, look at the Cheyenne and Sioux. They ran circles around the army. They knew more tactics than was ever written in any book."

Matt jumped Hicks's last checkers with one swoop.

"Dammit, Matt, maybe you ought to go to church. You'd learn to be more charitable."

Matt leaned back with a frown. "I wonder where Grant is."

"Well, Lacey was out to Silver Gulch yesterday. He said nothing was happening, except Little was having hisself a pretty good time with some freebies from the women."

"That's not good."

"I told Lacey to head back up there on Monday and tell Little to pay attention and stop fooling around. And speaking of fooling around, why are you avoiding Jennifer White?"

"What makes you think I am?"

"You're crazy about her, but you don't go see her."

Matt grinned. "You want me to play checkers or go courting?"

After two more games, Matt grew restless and left. He walked outside in the afternoon rain, water pouring off his hat and slicker. He had so much on his mind, he didn't know which way to turn. He found himself walking to the newspaper office. Inside, he found Henry alone at the type table.

"Miss White go to church?"

"No, she went riding with Ruben Smythe."

"In the rain?"

"Wasn't raining when they left this morning. I figured they'd come right back, but they didn't."

"Which way did they go?"

"Silver Gulch."

Matt, startled, spun on his heel.

He hurried out of the newspaper office, into the rain, down to the sheriff's, charging inside like a bull moose. "Hicks, that fool woman's gone riding with Ruben Smythe."

Hicks had his feet on his desk and was grinning with his arms folded. "That so?"

"They went to Silver Gulch."

Hicks growled and swung his feet down. "Dammit."

"She just had to find out what was going on, and she's using him to get her there. And the rain didn't turn them back. I'll borrow a horse from Eberley and get after them. You coming?"

Hicks nodded. "We'd better take a tarp and some grub in case we don't make it all the way."

"You know she could run into trouble."

"What kind? She's got a lawyer with her."

"You know what I'm talking about. Get off your rump, and let's go."

CHAPTER 13

In Silver Gulch, Ruben Smythe and Jennifer paced in Ferman's front office, listening to the rain rattling on the roof. Boner, working away at his desk, paid them little mind.

Deputy Little, a husky young man, six feet five with a round pink face and baby blue eyes, stood at the front window, staring out at the rain.

Boner, curious, looked at Jennifer. "I don't understand why you came back. Long way out here for nothing."

"It wasn't raining when we left," she said, annoyed.

"Well," Little said to Jennifer and Ruben, "you folks could stay with me in that shack the sheriff rents here, but it ain't much."

Jennifer, drawing her slicker over her coat and dress, shook her head. "I don't care how hard it's raining. We have to get back."

Boner ran his hand over his thinning hair. "It'll be dark in a couple hours."

"I have a paper to get out."

Red Ferman came out of his office in his shirtsleeves, his red hair unkempt as if he had been sleeping. He rubbed his eyes and looked at them. A cigar in his teeth, he shook his head.

He looked from Ruben to Jennifer to Boner and Deputy Little.

"What the devil brought you way out here?"

No one responded.

Ferman grabbed himself a cup of coffee and turned on Jennifer.

"Ma'am, I read your paper about the mines, and I don't like it one bit."

Her chin went up. "Men die down there, and it's time you cleaned it up."

"All you do is sling mud. That's not running a newspaper."

"Isn't it? Wait until you see my next copy. About that land grant of yours. I'm writing the US marshal in Denver so he'll investigate. I think you're taking over land you have no right to."

Ferman's face turned as red as his hair. "The grants were cleared by the judge."

"But how did you get your hands on them?" she asked.

Before Ferman could explode, Ruben helped her adjust her slicker.

"Let's go, Jennifer. The rain's not going to let up."

She pulled on her wide-brimmed hat with a chin trap and walked with Ruben to the door.

Boner, nervous, went to the supply room. Deputy Little looked as uneasy.

Ferman, full of pent-up fury, turned on Ruben.

"As for you, Smythe, I don't like them lies you say in court."

"What lies, Mr. Ferman?" Rube countered.

"You're gonna be real sorry, I promise."

Jennifer grabbed Ruben's arm and pulled him away.

Slickers and hats covering them, Jennifer and Ruben moved outside into the heavy rain. The mining camp and mountain, shut down by the storm, looked deserted. Up and down the street, doors and windows rattled in the wind. Three mules stood with their heads down near a saloon.

Ruben held Jennifer's mare as she mounted onto her sidesaddle. He swung astride his gray gelding, shaking his head as the rain pounded them.

"Jennifer, you'd better let me read that editorial before you print it."

She smiled and nodded. "I haven't written it."

"You sure set him on fire."

"I just couldn't resist, Ruben, but I think I'm on to something."

As they followed the trail, it rained so hard, they could barely see. The muddy road became dangerous. They had to ride on the slippery grass. The noisy storm deafened them.

Darkness came swiftly with the storm.

"We should go back and stay with Deputy Little," Ruben shouted.

Jennifer waved him off and kept riding.

Ruben's gray gelding slipped and slid on the wet grass. Her sorrel mare nervously fought the bit, tossing its head. The roaring wind pushed them sideways. They could see lightning dancing on the hills ahead.

"We're getting lost, Ruben," she shouted.

"This gray is so barn sour, I'll just let him take us home."

Suddenly, lightning struck in front of them, cracking the air like a whip, blinding them, spitting the earth.

Ruben's gray reared. Her mare jumped, twisted, and bucked, then slid sideways on the grass and rolled with her, throwing her so that it fell with its shoulder on her left leg. Her hat came off, dangling by the strap. Stunned, she lay pinned down in whirling water.

She screeched and fought to get the mare back up. The animal shuddered and couldn't rise. She had her right leg free. Her left leg lay smashed under the mare.

Ruben jumped to the ground, hanging on to his gray's reins, as he came to kneel at her side, rain pelting them. His words sounded far away in the noisy storm.

"My God, Jennifer, are you all right?"

"I don't know. Why won't she get up?"

He moved around in the dark, then came back. "Her right foreleg is broken. Hang on, I'll use my rope to pull you free."

He pulled his pistol and shot the mare, then took his rope from the saddle, tying it around the mare's neck. Fighting the fierce storm in the dark, he mounted. He dallied around the horn and started to back up.

The sudden loud crack of a rifle rang out as a bullet slammed into his back.

She stared in horror as he threw up his hands, jerked, and fell from the saddle. The gray spun around and tried to take off, but the rope held him to the mare a moment longer. Then the dally came free.

The gray jumped around and took off at a lope, disappearing in the dark rain.

Jennifer lay pinned under her mare. Rain fell so heavy she could barely see where Ruben had fallen. Her left leg lay numb under the dead mare, her body wet and cold despite her rain gear. Her chestnut hair lay soaked and across her face.

Barely conscious, her vision blurred, she saw movement in the rain.

Lightning flashed behind the shadow of an approaching rider, a rifle across his saddle. A big man, he wore a slicker with his hat pulled down tight.

Jennifer tried to see through the heavy rain. She could not move.

Helpless, terrified, she feared he would kill her. She closed her eyes and played dead, her only chance of survival.

Lying on the left side of her face, trying to hold her breath as rain tried to drown her, she lay as still as she could.

Through her lashes, she saw a horse's hoof.

The rider swung down and stood by her as she held her breath. She could only see the bottom of his slicker and heavy, muddy boots as lightning flashed again.

Now he kicked her right arm where it lay across her breast. She fiercely determined to show no sign of life. Her arm bounced, then lay still.

She fought the rain and hurt to pretend she was dead.

Finally, he turned and got back in the saddle. Afraid to look, afraid to move, she remained lifeless in the noisy rain.

He rode away. She dared to squint as she watched him into the black, heavy rain. Then she blinked and rubbed her eyes as they filled with tears.

Every time she tried to move the mare, however, she could feel sharp pain in her left leg. The cold rain kept her from feeling how bad it really hurt. She thought of digging under the horse, but she couldn't reach far enough.

She knew that everyone in Mountain Springs would assume they had stayed in Silver Gulch.

Unless Ruben's barn-sour horse raised the alarm, she had little chance.

If she had to lie here all night, she would die from exposure. Water ran off her face and through her hair as she shivered.

"Dear God."

She put her right knee on the saddle seat and pushed, then screamed at her pain.

She tried to pull her skirts and slicker back over her right leg, now nearly frozen. She could not reach her hat. Shivers ran through her. Terrified of frostbite, she pressed her fingers to her face.

The only light came from flashes of lightning in the hills.

Unable to move, chilled to the bone, she tried to be comfortable. She hurt all over. In a daze, she realized rain had turned to drizzle.

She felt grateful, until a swoop of wild wind brought heavier rain and chunks of hail that pelted her. Hail so big and driven, it racked her with pain as she whispered a prayer.

"Please, God, help me."

As the hail pounded Matt and Hicks in the saddle on their hurried ride toward Silver Gulch, Matt pulled his hat down tighter and hunched over.

"We won't find anything in the dark," Hicks complained.

Riding together, they hunched down in hail as hard as gravel. Their horses kept their heads down and were unsteady on the trail, so they had to move to the grass.

They had to shout over the loud storm.

"We're a couple of fools," Hicks yelled.

Matt leaned forward in the saddle. "Go back, if you want. I got me a bad feeling."

They could hardly hear each other, so they fell silent. The rain and hail now hit them face on, blinding them at times, and Matt wondered if Hicks was right.

Until a gray gelding came sliding up to them, so startled it spun and fell, legs every direction, then got up with a snort. It seemed glad to see them.

Hicks reached out and caught the reins. "It's Smythe's horse."

"Let him head for the barn. If we don't make it, they'll come looking."

Hicks threw the reins over the saddle horn. The gray took off again, winding its way east toward town, swaying from side to side and disappearing in the black storm.

Now Matt, scared down to his boots, had a knot in his stomach. Something bad had happened. He urged his bay mount onward.

The sheriff shouted. "I don't even know if we're on the trail now."

"No, we're OK. Keep going."

"Matt, if she's out here, we could ride right by her."

Hail pounded them in the dark storm. They were riding blind. Matt prayed they were still heading for Silver Gulch. He had about given up hope when his horse jumped aside and around.

"Something on the ground," the sheriff shouted.

Matt swung down, holding to the reins as he knelt in a black flood of whirling water. "It's a dead man, shot in the back."

With great effort, he turned the man over, finding it to be Ruben Smythe. Hicks came to kneel with him, hail beating at them.

"She's got to be around here somewhere," Matt said, so grim his face hurt. "Stay with the horses. I'll take one end of my rope and give you the other."

"All right. Work your way in a circle."

Five feet away from the horses, Matt could not see them anymore. He made a half circle at ten feet, holding the end of the lariat, then twenty.

At thirty feet, he stumbled on something, a horse's hoof. He felt the frozen leg. Terrified, moving his hands up to the neck and shoulder, he felt the saddle. There was a leg dangling over the horse's belly.

Frantic, he jerked on the rope, holding it as he guided Hicks toward him. He moved around the dead mare, feeling in the wet. His hand fell on a stiff arm, then a nearly frozen slicker and a woman's face. Jennifer did not respond to his touch.

He moved his hand to touch her face, finding her numb and lifeless with no warmth.

"Hicks!"

Hicks followed the rope, dismounted and came to kneel at his side. "Is she alive?"

"I don't know. There's a rope on the mare's neck, but it's stiff as a board. I'll put this one on, and you dally from the saddle. We've got to get her out of here."

Hicks helped him fasten the rope, then went back to the saddle, mounted and dallied, pulling hard until the mare moved away from Jennifer and slid across the grass.

Matt grabbed her. He knew her leg could be broken. He found a pulse in her neck and became excited. Hicks had found Smythe's Winchester in the mud. With saddle strings, they bound the rifle to her left leg, keeping it straight.

Matt struggled to lift her in his arms. She didn't stir. Hicks took her from him, and Matt mounted, so Hicks could hand her to him.

"She's hurt bad," Hicks said.

"But she's alive."

Matt, set in the saddle, cradled her in his arms. Hicks mounted. They fought their way through the driving rain and hail until they stumbled on a grove of aspen, praying the lightning would not return. Lots of big rocks gave them even more protection, away from the trees.

After tying the horses, they set up the tarp in a tent shape between the rocks. They huddled under it with Jennifer between them, wrapped in blankets.

When the rain slowed again, Matt went out to break small lower branches off the trees, snapping them together. He found enough rocks to surround a small fire pit under the tarp. He desperately fought with matches to start a fire.

When the wind swooped under the tarp and blew out the matches, he shifted position. Finally, Hicks went out and found some cow chips, which he brought back. One of the matches finally caught. Flames shot up from the hole. Matt pulled Jennifer into his arms, under his coat, cradling her against his chest.

"We've got to get her warm," Matt said.

"You hold her. I'll massage her legs and feet."

They did the best they could for her. Then Hicks covered her and Matt with blankets.

The storm raged around them. Every time the fire burned low, Hicks had to take his hunting knife to retrieve more of the small lower limbs. He gathered a bunch, which he heaped around them. They would break off twigs as needed. The wet wood made a smoky fire and didn't burn well, but when it caught, it crackled and spit.

The horses, tethered behind them, added some protection from the wind.

Matt silently prayed there would be no more lightning. Even the wind had stopped, but the hail and rain were brutal. The black storm threatened.

Matt cuddled Jennifer close against him, his hand against her cold cheek, and he whispered a prayer. As she lay asleep in his arms, he knew she might not survive.

Hicks caught enough rain and hail to brew some hot coffee, strong enough to break a man's tooth. They forced some between Jennifer's lips. Barely conscious, she fought to swallow. She turned and clung to Matt, who held her tight.

Hicks drank a cupful. "We'd better take turns sleeping. We don't want to freeze to death."

"I'll take first watch."

Hicks drew up his blanket. "I'd sure like to get my hands on whoever left her to die."

Matt nodded, held her tighter.

Hicks grumbled and curled up, trying to stay under the tarp.

CHAPTER 14

Matt, wide-awake in the night rain, held Jennifer against him, tucking the blankets around her as he sat up. Hicks slept nearby in an awkward position. About three in the morning, the rain and hail stopped as suddenly as they had started.

By daylight, the sun broke through, but the grass and ground were soaked.

Matt, stiff all over, found Jennifer warmer. Hicks sat up, rubbing his eyes.

"You didn't wake me."

"I couldn't sleep. Build the fire up."

Hicks gathered more branches and twigs, and then piled them up in the rock circle, fanning it with his hat. Soon the fire blazed again. Matt slid over as he moved Jennifer closer to it.

They massaged her legs and arms. Matt rubbed her face and forced more coffee into her mouth. She moaned and fought him.

"Jennifer?"

Matt shook her but her eyes didn't open. He drew her onto his lap, still stroking her face.

"That won't do it," Hicks said. He leaned close to her and shouted in her ear. "Wake up, dammit."

Jennifer jerked and twisted in Matt's arms. Her eyes opened. When she saw Matt's face looking down at her, she gasped and her lips moved soundlessly.

Then she tried to sit up and felt the pain in her leg. She screeched. Both men jumped in surprise. Eyes wet, Matt helped her slowly sit up. She tried to reach her left leg.

"Is it broken?" she whispered.

"We're not sure," Matt said. "Just lie down."

"I'm too cold."

"Can you feel your toes? Your fingers?" Hicks asked.

"I think so."

Matt drew the blankets more tightly about her. "What happened?"

They gave her coffee. She held it in both hands, sipping it. "My mare fell on me and broke her leg. Ruben shot her, and he was trying to pull her away with a rope when he was shot. His horse ran off, and I couldn't move."

"Did you see who it was?"

She drank more of the coffee, her voice stronger as she continued. "I saw a big man on a horse, but he was just a blur in the dark. He had a slicker and hat pulled down, and something over his face. He got down and kicked me in the arm, but I played dead, so he finally left."

Hicks frowned. "That was mighty brave of you."

"Any markings on the horse?" Matt asked.

"If there were, I couldn't see. But no, wait. I did see a front hoof, and there were no markings. Probably a left foreleg. Maybe a bay or a black. I don't know."

All around them, the rocks and wet grass glistened in the rising sun but ice formed everywhere.

They made a better cast for her leg with limbs and saddle strings. She grimaced with every movement.

"I don't think it's broken," Matt said.

Hicks warmed up some beans. Jennifer ate hungrily.

"We've got to get you back," Matt said. "Can you ride, if I hold you?"

"I think so."

They let her rest awhile longer. Then they broke camp. Matt was in the saddle. Hicks swung her up in front of Matt, as she winced in pain.

Matt held her in his arms as she rested against the pommel and him, blankets pulled around her. She nestled her left shoulder against his chest, her right arm sliding under his coat to grip his belt. Her legs dangled.

As they started back, Matt began to realize how terrified he had been because of her. He tried to tell himself he would have worried about any woman, but he knew he was fooling himself. He had been wild with panic.

"There's a wagon coming," Hicks said.

They could see it on the trail. Now it turned toward them. Sitting on the wagon seat were Gentry and young Henry, who held the lines, as they drew up near the riders.

"When Smythe's horse come back," Gentry said, "we figured we'd better have a look."

"Sure took your time," Hicks said. "Let me show you where he is."

When Hicks, Gentry, and Henry returned with Smythe, wrapped in the blankets in the wagon bed, Hicks also offered Jennifer a ride in the bed.

Jennifer refused to move from Matt's arms, claiming it would be too painful to ride in the wagon without springs.

Matt didn't mind holding her. He worried about her leg. When they reached town, he took her over to the doctor, whose office loomed above the post office. Hicks stayed with Matt to help Jennifer from the saddle.

Gentry took the body to the undertaker. Henry waited on the boardwalk.

Matt carried Jennifer up the stairs, Hicks following. Inside, the same elderly doctor who had looked at Banner came to help them. He had them lay her on a table in a back room, then ordered them to leave, while he cleaned his spectacles and prepared to examine her.

When they were allowed to return, the doctor smiled. "It's not broken—just badly sprained."

Jennifer, her left leg tightly bound with bandages and a splint, smiled up at them and reached for Matt's hand, drawing him toward her. "You were angels, both of you."

"Now get out of here," the doctor said to the men. "I want to watch her awhile. But Henry ought to get her house key and go start a fire in her stove so it'll be warm when she gets there. Ask Mrs. Ledbetter to be at her house to help her get settled."

Jennifer frowned at Matt, worried about the woman.

"It's all right," Matt said. "You were separated from Ruben in the rain. You got lost, and your horse fell. You nearly died, can't remember anything."

Hicks nodded agreement.

Jennifer reached in her belt purse and gave the key to Hicks.

"Come back in an hour," the doctor said.

As Matt walked back down the stairs with the sheriff, he realized, being Monday, he should have been at work. After giving her key to Henry, the youth left with instructions to warm the house and get Mrs. Ledbetter.

Hicks waited until Henry was on his way, then turned to Matt.

"I hope she doesn't let anything slip to that woman."

Matt shook his head. "She's too smart for that."

"I'll tell Eberley, after I talk to Ruben's brother."

"Thanks," Matt said.

"I'll take the horses."

Later, Matt, asleep in a big chair in the doctor's front office, suddenly awakened as the doctor called him into the back room.

Matt saw she had color in her cheeks and looked glad to see him. Now he could be angry with her. He gathered her up in some blankets.

As he carried her down the steps, he growled at her.

"You had no business going out there."

"It wasn't raining when we left."

"Just the same, you knew Silver Gulch was no place for you."

"I just wanted to see if anything was happening. I wanted to help."

Matt crossed the street, then stopped on the boardwalk in front of the newspaper office and glared down at her. Looking at her pretty face, he felt his anger waning.

He continued walking.

She nestled her face on his chest, holding on to him.

Matt grumbled, "Promise me you won't take any more chances."

"I promise, but I have to tell you, Ferman was madder than a wet chicken when he finally got around to reading my editorial about mine safety."

Matt stopped in the alley, his face hot. "I didn't see that one."

"I didn't actually accuse him. I just talked about how men were dying in shafts. What really made him mad was when I told him my next editorial would be about land grants. And that I was writing to the US marshal."

"Jennifer, you keep asking for trouble."

"Just get me home, Matt. I'm hurting."

He held her more closely and carried her up to her porch where Henry waited. Inside, a red-hot fire blazed in the iron stove. Matt stood, holding her by the couch, but he didn't set her down.

"Mrs. Ledbetter will be here in a moment," he said.

"Maybe I can find out something."

"Jennifer, she was a spy. Don't ask her questions. She's too smart for that."

"Just pull off my boots and go home, Matt."

Henry put her key on the table and left, leaving the door open. Matt still held her in his arms, gazing down at her.

"Jennifer, promise me. Don't give us away to her."

"No, Matt."

"And you'll remember you're not a man, right?"

She leaned back in his embrace, exhausted. She smiled, as she nodded, her green eyes shining.

He couldn't stop himself. He leaned down to kiss her soft lips, shivers running through him. She kissed him back.

"Now set me down, Matt."

"I'm sorry about Ruben."

"He was a good friend."

Mrs. Ledbetter's cheery voice came from the doorway. "There you are, always in trouble, Miss White."

Reluctant, Matt set Jennifer down on the couch.

When he was gone, he could hardly stay awake long enough to get to his room.

Monday afternoon in his private office at work, Frost looked weary from his trip to Alamosa. Eberley and Hancock took seats in front of his desk, the door closed behind them.

"Have you been home?" Hancock asked.

"No, but I'm on my way shortly," Frost said.

"How was Alamosa?"

"Thriving," Frost said. "Just like Canyon City and all around it. Here we sit in the middle of nowhere. I tried to get a spur up here, but all I can determine is Mountain Springs would have to subsidize it."

Eberley folded his arms. "Well, like you said, maybe we can get Grant to come down here for a celebration. That would help."

Frost nodded. "But nobody knows where he is."

"Jared," Eberley said, "while you were away, Ruben Smythe was killed."

"What?"

"He and Jennifer White had gone out to Silver Gulch."

"What for?"

"You know Jennifer. Always curious about something. Anyhow, they got caught in the hail storm coming back. Her horse fell on her. Then Smythe was shot in the back."

Frost leaned forward, hands together. "That's bad."

Eberley continued. "The killer rode over to her, then left her for dead. Luckily, Hicks and Matt Tyler went looking for them. She's going to be all right. Do you have any idea who would do that?"

"No," Frost said.

"Do you think it was Ferman or one of his men?" Eberley asked.

"No, I don't. Where is Matt?" Frost growled.

Eberley stood up and stretched. "Probably sleeping. He was up all night with her out there in the storm. Well, you're expecting Ferman, and I can't stand the man. See you later."

With Eberley gone, Frost and Hancock were alone.

Frost fumed, hands together on the desk.

"There was no need for Smythe to die. He was a nothing. What's the sheriff doing about it?"

Hancock made a face. “Nobody will tell us anything.”

“Just relax,” Frost said. “It will work out.”

Hancock paled. “You know I never wanted to get involved in this scheme in the first place. I think we ought to call the whole thing off.”

“I’m glad the colonel can’t hear what you’re saying.”

“Grant’s just an old man. I don’t want to die for an old man.”

“Milt, you worry me.”

“You really trust Ferman?”

Frost nodded. “He lost his plantation, and Black Friday took everything he had. Same as happened to us. That’s why all we have to do is stand back and wait for him to make it happen.”

It wasn’t long before Red Ferman, his face pink, joined them, closing the door behind him. Ferman looked innocent but rushed.

Ferman removed his heavy coat and sank on a chair near Hancock.

Frost studied him. “Why didn’t Smythe and Miss White stay in Silver Gulch when the storm hit?”

Ferman leaned back, crossing one leg over the other. He lit and puffed on a cigar. He looked from one to the other, always with a barely disguised disdain for lawyers and former officers. He spoke casually.

“She probably figured she wasn’t welcome. She made me mad as the devil. I could have strangled her. Didn’t you see her editorial about mine safety? That was bad enough. Then she says her next one will be about land grants, and she was going to have the US marshal investigate us.”

Hancock leaned forward. “Red, there’s nothing wrong with our land grant.”

Ferman grimaced. “I know, but she can make people start wondering how we got it, and I don’t want ’em digging into that. We’d have a fight on our hands with every miner we squeezed out.”

“So you ran her off?” Frost asked.

“No, but she knew she’d better leave in a hurry.”

“Then what?” Frost persisted.

Ferman scratched his chin. “I figured I’d better shut them up.”

Frost paled. “You did it?”

Hancock, speechless, got up and walked to the window to stare at the rain.

"Well, this is attorney-client privilege, isn't it?" Ferman grunted.

"Yes, but—"

"I got Smythe all right, but her horse fell on her. She was already dead, so I just left her out there."

Frost wet his lips. "Red, she's alive."

Ferman made a face. "How can that be?"

"You think she recognized you?"

"Not a chance."

Hancock, sweat on his face, turned and cleared his throat. "Hicks and Matt Tyler found them. She must have been pretending when you looked at her, because she wasn't dead."

Ferman shook his head, amazed. "What a woman."

"Smythe was shot in the back," Frost said.

"He was no account," Ferman snapped. "And I came here to do business, not listen to complaints. I did what I had to do, and nobody can prove anything."

Frost quickly pacified him. "We're just all worried, Red, and so's the colonel, and it's only natural."

Red Ferman folded his arms. "Nothing to fret over."

"Have you seen Crazy Albert out there?" Frost asked.

"No sign of 'im. I figure he's gone for good."

"There are too many loose ends," Hancock said, turning back to the window.

Ferman growled, "Well, I'd better not have any trouble with that land grant."

"It passed muster with Matt Tyler," Hancock said.

Ferman grunted. "That woman may get him to thinking how we got it. If he does, he'll make a mess of everything."

"You can't touch Matt Tyler just yet," Frost said. "Not until the job is done."

"I ain't never gonna rest until we make things right," Ferman said.

Hancock turned, agitated. “No reason to do anything to Matt Tyler.”

“He’s too nosy,” Ferman said.

That night, Matt found Hicks alone in his office and delighted to play a game of checkers. They sat by the iron stove with the little table between them. Hicks set it up. They played awhile in silence.

Matt jumped one of Hicks’s checkers. “My instincts are driving me crazy.”

Hicks jumped Matt’s last checker. “Well, come on, we’ll go for a walk, check some doors, think about something else.”

At midnight, they walked down the dimly lit street, lanterns flickering in front of buildings. The moon hid in the clouds. Stars glittered.

Except for the Grand Hotel, the town lay dark. But up on the distant hill, lamps burned in the Frost house.

As they passed in front of the hotel, they heard the sudden blast of a shotgun behind it, followed by shattering glass and then sudden silence.

Knowing Loring’s house stood behind the hotel, they pulled their Colts and broke into a run down the alley between the hotel and the courthouse.

As they neared the Loring house, they could hear a horse galloping south so fast on the grass, the sound quickly faded away.

They ran around to the open bedroom window where Pa Loring reached out with a lantern. Cracked glass hung around the frame and on the bare ground. They couldn’t see into the dark room.

“Mr. Loring,” Hicks said, out of breath. “Are you all right?”

“Yeah, but you’d better come inside.”

Matt and Hicks walked slowly as they went back around to the front door, both silent in their fear of what might have happened. Once inside the house, they went to the bedroom and found Ted Loring still alive and sitting up, rubbing his eyes in the lamplight.

Pa Loring, fully clothed, stood with his shotgun, shoving in two more shells. The stooped old man chuckled, as he sat down by the bed.

"He couldn't see me when he tried to get in the window, even with the lamp burning in the hallway out there."

"Who couldn't see you?" Hicks asked.

"Somebody with a hatchet, trying to pry open the window. Had his face covered. When I got up real sudden, it scared him. He turned around quick, but I blasted him right through the glass as he ran off. Don't think I got him too good, but I bet he can't sit down for a week."

"He was able to ride," Hicks said. "We heard his horse."

"I bet he wasn't planted in the saddle."

"So who was it?"

Pa made a face and leaned back. "He had a bandanna up over his nose and his hat pulled down tight. Don't think he was much over five feet, and he wasn't too husky either."

Hicks fretted. "So you don't know who it was?"

"Nope, but I bet he don't try that again."

"Crazy Albert's pretty short," Hicks said. "Was it him?"

"I don't know."

"What about his hat?" Matt asked.

"Just an old beat-up Stetson, all spotted with sweat around the band."

Ted drank water from the glass by his bed. "I can't just lie here, Pa. I don't care what the doctor says."

"We'll talk about it in the morning, but I'm gonna nail some boards over this here window."

"We won't get him tonight, so we'll help you," Hicks said. "Come daylight, maybe we can track him."

Matt and the sheriff carried in some loose boards from Loring's backyard. In a short time, they had the window nailed closed.

Later, they took a lantern and tried to trace the hoof marks. The signs wound through the houses, up the hill around the cemetery, and disappeared as they headed west.

Hicks grunted. "I'll have a look come morning, but it don't look like I'm gonna be able to track him. Just the same, I bet he headed for Silver Gulch."

"Or some doctor," Matt said.

"Two of those women at the cathouse over there—they used to be nurses. Bet that's where he goes. But I reckon any fool can dig out shotgun pellets."

"So what's your next move?"

"I'll send Lacey to have a look around."

Matt felt weary. "Time for some sleep."

"Go ahead. It ain't likely anybody's gonna try that again," Hicks said. "They'll wait until Ted's up and around and away from the house."

CHAPTER 15

When Matt came in Tuesday morning, he went to see Eberley, closing the door behind him. He sat down wearily, glad to see the older lawyer. Eberley, seated behind his desk, balanced his cup of coffee in his hands before speaking.

"I have a trip for you, Matt. The Horton ranch has just paid off its mortgage, and there are some papers to deliver. You can still see any smoke signal from their spread. In fact, you'll be a few miles closer to Needle Mountain. What's more, Horton's where you can buy a good horse if you still want to."

"You bet I do. Why don't you come along?"

"No, I'd better keep an eye on my partners. And I suspect Hicks will want to go with you. He's got a thing about the widow."

"Lucifer still sneaking around?"

"I'm watching him."

Matt thanked him and left the office. He didn't see Frost or Hancock, but Lucifer watched him as he left.

Matt had no trouble convincing Hicks to go out to the Horton ranch with him. The sun glistened in a clear sky of eggshell blue. No wind disturbed the fresh, clean air.

Matt rode the borrowed bay again. He liked the horse well enough, but he had a faster one in mind.

"You didn't tell me Mrs. Horton was the widow," Matt said as they rode side by side.

Hicks grunted with a little snort. "Wait'll you taste her apple pie."

"What if she hasn't made any?"

"She'll make it for us."

"Set her cap for you, has she?"

Hicks reddened a little. "Not without some invitation. I'm old for a lawman; you got to know that. I'm lucky to be alive as it is. When this is over, I'm going to ask her to marry me. If I'm still kicking."

"Then what?"

"Maybe I'll run for mayor. I don't want to just move in and take over her holdings. It'd look like I was retiring at her expense."

"She won't agree with you."

On rolling hills in close view of the high mountains, the Horton ranch had many stables and corrals. Men could be seen working colts and moving cattle. The long house had one rambling story and a long covered porch, shaded by aspens and yellow pine.

Emma Horton, plump and gray in calico, had a pretty face, round and pink. Large blue eyes constantly fixed on Hicks as she served them hot apple pie and coffee.

Hicks turned to Emma. "Matt here is looking for a horse."

"What do you have in mind?" she asked Matt.

"Just so it's fast," Matt said.

"Men," she said. "Well, I have a couple you might be interested in. Two four-year-olds. A black gelding and a buckskin stallion."

Hicks looked up slowly. "Buckskin stallion?"

"My foreman bought him a few weeks ago in Alamosa, but he's high strung. Jumps fences, opens gates, and you sure can't walk behind him."

Matt grinned. "Sounds interesting."

She looked him over. "You sure you could handle him? The black is a good horse and more fitting for a lawyer. You know how much trouble a stallion can be. No one will like you having it around."

But Matt insisted on seeing the buckskin.

About fourteen hands, flowing black mane and tail, the stallion had flaring nostrils and large brown eyes that watched Matt's every move, as he climbed onto the fence.

"They say he's fast," she said. "But the men are afraid to take him out of the corral."

"How's his mouth?"

"Tender. He has a good rein. And backs up faster than some go forward. The men call him Buck." She hesitated. "Matt, you know a stallion can cause trouble wherever it goes. Most cowmen won't have anything to do with one."

Matt waited until the buckskin was saddled. He swung astride. "Open the gate."

"Are you sure?" she asked, worried.

Matt insisted. She nodded to one of the men.

The gate swung open. Matt set the nervous stallion into a lope across the green hills. The buckskin's pent-up energy soon exhausted. It walked easily. Matt leaned over to stroke the powerful neck.

Then he reined it side to side and backed it up.

At the corrals, Hicks and Mrs. Horton waited, surprised he was still in the saddle.

Matt reined up near them and leaned on the horn. The buckskin tossed its head and stood quietly.

"His problem was he was busting with energy," Matt said. "He couldn't burn it up in a corral. How much do you want for him?"

Mrs. Horton folded her arms. "Well, I paid fifty for him, but only because the owner couldn't handle him. He's worth a lot more, and there'd be colts worth plenty. Make me an offer."

"Seventy-five," Matt said.

After much dickering to the amusement of Hicks and watching hands, Matt bought the stallion for one hundred and fifty. The saddle and gear cost him forty.

"That's a lot of money for a horse," Hicks said the next morning as they rode away from the ranch.

Hicks led the bay, because the buckskin wouldn't let anything trail it close. Matt enjoyed the ride with a big grin and a bit of boasting.

"I figure he's the fastest horse in Colorado."

They reined up to look back at the ranch and over to the mountains. They could see nothing from Needle Mountain.

Matt made a face. "I just had a thought. As soon as Grant sees old Buck here, he's going to want to buy him."

"Could Grant handle him?"

"He's one of the finest horsemen I've ever seen."

In late afternoon in bright sun, Matt and Hicks rode into Mountain Springs. Men and women stopped to stare at the stallion. Matt rode tall and proud in the saddle. They stopped in front of the firm just as Eberley walked outside.

Eberley stared at the stallion but kept his distance.

"Matt, that is one beautiful animal."

"Just don't walk behind him," Hicks said, grinning from the saddle.

"I'll break him of that," Matt said. "But he's sure a good fit."

They turned to see Deputy Lacey riding up the street on a sorrel. He led a bay horse with a dead body, half-covered by blankets, tied down on the saddle, and rocking with every step.

Hicks swung down and walked quickly to meet him.

"What happened?"

Lacey made a face. "I went to check on Little at the shack, and he was in there all right. Shot between the eyes. His gun was in his hand, already cocked, but he hadn't fired. Nobody knows anything. I didn't stick around, just got a couple fellahs to help me load him up."

"But why was he killed?" Matt questioned.

Lacey shrugged. "I don't know, but Boner said Little was asking too many questions around the camp."

Hicks grimaced. "Now I got to write his ma. What the devil can I tell her?"

Later that evening in the sheriff's office, alone with Hicks over a lazy game of checkers, Matt felt frustrated over the continuing turn of events. They sat by the stove having hot, thick coffee in a long silence, until Matt leaned forward.

"You notice both Witherspoon and Little were shot between the eyes. Almost a signature."

"Raddigan?" Hicks asked.

"Could be."

"Yeah, that'd be his style all right."

"But who shot Smythe?"

Hicks grunted. "Well, I don't know, but since Jennifer White made Ferman so mad, it makes you wonder if he followed them. He don't strike me as a woman killer, but he'd sure not hesitate to shoot a lawyer. "

"What I'm thinking is to divert attention from Silver Gulch," Matt said, jumping three of his checkers.

"How you gonna do that?"

"Since Mrs. Ledbetter thinks we don't know her leaning, I could feed her some information. Like putting Grant someplace else for a meeting."

Hicks grunted. "Well, give it a try, but you'd better stay away from Silver Gulch, if you want to avoid them figuring that's where he'd be. On the other hand, it's perfectly natural for me or Lacey to go looking for Little's killer."

That evening, Jennifer, alone in her house, decided to go to the office and pick up her notes for her next day's editorial, then bring them back home. As usual, she had a revolver in her purse. Wearing her cape, she went to the office around by the front door. She went inside, locking the door behind her. She turned up the lamp and went to her desk.

Gathering her notes, she paused. Had she heard something out back? Nervously, she turned down the lamp and headed for the front door, her heart thumping in her breast.

She unlatched it hurriedly. When she opened the door, a man forced his way inside. Jennifer gasped, backing up, as she stared at Raddigan, the killer who gave her chills.

"What do you want?"

He smiled, closing the door behind him.

She quickly turned up the lamp and held her purse in both hands, waiting.

"I just came to see you."

"You have news for me?"

His moustache twitched, his pale eyes shining like moons under his heavy brows.

"Miss White," he said, removing his hat, "I wanted to talk to you."

"About what?"

"Those stories you write about me."

Her face burned. "They're true, aren't they?"

"But they make me out a cold-blooded killer. I'd like a few changes."

"Changes?"

"Make me a little more colorful. After all, I never shoot a man who isn't pulling a gun on me. Those dime novels make heroes out of men who couldn't shine my boots. You could tell the world about me."

"I thought I already had."

"I figure I could outdraw anyone from Tucson to Deadwood. I want you to write that."

Her mouth felt dry as bone. "I can write you said it."

"Good enough."

"Now please leave."

He smiled, hooking his thumbs in his gun belt. "We're not through, you and me."

Her chin went up. She drew her revolver from her purse. In her haste, it slid crazily through her fingers. Frantic, she caught at it and missed. It crashed on the floor between her feet. It didn't go off. She drew a deep breath.

Raddigan looked down at the revolver. He looked at her a long serious moment. Suddenly, he laughed.

"That's the funniest thing I ever saw."

"I wasn't trying to entertain you."

"When I come after you, it'll be when all of this is over."

"When what's over?"

He smiled, tipping his hat. "Good night, Miss White."

Jennifer's legs wobbled as he closed the door. She stumbled over to latch it, now afraid to leave. She went back to the desk and turned down the lamp. She picked up the revolver and returned to peer through the curtains. She could see Raddigan mounting his horse. She watched him ride out of town.

Still frightened, she waited a long while, then closed up and hurried through the alley in the moonlight, her heart pounding. When safe in her house, her eyes filled with tears.

The next morning, alone with Frost in Frost's big office, Hancock paced the room. From his plush chair behind the desk, Frost watched with concern.

Hancock could not stop pacing. "Are you sure Mrs. Ledbetter heard Salida? It used to be New Arkansas?"

Frost nodded. "That's what Matt told her last night."

"How could Matt know that?"

"She said Matt heard it from someone riding through."

Hancock frowned. "So Grant turned around and went back?"

"I don't know, but that's where Grant supposedly rented his wagon in the first place."

Hancock made a face. "Do you think Matt Tyler's figured anything out?"

"He's nothing but a kid. He came here for the money, that's all."

"What about Eberley?" Hancock asked.

"Ignore him."

"What about your wife?"

"Morna? She doesn't know anything. Milt, I don't like you being so nervous. If the colonel knew how you were acting, he'd be worried about you."

There was a knock at the door. Lucifer entered with an announcement.

"Mr. Ferman's here."

"That so? Well, send him in."

Lucifer left but had hardly exited when Ferman came charging in, shoving the door shut behind him and charging up to the desk.

His face crimson like his hair, Ferman steamed.

Hancock backed away, pausing near the window.

Frost watched Ferman jerk around, pace, sweat.

"Red, sit down," Frost told him.

Ferman grimaced, squirmed, and plunked himself down in a chair facing the desk.

Hancock looked ready to climb out the window.

Ferman growled. "A friend of mine showed up last night, from Irwin."

Frost looked excited. "And?"

"Seems Grant had gone that way all right, traveling alone with a wagon and driver, and Routt, just as we figured."

Frost leaned forward, his hands on his desk. "And?"

"They were going to corner him in the canyon. A woman was going to do the shooting. But the town came to escort Grant in with a lot of noise, so her horse bolted, and nothing happened."

"Dammit," Frost said. "Where is he now?"

"Nobody knows. My friend was trying to track them but he lost 'em up there in the forest somewhere. And then the hailstorm wiped out all signs. He can't figure where they are. They sure aren't following Shockley's map, or they'd be in Silver Gulch by now."

Frost shrugged. "There's a possibility he's on his way to Salida."

"How can we be sure?" Ferman snapped.

"I'll take the afternoon stage," Frost said, "and see one of our clients there. One night in Salida's all I need to find out if Grant's gone or still on his way, or even where he is. Shockley will know."

"Something else I found out," Ferman said. "My friend from Irwin, he said Crazy Albert was up there again. Getting doctored and babbling. I figured we'd better shut him up for good, so my friend is going back to take care of 'im."

"He'd better watch out," Frost said. "They don't call him Crazy Albert for nothing."

Ferman turned in his chair to look at the closed door and made a face. "I don't like that Lucifer. He's uppity for a law clerk. You sure he can be trusted?"

"No," Frost said, "but he's so ambitious, he comes in handy. All he wants is to get his ticket as a lawyer and be a partner in our firm. He'll keep his mouth shut."

Hancock wiped his brow. "Remember our deal with the colonel, Red. We only brought Grant here with the understanding Jared and I would be completely out of it."

"Yeah, well," said Ferman, "you didn't complain when we finished off them law clerks to shut 'em up after you shot off your big mouths around here. You didn't make any noise when we got Choper to stop the newspaper."

Hancock paled. "We don't want to lose everything."

"You think I do?" Ferman growled.

Frost cleared his throat. "Just get it done, Red."

Ferman leaned back, glared at Frost and Hancock.

He hated their guts.

He didn't care how they came out of the ordeal with Grant.

One thing for sure, with Frost off to Salida, Ferman would be with that stuffy lawyer's pretty wife. The thought gave Ferman great pleasure and calmed him.

CHAPTER 16

RIGHT AFTER DARK ON FRIDAY night with Frost on his way to Salida, Ferman slipped out of his house and down the hillside, scurrying through the trees and into a back door of the Frost mansion, which had been left open for him.

He entered, set the latch, and hurried through the dark ballroom.

He could hardly wait to get his hands on Morna. It pleased him that the arrogant Frost didn't have the slightest idea about the affair. Maybe someday Ferman would jam the needle in the arrogant lawyer.

A lamp burned low in the fancy parlor in the silent house. Bounding up the stairs, three steps at a time, he could almost feel her in his arms.

He did love her, want her, and need her.

In the master bedroom, he found the lamps burning low, the bed turned down, and Morna in a pink silk gown, smiling at him from the dresser where she combed her shining hair. He could smell her French perfume.

Ferman hurried around to the left side of the bed and started peeling off his clothes and boots. Her smile faded. His actions reminded her too much of Jared.

He let his gun belt fall on the floor with everything else. He sat on the bed, still in his long underwear and waited for her, his legs dangling.

"As soon as Frost said he was going to Salida, this was all I could think about," he said.

She stood up and walked over to sit on the bed. He grabbed her and pulled her to him, kissing her hungrily.

She responded, until they heard a shout from the doorway.

"You bastard!"

Ferman and Morna turned to see Jared Frost standing there with his mouth wide open. Her husband's color changed rapidly from dark to white to red.

Jared Frost threw his carpetbag to the floor.

Morna struggled to her feet, backing toward the dresser.

Frantic, Ferman tangled with the covers, fell sideways and rolled over with a loud crash to the floor, right on top of his clothes, disappearing from Jared's view.

"I'm going to blow your head off," Frost said, pulling his shoulder pistol.

Ferman called out. "Dammit, Frost, the colonel needs us both."

Morna gasped. "Please, Jared, don't!"

Frost went charging around the bed with his pistol cocked.

Ferman had fallen on his gun belt, He drew his army Colt, fanned the hammer and rolled over. As he looked up at the fiery Jared and the barrel of the Smith & Wesson, Ferman had no choice but to pull the trigger.

The bullet slammed into Frost's chest, dead center.

Mouth open, Frost clutched at his wound with his free hand, blood spurting through his fingers. He dropped to his knees, still trying to fire his pistol, rage in his wild brown eyes.

Ferman cocked his revolver, got to his feet and waited.

Frost's eyes glazed over.

Morna covered her mouth with her hands, muffling her scream.

Frost fell facedown on the throw rug, bleeding all over it.

Colt still in hand, Ferman drew a deep breath.

Morna sat on the bed, tears in her eyes.

"Oh, Red, I never wanted this to happen."

"Me neither. Not this soon anyway."

"What are we going to do?"

He sat on the edge of the bed, still breathing hard. "Well, we sure don't want 'im found here, do we?"

Morna, in shock, could not look at the dead man.

"How did he get here?" Ferman asked.

"Do you think anyone heard the shot?"

"No, the house is too isolated, unless your handyman did, out at the stable?"

"He's nearly deaf." She wiped at her eyes. "What are you going to do?"

"I'll take him and his bag down the road, leave him just like somebody shot and robbed him. What about the dog? Do you think he untied it?"

"I don't think so, but please be careful."

"I'll go out the back door. I'll burn the rug. You just get ready to be mighty surprised when they come to tell you." He picked up the shoulder pistol. "I'll bury this so they'll think whoever robbed him took it."

Ferman hurriedly dressed, then rolled the dead man into the throw rug.

He stood and turned to give her a quick hug and a kiss.

With Morna's help, he threw Frost over his shoulder. She handed him the carpetbag.

"Did he have a briefcase?" Red asked.

"It'd be downstairs on his desk."

"From now on," he said, "we got to be careful. I get seen coming here, they'll figure it out, and I'll hang, so you be patient and don't look for me for a while."

He carried the body and bag out the door.

She followed him along the hallway and down the stairs.

Frost grew heavier by the minute. She found the briefcase and shoved it in the carpetbag Ferman had in his grasp. He had to get him out of the house and down near the road.

He looked kindly at the tearful Morna, then turned to the back door.

She let him out and closed it behind him with a sob.

Outside in the dark, Ferman saw no sign of the dog.

Carrying the body and bag, he slipped on grass and stumbled on rocks. He had to keep going. Once he leaned on a tree to catch his breath. Then as he neared the last few yards to the road, he heard a rushing sound behind him. He turned.

The gleaming yellow eyes of a bundle of fury charged, dragging its chain.

Ferman spun, threw the body full force at the big dog.

One hundred and seventy pounds of dead body crashed down on the animal and rolled with it, then away, leaving the dog crushed and lifeless.

Ferman picked up a rock and bashed in its head, just to be sure. Exhausted, he could hardly stand. He wasn't that far from the road. He had to give up on moving Frost any farther. He dragged the bloody rug off the dead man. He let Frost lie next to the carpetbag and the dead animal. He retraced his steps, carefully restructuring the grass and putting stones back in their pockets.

Then he dragged some brush everywhere he had stepped, all the way from the house. He carefully raised the grass up again. Drenched in sweat, he made plans to destroy the rug.

Back in the house, all alone, sitting on her bed, Morna wept. All of her flirting and selfish pleasures had suddenly exploded.

She knelt down to pray.

Her frantic prayer left her crying most of the night. Tears ran down her face and sobs jerked her breast. Remorse hung heavy.

Early Saturday morning at the newspaper, Jennifer worked at her desk, writing up some notes, while Henry sat on a stool in the back, replacing type in the individual boxes. That's how it worked, pick out the type, place it in a type tray, place the trays in a frame, and when the paper was printed, all the type had to go back into the slots. But it gave Henry time to think about a girl in his class at school.

Jennifer had trouble concentrating on her notes.

The front door opened.

Matt came inside to lean on the counter and smile at her. He always looked so full of life, so cocky, so darn handsome. He removed his Stetson.

"You getting around OK?" Matt asked.

Glad to see him, she stood up and limped over to the counter, her smile bright.

"Yes, Matt, I am, thanks to you and the sheriff. And if you asked real pretty, you could buy me a cup of coffee at Pop's."

"I'm asking."

"As a friend?"

He grinned. "That's our agreement."

Jennifer pulled on her gray cape and hat. Leaving Henry to his daydreaming, they went outside in the cold morning air. Her limp gave her an excuse to take his arm.

Matt paused at her side. "Someone's waving at you."

She followed his gaze to the man across the street.

"Ralph Smythe. Ruben's brother. He's been in a bad way."

"Just remember, my orders are secret."

"Don't worry."

Ralph, in his thirties, had the same round face and friendly brown eyes as his late brother. He wore a dark suit and no hat. He crossed the street to join them. The two men shook hands. They ended up in Pop's Café with coffee and blueberry pie. Ralph only had coffee.

She looked at Ralph's sadness. "Is there anything we can do for you?"

"No, but I sure hope they find out who shot my brother. "He turned to Matt. "Have you been looking into land grants?"

Matt tensed, fingering his cup. "Why do you ask?"

"Jennifer gets a sniff of something, she doesn't let go, and she's thinking maybe there's something wrong with the land grant Ferman claims to have purchased."

Matt shook his head. "It was authentic and given by Governor Armijo in the 1840s. In the treaty with Mexico, the United States had agreed to honor these."

Ralph folded his arms. "How many land grants do you suppose there were in this part of Colorado?"

"What are you getting at?"

"It seemed to me that the Sangre de Cristo grant covered the same territory as the Cochetopa, claimed by Ferman."

"Those grants became private property with the treaty, making them available for sale. I'm not aware of any conflicts."

They looked up from their coffee, as Hicks came walking in, a strange look on his face. He pulled up a chair and ordered coffee, then looked from one to the other.

"Another murder. Looks like robbery."

Jennifer drew back. "Oh, no."

The sheriff turned to Matt. "It was Frost."

Matt frowned. "Jared Frost?"

Hicks nodded. "Eberley was out walking his dog this morning. Found Frost's body not far from the road up the hill. The stage to Salida had turned back because of a cracked wheel and hub. Frost decided to walk home from the depot, I reckon. Whoever done it, killed Frost's dog at the same time."

Ralph Smythe made a face. "Who'd want to kill Frost?"

"He had a lot of money on him, his wife said. But it was all gone."

Ralph shook his head. "First the law clerks and now the lawyers?"

"And his dog," Matt said.

As the others talked, Matt's thoughts ran back to Moose and Grizzly, how they claimed when Frost was away, Red Ferman went in the back door.

Matt determined since there it was just gossip with no proof, he could not ruin Morna's reputation with further speculation.

He looked at Hicks and knew he would feel the same.

Toward evening, Matt found Eberley at Gentry's barbershop having his hair cut. No other customers were there. Matt sat with one leg crossed over the other knee and folded his arms, leaning back as he told them what Ralph had said about the grants.

"Wishful thinking," Eberley said. "It's my understanding the Cochetopa was legally purchased from former owners of the Sangre de Cristo grant. I don't think you'll find anything wrong with Ferman's title."

"Maybe it was obtained by fraud."

Eberley frowned. "Matt, you're reaching."

"Well, Frost won't be talking," Gentry said.

Matt pushed his hat back from his damp brow. "It sure doesn't make any sense, his being murdered like that."

"The town blames it on the gambling hall," Eberley said. "They say it makes for desperate men who've lost everything and are looking for victims like Frost."

Eberley thought about the night he caught Ferman on the run from the Frost mansion. Too much of a gentleman to ruin Morna's life without proof, he decided to keep it to himself.

Gentry handed Eberley a small looking glass. "All done. How about you, Matt?"

Eberley said good night, took his coat and hat, and left them.

Sitting in the barber's chair, Matt relaxed some as Gentry trimmed his hair.

"Matt, I heard you mailed a letter to the president's aide."

"Just thanking Harriman for helping me transfer my practice. How did you find out?"

"I gave the clerk a haircut."

"I wonder who else he told," Matt said.

"Matt, remember, I'll do anything to help. I'd give my life for the general."

Matt nodded. "So would I. That's what got me into this."

Late that night, downstairs in her parlor with the lamps down low, Morna stood fully dressed by the fire. Red Ferman, also fully dressed, put his arm around her. He wore a heavy coat.

Her eyes red from crying, she leaned against him.

"I can't stay long," he said. "I just wanted to see if you were OK."

She wiped at her eyes. "Jared gave me the house. His sons and I share what's in the bank, but we have nothing from the law firm except a trust fund. His partners get the rest."

"You'll be all right. Just keep your head."

"The funeral's tomorrow, Red. Are you going to be there?"

"Sure, I got no choice. But I'd better spend more time at the mines for a while. So don't look for me."

"But then what?"

"After a time, we'll get married."

Morna didn't answer, because she didn't want to offend him. She had no idea what she wanted for her future. She had been terribly disappointed in her marriage to Jared Frost.

She worried it would be the same with Red Ferman.

She had never felt so lost.

Sunday afternoon in the cemetery, most of the town turned out for the distinguished Jared Frost. The sunshine warmed them as the wind rose. A dismal scene, it evoked little fondness for Jared Frost, a feared, unpopular lawyer.

As the preacher gave his words over the closed pine coffin, many of the onlookers were wrapped in their own thoughts.

Milton Hancock worked his mouth, his nerves on edge. What would happen now? As much as he had hated Grant for destroying his fortune, he didn't want to face a firing squad or disgrace. Without the colonel driving them and Frost pushing him, he never would have been involved in Ferman's scheme. He had always been afraid they would learn he had let himself be captured back in the war. His bravado with them had been difficult.

"This was a man of honor," the preacher said.

Red Ferman stood with hat in hand, head bowed with sorrow painted on his face. In his thoughts, his passionate need for Morna. This had not been timely. Yet he now had a clear path to her. Frost had been one of those snooty officers, the type he had despised, so he wasn't grieving. Although Black Friday wiped Ferman out at the time, his wealth had returned through the mines.

Killing Frost had been untimely, but Ferman now had no regrets.

Ferman thought of Eberley the night he ran away from Frost's mansion. Eberley had no proof where he'd been, but Eberley could get him hanged, Ferman counted on the lawyer's Southern chivalry toward Morna. At the same time, Ferman considered Eberley a dead man if he said a single word about it.

"A highly respected member of the community," the preacher continued.

Matt Tyler held his hat in both hands, listening but carefully reading all the faces in the crowd. He hadn't liked Frost, but right now, he thought about Grant and wondered why Frost had to die. So many murders. So many questions. Matt had to protect the general, and yet he felt helpless.

Jennifer White also watched everyone, trying to spot any sign of guilt, even as her mind wandered. She had no family. Frank Choper had left her all alone. If she stayed a spinster, what would happen to her? She knew how lonely the rest of her life might be. It made her sad. Jennifer no longer limped, but the ordeal in the storm with Ruben murdered would haunt her forever. Losing her father, then Frank, and now Ruben. She looked over at Matt and worried about his safety. Losing Matt would be too much to bear.

"Leaving his beloved wife to mourn," the preacher said.

Morna had tears trickling down her face. Dressed in black under a navy cape, a veil draped from her hat, her head bowed, she clasped her hands at her waist. Every now and then, she would tremble with despair. She tried not to look at Red Ferman. She suffered with guilt and remorse. She saw no life for herself. Ferman loved her, but her regret stifled her feelings for him. She could not turn back the clock. She could only suffer.

Eberley looked from Ferman to Morna, for he had suspicions about their liaison. He figured there was more to Frost's death than met the eye, but he could only imagine what had happened. He had no evidence. Further, he could never humiliate Morna by exposing her to gossip. Even if he assumed the worst, that Frost had found them together, it would not change anything. The conspiracy to assassinate Grant would continue.

He also had been kept out of Frost and Hancock's circle, for as the only Yank in the firm, they didn't trust him.

Eberley knew it had been his personal fortune that had saved the firm. As a self-contained man, he had never expected gratitude, nor did he get it. At times, he regretted going in with them. On the other hand, he loved the Rockies.

"Vengeance is mine, sayeth the Lord," the preacher said.

Sheriff Hicks watched everyone in the cemetery, his hands gripping his hat but his mind working the crowd. He believed Matt about a conspiracy, and it had to involve Frost's death. There had to be more to the murders than was obvious. Hicks, a dedicated lawman, could not rest until he found the killers and could assure Grant's safety.

Gentry, leaning on his cane, looked around at the faces, searching for other than grief. He could see that many came for the show of it. Coming here from the South had been a good move for him. The town tolerated him, needed his barbershop and his inventions. Now that he had joined Matt's team to save Grant, he had a better and nobler purpose.

Judge Waller, a short gray-haired man who looked ready to leave, and all the lawyers in town, attended. McComb, the county attorney, stood with head bowed and hat in hand with the appropriate display of respect.

When the service ended and the crowd moved back on the path to town, Hancock caught up with Judge Waller and spoke quietly. "Your Honor, both Mr. Eberley and I have a full calendar, and some of the appearances in Denver will be a conflict."

"You have another lawyer, Mr. Hancock. Use him."

"But he's not familiar with the cases."

"I'm sorry about Mr. Frost, but there have been too many delays. Mr. McComb is our only county attorney, and he can't always be here. We have to work around his schedule."

Hancock wanted to protest, but the judge cut him off.

"That's my ruling, Mr. Hancock."

Judge Waller pulled on his hat, nodded farewell, and headed down the lane through the aspens, leaving Hancock frustrated and pink faced.

Hancock stood twirling his hat in his hands and grimacing. Frost had left him in a pickle. There would be a big mess now. Matt Tyler might well get a sniff of something he shouldn't. Hancock grimaced, worried and afraid.

Matt came to stand at his side. "Something wrong, Mr. Hancock?"

"You have to take some of Jared's cases, right away."

"I don't see any problem with that."

Hancock turned to look at him. "How easily the young face a challenge. Maybe ignorance is a blessing."

Matt frowned. "Ignorance?"

"I know you're a good lawyer, Matt, but you don't know what you're getting into."

"I'm sure I'll find out."

Hancock turned away and walked into the crowd moving down the hill.

Matt gazed after him. He had never cottoned to Hancock or Frost.

Jennifer caught up with Matt, walked at his side. "Something wrong?"

"I'm not sure."

"This is all so terrible, Matt."

"I'll walk you home."

"You could be next."

They fell silent, as she took his arm. They moved down the path, taking comfort in each other's presence.

Clouds moved over the sun. The wind rose, whipping the dust and trees.

As they walked, Matt counted the dead in his thoughts: three law clerks along with Frank Choper, Witherspoon, Ruben Smythe, Deputy Little, and now Jared Frost, all victims.

Matt had to wonder who would be next.

CHAPTER 17

On that same Sunday, Moose and Grizzly chopped wood and occasionally looked down from Needle Rock, toward the town far below to the north, where it nestled in front of Silver Mountain. Bright sun, often blinding, moved in and out of the clouds.

They scanned the surrounding ridges and trails with Moose's spyglass every day, and this particular morning, Grizzly grumbled, out of sorts.

"Even if we find Grant, what then? Ferman finds out, he'll have snipers down the front trail, and there ain't no cover. And the canyon, ambush for sure. Won't be no way out of here for the gen'ral."

"We'll take him down the back, down the cliff."

"You're loco, Moose. Nobody can get down there. There ain't enough ropes in Colorado to reach all the way down."

"We could try going down through the caves."

Grizzly suddenly laughed. "Yeah, lots of luck with that."

Grizzly sobered as he sat down on a stump with the spyglass, scanning the canyon and ridge to the north, far behind Silver Gulch. He scanned the rugged terrain and forest as they had been doing for days. But suddenly he stood.

"Hey, I see a camp over on Eagle Mountain. Look, where the pines are real dark there, near the aspens. Right on top. Near the ridge trail."

Moose also squinted through the glass. "Well, maybe."

"I saw a wagon wheel. Look real hard."

"Uh, could be. And someone walking around."

"Has to be Grant. Nobody else'd be fool enough to be way up there by themselves."

"Like us, you mean?"

Grizzly frowned. "You think it's prospectors?"

"I don't know, and neither do you. One of us has got to go look."

"All right, I'll get a mule and cut down through the back canyon."

"No, I'll go," Moose said. "You're a Southerner, remember?"

"All right, I'll watch from here, but when you get across there, you're out of range. I won't be able to help if you get in trouble."

"You can make plenty of noise."

Moose recovered the campaign hat and stuffed it inside his shirt.

It took Moose two hours on his mule, down through the steep canyon behind Silver Mountain and up onto Eagle Mountain. When he finally rode up through the pines in the early afternoon, he heard the click of a hammer.

Turning in the saddle, he saw Major Reis Williams, a man he didn't recognize, with a rifle, aiming at him. Williams, dressed in army britches with a heavy wool coat and felt hat, looked dangerous.

"Hold on, Mister," Moose said. "I ain't here for trouble. I saw your camp from our place on the mountain over there."

"What do you want?"

"I was looking for a cup of coffee and maybe we could talk."

"About what?"

"Matt Tyler."

Slowly, Reis lowered the rifle, his dark eyes narrowed. "What about him?"

"He got us working' for him."

"Get off that mule."

Moose swung down, reins in hand. "Just take it easy."

"Start walking through those trees. You'll see the wagon."

Moose's thick black beard twitched. He turned and walked ahead of the man. Soon they cleared the trees and moved into a small clearing near the wagon and tent.

There by the fire sat Ulysses Simpson Grant.

Moose stared at him in awe. "I never did think I'd see you face-to-face, General. Me, I fought with the Union navy. They call me Moose."

Grant studied him, then nodded. "Come and have some coffee with us. You've already met Major Williams."

Reis gestured. "He says he's working for Matt Tyler."

Moose sat down, accepted coffee, and stared at Grant as if he was a face in a newspaper. All through the war, he had heard of "unconditional surrender Grant." But here sat a quiet, soft-spoken man who could be anyone's grandfather.

Moose cleared his throat. "Yeah, me and Grizzly, we got a claim on Needle Mountain. Matt said if we was to see you, we was to signal him with smoke. He wanted us to stop you from going to Silver Gulch."

"Why is that?" Grant asked.

"Silver Gulch is all Southerners, including that there Red Ferman. And he still talks about losing his fortune on Black Friday."

"My God," said Grant, "that was all so long ago."

Moose grunted. "When it comes to gold, he's got hisself a long memory."

"You think they'll try something?" Reis asked.

"Matt thinks his law firm's gonna lay a trap for the general. Three law clerks was killed. He's real worried. Especially after what happened to Captain Witherspoon."

"Captain Witherspoon? Where is he?" Reis asked.

"Dead and buried."

Grant frowned, eyes darkening. "When?"

"After he saw Matt in town, he was shot on his way to Silver Gulch, that's what. Nobody knows who done it. Matt figures they didn't want you warned."

Moose reached inside his shirt, took out the campaign hat, and handed it to Grant.

Grant saw the lettering, fondled it in sudden sadness.

Reis Williams sat on his heels next to Moose. "What else did Matt tell you?"

"Just to keep you away from Silver Gulch and get you up to our place. Now my partner, Grizzly, he was a Reb, all right, but he's a good man."

"Where's Matt now?"

"He's over in Mountain Springs, waiting for us to signal with smoke if we saw you headed for the mines, but me and Grizzly, we figured if we could get you over to our cabin, it'd be better, and we'd get word to Matt some other way. Ferman's always watching us, waiting to see if we hit pay dirt. Ferman, he runs all the mines."

"Gold?" Reis asked.

"Yeah." Moose gestured. "Look over there at that there Needle Rock on our mountain. You can see the tip of it. And Silver Gulch is down below the next mountain."

Grant put his fingers together. "So Matt wants us to go with you."

"He don't want you in Silver Gulch or crossing all that open country in the daylight. He'd have our hides if anything happened to you before you got to Mountain Springs."

"I've been wanting to see him."

"Yes, sir, General. Now if you and the major here will come with me, I'll get you to our cabin afore dark. But you got to hide the wagon and ride the team over."

"Are you sure it's safe in Mountain Springs?" Reis asked.

"The town is full of Yanks, so Matt and the sheriff figure you'll be protected OK." Moose stood. "Right now, we got to be on the lookout for Crazy Albert. We think he done some of the killings."

Grant stiffened. "Crazy Albert?"

"Yeah," Moose said. "Little guy. Talks to himself."

"I think he was in our camp," Reis said.

Moose worked his mouth. "Well, sir, you're both real lucky fellows, then. Where do you think he was going?"

"Irwin, maybe," Reis said.

"He know who you was?"

"No."

"We'll tell the sheriff where he's headed," Moose said. "Right now, I figure we ought to get you over to our mountain where it's safe."

Back at the Frost mansion that evening, Morna sat at her late husband's desk, searching through the papers. Dressed in a dark-blue dress, she felt lonely and upset. Her husband had never allowed her in his office. Curious, she took her time.

She found a copy of the 1875 Denver newspaper with Grant's interview circled. It read, "The general said that Matt Tyler had saved his life at Pittsburgh Landing."

Then she found a startling drawing of a hanged man with a scribbled note, which she put inside her sleeve for safekeeping.

Morna frowned and kept looking, even as she heard a pounding at the front door. She stood up wearily and went to answer it, finding Hancock and Mrs. Ledbetter. She did not immediately invite them inside.

"I thought you'd want company," Hancock said.

"That's kind of you," Morna responded, "but I'm all right."

"Let us make you some tea, dear," the woman said.

Morna shrugged, reluctant, but nodded as she allowed them to enter.

Later in the parlor, Morna sipped her tea and looked from Hancock to Mrs. Ledbetter and back again. "I was going through Jared's desk."

Hancock frowned. "Nothing but law, I suspect. I'll clean it out for you. And the will, you know, is in our office."

"Yes, dear," Mrs. Ledbetter said, "please let Mr. Hancock help you. You don't want to deal with dreary old papers. It'll make you sad."

Morna set her cup down. "No, he was my husband. I'll take care of it."

Hancock leaned forward. "Jared may have had some briefs the office needs back. Mind if I go look?"

"When I've finished," Morna said.

"I hate to trouble you in your time of grief," Hancock said, "but on behalf of other clients, I must insist."

Morna frowned, suspicious. "I want to see anything you take."

"Agreed," Hancock said. He stood up, trying not to hurry to Frost's office.

"My dear," Mrs. Ledbetter said, "you should be upstairs resting."

"No, I can't do that. I'm too upset."

"Have you eaten, then?"

Morna shook her head. "I will, later."

"I really would like to stay with you tonight."

"No," Morna said, thinking of Ferman's possible unexpected visits. "I'll be fine. I want to be alone."

Through the open office door, Morna saw Hancock shuffling through Frost's papers at his desk.

Morna lost patience. She stood, walked into the office, and stood beside him. Hancock tried to appear calm as he stacked some legal documents.

He spoke with authority.

"This was a case he was working on. I need to take it with me."

Morna bent down and searched through the papers. "But you don't need this letter from his old friend in Denver, Dr. Webb."

Hancock swallowed hard. "It was just caught up in there."

"I haven't seen this before," she said, spreading the letter. "What does Dr. Webb mean: 'I pray no one learns of the colonel's scheme'?"

"Let me see. Well, the rest of the letter only talks about things in Denver. That last line, it means nothing."

"What scheme was Jared involved in? Who is the colonel?"

Hancock drew himself up. "Really, Morna, I don't know, and you are only tormenting yourself."

She took the letter and folded it before inserting in the envelope. "I'll keep this."

Hancock, his face sweating, sat back down and went through the rest of the drawers, carefully fingering every piece of paper. He stacked up some briefs, found some research notes and various client details.

"What about that?" she asked, pointing.

"Just a map of Colorado."

"But it's marked from Denver to Leadville."

"Doesn't mean anything."

"Isn't that where Grant was going?"

"Maybe so."

"Why would Jared trace his route?"

"Your husband wanted Grant to come to Mountain Springs for a big celebration. He wanted a spur up here from Alamosa, and he figured that maybe Grant's coming to town would be a good thing. Put the town on the map, so to speak."

"I'll keep this."

Hancock stood up slowly, taking the legal papers. "I guess this is all the office needs."

Morna walked them to the door. "Thank you for the tea, Mrs. Ledbetter."

"Dear, I really would like to stay."

"No, I'm sorry. I want to be alone."

When they were gone, Morna locked the door. She returned to the office and sat down at Jared's desk, her heart aching.

Jared had been harsh at times. He had wanted to control her, but he had taken good care of her. He had given her anything she wanted. He had left her well provided for, but she had no peace. She knew of his liaisons in Denver, but he had never embarrassed her in the town where they lived, keeping her on a pedestal. She had mixed feelings and great remorse.

At the same time, she sensed something going on about Grant. She was determined to find out, one way or another. If anyone so much as threatened her hero, she would have to do something about it, no matter who was behind it.

Outside in the cold night, Hancock helped Mrs. Ledbetter into his buggy. He swung up beside her, taking up the lines. He turned the team around and headed down the road toward town. She looked back several times, her mouth working.

"Milt, I'm worried," she said. "Morna's sniffing around, looking for something."

"She doesn't know anything. It'll all be over, before she figures it out."

"That war left my husband a dying man. I'm not letting some fancy lady get in the way."

"She won't."

"If she does, I want her silenced."

"You'll have to get past Ferman on that one."

"What do you mean?"

"Never mind. Just take my word for it."

"I don't care about Ferman. I just want this over and done with, if I have to do it myself."

Hancock drove on in silence. He didn't care for this woman's company. He didn't approve of anyone or anything. He longed to get out of this valley, go back East, start over. He just didn't know how.

Mrs. Ledbetter didn't care about the lawyers or anyone else. She could never rest until she avenged her husband's miserable death. That meant the general and former president had to die.

CHAPTER 18

MONDAY MORNING IN GOOD WEATHER, Eberley left for court in Denver.

The courtroom in Mountain Springs had benches in eight rows on each side, separated by a railing from the jury box and tables for counsel. The judge sat behind an elevated desk with the witness chair to his left. A clerk sat below to his right.

Hancock took both Eberley's appearances and his own. Hancock managed to dismiss one case and continue the others. Hancock then hurried out of the courtroom.

McComb's prosecution of a miner, dismissed for lack of evidence, left McComb free to leave. Instead, he sat down to watch the other cases.

Matt carried some of Frost's motions to dismiss two claims against Ferman.

Judge Waller, impatient, granted Ralph Smythe a continuance in both cases.

In the late afternoon, Jennifer entered the nearly empty courtroom and sat down in the back row with notebook in hand. She wore a blue cape over her calico dress. McComb came back to sit with her.

Matt stood in front of the grim Judge Waller, listening to a warning as his face burned.

"Any more frivolous actions, Mr. Tyler, and your firm will face sanctions."

"Your Honor, I will make certain."

"See that you do. Now there's one more action still pending. Bodecker versus Ferman. Mr. Smythe, do you have your witness now?"

Ralph Smythe stood up, papers in hand. "Your Honor, we are unable to locate him."

The judge listened to arguments, then spoke with dark, blazing eyes. "Mr. Smythe, you have sixty days to locate your witness. Otherwise, I will be forced to entertain another motion for dismissal of your client's claim."

"Your Honor," Matt said, "this is the third time you've given Mr. Smythe a continuance."

"Are you questioning my judgment, Mr. Tyler?"

Matt stiffened. "No, Your Honor, but in the interest of fairness, my client would like to see this resolved."

"Your Honor," Ralph said, "we have reason to suspect foul play and spoliation of evidence."

"That's why you're getting another sixty days, but I warn you, Mr. Smythe. Your allegations require proof to avoid sanctions. This court's time has been continually wasted, and I will not tolerate further delays without justification. Now, gentlemen, if there's no other matter pending, court is adjourned."

The crusty judge went back to his chambers.

Ralph followed Matt into the late sunlight, while Jennifer and McComb stood up and walked behind them. Matt swallowed hard, still smarting.

Ralph paused beside him on the boardwalk.

"You see what I'm facing, Matt?"

"I have a client, Ralph, just like you."

Ralph stormed off as McComb and Jennifer came to stand with Matt.

McComb smiled, his dark eyes friendly, his posture in a superior stance.

"So now you've been exposed to our judge."

"He's tough," Matt said.

"But I promise you, he's fair."

Jennifer looked disappointed there was not much news for her paper.

Hat in hand, McComb turned to her. "Another buggy ride on Sunday?"

"Ask me later," she said.

McComb went back into the courthouse

She turned to Matt. "The judge was giving you a bad time."

"What do you know about McComb?"

"Not very much. Why?"

"He's taking you for buggy rides?"

Jennifer smiled, tickled at Matt's annoyance. "Yes."

"Ruben and Ralph and now McComb. Is every man in town after you?"

"I hope so."

Matt scowled. "I wouldn't trust any of them."

She looked down at her notebook, thoughtful, a frown crossing her face. After a long moment, still staring at her papers, she spoke softly.

"Matt, I've put off telling you, but I had a visitor the other night. Bo Raddigan."

"What?"

"I went down to the office for some papers, and he came in to talk to me. He said he wanted me to write nicer things about him. Make him more colorful."

"And?"

"He frightened me, so I pulled my revolver."

"On a gunman?"

She flushed. "Don't worry. I dropped it. And Raddigan had a good laugh over it. Then he left. But he said after 'it' was over, he would come for me, but he wouldn't say what he was talking about."

Matt's face changed color in his anger. "He works for Ferman, and he could be involved in this thing with Grant."

"Don't look like that, Matt. Don't you see? He'd like to goad you into a fight, so he can kill you."

He hesitated. They broke off the conversation when they saw a rider coming. Grizzly rode up on a mule and reined up in the middle of the street. Matt and Jennifer walked out to him.

Grizzly leaned down to speak softly.

"We got Grant and some major up at our place. Nobody saw him, on account of we brought 'em over from the canyon, so we figured we'd better not signal."

Matt nodded. "Good. Let me get rid of this briefcase."

"Then what?"

"Let's talk to Hicks."

Jennifer and Grizzly waited in the street as Matt went back to the law firm's building.

Inside, Matt entered the reception area to find Lucifer standing at the window.

Matt knew the clerk had been watching him. "Still here, Lucifer?"

"Man wants to be a lawyer, he has to work hard."

Matt went back to his office and set his briefcase down, looking over his desk. He came back up front with a frown.

"Lucifer, where are those land grant transactions?"

"Oh, Mr. Hancock took them home with him."

"Why did he do that?"

"I don't ask foolish questions, Mr. Tyler. If the boss wants to do something, that's his business."

Matt took his coat and hat off the rack. He went back outside to join Jennifer and Grizzly. They walked to the sheriff's office to talk inside with Hicks. Jennifer sat in front of the desk. Hicks stood behind it.

With no one else in the office or cells, Grizzly told them how they'd spotted Grant and Williams, and how he had taken them through the canyon to the mountaintop.

"I can't get out there until Saturday," Matt said. "You've got to hold him down until then."

"Seems like they tried to kill him at Irwin, but it fell apart," Grizzly said, finishing the story in detail. "So the general wasn't hurt."

Matt stiffened. "Thank God."

"And some fellow named Shockley over in South Arkansas, which I reckon they call Salida now, seems like he cooked up this plan for Grant to go into the mountains by wagon with just a couple men. It was all figured to get him to Irwin."

"Shockley," Hicks said. "He used to work for Ferman."

Matt frowned. "It's coming together."

"We learned something else," Grizzly said, as they went to the door. "Grant said as how Crazy Albert stopped at their camp and maybe went on over to Irwin."

Hicks drew his heavy coat. “Looks like I’ll be headed for Irwin.”

“Be careful,” Matt said. “If he murdered those men, he won’t hesitate to kill a county sheriff.”

On Friday afternoon in her office, Jennifer worked with her apron over a faded green dress. Standing by the press, she thought over everything that had happened. She was worried. Henry stood in back, replacing type on the shelves.

The doorbell tinkled as Matt entered. She turned, glad to see him.

Henry took off his apron. He left, closing the door behind him.

Jennifer faced Matt across the counter, all the more fond of him. She couldn’t help herself. Even with his worries, he never failed to be lovable.

“Matt, I want to go with you, when you see Grant.”

“You wouldn’t be able to print anything until he was safe.”

“Agreed. And you have to realize, if I’m with you, everyone will think it’s a pleasure trip.”

Matt shrugged. “I guess you’re right. We’d have to leave before dawn in order to get back tomorrow night.”

“Do you really think General Grant would not make a good chaperone if we had to spend the night up there?”

“Since no one knows Grant is up there, who would know you have a chaperone? What about your reputation?”

“Matt Tyler, don’t you play tricks with me. I want to see General Grant, and I want to see him tomorrow.”

“When your face gets red, your freckles get white.”

“So am I going with you?”

“Well, maybe it wouldn’t look so suspicious if you came along, but not unless Gentry can go with us.”

“I’ll take a picnic basket. Fried chicken.”

“Grant never eats anything that ran around on two legs.”

She was thoughtful. “I’ll bake a cake, at least. Then I can hide what I need for overnight right under it. I mean, just in case.”

Abruptly, the door came open. Morna Frost stood there in a black cape over her dark-blue dress. A black lace shawl covered her golden curls. She had a strange look on her face, her eyes red from crying. She came inside and closed the door behind her.

"Matt, I've been looking all over for you."

"Mrs. Frost, are you all right?" he asked.

"I must talk with you."

Jennifer smiled. "I can step outside if you want to be alone here."

Morna hesitated. "Well, never mind. Maybe you should hear this as well."

Reaching into her silk purse, she drew out some papers. She spread them on the counter next to Matt.

"I found these things in Jared's desk. A map with chalk markings from Denver to Leadville. This strange letter from a Dr. Webb. And the newspaper with Matt's name circled."

Matt studied the papers, then the map. "I see Irwin circled."

"And the 'colonel's scheme'?" Morna persisted. "Who is the colonel?"

"I don't know."

"Then how about this?" She drew out another paper and read from some scribbled notes. "It says 'Grant,' and there's a drawing of a hanged man. What's going on, Matt?"

"I'm not sure, but I want you to write down that you found these in your husband's desk. List each one. Initial each exhibit. Then date and sign it. We'll witness it."

With the work done, Matt saw Morna's distress but had to question her.

"Did your husband ever say anything against Grant?"

"No, but he did fight for the South."

"Have you heard any of the partners or anyone else talk against Grant, I mean in a way that could be dangerous?"

"No, Matt. They never talked in front of me. Jared made sure of it."

"What about Red Ferman? He ever talk against Grant?"

"Not that I know of."

Matt folded the papers. "I'm going to take these to Judge Waller, but don't tell anyone."

Morna clasped her hands together. "All right."

He slid the papers into an inside pocket in his coat.

"You find anything else, put it in a sealed envelope and leave it with Jennifer, but put Judge Waller's name on it. Nothing will be printed until it's safe. Isn't that right, Jennifer?"

"Whatever you say, Matt. But can you trust the judge?"

"He's a mean cuss. But yes, I think so."

Matt turned to Morna. "Remember, keep this quiet. You could be in danger just asking questions."

"But, Matt, please, nothing must happen to Grant."

"It's under control. Don't worry."

Morna glanced out the window at her buggy and driver. "I have to go now."

At the door, she paused, looking from Matt to Jennifer as if in great need of encouragement. Sadly, she left.

Jennifer leaned on the counter, her hands clasped together.

She and Matt fell silent, gazing at each other in deep thought.

The door opened again. Travis McComb came striding inside, hat in hand. "Jennifer, are you ready?"

She flushed. "Matt, we're having supper at Pop's. Do you want to join us?"

"No, thanks. I have to be up early tomorrow."

Matt's annoyance made her sorry as he left.

She walked down the street with McComb, her hand through his arm.

"Mr. McComb, you realize you were very tricky in court last week."

"How is that?"

"You were getting in all kinds of hearsay."

"May I remind you that hearsay need not be given to tell the truth of what the witness heard, but it's admissible if he just says he heard it?"

"But your witnesses were not credible."

"Are you picking a fight with me, Jennifer?"

She smiled up at him. "I guess I am."

"That has to mean you like me."

"Mr. McComb, I like a lot of people."

"You know, Jennifer, you're a beautiful woman. You'd make a lovely hostess and a great first lady."

"First lady?"

"I won't always be a county attorney."

"You have ambitions? Then why are you still here?"

"I have some personal matters to clear up, before I move on, and you're one of them."

"Then you may be here a long time, Mr. McComb, because I'm much too busy with my newspaper."

"We'll see about that, but I won't rush you."

They smiled at each other. Jennifer enjoyed the attention but had other things on her mind.

Later that evening, Matt found Judge Waller in his chambers. The jurist looked annoyed at the interruption. He glared at Matt, who sat in front of his desk without being asked.

"What are you doing here, Mr. Tyler? You must know I cannot discuss any cases with you."

Matt felt awkward, hat in hand. He swallowed.

"It concerns General Grant."

"Is he coming here?"

"I don't know, sir."

"Then what can be important enough to delay my work, not to mention my supper?"

Matt withered some under the judge's icy gaze. "You know about the murders. Including Mr. Frost."

"Yes?"

"What you don't know is that General Grant sent a Captain Witherspoon to arrange a meeting with me in Silver Gulch. I told Witherspoon to keep Grant away from there because of the Southerners."

"That's reasonable. So?"

"Captain Witherspoon was murdered before he could warn General Grant."

Judge Waller leaned back, putting his fingers together, studying Matt. "Could have been a thief."

"But Witherspoon met me at the rooming house before he left, and I learned afterward Mrs. Ledbetter had been a Confederate spy."

Waller frowned with surprise. "You think she put the mark on him?"

"I don't know, but I'm told she probably knew who he was."

"Do you have any evidence against her?"

"No, Your Honor."

"Do you have any evidence of anything?"

"Sir, I believe the law clerks were murdered because they knew of a plot to assassinate Grant."

"Preposterous."

"President Hayes sent me here to investigate."

Waller leaned back, surprised.

Matt opened the folder he carried. "Morna Frost brought these to me. I'd like you to keep them safe, sir. The map tracks Grant's route. Irwin was circled off by itself, and I just found out there was a failed assassination attempt while he was there."

The judge's face darkened. "Now you have me worried."

"And this letter from a Dr. Webb, talking about a colonel's scheme. Are there any colonels in town?"

"Not that I'm aware of, but you have to remember, a lot of men have closed off the past to avoid trouble."

"And this drawing of a hanged man, right next to Grant's name."

Waller looked them over. "Are you trying to tell me Frost was killed because he was involved?"

"I hope not, Your Honor, but the sheriff is out of town, and I have to trust someone with these papers. I've asked Mrs. Frost to put anything else she finds in a sealed envelope with your name on it. No one must know. Not even McComb. He's a real Southerner."

"I don't like this, Mr. Tyler."

"Nor do I, Your Honor. But I don't think the war's over at Silver Gulch."

"And I'm a Virginian."

"I know, sir."

"I stayed out of the war," Waller admitted. "I thought the issue of states' rights should have gone to the Supreme Court."

"I don't think that would have stopped the war," Matt said.

"Maybe not."

"Sorry to burden you with this, Your Honor."

Waller took a long time to answer. Matt waited, concerned.

At length, Waller cleared his throat. "I accept this trust."

Before daylight on Saturday, Jennifer led Eberley's bay to the tack room at the livery. Matt and Gentry already had their horses saddled. Gentry took the picnic basket from her and tied it to his saddle.

Wearing a blue cape over her riding outfit, a wide-brimmed hat cocked sideways on her head of chestnut hair, she could see that Matt worried.

"Jennifer, this is not a good idea."

"Now, Matt, you have to take me. I know too much."

Matt grimaced. He helped her with her sidesaddle and gave her a leg up, her boot on his knee. Once she had mounted, he and Gentry swung astride.

Matt turned in the saddle. "Jennifer, I want you to promise me. Any sign of trouble, you head back to town."

She smiled brightly. "Whatever you say, Matt."

He did not believe her for a minute.

Late morning, they sighted Silver Gulch in the distance to the north, and up on the high Silver Mountain, a lot of activity. To the far south of the town, they could see Needle Rock against the sky on Needle Mountain.

They rode into busy Silver Gulch as a ploy and stopped at Ferman's office.

Inside, Boner told them he had not seen Hicks or Ferman that morning. He gave them coffee and chatted for some time. Boner expressed his own frustrations about having so much work to do with little appreciation.

When Matt, Gentry, and Jennifer left the office, they saw Bo Raddigan standing on the warped boardwalk, thumbs in his gun belt, feet apart, and hat pushed back. Raddigan had an air about him. He showed no fear.

"Mr. Tyler, we meet again."

"You know where Ferman is?"

"No, I don't."

Raddigan tipped his hat to Jennifer as his eyes scanned her. Matt stepped between them, his face grim and hands ready for a fight.

"You ever bother Miss White again, you'll answer to me."

Raddigan smiled. "The feeling is mutual, Mr. Tyler."

Matt turned to the hitching rail to take up the buckskin's reins. Raddigan gave a long look at the stallion.

"Want to sell him?"

"Nope."

Gentry helped Jennifer mount while Matt kept his gaze on Raddigan. Matt knew the man was a killer, but he would not expect anything but a fair fight from him. Raddigan's arrogance would not allow otherwise.

Raddigan turned to look up at Jennifer, a crooked smile on his face. "Miss White, I will be seeing you."

Chilled through, she turned her horse away from him.

Matt, furious, turned his buckskin so that he bumped Raddigan, forcing the gunman to stagger back.

He glared down at Raddigan, who sneered.

"All in good time, Mr. Tyler."

Raddigan, eyes gleaming, watched after them as they rode away.

Later, as Matt, Jennifer, and Gentry rode the steep, mostly barren trail up Needle Mountain, she kept looking back at the wondrous view in the afternoon sun. They rested at the base of Needle Rock. Gazing across the vast green valley, Jennifer smiled, impressed as before.

"No wonder men love the mountains."

Gentry lay back on the grass, his hands behind his head, and nodded.

Matt stood up. "Maybe that's why Grant keeps coming back to Colorado. To distance himself from what's down there."

"He could do some hunting," Gentry suggested.

"Grant never was a hunter. He didn't like blood, and that's why he had a rough time during the war. With the hospital tents."

"And you?" Jennifer asked. "And Mr. Gentry? How did you handle the war?"

Matt shrugged and glanced at Gentry. "We gritted our teeth or threw up, whichever was appropriate at the time."

Gentry nodded. "Or worse."

Jennifer looked from one to the other. She knew she would never feel what they had experienced. She envied them. Whatever had happened during the War between the States had shaped them into the men they were. They had survived more than they would ever say.

They soon mounted and made their way up the ever steep, winding trail.

At times, it felt like no man or animal could make it to the top.

The trail had no cover. A sniper could pick them off easily, and they knew it.

Jennifer, fearful, clung to the horn and mane.

Their mounts climbed slowly, deliberately.

When they finally reached the wide, grassy plateau, their horses winded, they dismounted in sight of the distant cabin. Mules and two horses with harness marks were grazing nearby. All appeared serene.

From the plateau, they enjoyed the view of the valley and snow-crested Rockies.

They finally remounted to ride up to the cabin. They saw no one.

Matt and Gentry took care of the horses, loosening the cinches and hobbling them to graze near a trough.

Jennifer took the cake inside the empty cabin.

Matt stroked his buckskin's neck. He worried.

He would have no problem recognizing Grant, but Matt had been only one of many thousands of troops reporting to him. Would the general even remember him? It would mean a lot to Matt if he did.

Gentry looked around the plateau. "Where do you think they are?"

"Right here," a husky voice called.

Moose was coming out of the rocks over by the trail to the mine. Grizzly was right behind him. They waved.

CHAPTER 19

UP ON NEEDLE MOUNTAIN, JENNIFER came outside the cabin and stood on the porch with Matt and Gentry. They shaded their eyes from the bright sun.

They watched anxiously as another man stirred in the distant rocks behind Moose and Grizzly, who already walked toward them.

Reis Williams, carrying a Winchester, moved past the two miners. His strides long and quiet, like a stalking animal, he had a smile on his face as he reached them.

"Matt Tyler, is it? Reis Williams."

Matt came down from the porch, shook his hand, introduced him to his companions as Major Williams, and continued to watch for Grant.

When the general appeared from the distant rocks, Matt stared with delight. Grant looked the same, slight of build but muscular, his graying brown beard and moustache neatly trimmed, the same sad, soft blue eyes.

Grant wore tired, sloppy clothing. He had a small-brimmed hat and long coat. He looked astonished when he saw Matt. He nearly dropped his cigar.

"General," Reis said, "this is Matt Tyler."

Grant could not believe it. He came closer, staring up from his five feet seven inches to Matt's six feet and big shoulders.

"Matt," he said, shaking his hand, "you sure got big."

"You haven't changed, sir."

"A lot older, but not any wiser."

"General, this is Ulysses Simpson Gentry. He fought for the Union with the Fifty-Fourth."

Gentry nearly stumbled down the steps.

Grant smiled and shook Gentry's hand. "Proud to know you."

"And this is Jennifer White," Matt said. "She runs the *Mountain Springs Recorder*, but she won't be printing anything until you're safe."

Excited, Jennifer smiled from the porch as Grant removed his hat and bowed slightly.

Moose cleared his throat. "Well, let's go inside. I'm ready for some coffee."

As the others moved inside the cabin, Grant stood on the porch, gazing up at Matt. "I'm proud of you, son."

"Thank you, sir."

"How do you like being a lawyer?"

"I'm not so sure anymore."

"Yes, I met Mr. Frost. He looked like a hard taskmaster."

"He's dead, sir. He was murdered."

Grant frowned. "I heard about the others and Captain Witherspoon. And now Frost? What does it mean, Matt?"

"Nothing we can be sure of, but you could be in danger."

"I hear this Ferman is also a bitter man."

"He lost his holdings in Georgia, as well as his fortune on Black Friday. And he's got a pack of Southerners in Silver Gulch. That's why I wanted to talk with you first."

"I can't be watching my every step. Life is too short."

"All I ask is you stay up here until we figure out what Ferman's going to do."

"All right, Matt. But I had in mind to go to Mountain Springs."

"We can do that when it's safe."

Suddenly, Grant stared past Matt with his eyes wide open. "Matt, that stallion."

"Mine, sir."

"I've got to look at it."

Matt swallowed nervously and followed the exhilarated Grant down to the hobbled buckskin, which threw its head up and flared its nostrils with a snort.

"Magnificent," Grant said, moving closer.

"Be careful, sir. He can be dangerous."

Grant walked right up to the stallion and held out his hand as the animal stuck its nose in his palm and nuzzled it. Grant stroked the great head and neck. The stallion snorted again, stamping its right foreleg.

Grant grasped the halter and scratched behind its right ear. "Matt, this animal is priceless."

"I know, sir."

"I always liked big, powerful animals like this."

"Yes, sir."

"He a troublemaker in town?"

"No, sir. Just don't walk behind him."

It took time to get the general to leave the buckskin and go inside the cabin.

After a quick lunch of bread, cheese, and ham, they devoured servings of Jennifer's delicious chocolate cake. Grant and Williams told of their mountain travels as they all sat about the iron stove. Moose built up the fire.

"General," Matt said, "Frost's wife found a piece of paper with your name on it, and alongside it was a drawing of a hanged man."

"Doesn't sound too good, does it?"

"Frost and Hancock were Confederate officers. And they lost their fortunes on Black Friday, same as Ferman. Worse, they had barely recovered and lost money when the government stopped buying silver."

Reis shrugged. "Irwin was a shock. And now this."

"A hanged man," said Grant. "So that's what they have in mind for me. Not even the dignity of a firing squad."

"We don't know anything for sure," Matt said. "But there was also a letter about a 'colonel's scheme.' Do you know of any colonel with a grudge against you?"

Grant smiled. "Half of the Confederate leaders."

Jennifer cleaned off the table and returned with the coffee pot, serving each of them. "It's just bits and pieces, but it's a worry," she told the general.

"Whatever happens," Grant said, "it was worth a slice of your cake, and I'll have another, if you don't mind."

She beamed and served everyone again.

Matt turned to Moose. "Can you put us up for the night?"

"Uh, sure, but Miss White—"

"I'll be chaperone," Grant said.

"What I mean is," Moose said, "nobody knows you're here, General. Folks may talk about Miss White if she stays."

Jennifer smiled. "The truth will come out later, and I'm not leaving a story like this."

Grant reached over and squeezed her hand. "You're a fine lady, Miss White. You remind me of my daughter, Nellie."

That evening, around the hot stove, they heard stories about Matt's time on the trail drives. Jennifer had stories about outlaws she had seen in Tucson years back.

Then the war brought a lively round of memories from Moose and Grizzly.

Grant became misty-eyed more than once. They reveled in the man's stature. Jennifer smiled with delight with what she could someday write.

Now Grant told of how Matt had saved his life.

"A bullet had already hit my saber," Grant said. "But when they hit us again, Matt saw the sniper. He jumped right in front of me and took the bullets in his side and his right leg. And then, bleeding all over, he turned around and went out there and got the sniper."

"He should a got a medal," Moose said with a grin. "But look how he turned out. Just another dandified lawyer."

At her mansion late Saturday night, Morna Frost tried to keep her composure. She was at the back door, fully dressed, when Red Ferman came through the darkness and hurried inside.

She slowly warmed to him because she needed comfort, but she didn't feel the same wild urge as in the past. She felt strange, separated from him emotionally. They stood in darkness but light from the parlor filtered through and lit their faces. He embraced her but with worry.

"I took a chance coming here," he said.

"I'm having terrible nightmares about Jared."

"They'll go away, Morna."

"Red. I went through Jared's desk and found some things I didn't like."

When she told him about the papers she had found, he tried to hide his annoyance. "You're making a lot out of nothing. Besides, Grant's not even around here."

"But I think he is."

Ferman swallowed. "What makes you think so?"

"I'm not sure, but I think Matt Tyler knows something he's not telling me."

"Is Tyler in town now?"

"No, he went to Silver Gulch. With Jennifer White and Gentry—something about a picnic."

Trying to remain quiet and calm, Ferman held her tighter against him. "Are they back?"

"I don't know," she said. "I'm just worried about Grant."

Ferman forced a smile. "I wish Grant would come here. I've always admired him."

He kissed her gently.

"I have to go, Morna. We don't want anyone to catch on, remember? I'd look pretty silly hanging on that cottonwood down by the creek."

"Please take care of yourself, Red. I don't want anything to happen to you."

Ferman could hardly wait to get out of the house and go home. His heart pounded as he ran up the hillside. He saddled his horse and rode down into town. He reined up in front of the gambling hall, which had lamps burning inside, even though it was past closing time.

He left his horse at the hitching rail and hurried inside, looking for Bittner. Ferman had no respect for the former slave trader, but he needed him.

The bartender and two of the dealers busied themselves closing up the tables and yawning. They paid no heed to Ferman.

Bittner busied himself in his back office, at his desk, counting his money.

Ferman came through the door in a hurry. "We've got to talk."

He closed the door behind him and sat down.

"Have a drink," Bittner said, pouring two glasses of whiskey. "You look like you need one."

Ferman downed his drink. "I think Grant's meeting Tyler in Silver Gulch."

"So what now?"

"I've got to get out there, but I need you to keep a watch in town, just in case Grant shows up here after all."

"And do what?"

"You've got men. You know what to do."

"In town, with all these Yanks? The whole idea was to get him in the mountains so nobody would get caught. I can't help it if they messed up at Irwin."

Ferman refilled his own glass. "I want you to keep an eye on Hancock."

"He's a weak sister."

"I know, but we need him right now."

Bittner scowled. "What about Matt Tyler? I mean, when it's over."

"He saved Grant's life. What do you think we're going to do with him?"

"Red, you have more than a couple hundred former Confederates out there. Are they all behind you in this?"

"Not many. About forty, but not all Southerners. A few are bad ones who just want the money. But we'll get it done."

"Lee's been dead ten years now. I wish he was alive to see the end of this." Bittner held up his glass. "Well, here's to the colonel, the Confederacy, and General Robert E. Lee. And to Georgia."

"And to all who didn't make it," Ferman said.

"And here's to the last of General Grant."

"And wiping the slate on Black Friday."

They drank, and Ferman smiled. "This has been a long time coming."

CHAPTER 20

SATURDAY NIGHT ON THE MOUNTAIN found everyone sleepless and full of conversation for hours. At length, they were weary. Grizzly gave his room to Grant, who turned in, while Jennifer had Moose's room.

Reis, Moose, Grizzly, Gentry, and Matt were wrapped in blankets around the hot stove. Matt took first watch and spoke softly to Reis while the others slept on the floor.

"The general looks fine."

"Thanks to you."

Matt balanced his Winchester. "All of us had it rough, but Grant was right there with us. He never took a step backward."

"Did you know that was one of his superstitions?"

Matt grinned. "It doesn't matter how he made his decisions. They were all on target."

Reis stretched out away from Moose and Grizzly, who snored like donkeys, and moved alongside the quietly sleeping Gentry. Matt sat nearer to the stove so he could reach the coffee.

This had been one of the greatest days of his life, better than saving Grant, and even better than being admitted to practice law.

This day had been a gift. He savored it. He felt proud to be a lawyer and full grown in Grant's eyes. He felt so content right now, he could give Grant the stallion for free. Of course, he knew he'd get over that idea come first light.

Outside, in the morning, in bright sun, a breeze rose from the west.

Inside the cabin, a hearty breakfast of bacon, beans, and steaming-hot coffee. Moose and Grizzly were very talkative while the others were still sleepy.

Reis sat next to Grant, with Jennifer on his other side.

Gentry enjoyed great conversations with the general.

Matt had concerns, however. "Red Ferman must be wondering where the general's been since Irwin. He'll have men watching every trail and every possibility. Including this place."

Moose grunted. "Even if they come up that side canyon, they can't get on the plateau without being seen. And we couldn't go down that way without them seeing us. And they'd spot us miles away if we went down the main trail in front. And it ain't all that safe at night."

"They'll be watching for us," Matt said.

"What do you suggest?" Reis asked.

Matt turned to Moose. "Didn't you say something about some caves up here?"

"Sure, they go downhill all right, but they got bats in 'em, and we got no idea how far down they go. A fella could get lost in there."

"Show me," Matt said. "We'd better find some other way off this mountain just in case."

Grizzly chuckled. "I'd better take you, Matt. Ole Moose here, he's scared of bats. Me, it don't make no never mind."

Jennifer winced. "I'm with Moose."

Gentry knew his leg was a handicap. "I'll stay and take a turn at watch. Me and the major and Moose, we'll take care of any trouble. But you watch out. Caves can be tricky and have a lot of holes in 'em."

Grant nodded. "In Mexico, after that war, we went into the great caves with guides, candles, and rockets."

"We have no rockets," Matt said, "but we'll make do with torches. You're welcome to come with us."

Grant shook his head and smiled. "I'll wait to see if I have to rescue you."

"Same here," Reis said.

With Jennifer trailing, Matt and Grizzly took lanterns, torches, leather gloves, ropes, and knives to mark their path so they would be able to find their way back. The cave entrance lay hidden beyond the mine in a pile of boulders. The small opening led to big deep caverns.

"We think it goes all the way down to the cliff bottom, but we ain't sure," Grizzly said. "And you got to be careful on account of the floor's wet in places. There's stone growing down from the ceiling and up from the bottom."

Matt nodded. "Mineral deposits."

"You hit your head on one, you'll think different."

"Let's see how far it goes."

Jennifer found a shady spot to wait, away from the entrance.

At the same time on Sunday morning, Sheriff Hicks met with the mayor of Irwin, a little mining town crowded in high terrain. He sensed he wasn't welcome.

Mayor Travers, short and stumpy, an avowed hater of the North and Grant in particular, took credit for stopping the assassination attempt.

"I had no love for Grant," Travers admitted to Hicks in his office, "but I'm the one who sent the citizen's group out to surround and protect him. Didn't want our town on the map for an assassination."

Hicks studied the mayor, finding no reason not to believe the man.

"At least he was here," Hicks said.

"You bet he was. Even saw the Ruby Chief Mine. We put on a good show. Didn't have no band, but we had drums, which made a lot of noise. But what he liked the best was just being with the men at the Irwin Club. Grant enjoyed it so much, he stayed two days. Makes for some mighty good publicity."

"So where is he now?"

"I got no idea. But you didn't come here to talk about Grant. What are you looking for?"

"A little man called Crazy Albert."

"He was here, scared everybody, but he left."

"Do you know where?"

"I don't know, but it must have had something to do with your visit."

"Why do you say that?"

"The barber told me Crazy Albert lit out early this morning, and you just got here last night."

Hat pulled down tight, Sheriff Hicks continued riding back along the steep ridge trail alongside Eagle Mountain. To his right a drop of several hundred feet. To his left, great boulders, timber, and brush.

Weary, he contemplated a noon break. The warm sun made him sleepy.

A rifle cracked from his left.

A bullet slammed into his left shoulder. In shock, Hicks bent low in the saddle, trying to draw his six-shooter, but his horse shied.

Another shot struck the animal on the left side of its neck. It spun, lost its footing.

Hicks and his mount flew in the air, suspended a brief second off the face of the cliff. They plunged down the steep bank in a terrible drop toward the valley floor below.

Up on Needle Mountain, Matt and Grizzly moved through the cave entrance into the first cavern while Jennifer waited outside in the shade of the trees. They carried torches and ropes.

Matt felt an icy chill. The damp cave had stone formations hanging down and sticking up from the floor. Their flaming torches made it all the more eerie as the light hit the bats hanging on the ceiling far above.

"Creepy in here," Grizzly said. "Now if we go much farther, it starts going downhill, and I ain't sure we'd ever get back up again."

Matt pretended to be brave. "We've got to know."

"We got plenty of rope. I can let you down, and if you get in trouble, I can pull you back up, on account of I'm bigger."

They secured the end of the first rope to stone formations rising from the floor.

They then fastened that first rope to Matt, around his waist and shoulders like a harness. They tied several lariats together with Grizzly in tight control and ready to loop them around another formation if needed.

With the torch, Matt started slowly down the cavern. There were no side exits, just one long winding hollow, as if some ancient lake had drained through it.

He slipped and fell more than once but kept the torch going. He saw no more bats, just wet walls, mineral formations rising from the floor or hanging from the ceiling, and sloping floor. He thought he might suffocate until a breath of air struck him and flickered the torch.

"You still there?" Grizzly yelled, his voice echoing for a full minute.

Matt shouted back. "I see light below."

Matt's voice echoed back. He kept going until he saw a crack in the wall. Peering through, he saw the canyon below and the next mountain. Right at the cliffside, he could see a mighty long drop below.

He figured he had come down a thousand feet. There was almost that much left to the canyon floor. He continued down, slipping and sliding. It seemed an eternity before another breath of air hit the torch.

He saw bright light below. He became excited.

The cave wound down like a funnel. A man could slide down there like an otter, but there was no telling how he could stop or where he would end up.

"Matt, where are you?" came the bouncing echo of Grizzly's voice.

"I'm coming back."

Matt's voice echoed on up through the cavern as he picked up his torch. All the way back up, using his feet and pulling himself with the rope and Grizzly's help, he grinned to himself.

When he got to the entrance cave where Grizzly waited, he sat exhausted on the damp floor. He looked happy.

"Matt, what are you grinning at?"

"There's an opening all right. But it'll be a devil of a ride through a funnel, just like a cork screw. Give me some more rope. I want to go back down."

"Are you sure?"

"We've got to know."

They refastened a lot more of the ropes to Matt.

Matt started down the circling funnel, hand over hand, wondering again if he could ever get back up. He lost his footing several times, slid part of the way. Suddenly he found himself on the floor of a narrow cave by a natural hole in the wall.

He leaned out to see the valley floor some twenty feet below. Pines clustered at the drop, making great cover.

With great effort and Grizzly's help, he made his way back up to the upper cave floor.

Out of breath and sweating, he sat down. "There's a big window just twenty feet above the trees."

Back at the cabin, Grant smiled with enthusiasm. "Matt, that was brave of you going down there. But by glory, I remember my youth and vigor, and if I were younger, I would have sailed down the funnel."

Matt grinned as Jennifer served him coffee. "It looks like a way out, all right. Just in case, we'd better have enough ropes all ready and fastened together."

"But dangerous," Reis said. "All they'd have to do is fire a few rounds down the cavern, and the bullets would be bouncing around like flies."

"But," Jennifer reminded them, "this is all speculation, and I think we should relax and have a good time."

"With one man on guard," Matt said.

"Matt, what about your job?" Reis asked. "This is Sunday afternoon."

"That's a problem. I trust Eberley but not Hancock."

"We have to go back," Jennifer said. "Otherwise, they'll think we're with the general."

Grant put out his cigar and coughed. "She's right, Matt, but I want to see more of you."

"I'll figure a way, but will you stay put?"

Grant scratched his beard. "For a while. If Moose and Grizzly don't mind. I've been all over the world, but there's nothing to match the Rockies. And this is one terrific view up here."

"I read you saw Queen Victoria," Jennifer said. "What did you think of her?"

"A grand lady with strange ideas, but there was a bit of a to-do. They wanted my son Jesse to eat with the servants. Now Jesse, he was nearly twenty, and he put up a real fuss. He ended up eating with us and the queen. Afterward, she said he was a 'very ill-mannered young Yankee.'" Grant chuckled at the memory.

"How did she and Mrs. Grant get along?"

Grant laughed this time. "When the queen was going to retire, she was saying how horribly tiring her job was, and Julia, not to miss a bet, up and said, 'Yes, I can imagine. I too have been the wife of a great ruler.'"

Jennifer was delighted. "I like your wife already."

"Well, Julia liked all the fancy surroundings, but she's a good American patriot at heart. The British are still mindful of station and place. They'd never survive over here."

"Of all your travels, what did you like best?" she asked.

"Coming home."

"And Mrs. Grant?"

"She likes excitement, and I've gotten used to it. It's addictive. We have a lot of fun in our travels and are bound to keep going as long as we're welcome. But these mountains are where I get back to normal. I like the silence."

"That's why you rented the wagon?" she asked.

"Are you interviewing me, Miss White?"

She blushed. "Yes, sir."

"Well, some merchant named Shockley had the idea first, but I took right to it."

"Weren't you afraid?" she asked.

"Miss White, after two wars and the presidency, there's not much left to rattle my bones."

"We're running out of time," Matt said. "We have to get Jennifer back before dark, if we can."

"I didn't come along to be a problem."

"Just get ready."

Her chin went up. "Matt Tyler, will you please stop ordering me around?"

Grant chuckled. "Yes, sir, I do like it up here."

———

Moose went down the trail with Gentry, Matt, and Jennifer. Slow going on the steep grade made it a longer trip. Sunshine and drifting clouds covered the blue sky.

The view, ever beautiful, kept their attention.

At the foot of Needle Mountain, they saw Ferman and seven of his men riding toward them from Silver Gulch.

"Oh, oh," Matt said.

They reined up and waited.

Gentry gestured at a flash in the sunlight on Silver Mountain.

"Spyglass," Gentry said.

"More than one," Matt agreed. "They've been real curious about us and where Grant's been since he rode out of Irwin."

"Yeah," Moose said. "They even got a camp over in them aspens across the way."

They watched as Ferman and his men approached.

CHAPTER 21

At the foot of Needle Mountain, Matt, Gentry, Moose, and Jennifer reined to a halt and rested their mounts. The warm sun fought off the cold wind.

Matt sat straight in the saddle, watching Ferman approach from Silver Gulch with seven men. Jennifer and Gentry held back. Moose sat astride his mule with a Winchester across his saddle.

Ferman reined up. "Miss White, you're in bad company."

"It was too late to come down last night," she said.

"Who you got up there?" Ferman asked.

Moose leaned on the pommel. "Grizzly's up there working. Someday we'll find a glory hole and buy your whole outfit."

"Says you.," Ferman grunted and turned to Matt. "That Crazy Albert came back. He killed Boner, tore my office apart looking for money, and nearly cut Carruth's arm off."

The news stunned Matt and his companions.

"We haven't seen him," Matt said. "We'll tell the sheriff when we get back."

"No use in that," one of Ferman's men said.

Ferman nodded. "Carruth said Crazy Albert was wearing Hicks's badge."

Matt felt his heart stop, then thump like crazy. "Which direction did Albert come from?"

"He came down Eagle Mountain from Irwin and the men scattered. He went right to my office," Ferman said. "He was last seen heading south. We plan to shoot him on sight."

Matt figured Ferman had plans to make sure Albert never talked.

Ferman and his men turned south and headed over the rolling hills toward the Horton ranch, which worried Matt, as he thought of the widow.

"Not good," Matt said. "He'll tell her about Hicks."

Moose removed his hat. "The sheriff was a real man."

"I've got to find him," Matt said.

Gentry gestured. "Someone has to see Miss White back to town, because I'm going with you."

Moose looked back up Needle Mountain. "I got to warn 'em about Crazy Albert."

Matt turned to Jennifer. "Somebody's got to tell Judge Waller not to hold me in contempt tomorrow."

"Well, there's your messenger," Gentry said, pointing at a distant horse and buggy.

Hancock, on his way to Silver Gulch, drew up his buggy when he saw them.

Matt nodded. "He can take Jennifer back."

"I don't want to go back," she said.

"You're going with Hancock," Matt said, "Moose is going back up to watch out for Grant. Gentry and me, we're going to find Hicks."

"I'm not leaving," she said.

"If you don't turn back, where will you go? Back up to Grant, so the town'll wonder why you're up there with Moose and Grizzly? What about your reputation?"

She made a face. "I hate it when you're right."

They rode over to Hancock, who agonized on hearing of Crazy Albert's rampage.

"My God," Hancock said, "Boner was a family man."

"Gentry and I will try to find Hicks," Matt said. "That means I may not be back for court in the morning."

"Don't worry about it, Matt," Hancock said. "But if Albert was wearing Hicks's badge, you're not going to like what you find."

"Will you see Miss White back to town?"

Hancock nodded. "I came to see Ferman, but since he's on Albert's trail, that doesn't seem likely. I hate to think of that crazy little man heading for the Horton ranch."

Matt agreed. "But Ferman has seven men with him, and the ranch has a couple dozen or more."

"Albert's like a weasel," Hancock said. "He might hole up. But come along, Miss White. We'd better get you back to town. Why don't you ride with me?"

With Jennifer in Hancock's buggy and her horse trailing, the two headed back to town. She kept turning in the buggy to look back. She soon lost sight of Matt and Gentry.

With Hancock and Jennifer on the way back to town, and Moose about to ride back up the mountain, Matt sickened, his mouth dry as cotton.

He and Gentry worried if they would find Hicks alive.

Gentry frowned. "All we can do is pray."

Matt prayed, deep in his heart.

"You be careful," Moose warned, as he reined near the trail to Needle Mountain. "You don't have any friends in Silver Gulch."

"Just take care of the general."

"You can bet on it."

Matt turned his stallion toward Silver Gulch. Gentry, riding at his side, pointed beyond the town.

"That's Eagle Mountain with the road running along its side to Irwin. Pretty steep up there. And narrow. But the first place we got to look."

They could see the trail, a narrow ledge, on the mountainside.

In Silver Gulch, they stopped at a store to acquire provisions and a tarp. The storekeeper, a little man with a big voice, grunted as he gathered their goods.

"Carruth, he won't be losing his arm."

"Boner didn't make it, I hear," Matt said.

"No, and Carruth said Albert had Hicks's badge. What can anyone do about a crazy man like that? I'm lucky he didn't come in here."

Matt, nauseated as he and Gentry rode north out of town, thought of Hicks. The sheriff had been a good friend, a man you could trust. He remembered the checker games and long talks, His eyes misted. He should have let Hicks win more often.

On the way back to town, Jennifer sat next to Hancock as he drove, the bay pony trotting easily on the wagon road. Cold and worried, she resigned herself to returning to town. She wanted to be back at Silver Gulch, helping Matt find Hicks. Yet she still had nightmares about seeing how Frank had died. Being tough had its drawbacks.

She had learned the hard way that there were no simple answers in life. Rationalizing her need to serve her father's memory and keep the paper alive and fighting, as opposed to the excitement she felt whenever she was around Matt, along with her woman's instincts, was impossible.

Hancock's voice startled her. She straightened.

"You stayed overnight on Needle Mountain?" he asked.

"It was so late when we got up there on Saturday, we were forced to stay, but you don't have to tell everyone in town. They were all perfect gentlemen."

"Miss White, you have the highest reputation, and I would never do anything to change that."

"Thank you."

"You and Matt, is it serious?"

Jennifer glanced at him. "We're good friends. Why do you ask?"

"It just seems you're together a lot."

"Mr. Hancock, are you flirting with me?"

Embarrassed, he smiled. "Maybe so. I guess I've been a widower too long."

"How long has it been?"

Hancock sobered. "Sixteen years. She died in childbirth. Lost them both. Frost's wife died of the fever not long after. The war kept us from being there."

"I'm sorry," she said.

Jennifer gazed across the rolling hills, realizing it would be dark before they got back to town. She didn't want to alarm Hancock and kept him talking about everything except Grant.

"Did Mr. Eberley's wife die during the war also?"

"Yes, but he was with her the whole time in Washington. She'd been sick for years."

"How sad, for all three of you."

"When we came west, Jared met Morna in Kansas. She was a widow and gorgeous, like she is now. He would not go on without her, so they were married."

Hancock slapped the lines on the rump of the bay. The wind rising, she pulled her hat down tight. She turned to glance toward the north, remembering that terrible storm. She shivered at the memory of Ruben's death and of the rain and hail that had nearly ended her life.

She looked at the sky. "It's going to storm."

Hancock frowned. "Well, we'll beat it to town."

"Matt and Mr. Gentry, they'll be right in it."

"They won't find the sheriff alive."

"I hope you're wrong," she said.

As Matt and his friend Gentry rode up the steep Eagle Mountain road, the storm broke.

Rain and hail beat on them. The wind began to howl.

They had their slickers on and hunched forward in the saddle in the cold.

"We'd better find a place to camp," Matt said.

"Up ahead. Looks like some shelter there off the side of the road."

On their left, a terrible drop fell to the valley floor.

On their right, boulders guarded a small open space. They found high ground in the rocks to avoid any flash flood. They set up the tarp. They built a small fire under it with brush and horse dung they picked off the trail.

"It's too darn cold," Gentry said.

"Look, there's some empty shells here."

"Winchester, looks like."

They had beans and jerky and soon rested with their coffee, as the rain poured around them. Matt, sick with worry over Hicks, tried to think positive. He warmed his hands over the fire and glanced at Gentry, a man he greatly admired.

"You all right?"

Gentry pulled a blanket around him. "As you get older, your bones get creaky."

"I can't tell you how glad I was to see the general. He hasn't changed."

"A little older, maybe. And he's got a cough."

"Not much of one. But consumption did run in his family, I believe. And those cigars can't help."

"I'm real proud to have met him," Gentry said. "He did a lot for us, but it's getting brutal in the South now. A lot of us come west. We seem to be naturals with horses and cattle. And pretty good with a rope."

"You've done well, making a new life for yourself."

Gentry leaned back, his hands behind his head. "I was young and pig-headed. The first time a whip crossed my back, I took it away from the man and wrapped it around his neck so tight, it's probably still there. I ran off and never looked back. I hid out until, all of a sudden, there was a war, and Father Abraham was calling. That led the way to freedom, but we ain't gained much ground otherwise."

"You're the most free man I know, Gentry. You don't take anything off of anybody."

Gentry laughed. "You noticed that, did you?"

"But it must take a lot of restraint to be around Carruth. And Bittner."

Gentry scowled. "Some things you can't do nothing about."

They talked about Grant for a while, and then Matt took the first watch, as Gentry slept. Freezing rain lasted all night with little warmth from the fire.

At daylight, as the storm drifted on, the sun brought some warmth.

They enjoyed their breakfast and the view far below.

Matt stood up with his coffee in hand. "Look, Gentry. That's a meadow made for cattle, and nothing on it."

"They'll get to it."

"Makes a man feel good to know there's some land left."

Gentry stood up. They walked across the muddy road to gaze at the meadows far below. "Really something."

Matt nodded and walked closer to the edge. "Look here. Something tore this brush away, and it wasn't the rain."

Gentry stood on a rock farther out. "Matt, there's a dead horse down there, about three hundred feet. Could be Hicks's."

Matt caught his breath and climbed out farther.

"I've got to take a look."

"You'll break your neck getting down there."

"Get the ropes. They'll take me partway."

They worked feverishly to set up a trail of ropes from the rocks alongside the wagon road. Matt put on gloves and started working his way down the cliff, his leather coat protecting him from the brush.

When he rested on a narrow ledge some twenty feet down, he saw that more brush had been torn away. And a six-shooter stuck in the mud. And a hat.

"Looks like there was a fight here," he shouted.

Gentry became frantic. "Keep looking."

Matt took up the hat. It could be Hicks's battered Stetson. But the army Colt, the same as Hicks had carried, heightened his anxiety.

A prayer on his lips, Matt continued down the cliff, frantic for sign of Hicks. The horse lay another two hundred feet down the incline. It looked like the sheriff's mount.

The heavy brush could have broken a man's fall. He had to figure Hicks was dead, and he prayed that Crazy Albert had not cut him badly. Hicks would have bled to death, like Banner.

After another fifty feet, the rope ran out. Slipping and sliding and seizing at the wiry brush exhausted him. He rested before continuing without the rope, knowing he could plunge to his own death.

And then he saw it, a boot sticking out of the brush, its toe in the mud, to his right.

Excited, Matt shouted.

"Hicks? Hicks, talk to me!"

Frantic, Matt slid down to the boot. He tried to clear the brush away but couldn't. It forced him to drag the body away from the brambles.

CHAPTER 22

On the side of the cliff on Eagle Mountain, far below the ledge, Matt struggled with the brush, fighting to free the body, praying he didn't find the sheriff's head split open.

Gentry hovered over 150 feet above, watching and waiting. Gentry held on to the rope that dangled down near Matt.

Drenched with sweat, his heart pounding, Matt jerked on a boot.

A growling voice responded. "Ow, dammit, you're breaking my neck."

Matt gasped with joy. "Hicks?"

Matt pulled more slowly, helping the sheriff twist about and sit up.

Hicks's shirt ran with blood, his face badly scratched, hands bleeding. He looked in horrible shape. His badge had been ripped from his vest.

"God, you're beautiful," Matt said, grabbing his arm. "Are you shot?"

"My left shoulder."

"Why were you just lying there?"

"Playing dead. How'd I know it wasn't Crazy Albert coming back?"

"How'd you end up here?"

"I landed on that ledge up there, and I was half-conscious. When I come to, I see that crazy man with my badge in one hand and a hatchet in the other. My six-shooter was gone, and he was out of his head, coming at me. When I rolled away from him, I fell down off the ledge. I think every bone in my body is broken."

"Why did you stay here?"

"I just come to a while ago. I heard voices up above, and I was scared to make a move. Until I saw your ugly face."

"You look all right."

"I'm not sure I can pull myself up."

"We'll do it together. We got a rope here. Gentry will help."

Matt got the rope around Hicks while Gentry mounted and put a dally around the horn.

With great effort, Hicks moved up the climb with Matt, until they reached the dangling rope. Matt tied it around the wounded man's waist. Hicks shivered, his body cold under his leather coat and wet clothes. Matt knew they had better get him warmed up fast.

Gentry backed his horse to help them up the steep climb.

It took over an hour with Matt helping Hicks move up the rope, praying it would not break under their weight. When they reached the road at last and were dragged to safety, Hicks fainted. Gentry dismounted and knelt by them.

"We got to warm him up in a hurry," Gentry said.

While Matt and Gentry frantically tried to save Hicks on Eagle Mountain, Jennifer was at her office alone. She had just sent Henry off on an errand, when she had unexpected company.

Morna Frost entered, wearing her black cape, a veil over her golden hair, and looking pale.

"Morna, I didn't expect you. It's going to rain before you get home."

"I was worried."

"Come over by the stove. You look cold."

Jennifer stoked up the fire and poured coffee for both of them. Then she pulled chairs over, close to the heat. They looked at each other as two women who had never been friends. In fact, they had never liked each other, not until Morna had brought the papers to help save Grant.

Morna warmed her hands. "I'm troubled."

"Why?"

"Saturday night, Red Ferman came to see if I was all right. I can't remember the conversation, but I know he thinks Grant's in Silver Gulch. I feel responsible."

"Morna, listen to me. Whatever happens, it will happen without you or me lifting a finger."

"So I didn't do anything wrong?"

"No, of course not." Jennifer saw tears in the woman's eyes. "Morna, you seem very depressed. Why don't you go to Denver for a while? You have friends there."

"I don't have any friends, Jennifer. I've been rude and pushy and overbearing to everyone, riding on my husband's coattails. When he died, I realized I was nothing without him." Morna sipped her coffee. "Jared wouldn't let me do anything. I couldn't even go in his office at home. He had two sons, so he didn't want any more children. I was just his china doll."

"But you seemed happy."

"I was at the beginning, but now, here I am. What do I do—get a cat and give piano lessons?"

"Morna, I'm sure you will remarry in no time at all. There are very few available women out here, especially any that look like you."

"I guess so, but I hate being alone."

"Then come stay with me."

Morna realized she was cutting herself off from Red's possible visits, and she pulled herself together. "Thank you, Jennifer, but I'll be all right. I guess I just got lonely."

"Why don't you have lunch with me tomorrow? About noon. We'll invite some of the ladies and have it at my house."

"Are you serious?"

"Why not? I think you'll discover that no one dislikes you. They just don't know you. There must be more to you than looks."

Morna smiled. "I think I'll go home now. You made me feel so much better, Jennifer. I'm sorry about all the things I said about you."

"So am I. It goes both ways."

Morna stood up and went to the door, Jennifer following.

"My driver's waiting up the street," Morna said.

"Well, you're just going to make it before it rains."

Up on Eagle Mountain, camped off the ridge trail in hazy sunlight, Matt and Gentry discovered rescuing the sheriff had its drawbacks.

Hicks turned out to be an impossible patient. As they tried to get the bullet out of his left shoulder, he cussed them every few minutes.

"You know, Gentry," Matt said, "we ought to just bury him and get it over with."

"Yeah, I tend to agree."

Hicks snapped at them. "Just get the blasted thing out afore I bleed to death."

"You ain't never gonna die," Gentry said. "Even the devil won't want you, so you got no place to go."

"Yeah, well, just get on with it. Ow!"

Hours later and near the fire, Hicks rested in blankets, comfortable, no longer complaining. He finally warmed up and had more coffee.

Matt told him about Grant and Reis. He told of Crazy Albert's killing Boner and wounding Carruth in Silver Gulch not long after Hicks was shot.

"So where is he now?" Hicks asked.

Matt shrugged. "Ferman and his men went after him. They think he headed south."

"South? To the Horton ranch? We got to get there."

"Hold on," Gentry said. "You're all busted up. You want to start bleeding inside?"

"I got no more blood, but I got to get to Horton's."

"You mean, Mrs. Horton," Matt said.

"Dammit, you know what I mean."

"There's no way you can ride," Gentry said. "Not for a day or so, but I can ride down to make sure she's all right. That is, if you think Matt can handle you."

"Just get going," Hicks snapped. "And when you get down to Silver Gulch, send a wagon for me. No way I can sit a saddle."

Gentry grunted as he saddled his horse. "Hicks, you're a cantankerous old goat."

"Yeah, well, you get shot and fall a hundred feet down a cliff and bounce off a few rocks and tangle with brush and see how you feel."

"You know, Matt, I think he should get married. He needs some woman to mother him."

Hicks glared at Gentry and then laughed with a snort.

When Gentry had ridden away, Hicks lay back, gritting his teeth.

"Hurts like the devil, Matt."

"We'll get you fixed up. Maybe you'd like to recuperate out at Mrs. Horton's."

Hicks moistened his lips. "Apple pie."

"As soon as the doctor says you're OK, we'll take you out there."

"But what about Grant? We got to make sure he's all right, don't we?"

"Right now he's safe. Moose and Grizzly, they're dead shots. As long as Grant stays there, we don't have to worry just yet."

"I want to meet him."

"You're in no shape right now."

"Dammit, Matt—"

"That's another thing. The general hates foul language."

"Well, you ain't the general."

As Gentry rode into Silver Gulch, he saw Ferman and his men dismounting in front of Ferman's office. He knew they hated him, because he was colored and had fought for the Union. Yet he didn't give a darn what they thought. He had made a place for himself.

He rode over to them and reined up, leaning on the horn.

"We found Hicks, and he's shot up. I think he'll make it, but we need a wagon."

Ferman gestured. "Take that one across the street. You see Crazy Albert?"

"No. Mrs. Horton all right?"

"Yeah, sure. And she has plenty of men with her."

"Then I'll drive the wagon myself."

When Gentry drove away, his horse trailing, Ferman scowled and turned to Bulldog, nodding to him to come into the office. Inside, Ferman sat at his desk. Bulldog, a little big for the available chair, remained standing.

"Grant's got to be somewhere around," Ferman said. "We know he was headed for here, so where is he?"

"I don't know, but Tyler was awful friendly with Moose and Grizzly."

"Any signs on Needle Mountain?"

"Can't get up there to find out," Bulldog said. "And we can't see nothing through the spyglass. But we got men all around it, watching. They can't come down without our seeing 'em."

Ferman leaned forward, fingertips together. "Matt Tyler has something going on, and I know full well it involves Grant. Mrs. Ledbetter recognized that Witherspoon, and he wasn't there for nothing. Raddigan went and shot him before we could find out anything."

Bulldog stood waiting, and finally Ferman continued.

"What about the men? We need all we can get."

"A bunch of 'em are with us," Bulldog said, "but they want to be paid."

"That gripes me."

"Some ain't even from the South."

"This mountain is crawling with Southerners," Ferman complained.

"They listen to Hennesy. He tells 'em they got to get on with their lives."

"I'll work on him. Now get me Raddigan."

CHAPTER 23

Bo Raddigan had nothing but disdain for Red Ferman as he sat in front of Ferman's desk at Silver Gulch. Twirling his hat in his hand, the sunlight from the window dancing on the conches, Raddigan wore his constant sneer. He wanted a lot of money from Ferman for doing what he did best. He didn't have to like him.

"You wanted to see me?"

Ferman put his hands together. "You know Crazy Albert better than anyone. Is he coming back here?"

"I don't know. Scared?"

Ferman leaned forward, his eyes narrowed. "Listen to me, Raddigan. I pay you to follow orders and not smart off."

"This isn't the army, Ferman."

"No, in the army, I'd have you shot."

Raddigan smiled. "I've done two jobs for you and been paid well. But I'm still ready to do Matt Tyler for free."

"Don't underestimate the enemy. He's no slouch with a firearm."

"How do you know that?"

"Instinct, Raddigan. Something you lost a long time ago."

The gunman leaned forward, one hand on the desk. "My instinct's always working, Ferman. And I tell you, this plan of yours is going to blow sky-high. Frost was the only one with any brains, except for your fancy colonel. And your plan didn't do so well at Irwin."

"Some actress leaked the word to a miner, who blew the whole thing by telling the mayor. That ain't going to happen here."

With a lazy smile and movement, Raddigan got to his feet, pulled his hat down tight, adjusted his gun belt, and slowly walked to the door, where he paused and turned.

"Remember, Matt Tyler, for free."

Ferman glared after him and continued to glare at the closed door.

In Mountain Springs, at the law firm, Hancock squirmed at his desk in his office, his heart pounding a little too fast. He didn't like anything that was happening. He didn't trust Bittner or Ferman. With Frost gone, all steam for their plans had dissipated. He felt certain Eberley suspected some kind of plot.

He also wondered why Matt Tyler had not returned.

Hancock wanted to withdraw from the conspiracy, yet he knew the colonel would never let him out of it alive. It had seemed so easy. Just get Tyler here and pay a lot of money into the plan. The lawyers, supposed to stay clear of any blame, could now just as easily hang.

He sweated, terrified.

He jerked to attention with the knock on the door.

Lucifer entered with a stack of papers, which he placed on the desk. "Don't forget, you have two appearances in the morning."

Hancock leaned back. "Sit down, Lucifer."

"Yes, sir." Lucifer sat facing him.

"You want to be a lawyer pretty bad, I take it."

"Yes, sir."

Hancock studied him. "I need to know that I can trust you, Lucifer."

"You can count on me, sir."

"You were loyal when you told me Pocket had heard me and Frost making plans in the library. I'm sure you've put it all together, with Mrs. Ledbetter feeding you messages. But I'm counting on your loyalty."

"Yes, sir. I'm with you, sir."

"You hear anything in town, you let me know."

"You mean like a letter Matt Tyler sent to Washington?"

Hancock, surprised, mulled it over.

"Well, he did have a practice and maybe it was to whoever took over his files."

"Did the president's aide take his files?"

Hancock got nervous. "Who are you talking about?"

"Colonel Harriman."

Hancock tried to calm himself. "That's bad news. We should call the whole thing off."

"You want to back out, sir?"

"No," Hancock said quickly, because he didn't trust Lucifer. "It could mean nothing whatsoever. Just keep your eyes and ears open."

"Yes, sir."

"And tell me, Lucifer, what about Ted Loring?"

"I don't think he knows anything. The other three hardly talked to him. And Ted asked me what was going on. Of course, I said I didn't know."

"Good. Now all we have to worry about is Matt Tyler and Eberley. You watch them, will you?"

"Yes, sir, every chance I get."

"I'll make it worth your while, Lucifer."

"Thank you, sir."

When law clerk Lucifer left, Hancock realized he had talked too much. He missed having Frost to discuss the matter with, because his partner had been with him for so many years and understood. He could never talk like this to Ferman. All he could do now was deny he said any such thing to Lucifer.

After midnight, a wagon came rolling into Mountain Springs and stopped in front of the general store, where the elderly doctor had an office upstairs.

Gentry held the lincs. Matt rode around them, leading Gentry's horse. Sheriff Hicks, wrapped in blankets, lay down in the bed.

Matt and Gentry stepped down and dropped the tailgate to slowly move the cussing Hicks. Their patient had such a miserable disposition, all Matt and Gentry could do was hide their grins. Hicks groaned as they dragged him forward to help him sit up.

"Before you kill me, why don't you make sure the doctor's home?"

"There's a light on up there." Matt said.

"Ow, you're breaking me in half."

Matt grunted as he and Gentry helped Hicks to his feet.

Hicks moaned. "You're killing me."

Matt tried not to laugh. "Hicks, you're a crybaby."

"Yeah, well, you get busted up like me, and let's see how you make out."

They struggled with Hicks, walking him across the boardwalk and over to the stairs.

Gentry, with his bad leg, remained on the boardwalk. Matt, his own right leg hurting, managed to help Hicks up the steps, one at a time.

"You ain't helping much," Hicks said.

"You're waking up the whole town," Matt told him.

"Yeah, well, good."

At the top of the stairs, Matt reached out to knock on the door. The elderly doctor, in his nightshirt, let them inside.

His spectacles at the end of his nose, the doctor shook his head, as Hicks reclined on a table. He checked Hicks's shoulder wound.

"Sheriff, it was only a matter of time. I'm surprised you're not dead. Look at you. What a mess."

"Doc, I don't have time to listen to a sermon. Ow!"

"You'll hurt a lot worse by the time I get finished."

"What?"

The doctor grinned. "I just wanted to shut you up."

"We've been trying to do that for hours," Matt said.

"Your wound's healing fine," the doctor said. "They did a good job of taking out the bullet and cleaning it up."

"Yeah, well, they near killed me."

As the doctor felt around Hicks's arms and legs, he kept mumbling, while Hicks kept complaining. Then he examined the sheriff's back and chest, listening to his heart with a new stethoscope.

"Well, I tell you what you got, Sheriff."

"What?"

"You got two cracked ribs."

"And what else?"

"A stick of ornery up your rear end."

Matt stifled his laughter.

Hicks grumbled. "A lawman gets no respect around here."

Matt came to squeeze Hicks's good shoulder. He turned to the doctor. "What do you think about him resting up at the Horton ranch?"

"Well, Emma's a good nurse, all right, but could she stand him?"

"All she has to do is keep shoving apple pie in his face."

"You leave him here," the doctor said. "I'll let you know tomorrow."

Weary, Matt left to join Gentry down in the street.

Late morning, Matt went to the office to find that Hancock had gone to court and Lucifer was interviewing clients. He went back to Eberley's office.

Eberley waited quietly at his desk, as Matt closed the door behind him.

Matt sat down facing Eberley and brought him up to date.

"So Hicks is going to be all right?" Eberley asked.

"Yeah, but he's sure noisy about it."

"Matt, I'd sure like to see Grant."

"We can't have a trail of visitors up there. It'd give things away. If Ferman suspects, he'll be watching like a hawk."

Eberley frowned. "I wonder what happened to Crazy Albert."

"It's anyone's guess, but he never showed at the Horton ranch."

"I'd better bring Judge Waller up to date on what's happening now."

"Do you think we can trust him?"

"He was a Southerner, Matt, but he was always a good lawyer. He wanted the courts to settle everything, and he refused to wear a uniform. It was a hard road for him to follow, but he has strong beliefs."

"What's your impression of McComb?"

"He was in the Confederate army and has strong feelings he tries to hide. He does his job as county attorney, but that's all. I get the impression he looks down on the rest of us."

"Well," Matt said, "right now, I've got to be sure Grant stays on the mountain."

"Let me warn you, Lucifer is sniffing around like crazy. Don't trust him."

Late that night, Morna sat in her parlor in a white French dressing gown, her hair freshly washed and done up in curls. She heard a knock at the back door. She went to allow Red inside.

"Red, I'm glad you came."

He hugged her and gave her a kiss on the cheek.

"I'm taking a real chance every time I come here."

As they walked into the parlor, she told him of her luncheon at Jennifer's.

They sat on the couch with his arm around her.

"The ladies were very nice to me," she said.

"I guess you heard about the sheriff."

"Yes, I'm terribly frightened. Suppose this Albert sneaks into town some night?"

"He's probably long gone," Ferman said. "What did Jennifer say about her visit to Needle Mountain?"

"Oh, just what a beautiful sight it was up there. When she was out of the room, the women all whispered about her being gone overnight with Matt Tyler and Gentry."

"Who was up there with them?"

"Oh, I guess those big men. Moose and Grizzly."

"I was hoping Grant would be there."

"No, but I wish he would come here."

"I got to go."

Morna stood up with him and soon locked the door behind him.

She no longer trusted him about Grant.

She went upstairs and lay alone on her bed in the lamplight.

Morna, with all her mannerisms and selfish ways, had never been happy in her entire life. She had been skinny and gangly as a teenager. She had barely become a full-grown woman when she was first married. He had treated her just as Jared had, but he had been shot dead in a saloon.

She wondered what it really would be like to be with a man who saw her as a real woman—a man she could talk with long into the night, as she lay in his arms—a man who would give her children.

Turning on her side, pressing against her pillow, she began to cry.

CHAPTER 24

Up on Needle Mountain the next day, Grant enjoyed the rain and hail that hit suddenly. He stood on the sheltered porch, Reis at his side. Moose and Grizzly came running from the mine, dripping wet, to join them.

"Wow, that came out of nowhere," Grizzly said.

"I'm afraid," Grant said, "that when the rain stops, we have to leave."

"You can't leave," Moose said. "Matt will kill us. And I know Ferman's got men watching the canyon and the face of the mountain. You'd be spotted either way."

"We should wait for Matt," Grizzly said. "There may be things going on we don't know about."

They went back inside, and Grizzly built up the fire. Grant frowned, obviously restless. Moose, worried, sat near the general.

"I thought you liked it up here."

"I do, but I'm getting cabin fever."

"If that's all it is, you can camp outside the house."

Grant laughed. "I didn't mean to go that far."

"Tomorrow," Moose said, "I was planning on making buckwheat pancakes with maple syrup. And I'm right good at it."

"You're a great cook," Grant admitted. "That succotash was very good last night."

"Tell you what," Moose said, "if you stay until Matt comes back, maybe you can talk him out of that buckskin."

Grant's eyes lit up. "Do you think so?"

"I'll bet on it," Moose said.

"He'd do anything for you, sir," Grizzly said.

Reis made a face. "They can't promise anything, Ulysses."

Grant smiled, intrigued. "It's worth waiting around to find out. I haven't had a horse like that since I was in Washington."

"You're a good horseman, general," Reis said, "but you're forgetting that a couple of 'em fell on you during the war. One nearly laid you up for good. And remember another time in Washington. Your leg was all cut up."

"But with the buckskin, it'd be worth it."

The next day, when the rain stopped, Gentry came to see Hicks, who made noise up at the doctor's office.

The disgruntled doctor left them together.

"Good news, Sheriff. Mrs. Horton says to get yourself out there pronto."

Hicks sat up, immediately cheerful.

By noon, Hicks reclined in a wagon bed, with Gentry driving and Matt following on his dancing buckskin.

At the Horton ranch, the widow, wearing a calico dress and white apron, came rushing outside, her face red and eyes shining. "Sheriff Hicks, you'll catch your death of cold. Now come on inside, where I can fix you up."

She fussed with him, as he was brought down on his feet.

Hicks let Matt and Gentry walk him into the house. He moaned.

They brought in his carpetbag.

Hicks, in seventh heaven, groaned and grimaced while Emma helped him into a soft chair. She stroked his cheek. She covered him with a quilt.

"Now you sit right there until your room is ready."

"Lying down hurts," Hicks said. "I'd rather sit here awhile."

"He's right," Gentry said. "Lying hurts."

Hicks growled. "You two go on back to town."

"Now, Willoughby," Emma said. "You just rest while I serve us all some apple pie and fresh coffee. Your friends deserve thanks for bringing you all this way."

She hurried away to the back kitchen.

Matt grinned. "Willoughby?"

Gentry fought his chuckle.

Hicks's face turned several shades with embarrassment. He snapped at them.

"Sheriff Hicks, to you. Just eat your pie and get out of here."

Emma returned with a fresh hot apple pie.

Gentry sobered, hat in hand, and turned to Emma. "Listen, you watch out for him."

"Don't you worry, young man. I have a lot of men on this ranch, and I also have a very large shotgun." She gestured. "Now come to the table."

Later that evening, Jennifer finished up in the newspaper office, getting ready to close, while Ralph Smythe stood waiting at the counter. She wore a green dress with lace at the collar. She removed her apron.

"This is too hard on you, Jennifer."

"No, Ralph. Nothing you care about is too hard."

"Why are you so driven?"

"We both are, but we take different roads."

Ralph frowned at her. "I stood back because of Ruben, but you know how I feel. And I'd rather you be at home with our children."

Jennifer smiled and came to the counter. "You're a nice man, Ralph, but I would never see you. You are always in your office or in court, or you're out with your clients."

"But that's my job."

"And this is mine."

"You're just a woman, Jennifer. Maybe a hundred years from now, this would be right for you, but you're going too far in a man's field."

"There are a lot of women working in newspaper offices. They're much faster at setting type."

"But they're not writing editorials."

The door opened with a jingle. Matt, hat in hand, entered.

She smiled at him. "Hello, Matt. Won't you join us for supper at Pop's?"

"Yeah, sure."

"Is Sheriff Hicks settled down at Mrs. Horton's?" she asked.

Matt grinned. "And how."

"And Deputy Lacey's in charge?" she asked.

"Yes, but the town is pretty quiet."

All through supper at Pop's, Matt seemed annoyed. Jennifer dared to believe Ralph made Matt jealous.

However, Ralph only wanted to talk about litigation and cases coming up on calendar.

All the while, she thought of her luncheon with Morna and the ladies. The women had been excited every time they had talked about their children and their homes. They had swapped recipes, talked about remedies, and the possibility of getting one of those new wringer washing machines.

As she listened to Ralph and Matt, her mind wandered. She didn't want to marry, but she wanted all the things marriage would give. Torn between dedication and maternal thoughts, she felt herself weakening every time she looked at Matt.

"The next time," Ralph said to Matt, "I'm going to prove Ferman's a claim jumper. So you'd better watch out."

"Eberley and Hancock are handling those cases."

"How do you earn your pay?"

"I'm too valuable to get worn out. They're saving me for the big stuff."

Ralph smirked. "The big stuff being?"

"Well, it's a surprise."

After coffee, they stood up, as they helped Jennifer with her cape.

Ralph took her arm. "Come on, I'll walk you home."

"Never mind," Matt said. "I'll see to it."

Ralph stood taller. "I invited her to supper."

"And she invited me."

"So you were here. Now go."

"I think you should go," Matt said.

"You got some claim on Jennifer?"

"I'm looking out for her."

Ralph made a face. "You're her father now?"

"I have to make sure she doesn't get mixed up with the wrong people."

"And who are the wrong people?"

"Stuffed shirts."

Ralph sneered. "What? Your outfit's the one with the stuffed shirts. You and your Harvard lawyers. Only the rich go to law school, and they think nobody else knows anything. But the real smart ones learn it the hard way."

"Then I'm real smart."

"They hired you, and you didn't go to law school?"

"That's right."

Ralph frowned. "That doesn't make sense. They made such a big deal out of their elitist attitudes, looking down on the rest of us."

"Maybe they like me."

"No, I figure you're just temporary."

Matt grinned. "We all are."

"Look, you just go on home. I'll take care of Jennifer."

"What are your intentions?"

"What are yours?"

They glared at each other.

They looked at Jennifer, who had the sweetest smile on her face. She drew her cape about her.

"You can both walk me home."

Grim, they walked on either side of her, taking her arms and almost carrying her up the boardwalk and down the alley. At her porch, she turned with a shine in her eyes.

"Thank you both."

She went inside. They heard the bar slide down across the door.

Matt pulled his hat down tight. "Well, you messed that up. I might have gotten a good night kiss."

"From Jennifer? You've got to be kidding. She'll never kiss anybody. Not until she's betrothed. You can bet on that."

Matt grinned to himself as he headed for the rooming house. Jennifer's kiss made him one up on Ralph Smythe and everyone else.

As he entered the lobby, he found Mrs. Ledbetter waiting with a big smile. "Matt, you missed supper."

"I ate downtown."

"With Miss White?"

"And Mr. Smythe. Why?"

"Oh, I just worry about you."

He considered her beaming face and decided Eberley could be wrong. She probably had been a better spy than anyone had guessed back in Washington.

"Come and have some pie," she said.

They sat alone at the dining room table. Her lemon pie tasted all right, but nothing like Mrs. Horton's apple. She refilled their coffee cups.

She leaned back with a bright smile.

"Now then, Matt, I hear you went picnicking on Needle Mountain. That was a far piece."

"You can see everything from up there."

"So Jennifer said. My, it must have been crowded in that cabin."

Matt wanted to laugh. The spy was more concerned about Jennifer's sleeping arrangements than the general.

"Jennifer had her own room. With a lock on the door."

"Oh, my, I didn't mean to imply any impropriety. Miss White is a real lady."

"That she is. Anyone says different, they have to answer to me."

Mrs. Ledbetter quickly changed the subject.

"But, Matt, when will you be meeting Grant?"

"Who said I was?"

"I just thought, I mean, because Captain Witherspoon came to see you."

"How did you know who he was?"

She flushed. “Oh, he didn’t know me, but I recognized him from when I lived in Washington.”

“The captain’s a friend.” Matt downed his coffee. “Thanks for the pie.”

“I just know you’re keeping a secret, Matt. Please, where is Grant? We just have to have him here.”

“I don’t know where he is. For all I know, he’s back in Denver.”

“Oh, that would be dreadful.”

“Yes, it would.”

And Matt went to bed, leaving her staring after him.

Down the street at the gambling hall that night, Lucifer met with Bittner in his office. Neither man liked the other. Lucifer, looking down his nose at Bittner, a former slave trader—so beneath him. At the same time, Bittner hated the snooty clerk, wanting to gut him.

Lucifer sat down, hat in hand.

Bittner settled back in his chair. “Well, what do you have for me?”

Lucifer crossed one leg over the other. “This one will cost you a lot more.”

“You’re a greedy bastard.”

“Only the ignorant are forced to use foul language.”

Bittner straightened in his chair, eyes blazing. “Blast you, Lucifer. Either ply your wares or get out of here.”

Lucifer smiled. “All right. It’s Hancock.”

“What about him?”

“He’s folding.”

“What makes you think that?”

“I told him how Tyler sent a letter to the president’s aide in Washington. He got very upset.”

Bittner scowled at the news. “Yeah, well, I don’t like it either.”

“He was ready to toss in his chips.”

Bittner scowled. “Maybe he was just talking.”

“He was pretty shaky.”

"Did you tell this to the colonel?"

"Yes, and he said for you to do whatever you think necessary."

"Actually, we don't need Hancock anymore."

"That's what the colonel said."

"All right, here's your pay."

Bittner tossed him a handful of double eagles.

Lucifer caught them gleefully. More than he had expected, it made him all the greedier.

Bittner glared at him. "Now get out of here, and keep your mouth shut. You see Hancock talking to the sheriff or the judge outside of court, you let me know."

"The judge. Now that's a thought. Maybe you ought to get rid of him too."

Bittner's face turned red. "I don't like your sense of humor. Get out of here, before I get my shotgun."

Amused, Lucifer stood up and left.

Bittner slammed a fist on his desk.

Later that night at the face of a mountain overlooking the distant Horton ranch acres, a small camp rested in a hollow some hundred feet up from the valley floor. Crazy Albert, wearing Hicks's badge, had a spyglass and had been watching everything, including the lights at the Horton ranch and the distant twinkle of Mountain Springs.

"Yeah, I seen you, Sheriff. You think you're getting away, don't you? Well, I'm just gonna rest up here, and then I'm gonna get you and anybody else I feel like. And they don't got to pay me no more. I'm just gonna do it."

He downed some coffee and lay back by the flickering fire, chuckling to himself.

"I sure did scare you, didn't I? Yeah, and I'm gonna wear your badge. Everybody's gonna think I'm sheriff. Maybe I'll arrest somebody."

He drew his blankets around him, his hatchet at his side. "But you go ahead and get fixed up, Sheriff, because I'm gonna take my little hatchet and fix you better."

Chuckling, he curled up. "Yeah, and maybe I'll take care of the widow too. And that woman what shot at me."

Cackling, he pulled his hat down over his face.

"I ain't done with you or anybody else. No, sir. I got to leave my mark."

Flicking a bug off his arm, he laughed, scratching himself. "Yeah, I'm gonna get you. All of you. You ain't seen the last of ole Albert."

In Mountain Springs later that night, Bittner stopped to see Ferman at his mansion. Sometime later, Bittner left, then moved on to Hancock's house, where he pounded on the door.

Hancock answered it, annoyed and only half-dressed with a robe around him. He intensely disliked this man, who had been a brutal slave trader so long ago. A shared past Hancock wanted desperately to forget.

"Bittner, what are you doing here so late?"

"You want me to come in the daytime?"

"Absolutely not. Come in. I'll fix you a drink."

They sat facing each other in the plush parlor. Hancock yawned, waiting for Bittner to talk. He rubbed his eyes.

"Hancock, I have to tell you, Lucifer came to see me."

"Lucifer? What did that little worm want?"

"Money."

"For what?"

"To tell me about you."

Hancock frowned. "What the devil for?"

"He says you're backing out."

Hancock postured. "I'm not doing any such thing."

"So you haven't changed your mind."

"Of course not. I'm behind the colonel all the way. So don't listen to Lucifer. He's just a law clerk. With a big ego. Out for anything he can get from anyone."

Bittner smiled. "Well, I suppose you're right."

"Besides, it's too late for any of us."

"Too late?"

"By getting Matt here to draw Grant, I'm an accessory."

"So, if they questioned you, you might fall apart and blow the whistle on us."

"I wouldn't do that."

"Not even to avoid a firing squad?"

"Bittner, I don't like the way this conversation is going."

"Well, I've just been thinking about what Lucifer said."

"Forget that little worm. Have your drink and go on home."

"Frost told me you were a weak sister."

Hancock's face went red. "I never liked Frost—did you know that? We worked well together, but I never liked the man. He's the one got me in with Fisk. If you recall, he also dragged you into the gold market, and you lost everything, same as we did."

"I remember," Bittner said.

"If it hadn't been for Eberley's money, I'd have split."

Bittner nodded. "But when Frost wanted to take Grant down, you went along with him on that."

"Well, sure. I wanted revenge, just like you."

"Your hands are shaking."

Hancock grimaced. "Just nerves. And I'm usually asleep by now."

"Nerves?"

"You know what I mean."

"I'll have another drink."

"Look, Bittner, why don't you go home and drink your own whiskey?"

"Get me another drink, and stop your fidgeting."

Hancock obliged, agitated. They sat down with their drinks. Bittner kept watching him.

His face flushed, Hancock crossed and uncrossed his legs. He ran his hand over his hair and tried to sip his drink without spilling it, but he knew he was squirming.

"I know about you," Bittner said, abruptly. "One of your sergeants told me, how you got yourself captured to get out of the war. I guess that was better than desertion."

"I don't know what you're talking about."

"Yeah, you do, and you're lucky I never told no one else. But it shows what kind of coward you really are. So why do you think I'm worried now? Because you're about to fold."

"Look, Bittner, you're wrong. There's no problem. The wheels are in motion. I'm not going to stop you."

"Have you considered stopping us?"

"Why should I?"

"Lucifer said you might sell us down the river."

Hancock laughed awkwardly, his face flushed. "I told you, he's a worm. He takes everything out of context."

"All right. I'm satisfied there's nothing to worry about."

Hancock drew a deep breath as Bittner downed his drink. He waited anxiously for his visitor to leave. He knew his jaw was twitching.

Now that Frost was gone, Hancock wanted to wash his hands of the whole thing, to be free of it, and yet he wasn't sure he was brave enough.

They stood up and walked toward the door, Hancock leading the way, anxious for Bittner to leave. His heart thumped in his chest.

Bittner moved slowly behind him, then reached inside his coat and drew a long knife.

In a moment, Hancock's worries would end.

CHAPTER 25

THE NEXT MORNING, MATT MET with Eberley in the older man's office. Shortly thereafter, both men walked up front, where law clerk Lucifer sat, pretending to be studying his law books.

Lucifer hated Matt for his self-confidence and strut. He resented Eberley's education. Yet he had to come up on top around here, one way or the other. He knew how to work people.

"We'll be back later," Eberley said.

Just then, a distraught and flushed Deputy Lacey came rushing inside. "Oh, Matt, there you are. And Mr. Eberley. I got real bad news."

They all stared at him, wondering what was next.

"It's Mr. Hancock. He was murdered last night. Stabbed in his own parlor. Right in the back. The housekeeper found him this morning. He's over at the undertaker's right now."

Lucifer tried to look surprised as he thought of Bittner's quick action. Then he realized Hancock was the last one who was sure to bring him into the firm. He would have to start working on Eberley. Lucifer stood.

Matt, stunned, gathered his thoughts.

Eberley shook his head. "My God, what next?"

"It doesn't make sense," Lacey continued. "The housekeeper says he never had night visitors, because he went to bed early, and he was real safety conscious. Never let anyone in that he didn't know. And there was no sign of a break-in. And no robbery."

Eberley frowned. "So he knew the killer well enough to turn his back on him. Lucifer, was he on calendar this morning?"

Lucifer sat down, fussed with the calendar book. "No, Mr. Hancock didn't have anything else this week. Neither did Mr. Frost. Just two for you, Mr. Eberley. One's a settlement conference. The other's a motion."

"Thanks, Lucifer," Eberley said. "Now, Matt, I can handle things here. You go on and take care of that business you had in mind. I'll see to Hancock."

Lacey worried. "Matt, I have to talk to you."

"All right, let's go to your office."

Lucifer turned to Eberley, professing his devotion and how hard he would try to keep things working in the office. Lucifer never saw himself as a lowly law clerk.

Outside, Matt walked down the street with the nervous deputy.

In the empty jail, they sat down with coffee near the iron stove. Lacey tried to be calm, but his young face was pale, his hands twitching.

"I'm not ready for this, Matt."

"I'm sure you can arrange for more help until Hicks comes back."

"But I don't know what to do."

"About what?"

"All these murders. First, three law clerks. Attempted murder of another one. Then Choper. And Frost. Smythe. And Little. They almost got Hicks. And now Hancock. What next?"

"Maybe you should go out and talk to Hicks."

"Doc said it'd be a while yet before he'd let him up and around, and you know how cantankerous Hicks can be."

"Then I have to fill you in on Grant."

Matt told him about Witherspoon and filled him in on all the details about Grant. Just hearing it all out loud made Lacey sweat all over.

Matt shook his head. "All we know for sure is, there will be an assassination attempt."

Lacey bit his lip. "My God."

"That makes it federal. I suggest you send for the US marshal, but not by telegraph. I'd use a courier."

"Could take forever, but all right."

Matt walked to work the next morning in the hazy sun.

On the way, he saw Moose riding into town on a mule. He panicked. Moose would have had to leave in the middle of the night to be here so early. He hurried into the street to stop him.

Moose leaned down, muttered, "Grant's getting restless."

"You've got to keep him there."

"Well, so far I have, but you won't like how I done it."

"What do you mean?"

"I told him if he stuck around, there was a chance he could buy that buckskin off you."

Matt made a face. "What did he say?"

"He near jumped with joy."

"Yeah, I bet."

"Are you coming Saturday?"

"Yes, but I sure don't want to walk back to town."

"You could have one of our mules."

"Thanks a lot."

Moose grinned. "We've really been having a time up there. Grant and the major, they sure been everywhere, and we're all Republicans, even Grizzly, so we can agree on most everything. And he plays a fair game of poker."

"Well, keep him busy."

"If you don't come Saturday, I don't promise I can hold him."

"I'll be there, but I'll swing around and see Hicks on the way. That might throw Ferman off."

"They're still watching the canyon and front trail."

"Well, they won't do anything until they know for sure, so you keep Grant inside during the daytime. Or at least out of sight."

"That's not easy."

"Just remember, you're not the only one with a spyglass."

"I'll try to sit on him, but he sure loves watching them mountains."

"And I'll need your help, Moose. I've got to set up a fake meeting with Grant. Maybe we can smoke 'em out."

"That's a good idea, and I know just the place."

"Are you in town for anything else?"

"Supplies, yeah."

"Well, you tell Grant I'll be there Saturday for the noon meal at least."

"Will you sell him the buckskin?"

"I don't know."

Moose chuckled and straightened in the saddle, then frowned. "That law clerk of yours is watching from your window."

"Probably wondering if I'm next. Hancock was murdered the other night. Stabbed in the back in his own house."

"Holy cow. What do you figure that means?"

"If there is a conspiracy, they're cutting down on the members."

"You be careful, Matt. No telling what they got planned for you."

"You just keep an eye on Grant and the major."

"Don't worry. We keep our guard up."

Matt worried and talked with Eberley, then Lacey. That night, at the barbershop, Matt filled Gentry in with the latest. They agreed Gentry had better stay in town and make sure no one ambushed Lacey or bothered Jennifer.

On Saturday morning with hazy sunlight, Matt saddled his buckskin stallion and grumbled to himself. If he had to sell, it would only be to Grant. Even that put a knot in his gut. He had waited a long time for an animal like this, even though it still enjoyed kicking if anyone got around its tail.

He rode out to the Horton ranch to find Sheriff Hicks sitting in the front room by the hot stove, Emma fussing over him. When she left the room, Matt sat down with a chuckle.

"You're sure comfortable."

Hicks looked over his shoulder to be sure they were alone. He laughed with a snort. "I'm glad to see you, Matt."

"Did you hear about Hancock?"

"Yes, I did. Lacey sent word last night. Who do you think got him?"

"I don't know, but Ferman lives near him."

"I don't see Ferman as a knife killer."

"When are you coming back to work?"

"Monday, I guess."

"I'm going to set up a fake meeting with Grant. I'll let you know when we have it figured. That could smoke them out."

Hicks frowned. "You may need someone who looks like Grant."

"Got any ideas?"

"Judge Waller's close enough."

Matt grinned. "Now that would be a kick."

Matt left after more pie. He wasn't smiling as he rode away across the hills. He worried, but he would also have been right nervous if he knew Crazy Albert, hiding on the ridge, had a spyglass on him.

When Matt reached the foot of Needle Mountain, Matt saw a rider on a nearby hillside. He figured it had to be one of Ferman's men.

He rode up the mountain and arrived before noon.

Moose ran out to greet him. "Hurry up, Matt. I can hardly keep the general inside."

When Matt entered the cabin, Grant jumped to his feet and shook Matt's hand with fervor. "Glad to see you, son. Have some coffee."

"I'm goin' out to get Grizzly from the mine," Moose said. "He's been down there too long. Ain't healthy."

Reis poured the coffee and sat next to Grant, with Matt across from them. Moose had already told them about Hancock.

Reis frowned. "This fake meeting, how will you work it?"

"We'll get someone to impersonate the general."

"Who'd be fool enough to do that?" Reis asked.

Matt grimaced. "Well, we'll figure something. Anyhow, Hicks is a lot better. He's just having too much fun to leave the widow. But now he knows what's going on, he'll get back in the fight."

Grant leaned forward. "Did you bring the buckskin?"

While Matt danced around Grant's interest in his stallion, up on the mountain, Ferman, in Silver Gulch, sat at his desk with Bittner across from him.

Red Ferman looked down on Bittner, seeing him as nothing but a nasty slave trader, a man at the bottom of the pit.

Bittner resented Ferman's sense of superiority. He controlled himself, as he told Ferman of how he had dispatched Hancock.

"He was falling apart," Bittner said. "Mostly on account of that letter."

"What letter?"

"Lucifer found out Tyler wrote to the president's aide."

Ferman leaned forward. "What does it mean?"

"Maybe nothing about us," Bittner said. "If it had been, the cavalry would have been in town real fast. We'd all be standing in front of a firing squad. But all has stayed real quiet."

Ferman, rattled, had no answers.

"So I don't think there's any worry about it." Bittner leaned back. "You keeping things stirred up out here?"

"A lot of 'em just want to forget the war. Especially Hennesy. But he's one heck of a fighter and the best rifleman out here. If I can get him in on it, a bunch more will follow."

"How you gonna do that?"

"Play on his loyalty. Promise him no harm will come to the general."

"You think he'd believe that?"

"He owes me. I was his sergeant in the war. And there were times I loaned him a lot of money, which he used to take care of his sick wife down South before she died."

"Well, good luck." Bittner glanced at the door. "I wonder what's keeping Raddigan. He sure gives me the creeps. I'll bet he could shoot a dozen men, have his supper, and use one of 'em for a footrest."

The door suddenly opened.

Raddigan entered, his arrogant smile annoying, as he remained standing. He always acted superior to them.

"First off," Ferman said, "Hancock is dead."

"Who got him?"

Bittner frowned. "I don't know."

"Well, you couldn't count on him," Raddigan said. "He had no stomach for this."

"I'm getting tired of it myself," Bittner said.

Ferman was angry. "We're all in this together, and nobody's backing out. We get Grant, we'll sleep a lot better."

"Grant really made you mad, did he?" Raddigan asked.

"You went right along on this," Ferman snapped.

"For the money."

Raddigan stood with his hand on his holster. He looked from one to the other in mocking silence. His air of superiority grated on them.

Bittner cleared his throat. "We don't even know where Grant is for sure. And I'm real tired of all this waiting around."

"Well," Ferman said with a sneer, "you go on up Needle Mountain, and see if Grant's up there."

"I'm not that stupid," Bittner said.

"There's nothing we can do but wait," Ferman said. "Besides, if he's up there, he's got to come down sooner or later."

"I'm no good at waiting," Bittner said. "And what about Crazy Albert? Where is he?"

Ferman frowned. "I sure wish I knew. He shoots off his mouth, he could get us all hanged. Or shot. The boys have hunted all over the valley for 'im."

Raddigan pushed his hat back. "I don't think anyone would believe him. He's loco."

Bittner grimaced. "That Lucifer's watching real close for us. But I don't trust him."

"He's someone else could get us hanged," Ferman said. "We sure won't want him around when this is over."

"What about Eberley?"

"He doesn't know anything," Ferman said. "He's an old fool, and he'll believe anything we tell him. Mrs. Ledbetter's convinced us of that. And we're going to need at least one lawyer on our side."

"And that newspaper woman?" Bittner asked. "I hear she's printing up stuff about land grants for Monday's paper."

"There's nothing wrong with the grant," Ferman said.

Raddigan smiled. "You leave her to me."

"You're out of this one," Ferman said. "I'll send Bulldog. They're real used to his being in town at night. He can sneak over there and burn the place down, press and all."

Raddigan left them. The door closed behind him.

Bittner turned to Ferman. "What are we going to do about Raddigan?"

"Maybe Matt Tyler will take care of him."

CHAPTER 26

SATURDAY NIGHT, JENNIFER WORKED AT her desk with the curtains drawn. Nervous, she had a revolver sitting by her elbow. She scanned the ready print.

She set down the paper in sadness. Her father's death had changed nothing.

Her own would have no effect at all. What was wrong with her, anyway? Did she want to end up an old, old spinster, shuffling newspapers? By then, the West would be tamed. She'd be writing about ladies' hats and theater. And she'd be all alone.

Without children, what would she leave behind?

Somehow, she had to get over Richard's failure and take a good hard look at Matt Tyler.

Except he would be one hard man to corral.

With a sigh, she stood up and took off her apron, then checked the lock on the front door. She turned out the lamp on the counter and turned, ready to leave by the back door.

Picking up her revolver, she reached for the handle of the still burning lamp she would carry home, but she paused.

She heard a noise outside the back door. She turned the lamp down low and left it on the desk. Then she took the revolver and moved for the front door and escape when the back latch jiggled.

She made it behind the counter and crouched out of sight just as the back door burst open. She stayed down, heart crazy in her breast, until she heard a match being scraped. There was the sudden crackling of flames.

Jumping up, she ran to the railing, the revolver in both hands.

She saw no one. The back door swayed wide open to the night.

Her new edition, stacked by the press, burned bright. She ran through the little gate, lifted her skirts, and tried to stamp on the flames. She still had her pistol.

Suddenly, a big shape came from behind the boxes near the press, a big man trying to get away. She raised her weapon and shouted.

"Stop!"

He headed for the back door. She fired over his head, the shot so loud in her ears, it hurt.

He spun around and charged her like a bull. She gasped, trying to cock the hammer, just as his big hand slammed across her face, knocking her down. He grabbed the lantern off the desk. He raised it to throw against the press. Jennifer rolled over and fired again.

This time, the bullet hit him in the middle of his chest, stopping him in his tracks. As his blood spurted, she cried out in horror.

"Dear God."

With a roar, the man charged toward her, dying even as he fell on her legs like a huge boulder, hurting her. She scrambled frantically, trying to free herself.

The lamp had crashed down on the desk, bursting into flames and swallowing up the papers she had been reading. Smoke filled the room.

She managed to roll him away and get to her feet, only to discover her skirts were on fire. She gasped and cried out.

"Help!"

Her voice weak, she tried again, crying, "Help!"

She peeled off her skirt, letting it drop and jumping free in her petticoats. She grabbed the pitcher of water off the table and threw it at the flames eating up around the press.

Coughing, still dazed from his blow, she knew if she didn't get out of there right now, she could die, unless she made out the back door, the closest exit.

"Dear God, help me."

She dropped to one knee, knowing she had to get out or suffocate on the smoke. Yet she scrambled back to her feet and tried to move the heavy press away from the flames.

Unable to budge it, she dropped to her knees again and started to crawl toward the open back door, which sucked at the smoke and fed the flames.

Gasping for air, she crawled through the doorway.

Suddenly, hands pulled her up, lifting her. It was Matt, cradling her and spinning her away from the smoke. She clung to him as he carried her into the cold moonlight.

Now men rushed around with buckets. Matt got out of their way, carrying her off to the damp grass where he set her down. He took off his coat and put it around her shoulders. He turned and rushed back to help with the bucket brigade. Two men had dragged out Bulldog's huge body.

Jennifer tried to stand but failed. She coughed and collapsed.

When the fire was out, Matt came back to kneel at her side. "Jennifer, are you all right?"

"Who was that man? I couldn't see his face."

"Bulldog. He works for Ferman."

"Is he dead?"

Matt nodded. "Sure is."

As she calmed down, she looked at Matt's anxious hand on her arm and the concern on his face in the pale light. She felt a lot safer with Matt at her side. She shivered.

All of a sudden, she had tears in her eyes.

"Did he hurt you?" Matt asked.

"He struck me, and then he tried to burn the place with me in it. I didn't want to kill him. I just wanted him to stop." She paused, frantic. "Is the press all right?"

"Seems to be, but whatever papers were next to it were burned."

"My new edition."

Lacey and Gentry came over to them. Lacey knelt.

"Smoke's clearing out now," Lacey said. "We'll bar the back door from the inside. You'll have to use the front door until you can get another lock for the back one."

Ralph came hurrying around from the alley and paused to stare down at her. "Jennifer, are you hurt?"

"No, not very much."

"Let me take you home," Ralph said to her.

Matt quickly stood up and lifted Jennifer in his arms.

"I can walk," she said. She bit her tongue and settled into Matt's embrace, enjoying it. He carried her to her porch where he set her down. Ralph came right there, making sure they behaved themselves.

She smiled up at Matt as he set her on her feet. "Thank you."

"You want a woman to stay with you?" Ralph asked.

"No, it was the press they wanted. He didn't even know I was there. I'll be all right. And thank you both."

Matt worried. "You've just killed a man, and that's going to be tough. Are you sure you want to be alone?"

"Yes, Matt."

The two men stood back. She closed the door behind her. Ralph glared at Matt.

"Just what are your intentions, Mr. Tyler?"

"What are yours?"

"I want to marry her," Ralph said.

"So why haven't you?"

Grim, Ralph pulled his hat on tight. "You stay away from her. She's a good woman." He turned and stomped off.

Matt stood a long moment in the night. Then he walked around her house, looking for trouble. Everything seemed safe enough. Weary, he headed for home.

Mrs. Ledbetter waited alone in the rooming house parlor. She insisted on giving him pie and coffee in the empty, very plain dining room. All others had turned in for the night.

He removed his hat to sit at the table. She served lemon pie and coffee.

Her fawning bothered him, but he played her game.

With her own agenda and devious plans, she kept after him.

"You look so tired, Matt. Aren't you weary of going back and forth to Needle Mountain?"

"How did you know where I went?"

"Oh, I just assumed, since you were gone all day, and you're such good friends with Moose and Grizzly." She smiled easily. "How is the lemon pie?"

"Wonderful," he lied.

"So where is your next trip taking you?"

Matt shrugged. "Someplace you never even heard of."

"Try me."

He swallowed some coffee to wash down the pie. "Mule Creek Canyon. I understand there's an old cabin there."

She made a face. "Mule Creek? That's way south of Silver Gulch and Needle Mountain." She thought a moment. "Yes, right at the highest ridges. A lot of canyons there. But why on earth would you go to a lonely place like that?"

"Wasn't my idea."

"Oh, dear, that's too bad. Business?"

"Just meeting some friends."

"When are you going?"

"As soon as I get the word. Next week maybe."

"A whole bunch of you?"

"No, maybe two or three. Why?"

"Oh, Matt, I worry about you with all these murders. You're like a son to me. Is that so bad?"

"No, ma'am."

"I always feel like tucking you in."

He grinned. "I can do that myself."

As he started to stand up, she leaned over and patted him on the arm. He smiled and went up to his room, where he sobered fast.

With Hancock gone, he wondered how she would get the word to Ferman. He needn't have worried.

Mrs. Ledbetter charged out the front door. She walked in the moonlight to the next house over. No lights could be seen behind the curtains.

She knew which room Lucifer rented in the back. She tapped on his window.

On Sunday morning, Jennifer returned to the newspaper office. She wore her faded blue dress and heavy apron. Gentry hobbled about, helping her clean. The smell of smoke hovered even with both doors and the windows open. Matt soon appeared, hat in hand.

Delighted to see him, she poured coffee in mugs at the table. She sat with Matt and Gentry and enjoyed their company. It no longer pleased her to be a woman fighting the world alone. Men were not so bad after all.

Matt smiled at her shining green eyes. "You look all right."

"Yes, thanks to you. Now what's going on?"

Matt told them what he had leaked to Mrs. Ledbetter.

"Mule Creek?" Gentry asked. "Where did you come up with that?"

"Moose suggested it. There's an abandoned cabin in it."

"Then what? They could be waiting on the walls."

"We just wanted to be where nobody else would get hurt."

Gentry frowned. "Matt, have you thought this through?"

"I'm getting advice from the best strategist I know."

"Grant? But he doesn't know that area."

"It never made any difference before."

Jennifer fretted. "But Matt, Mr. Gentry is right. You name the place, they'll be waiting for you. It'll be an ambush."

"That's the idea," Matt said. "I'll fill you in when the time comes."

"Well, you let me know," Gentry said. "I'll do my part, whatever it is."

"You have any idea who killed Hancock?" Matt asked.

Gentry, shrugged, thoughtful. "No, but the night he was killed, I saw Lucifer going in the gambling hall."

"And?"

Gentry sipped his coffee. "Well, like I told Lacey, I got real interested. Pretty soon, I saw Lucifer leave. And later on, Bittner got on his horse and rode north toward the houses on the hill. He could have gone to Hancock's."

"If you're right, that means Bittner's one of them."

"I was always sure of that," Gentry said.

Jennifer worried, both hands around her cup. "Matt, you're surrounded. Lucifer, Bittner, Red Ferman, and who knows who else is in on it? Like this mysterious colonel."

"Well, there's one thing for sure," Matt said. "Anyone finds out about their plans, they get killed. And so does anyone who backs out. I just hope that Morna Frost is careful."

Late Sunday evening, Moose showed up at the boardinghouse. Mrs. Ledbetter, delighted to see him, had hopes of learning more.

Moose, hat in hand, bowed slightly.

"Matt invited me to spend the night with him, Ma'am. I hope it's all right. I'd be glad to pay."

"Oh, dear no, not for the room. Matt's already paid."

Moose went upstairs and pounded on Matt's door.

Half-asleep, Matt let him inside. As they had arranged, Matt shook his hand and invited him to take the other bed for the night. Although the door remained closed to the hallway, they assumed she would be listening somehow. They spoke in normal voices.

"Mrs. Ledbetter makes a great breakfast," Matt said. "Eggs, potatoes, sausage, cheese, bacon, and flapjacks."

"Well, I didn't come to eat, but that sure sounds good."

"So what's the word?"

"Wednesday in Mule Creek Canyon. They'll meet us there about sunset. We'll bunk in that old cabin and wait for 'em."

"That's good news, but we got to keep it quiet."

"Hey, I don't want nothing to happen to the general. I sure look forward to seeing him. Always wondered if he looks like the pictures."

Matt sat on his bed. "I haven't seen him for fifteen years. I tell you, it's going to be one heck of a thrill."

"Well, I'm worn out. Bother you if I go on to sleep?"

"No, I could use a little of the same."

They both sat quiet and stared at the walls and door.

CHAPTER 27

At work on Monday morning with Moose having left town, Matt walked past Lucifer who was walking down the hallway. Matt went into Eberley's office and closed the door. He gave Eberley a hush signal with his hand. Matt figured Lucifer would eavesdrop.

His words had to cover the real meaning.

"Mr. Eberley, I need Wednesday afternoon and Thursday for some personal business."

"That so?"

"Yes, sir. I have to meet some friends."

"Where are you going?"

"Mule Creek Canyon."

"My gosh, Matt, there's nothing there."

"It's real important, sir."

"All right. You have a clear calendar this week and no rushes," Eberley said, looking past Matt at the closed door.

"Thanks, Mr. Eberley."

"I'm thinking of bringing in another lawyer from Denver to help out for a while, but not right now. We have no backlog at the moment, so there's no rush."

That evening in the newspaper office, Henry and Jennifer cleaned the press.

Matt arrived with the tin sound of the doorbell. Hat in hand, he came to the counter with his nice smile. She responded with her own sweet expression.

"Papers were all delivered today," she said, hands on the counter.

"And?"

"I toned it down. I didn't think this was the time to start another ruckus."

"But you're all right?"

"A little disgusted, that's all."

"I've invited Gentry and Hicks to supper at Pop's," Matt said, "but first, we're meeting at the sheriff's office. Why don't you join us?"

She peeled off her apron. "Lock up, Henry?"

Matt helped her with her coat. She walked outside with him. Though yet daylight, they could feel the chill of night. She took his arm as they started down the street. Only a few citizens were in view and none within earshot.

Jennifer leaned close. "Matt, I'm worried."

"About me?"

"Of course not."

"Not even as a friend?"

"Well, maybe a little."

She smiled up at him. When they reached the jail, they found Gentry and Hicks seated by the stove, playing checkers. The empty cells out back added to the quiet.

Matt grinned at Hicks. "You've gained some weight."

Hicks rubbed his stomach. "It was worth it."

"Have you set a date?"

"None of your business."

"So you haven't asked her yet?" Matt persisted.

"Maybe I want to make sure I'm going to be alive first. Now, what's going on?"

Gentry jumped Hicks's last checkers and chuckled, while the sheriff glared at him.

Matt pulled up chairs for himself and Jennifer. "I'm taking Wednesday afternoon and Thursday off. We just need to find the right man for the job. I'm not so sure the judge is the right choice."

Abruptly, the door opened. They fell silent.

A stranger appeared. A man of average height and weight with gray hair, moustache, and beard, he had a slight limp. His trail clothes and long black coat were a bit sloppy. He closed the door behind him.

As he opened his coat, they saw the badge of a deputy US marshal.

"Sheriff Hicks? I'm Marshal Brady."

They all stared at the visitor with the same thought.

Matt stood up with a grin.

"Sheriff, I think we have our man."

On Wednesday afternoon with the pretense of a picnic, Matt saddled up his buckskin. Gentry swung astride his gelding. Jennifer perched on Eberley's bay gelding. They all glanced around the livery barn, wondering who might be watching.

A basket hung from her saddle horn. It contained overnight clothes instead of food.

"We'll stop at the Horton ranch for some pie," Matt said. "Maybe take some with us."

Gentry nodded. "Good idea."

Soon they were out of town and heading southwest toward the Horton ranch. The town faded behind them. No one appeared to follow.

Matt turned in the saddle to look at Jennifer.

"Remember, you're only going as far as the Horton ranch. If we're not back by tomorrow noon, you get one of the cowhands to take you into town."

"If I was a man, you'd let me go with you."

Matt grinned. "Probably."

"I can hit what I aim at."

"I just don't want any dead women around."

Gentry shrugged. "Well, right now, Hicks and Marshal Brady had better be at the ranch waiting for us. I sure hope it works."

Matt tugged at his hat brim. "Grant has it all figured out."

"Yeah, well," Gentry said, "he's not going to be there to fix it if something goes wrong."

A sunny day without wind made the rolling hills all the more green and beautiful. On the northern horizon, they saw dark clouds forming.

"I hope that storm goes somewhere else," Matt said.

When they reached the Horton ranch, they dismounted and entered the house.

Sheriff Hicks and Marshal Brady were inside, already feeding their faces with apple pie.

Hicks wore range clothes and a new hat, his badge hidden.

Marshal Brady's beard, now closely trimmed, along with a long dark coat and a campaign hat, all gave the illusion of Grant. Brady appeared to have no trouble with their plans. In fact, Brady liked the idea and showed it.

Matt grinned at Brady. "From a distance, you'd sure look like him, all right."

"Yeah, a real target," Brady replied. "But this pie makes it all worthwhile."

"I have two wonderful trees," Emma said with pride.

Emma stuffed them with pie and coffee, so much so they had trouble getting up from their chairs. Emma got smiles and hugs, loaded with praise.

The four men went outside to their horses.

Jennifer and Emma followed. They waited on the porch in silence as the four men mounted and headed toward the mountains in the southwest. This late in the day, night would soon follow.

The two women watched them ride out of sight.

Emma frowned. "What are they up to?"

"I'll explain later."

"Well, come inside. I'm glad you're here. With that Crazy Albert running loose, the house is very empty."

"I have a revolver."

"Revolver? I sleep with a shotgun."

Jennifer laughed. "I'll bet you are a good shot."

"Honey, with a shotgun, it don't matter."

Up in Mule Creek canyon, Ferman and Bittner had spread a dozen men along the high walls in trees and rocks. The canyon, narrow and long, made a perfect spot for ambush.

By late afternoon, they settled down for cover. Below they could see the old cabin and had a perfect line of fire into the entire area.

"Be dark afore long," Bittner said.

Ferman grinned, as he settled down behind a rock.

"Like a turkey shoot."

"Yeah," Bittner said, wetting his lips. "Too bad the colonel ain't here to enjoy it. But I'm surprised you didn't bring more men. I thought you was gonna get Hennesy stirred up."

"I'm working on him, but he's too wrapped up in working his claim and saving to get himself a ranch. They're all trying to forget."

Bittner, the former slave trader, sipped whiskey from a flask.

"Yeah," Bittner said. "They never had nothing to start with."

Ferman shifted his weight on his blankets. "But they did fight for the South."

"Not the way we did. The fools say they fought for their outfits," Bittner said. "And their state. A whole bunch of flag-wavers."

"Whatever the reason, we can't count on 'em, but we have enough for tonight." Ferman wiped his brow. "I can get more later. All it takes is money."

"Yours, not mine."

Ferman ignored the comment. "Now remember, half of us aim right at Grant, and none of us had better miss."

"Yeah, and the other half aim at the man who saved his neck. We've waited a long time for this."

Ferman grunted. "Bulldog sure didn't. I bet he sure was surprised, breaking in and finding her there with a six-shooter."

"Shadows are getting long," Bittner said. "Where the devil are they?"

"I don't know, but look over there toward the Horton place."

Ferman squinted through a spyglass. "I see something, all right. Four riders?"

"Coming this way?"

"Yeah, but I can't make 'em out."

The two men nestled down, Winchesters cocked.

In their minds flashed visions of the War between the States.

Ferman thought grimly of what he had lost in Georgia, of the bloody battles of the war, and of Black Friday and financial ruin he had suffered at the time. Grant had done that to him.

After Black Friday, they had tried several times and failed to extinguish Grant as either general or president. This time, there would be no failure.

In the Southern camps, Grant had been the fearful one to beat, "unconditional surrender" Grant, the leader who never turned back and had run over thousands of Confederates like a battering ram, the general who sent Sherman south through Georgia, the man Tyler had saved.

Ferman and Bittner were as anxious to kill Matt Tyler as the aging Grant.

"Frost should have been here to see this," Bittner said.

Ferman, a little nervous at Frost's name, didn't answer.

"They're getting closer."

Ferman peered through the glass. "By golly, I think Grant's with 'em."

In Lone Willow Canyon, the next canyon farther south of Mule Creek Canyon, Moose and Grizzly had also settled in about sixty feet up the rocky walls. The chill of night approached. They wrapped themselves in blankets with rifles ready. The narrow canyon, brush and trees scant, came to a dead end in a group of boulders.

"Awful cold," Grizzly said.

"It's colder at sea."

"So you say."

"Listen, I've been on the north seas where a man could freeze between his cabin and the wheel. That's when it's cold as blue flugin."

"What's that mean?" Grizzly muttered.

"To a landlubber, cold enough that fire freezes."

"Well, like now. I sure wish I had some coffee. My rump's turning to ice."

Back at Mule Creek Canyon on the walls with the day ending, Ferman wiped his brow. He wasn't cold. Fever ran through him. He had waited a long time for this. As he lifted his rifle, he spoke softly.

"This is for a lot of good men. And Robert E. Lee."

Bittner nodded. "And a way of life they took from us."

Once a rich slave trader who barely saved his fortune after the war, Bittner ended up losing it all on Black Friday. He had nothing but hate left in him.

Ferman, once a rich plantation owner, whose fortune survived the war, had also gambled on the gold market and lost everything on Black Friday because of Grant's actions as president.

Ferman's thirst for vengeance loomed so close, he could taste it.

They watched anxiously as the four riders neared the canyon entrance in direct line for the cabin. Bittner grimaced and fingered his rifle. Ferman kept moistening his lips, his throat dry.

They saw what they thought was Grant, riding with Hicks, Gentry, and Matt.

"It's Grant, all right," Ferman said.

The riders kept coming, Now they were close to the canyon entrance, almost within rifle range.

Ferman and Bittner, along with their men, prepared for a slaughter.

Abruptly, the four riders turned from outside the mouth of Mule Creek Canyon and headed south instead.

Bittner cussed furiously.

Ferman got to one knee. "What the devil?"

"They kept going," Bittner said. "Let's get 'em."

"It won't be so easy out there. We've lost the advantage."

Bittner got to his feet. "There's over a dozen of us and only four of them. Let's get the horses. They got to camp somewhere."

Ferman's mind worked fast. He stood up, lost his balance, and dropped to one knee. "Yow!"

"What's the matter?"

"My bad knee. Go ahead. I'll catch up."

"All right, but hurry. You're going to miss all the fun."

Ferman sat on a rock, holding his knee in false pain. He watched as Bittner and the dozen men dropped down into the canyon, mounted, and went charging toward the entrance as twilight fell.

Ferman, relieved, went down to his horse and swung astride, rifle across the pommel. Slowly, he rode to the entrance of Mule Creek Canyon. He reined up, short of the entrance, waiting for the sound of rifle fire to the south. He kept out of sight in the pines.

At twilight in the next canyon known as Lone Willow, four riders rode into its narrow passage. Unknown to Bittner, they included Sheriff Hicks, Matt, Gentry, and Marshal Brady dressed as Grant.

Bittner and a dozen men chased after them.

Just outside the entrance, Bittner reined up, holding back behind junipers.

His men charged deep into the canyon.

Their prey disappeared behind the boulders at the deep end.

The dozen riders reined up inside the canyon, suddenly afraid of ambush.

From cover on the south wall, Sheriff Hicks shouted down to the raiders.

"Reach! You're all under arrest."

Safe and hidden back outside the canyon entrance, Bittner winced, expecting surrender of his force and their possible talking to save themselves.

Instead, the dozen riders spun their horses and started firing back.

Within minutes, gunfire exchanged so rapidly, sparks and flashes lit the canyon.

Bittner eased forward to have a look. He saw his men falling from the saddle like flies.

When four survivors came charging out of the canyon, Bittner turned his horse with theirs. They rode north at a gallop in the twilight, back toward Silver Gulch.

Inside Lone Willow Canyon as night fell, eight Southern men lay dead. With torches, they were surveyed on foot by Hicks, Gentry, Matt, and Marshal Brady.

"They work in the mines," Hicks said, "but it don't prove Ferman was in on it."

Grimly, they loaded and tied the bodies on the horses, swatted the animals on the rumps, and sent them home. The horses spun out of the canyon and headed north toward Silver Gulch.

Matt grimaced. "We'd better talk to Ferman just the same."

"All right," Marshal Brady said. "But let's get some sleep first."

They set about making camp in the high rocks. Moose and Grizzly took turns on watch.

In his blankets, Matt lay quiet, staring at the twinkling stars above.

So much had happened so fast. Three law clerks murdered, along with Frank Choper, Captain Witherspoon, Ruben Smythe, Deputy Little, Jared Frost, Boner, and Hancock.

They had almost lost Sheriff Hicks.

He worried who would be next.

Back at the Horton ranch late that same night, Jennifer and Emma talked long into the evening. They sat by the fire in the hearth.

"When I lost my husband," Emma Horton said, "I thought my life was over, but this was his family homestead. I had to keep it going. Now I'm glad I did."

"Are you going to marry Sheriff Hicks?" Jennifer asked.

"Yes," Emma said.

"Does he know it?"

"Not yet," Emma said with a laugh. "What about you?"

"If I was ever to marry, I'd like it to be Matt Tyler."

"Does he know?"

Jennifer laughed. "Not yet."

At length, they turned in, expecting a restless night.

Jennifer, wearing a soft white cotton gown, slept in Emma's spare room, which was simply decorated with white curtains. She worried about Matt, as she fell asleep.

Around midnight, her lamp burning low, Jennifer suddenly opened her eyes, her heart pounding. She had heard something. She squinted.

And now there was a cackle.

She looked to her left and saw Crazy Albert, grinning like a wild man, his eyes round and glassy. A monster in shabby clothes, horrifying to look at, he cackled again.

She screamed at the top of her voice.

He slowly raised a hatchet, the horror of his deliberate movement freezing Jennifer.

As he came at her, she rolled aside, pulled the revolver from under her pillow, jerked back the hammer, and fired point-blank.

Her bullet hit him in the left shoulder.

He shrieked and kept coming.

She rolled off the bed, crashing to the floor with a gasp and getting up, as she frantically tried to recock the revolver, her heart crazy wild.

She staggered backward in horror.

The hatchet slammed down into her pillow. When Albert jerked it free, feathers flew.

He cackled, loud and wild. He delighted in teasing her.

Jennifer, heart in her throat, breath gone, lifted her revolver.

"God help me," she whined.

He charged across the bed, hatchet raised.

She saw his bloodshot eyes.

She fired again, hitting him in the chest. He didn't stop.

She leaped aside, as the hatchet whistled by her ear.

She turned, as she cocked her revolver and ran in her bare feet toward the door to the hallway.

He cackled again with eerie laughter, giving her room, as he chased her, like a cat after a frightened mouse.

She jerked open the door and ran into the hall.

She tripped on her gown and went crashing to the floor, holding on to the revolver, and rolling sideways in terror. She slammed against the wall, stunned.

Looking up, she saw the man slowly moving toward her. He savored every second of the kill. He smelled of death, each step deliberate, driving horror through her.

She fumbled with her weapon.

From behind her came the sudden blast of a shotgun.

The blast roared, bouncing off the walls. Deafened, Jennifer gasped for breath.

Blood spread all over Crazy Albert as he staggered forward, doubled up.

Eyes crazed in disbelief, he spun around. He crashed against the wall.

He slid down to the floor in a bloody heap, his eyes glassy. His moan ugly, he spat blood.

Jennifer, hysterical, gripped the revolver and got to her knees. She squirmed to move back, aware Emma had her shotgun ready behind her.

Albert, a bloody mess, suddenly got up.

He raised the hatchet and staggered toward her with a shriek.

Jennifer fired again. This time, she shot him square between the eyes.

Albert stood frozen, crazy with death claiming him.

She squealed, got to her feet, and backed away to where Emma Horton stood ready with another blast from the shotgun. Jennifer had been in the line of fire, stopping Emma from firing again. But it was over.

Albert just folded up dead and collapsed.

Jennifer leaned on the wall in hysteria.

The two women, numb, could no longer move.

A pounding rattled the front door, followed by a half dozen hands breaking in to help.

Emma went to bring them into the hallway.

Jennifer, unable to let go of her pistol, remained in shock.

Three of the hands took a blanket Emma offered. They rolled Albert into it, and prepared to carry him away.

Emma helped Jennifer and led her away from the bloody scene, getting her to a chair near the fire and bringing her a robe.

The men, stunned by what the women had done to a crazy, wild animal, paused in amazement. The most feared killer in the valley had met his match.

Three hands picked up the blanket holding Albert and carried it into the front room and out the front door. The other three used old rags, which Emma provided, to clean some of the blood from the hallway. They soon left, but shock remained in the house.

A silence haunted the women.

Emma built up the fire and warmed the coffee.

Jennifer, numb, sat at the table. She still held the revolver.

Nothing in her life had prepared Jennifer for this night.

Emma, less shaken, having fought her share of Indians, rustlers, and bad men, concentrated on Jennifer, who now sat with a hand over her eyes.

Emma brought coffee. Neither spoke.

Jennifer finally set the revolver aside to hold her cup in both hands.

After a long, horrifying reflection of the fight, Jennifer shuddered.

She looked at the calm but weary Emma with admiration. It had all happened so fast, it had left her breathless.

"My God," Jennifer whispered.

"Exactly."

CHAPTER 28

Late that night In Silver Gulch, inside Ferman's office, he knelt at his safe. He shoved cash into a gunnysack and got to his feet. He heard horses outside, and the front door yanked open.

Ferman drew his revolver.

Bittner came charging inside. "Blast you, Red, you left us to die."

"I don't see you back in the canyon."

Bittner grimaced. "It was a slaughter. Those fools didn't know how to surrender, and eight of 'em got shot out of the saddle. Only four got away. So now what?"

Ferman holstered his weapon. "If any of the men survived, they'll be talking up a storm."

Bittner grimaced. "You're right."

"We'd better get out of here and swear we were in town."

"What about Grant?" Bittner asked.

"There'll be other chances."

"Yeah," Bittner said, "but one of the men who got away, he said he didn't think the man was Grant."

"What?" Ferman asked. "Why?"

"He remembered Grant pretty well, and he said this fellah was too husky."

Ferman steamed. He hated being tricked. No one had ever dared, when he had his own plantation and ran it with an iron hand. He hated not being in total control.

Bittner helped himself to some rye whiskey.

They turned to see Raddigan standing in the doorway, a sinister smile on his face. "Told you they'd pull a fast one."

Ferman and Bittner hated Raddigan but feared him.

"Never mind now," Ferman said. "And we haven't been here."

"Fine with me. Except whoever you saw in the canyon, it wasn't Grant."

"What are you talking about?"

"He's up on Needle Mountain. I saw him through the spyglass."

"So now what?" Bittner asked.

"We thought it was him in the canyon," Ferman said, skeptical. "Now we think it's him up there. It could be Grant's nowhere around here. Just men dressed up to look like him. They got us running in circles."

"You could be right," Bittner agreed.

Ferman looked certain of it. "Whether it's Grant on Needle Mountain or some look-alike, our snipers can take him out if he comes down," Ferman said. "There's no cover on the trail. And we'd ambush 'em easy in that back canyon."

"You're just gonna sit and wait?" Bittner persisted.

"I have a feeling," Ferman said, "that Grant's nowhere in this valley or on any mountain. They have something else cooked up. He may just show up in Mountain Springs."

"And then what?" Bittner asked.

"I have a plan," Ferman said.

"What about Tyler?" Bittner grunted. "He's no fool."

Raddigan smiled. "Leave him to me."

A half hour later in Silver Gulch, rain fell in the dark night. Lamplights under the eaves flickered in the wind. A miserable night that followed a disaster in the canyon to the south.

Bittner and Ferman stood on the porch in front of Ferman's office.

In front of them, on his mule, sat Hennesy, a big burly, clean-shaven man. Rain ran off his hat brim and slicker. He looked disinterested as Ferman talked.

"We were counting on you," Ferman growled.

"No, thanks," Hennesy said.

Hennesy had no intention of messing up his life. He made no secret he hated Bittner, the slave trader, and Carruth, the slave enforcer. He owed Ferman, but he didn't respect him. These men had made themselves rich without honor.

Hennesy loved the Old South, but not what they represented.

They heard horses coming at a trot along the crooked street.

Ferman and Bittner drew their weapons. Hennesy didn't react.

Now they saw eight dead men strapped over saddles, their mounts slowing to a halt with snorts and tosses of their heads. Carruth and three men came from a shack across the street to help catch up the horses. Hennesy stayed on his mule, watching.

Hennesy wanted as little to do with Carruth as possible. He knew Carruth had been a brutal slave enforcer. Hennesy had Southern pride that could never include a man like this.

Carruth looked the dead over while Ferman and Bittner stood back.

Watching and listening, Hennesy made a face and turned his mule away.

Both Ferman and Bittner arrived in Mountain Springs long after midnight.

Ferman went home to his mansion on the hill.

Rain pounding the roof, Bittner hid in his office behind the gambling hall, counting his money and trying to calm himself. Still breathing hard, sweat on his face, he knew he had come close to losing his life because of a thirst for vengeance. The war had destroyed his way of life. Black Friday had taken his riches. Yet it seemed so long ago.

Now he wondered if it was worth the chance he was taking.

He put the money in his safe and locked it.

As he opened the back door to leave, he paused, staring at Lucifer, rain pouring off the clerk's hat and slicker. Bittner hated Lucifer, seeing him as a worm and not a man.

"What are you doing here now?" Bittner growled.

"I've been waiting all this time to see what happened. I couldn't sleep."

"It was a trap. Eight men were killed, and we don't figure they lived long enough to talk, but just in case, I'm going to Alamosa for a few days."

"Wait a minute," Lucifer said. "I did everything the colonel wanted. Now you're saying, we could be in trouble, and that means I'll be right in it with you. So you're not leaving without paying me a lot more money, so I can get out of here if it all blows up."

"We paid you."

"I want five thousand, and I know you have it."

"I'll give you another hundred and that's it."

"Why don't you ask the colonel?" Lucifer persisted.

"He'd tell us to clean up our own mess. Now take the hundred."

Bittner stood out of the rain in the doorway, his face grim, saddlebags over his shoulder, sack in his left hand. His right hand shoved his slicker back from his holster.

"That's not enough," Lucifer said.

"It's all you get. Take it or leave it."

"I risked everything for you and the colonel."

"Sure, but we had our reasons, and we fought for the South. The only thing you're interested in is your crazy ambition and your greed for our money. Well, I'm sick of it."

Lucifer's mouth twisted. "I'm almost a lawyer. I'm better than you scum will ever be. Ferman bought slaves from you and you both got rich off 'em. And Carruth whipped them. At least I'm civilized."

"You're something we find under rocks. Now get out of my way or take the hundred."

Lucifer snarled and suddenly pulled his revolver to threaten Bittner.

Bittner drew faster, firing as it cleared the holster.

Lucifer gasped as the bullet struck his left shoulder and spun him around. Instead of firing back, he jumped out of Bittner's view and disappeared in the dark rain.

Frantic, Bittner went after him. Lucifer, younger with long legs, outran him.

Bittner looked all over the back streets, even to Lucifer's rented room, where it was still dark and the house locked. Rain and wind tore at him as he searched.

Drenched with sweat, even as the storm pounded him, Bittner hurried back to his horse. He tied on his saddlebags and sack. He mounted, then rode into the street and up the hill toward Ferman's house. He avoided anyone seeing him.

He saw a light in the front window and reined up to dismount. Rushing to the door, he pounded until Ferman, still in his slicker, opened up to allow him inside.

"I was just going out," Ferman said, annoyed.

"Lucifer turned on us. We got to find him."

Lucifer hid in an alley across the street from the newspaper office. Bleeding and in pain, he leaned against the wall of the saddlery, knowing Ralph Smythe's office and sleeping quarters were upstairs.

Rain and wind persisted in the late night.

Lucifer had seen Bittner cross the street and ride up the hill, probably to Ferman's.

He shivered, bleeding, hurt, and terrified.

He looked around, but he saw no one on the street.

Up the stairs he went, hurting so badly he could hardly breathe. He made it to the door and pounded, then kicked.

It took a while before Ralph lit a lantern and came to the door to peer out at him.

“Lucifer, what the devil?”

“I’ve been shot, and I need a lawyer.”

“I’ve got too big a case load now. You need to see the doc and use your own firm.”

“Do you want to tear down Frost, Hancock, and Eberley? Do you want to get Red Ferman once and for all? And Bittner? And the whole town?”

Ralph moistened his lips. “Come in, quick.”

Later that night in Mountain Springs, Ferman and Bittner gave up looking for Lucifer.

They stood in the rain near the gambling hall.

So much seemed to be falling apart. They felt drained.

Ferman pulled his hat down tight. “No use. You think you shot him enough he’s dead?”

“I sure hope so, Bittner said. I’m heading for Alamosa for a few days.”

“You’re running out?” Ferman growled.

“Lucifer could nail me for Hancock.” Bittner said. “We got to kill him.”

“He know you’re going to Alamosa?”

“He sure does,” Bittner said, hesitant. “All right then. I’m going to Silver Gulch, and you’d better hide me for a while.”

Ferman nodded. “See Carruth. He’ll find a place for you. Right now, I’ve got to see the colonel, and then I’ll find Mrs. Ledbetter. If Lucifer’s gone to the law, she can make a deal with him.”

“He wanted five thousand,” Bittner said. “Maybe more now.”

They reflected on the dire situation. Both men had lived their lives with the idea that money could solve every problem. Now they knew Lucifer could not be solved with gold. The worm would have to die.

Ferman gave Bittner his office key, then watched Bittner mount and ride back through the alley in the rain.

Ferman felt superior to Bittner, but right now, he needed him.

Ferman mounted and rode up in to the hills north of town. He bent low in the wind and rain. He had a yearning for Morna but restrained himself when he saw no lights in her mansion.

Ferman rode on up to his own mansion. Complications had set in, messing up his plans, thanks to Lucifer. He wondered how many phony claims and grants they would toss back at him. Every Yank who had ever filed a claim at Silver Gulch had lost it, one way or another. Now they'd be back to haunt him.

Richer than anyone in the valley because of the mines, he told himself he would prevail, somehow, no matter what it cost in money or people.

And no matter what, the real Grant would soon be dead.

In the morning rain, the small posse of Moose, Grizzly, Marshal Brady as himself again, Sheriff Hicks, Gentry, and Matt came to Silver Gulch, where no man remembered anything.

There was no sign of Ferman, Bittner, Raddigan, or Carruth.

Moose and Grizzly went back up the mountain to be with their visitors.

Marshal Brady and Gentry turned back to town.

Rain and wind persisted, as Matt and Sheriff Hicks headed for the Horton ranch to pick up Jennifer. Weary, they had little to say as they hunched over in the storm.

Rain continued to drench them as they reined up by the corrals.

Two of the hands came to take their horses and tell them what had happened with Crazy Albert. They dressed up the story with the women's heroism.

Listening in dismay, Hicks and Matt were speechless.

"Yeah," one old timer said, "they shot heck out of him."

"Pistol and shotgun," another man said. "Messed him up real good."

"The women didn't get hurt," the old-timer added.

Frantic, Hicks and Matt hurried to the house, removed their slickers under the porch roof, and pounded on the door. Hats in hand, they waited.

Emma, wearing an apron and holding a towel, opened the door.

Surprised, she rushed to throw her arms around the startled Hicks, hugging him, her face reaching to his chest. She drew them both inside.

Matt shut the door against the storm.

Overwhelmed, Hicks held her as she trembled.

"It was awful, Willoughby."

Hicks swallowed hard. "The men told us."

"First Jennifer got him, and then I blasted him with the shotgun, but he kept coming, so Jennifer shot him right between the eyes." Emma took a deep breath. "He was so terrifying."

Matt turned around, looking for Jennifer. She came out of the other room, wearing an apron. Her chestnut hair on her shoulders, she looked half-asleep. When she saw Matt, her pale face lit up with joy. She rushed to him, falling into his arms, her face at his shoulder as she hugged him.

"Matt, I'm so glad you're alive."

"We heard about your visitor."

Jennifer backed away, still shaken, and ashen. "Now I've shot two men."

She sat on the couch, dabbing at her eyes.

"He was no man," Emma said, turning from Hicks's arms. "He was a varmint."

"But it doesn't answer all our questions," Hicks said, letting Emma lead him to a chair as she handed him his badge. "And we can't keep Grant up on that mountain much longer."

"Bring him here," Emma said, sitting next to him. "I have more than twenty good riders on my ranch, and every one of them was loyal to the Union. My husband made sure of it before he hired them."

Hicks nodded agreement. "Except we know Ferman's men are waiting for him to come down. It won't be easy."

"It can be done," Matt said.

Matt thought of the cave and the danger. Yet he would never let anything happen to Grant, whatever it took. At the same time, he felt he had failed Jennifer.

Emma and Jennifer served them coffee, bread, and ham.

Matt could not take his eyes from Jennifer.

Hicks kept smiling at Emma.

Both men felt humble with admiration.

Matt felt for Jennifer and her ordeal. He had a need and desire to protect her, to keep her close always, and it scared him plenty.

His burden to protect her and Grant lay heavy on his shoulders.

CHAPTER 29

THE NEXT MORNING IN MOUNTAIN Springs, the rain having stopped and the sky cleared, townspeople moved about in their daily activities.

At Sheriff Hicks's office, Marshal Brady waited with Gentry.

Brady dozed in the chair behind Hicks's desk.

Gentry paced. The door to the cells remained closed.

Gentry made a fresh pot of coffee and paced some more.

Matt and the sheriff arrived late morning. They came inside with a rush of wind, awakening Marshal Brady as they dropped their gear. They headed for the stove and hot coffee.

Gentry, relieved to see them, poured himself a cup.

Brady got up, stretched, and also wanted coffee.

Hicks placed his saddlebags on his desk. "Where's Lacey?"

"Keeping an eye on Lucifer," Gentry said. "He's in protective custody up at the doc's until he's able to come here."

Matt, startled, lowered his cup. "Lucifer is?"

"By order of Judge Waller," Brady said. "Seems Bittner tried to kill him. Lucifer wants to turn state's evidence in exchange for what Ralph Smythe says will implicate Frost and Hancock and half of Silver Gulch in an assassination plot against Grant."

"Sounds like a real break for us," Matt said.

Brady nodded. "But Lucifer wants both state and federal immunity, so he's not opening up. As soon as we get confirmation from Denver, we can make a deal."

"I'll be," Hicks said.

"Lucifer did say that Crazy Albert killed Choper and the law clerks," Gentry added.

"We don't have to worry about Albert," Hicks said. "The women shot him full of holes at the ranch."

Brady and Gentry stared at Hicks and Matt, who sipped their coffee with big grins. Brady, amazed, just shook his head.

"No fooling?" Gentry asked, delighted and doing a little dance.

Matt went to a window to check the street.

Hicks sat at his desk. He got serious and turned to Marshal Brady. "So about Lucifer?"

Brady cradled his cup in his hands. "He promises to talk about some mysterious colonel. Meanwhile, I'm on my way to Alamosa to pick up Bittner. That's where Lucifer said he went."

Hicks grunted. "What about Mrs. Ledbetter?"

"Seems Lucifer insists she has nothing to do with this," Brady said.

"Did Lucifer tell Ralph who killed his brother?" Matt asked. "Or who hired Crazy Albert?"

Brady shook his head. "Lucifer won't say anything more until he gets a deal."

"Ralph's real bitter," Hicks said. "He'll blow this wide open, if he can."

Matt stood up. "I've got to tell Eberley."

"He already knows," Brady said. "He's at the office right now, going through all the personal files on his dead partners."

Hicks turned to Gentry. "I need someone I can trust to work with me and Lacey to keep Lucifer safe in jail."

"I'll help," Gentry said. "Soon's they get here."

Matt knew that by now, Ralph had filled in Jennifer with relish. He went outside where he took a deep breath in the sunlight.

Then he hurried along the street to his law firm.

Matt entered the law firm's building, expecting the reception area to be empty.

Instead, he saw Pa Loring sitting just inside with a shotgun.

They grinned and nodded at each other.

"Don't you worry none," Pa Loring said.

"I have to tell you, Crazy Albert is dead. Jennifer and Mrs. Horton got attacked at the ranch, and they shot him dead."

"Great balls of fire," Pa Loring said with delight. "I've known Emma Horton a long time. She's a real tough one."

"She got him with a shotgun. Jennifer shot him between the eyes."

"Heckfire," Pa Loring said. "Women don't need us no more?"

They both laughed.

Matt sobered when he entered the back hallway. He soon found Eberley searching in Frost's office file cabinets. Eberley looked exhausted from the strain.

"You find anything?" Matt asked.

"No, they were too careful, but Ralph is on this like flies on a hog."

"All he has for sure is Bittner's attempted murder of Lucifer."

Eberley nodded, sitting down wearily behind the desk. "But I have a feeling he'll manage to blow it up when Lucifer talks."

Matt pulled up a chair. "I'm sorry about your partners."

"They were good lawyers. Yet they threw it all away for revenge. And it wasn't even the War between the States—can you believe it? They wanted Grant dead because of Black Friday. The conspiracy shows what kind of men they really were. And it doesn't matter which side they fought on." Eberley shook his head. "It wasn't over any kind of conviction. It was all over money."

"I know," Matt said.

"Isn't that kind of sad?"

"Lucifer's implicating your partners, because they're dead—do you realize that?"

Eberley nodded. "I just hope you can get Grant safely to town."

"With Lucifer foaming at the mouth, maybe the others will back off."

"Don't be too sure. It only takes one bullet if the opportunity arises," Eberley said, "but I sure hope they find Crazy Albert."

Matt grinned and told him how the women took him down.

"My God," Eberley said, amazed. He leaned back, shook his head. "What a terrible experience for Jennifer and Mrs. Horton."

"I think it was worse for Albert."

Eberley chuckled. "You're right."

"I'm sorry you got caught up in this," Matt said.

Eberley nodded. "So am I. Our major client was Ferman and his associates. Now I'm finding some indication Ferman used fraud to obtain that land grant after all."

"That'll tie up the court for years."

"Maybe when this is over, I'll sell the practice and move to Denver."

"The town knows you're an honest man, and you're clean in this."

"I'm getting tired, Matt. The law has been my life, but this is leaving a bad taste in my mouth."

"Maybe we could start our own firm. Eberley and Tyler."

"Eberley, Tyler, and Loring," Ted Loring, law clerk, said from the doorway.

"Maybe so," Eberley said, turning to Matt. "Ted didn't know what was going on, but he's helping me clean up this mess. And Pa Loring's making sure we're not disturbed."

"But we haven't found anything," Ted said.

"As soon as Lucifer's in a cell, we may get some answers," Eberley added.

Matt left them reluctantly and returned to the boardinghouse for some sleep.

Hours later, Mrs. Ledbetter, wearing a cape over her blue checkered dress, found Lacey in charge of the jail, eating his lunch at the desk. He stood up to greet her, noticing she carried nothing in her hands. She talked sweetly, friendly.

He allowed her to walk back to where Lucifer sat in his cell. Lacey returned to his meal but kept the door to the cells open so he could watch.

In the last cell, Lucifer, pale but arrogant, sat with his left arm in a sling.

Mrs. Ledbetter couldn't stand this weasel of a man who wasn't fit to have lit her husband's pipe, but she had a job to do. She pressed against the bars and glanced toward the open door to the front office, then whispered.

"Lucifer, Mr. Ferman wants to make a deal."

Lucifer got up and came close, his voice low. "I'm sure he does. That's why I kept you free of the whole thing, because I knew you'd come to see me."

"What have you told the law?"

"Just that Bittner shot me, and that Crazy Albert did some of the killings. I told them there was an assassination plot, but I haven't given any names except Hancock and Frost, and they're dead."

"Good. Do you have a price?"

Lucifer frowned. "I'm thinking."

"Mr. Ferman suggests that you tell the sheriff it was all a mistake about Bittner having shot you; you really couldn't see who it was because of the rain."

"What's it worth?"

She leaned closer. "Mr. Ferman says he'll give five thousand for you to clear Bittner and leave town."

"Ten."

She frowned. "He said you'd double it, but that's all right."

"I want the money now."

Her back to the door, she reached under her skirts and pulled a fat envelope from her stockings. "Two now. The rest when you've done what we asked."

Turning his back also, Lucifer greedily counted the greenbacks, then slid them inside his shirt.

"All you have to say," she continued, "is that the plot stopped with Hancock and Frost. And it wasn't Bittner who shot you."

He turned. "What about Crazy Albert?"

"He's dead, so you can say Frost and Hancock hired him. But you can't prove it."

"All right, but when I walk out this door, I want that in gold and my horse saddled and waiting. A safe ride out of town, or I'm changing my mind."

"Mr. Ferman says the ten is the end of it. He doesn't want ever to hear from you again."

Lucifer smiled. "The best way to be sure of that is to double it."

CHAPTER 30

LATE MORNING, MATT LEFT THE rooming house where he had been sleeping and headed straight for the jail. Sunshine warmed him. He prayed things would go better now with Lucifer ready to talk.

Deputy Lacey let him inside.

Behind the closed door to the cells, Lucifer remained in custody.

Lacey lounged at the desk as Matt paced, his hand on his holster.

"The sheriff went over to Pop's to eat," Lacey said.

"Lucifer have any visitors?"

"Just Mrs. Ledbetter."

"That's interesting."

Lacey nodded. "I couldn't hear what they said, but when she left, Lucifer sure looked happy."

"Just watch yourself."

Matt went back outside. He crossed over to Pop's Café, where Sheriff Hicks and Eberley ate with Jennifer at a back table. When she saw Matt, she half-rose from her chair with delight.

He came to sit between her and Eberley. He spoke low even though there were no other diners and Pop remained in the back.

"Tomorrow night," Matt said. "We'll need help from the Horton ranch."

"You sure about the cave?" Eberley whispered.

"Ferman's men are lying in wait," Matt said. "Even if we had help, we'd all be an open target coming down that mountain. A long rifle could pick us off easy. And the back canyon would be worse."

"Marshal Brady could call in the army," Hicks said. "When he gets back."

"No," Matt said, "we don't want to fight the war all over again."

Later, Jennifer walked with Matt to the newspaper office in the afternoon sun. She enjoyed his nearness, wondering if he knew how much she admired him.

When they entered, Ralph Smythe stood waiting at the counter and seemed visibly annoyed. His lawyer demeanor never let up.

"I've been waiting for you, Jennifer."

She went behind the counter. "When is your client going to talk?"

"Whenever he gets immunity."

Matt pushed his hat back. "Just what exactly is he going to say?"

"You know I can't divulge that information."

"Is he going to say Ferman killed your brother?"

"He doesn't know who killed my brother."

"I'd say Lucifer knows everything."

"Why do you think that?" Ralph snapped.

"He was the messenger, remember?"

Ralph turned to Jennifer. "I'll be back when this man is gone."

Jennifer watched the door slam behind Ralph. "I'm sorry, Matt. Can't you two get along?"

"Lucifer's lying to him."

Out in the street in the bright sun with a rising breeze, Ralph stormed down the boardwalk and crossed over to the jail. Lacey let him inside.

Ralph charged past the startled Lacey, slammed the middle door behind him, and walked over to the cell where Lucifer sat on his bunk.

Ralph gripped the bars with both hands.

Lucifer stood up with a yawn. "Something new?"

"Who killed my brother?"

"I'm not talking until I get full immunity."

"So you do know."

"No, I don't."

Ralph pounded the bars, startling Lucifer, who backed away.

"You're lying, Lucifer. If you think you can protect the rest of them, you'd better remember that they'd be a lot happier if you were dead. Your best bet to stay alive is by telling the whole truth. You'd be protected."

"I'll do whatever I think is necessary."

"And if the federal immunity comes through?"

"Then we'll talk about it."

The door opened. Lacey stood watching.

Ralph turned angrily. "I have a right to be alone with my client."

"Just checking," Lacey said as he closed the door again.

Ralph drew a deep breath. "Lucifer, anything you tell me will be kept in the strictest of confidence."

"Except when it's a fraud on the court?"

"Blast you, Lucifer, who killed my brother?"

"I'm not saying anything else."

"Then you'd better get yourself another lawyer."

"Hey, you can't abandon me."

Ralph started for the door. "Just watch me."

"Hey, wait."

Slowly, Ralph turned. "Yes?"

"You're the best lawyer I can get."

"And?"

Lucifer made a face, but he shook his head. "I don't want to die. I can't say any more."

"I'm asking the judge to be relieved."

Ralph jerked open the door to the front office and barely avoided a collision with Mrs. Ledbetter, who, startled, jumped back. He stormed past Deputy Lacey and left without another word.

Mrs. Ledbetter frowned. She left the middle door open and walked back to the cell where Lucifer hung onto the bars with tight fists.

"What happened?" she whispered.

Lucifer slammed his palm against the bars, and then drew back, holding his painful hand. Then he leaned close, whispering.

"That crummy lawyer is backing out on me."

She leaned close, murmuring, "You clear Bittner and keep the others out of it, you can leave tonight. The gold will be on your horse behind the livery barn."

Lucifer frowned. "I want to talk to the colonel."

"You know that's not possible right now. But let's look at your situation. Eberley's never going to hire you after this. So let's do what's best for you."

"I don't think ten thousand's enough to start over someplace else."

Lacey appeared in the doorway, checking on them, then walked out of sight.

Mrs. Ledbetter spoke even more softly.

"I can get you another five thousand in greenbacks."

Lucifer wet his lips. "I can make out with another ten."

"All right, but you clear Bittner right away and get out of here. Be at the livery at midnight. Your horse will be saddled, and there'll be a pack horse. And the rest of the money, provided you have done what we ask."

"It's a deal."

She backed away. She hurried to the door and out into the office. Lacey watched her go, closing the door behind her. He walked back to where Lucifer stood with arms folded.

"What's going on?"

"I want to get out of here."

"The sheriff says we got to protect you."

"Well, you tell him I made a mistake. It wasn't Bittner. It was dark and raining, and just because I was near his place, his name popped to mind. But it wasn't him. So either charge me with something or let me out."

Lacey grimaced. "When Hicks comes in, I'll ask him."

"I want out of here by tonight."

"I'll let you know."

Lucifer glared after the deputy, then turned away with a smile.

He would have more money than he could earn in a lifetime. Money for play, for stature, for a new life. Women would flock to him.

Later that afternoon, Sheriff Hicks and Matt were with Judge Waller and McComb, the county attorney, in the judge's chambers. The judge sat at his desk and looked weary.

"Lucifer's right," Waller said. "You have to charge him or let him out."

"Where's his attorney?" Matt asked.

"Ralph Smythe wants off the case," Waller said.

"Just as well," McComb said. "The only evidence we have is whatever Lucifer tells us, We have nothing. And he's not really a material witness to his own shooting when he says he couldn't see who did it. So let him go, Sheriff."

Hicks and Matt were quiet but angry.

"If Brady brings Bittner in," McComb said, "we'll have to let him go. Lucifer's cleared him."

Matt, disappointed, fell silent.

Later that evening, Lucifer left the jail a free man. Mrs. Ledbetter escorted him down the street, Jennifer on their heels. Matt walked slowly behind them.

A chill wind followed them under a starry sky.

Even as Jennifer tried to interview Lucifer, the law clerk continued at a face pace with Mrs. Ledbetter urging him onward.

"Mr. Rawlins," Jennifer insisted, "you must have a statement for the press."

"So you can crucify me like you did the firm?"

"I only print the truth, Mr. Rawlins. Now, what about your complaint against Mr. Bittner?"

"I told the judge I was mistaken. It was dark and raining. I didn't see who did it. I just thought it was him. I didn't want an innocent man charged."

Jennifer, out of breath, tried to keep up. "But what about the conspiracy?"

"What conspiracy?"

"The one that Frost and Hancock had planned against Grant."

"They're both dead, and so's the conspiracy. I told that to the judge as well."

Mrs. Ledbetter and Lucifer came to a sudden halt as Ralph Smythe appeared out of nowhere and confronted them. The young lawyer turned furious.

"What's going on here?" Ralph demanded.

"You dropped me," Lucifer said, "so what do you care?"

"Why are you free?"

"I made a mistake," Lucifer said. "It wasn't Bittner. I don't know who it was."

Lucifer and Mrs. Ledbetter turned and crossed the street.

Jennifer came up to Ralph. Matt joined them, and all three watched the pair head for the alley by the courthouse on their way to where Lucifer lived.

"Well," Ralph said, "that's that."

Jennifer folded her arms. "So what happens now?"

"It's time we filled Ralph in," Matt said. "And I'm hungry."

Later that night, at Pop's over supper with the other tables now empty, while Jennifer listened, Matt told Ralph his story. He told him about President Hayes, Grant, and the action in the canyons. He revealed his plan to get Grant secretly off the mountain.

Ralph frowned. "I'm glad you told me, Matt, but without Lucifer, how can you prove Bittner and Ferman are involved? Or who killed my brother?"

"We don't know," Matt said.

Ralph grimaced. "I suspect Lucifer is about to be a very wealthy man."

Matt nodded, leaned back. Jennifer sipped her coffee and stared out the window, into the night.

Ralph continued to steam.

Matt and Jennifer were just exhausted from all the mystery, the stress, and the danger.

Even later that same night in his room, Lucifer had a pocket full of money. He knew the rest would be at the livery. His excitement spun his imagination as he packed his things.

He smiled to himself. He sure didn't need to rush to practice law now. He would be set for life. Oh, he would make sure he was admitted to the bar. He would take some important cases, just to impress everyone.

He thought of all the grand ways he would be living. Maybe he wasn't handsome, but with money, he could likely find him a pretty woman and settle down. He could have luxury and prestige and position. Money would do that. All he had to do was find himself a nice little town.

At midnight, Lucifer slipped through the back alleys behind the courthouse, hotel, stage depot, and laundry, making his way with his carpetbag to the boardwalk, where he had to cross. He saw no one in the lights of the hanging lamps up the street. The jail looked dark a few doors down.

Sweat on his brow, he hurried over to the other side but stayed on the dirt to be quiet, his eyes scanning the closed farm supply and wheelwright. He made it to the livery barn where the outside lantern burned low.

Inside, he heard snoring in the loft. He walked softly on the straw and dirt, heading for the back of the barn. In lamplight, he could see his saddled horse in the corral, along with a pack mule already loaded.

Lucifer smiled. He had the world by the tail with a downhill pull.

In the hush of the night, he had no fear. He paid no heed to moving shadows, the rustle of some varmint in the straw, the glow of the passing moonlight awaiting him in the corral.

He tugged at his hat, his joy unbounded. A rich man, he could live the rest of his life in pleasure. No restraints. No one bossing him. Everyone jumping at his bark.

Lucifer could not stop grinning.

As he walked out of the barn, he heard a swish.

The swish of a large knife coming down at his back.

CHAPTER 31

On Needle Mountain, at one in the morning, Reis Williams and Grant followed Matt, Moose, and Grizzly into the icy-cold night. Stars glittered overhead.

They entered the cave and lit torches. Inside more ropes had been stacked.

"You really think this is necessary?" Grant asked.

"General, they're watching us like hawks, because they still got it in their heads you was hiding somewhere up here," Grizzly said. "There's twenty men in the back canyon, and they got a bunch of snipers watching the trail out front. I'm just sorry you have to go down that funnel. Must be four hundred feet of it."

"We have a harness rigged," Matt said. "It'll be fine."

They moved down through the cave to where it dropped into the deep chasm.

Reis Williams went first in rope harness. Down the chute, hand over hand in the darkness, sweat covering him, he finally dropped into the cave floor and saw the moonlight at the window.

He lit a torch and shouted for Grant to come down.

Slowly, in a rope harness, wearing gloves and bracing his boots on the curved walls, Ulysses Simpson Grant began his descent. Torchlight followed him from above and more light waited on the cave floor with Reis.

Grant coughed and stopped, then continued. His arms ached, and his heart pounded, but it was exhilarating.

He wished Julia could see him—and his sons.

They'd be just as excited.

Halfway down, Grant heard something tear.

Moose shouted from above. The knotted rope had come apart halfway down the shaft. Grant, falling, tried to brace himself from wall to wall but failed.

Grant went sailing down through the funnel.

Bouncing, spinning, Grant spun around and around.

The wet, cold walls threw him side to side.

Shouts from above echoed down the funnel with him.

Grant spun, jerked, hit, whirled, dropped, and slammed in all directions.

Reis Williams heard the shouting far above. He braced himself as he heard something careening down through the funnel.

"My God," he gasped.

A body came down in a spin through the chasm. Any moment, alive or dead, it would reach the bottom. Reis reached for the shaft in terror.

Grant spun out of the funnel and into Reis's arms.

They both slammed back against the cave wall and collapsed in a heap.

Terrified Grant had died in the fall, Reis shook the general.

Grant sat up, out of breath, his face flushed in the light of the torch. He turned and looked up the black chasm. He gasped for air, wiping his brow.

Suddenly, Grant chuckled with delight.

"Reis, that was one wild ride."

"General, you scared me pretty bad."

"I had a great time!"

Reis drew a deep breath. "Well, I didn't."

Moose shouted. Reis called back that Grant had survived the fall.

Reis got to the natural window. Below in the dark, he could see a dozen of the Horton men with horses. He waved to them, and then crawled back as his and Grant's gear came whirling down the funnel. Then the rope itself, let go, came down in a whirling heap.

"Men are waiting for us," Reis said.

"What about Matt?"

"They'll ride him out OK tomorrow."

Reis set about fastening rope to stone formations.

Grant grinned. "I can hardly wait to tell my wife."

Reis shook his head but had to smile in relief.

At midday, with clouds covering the sun, Matt rode his buckskin down the Needle Mountain trail. Cold and weary, he slumped in the saddle.

Moose and Grizzly, well armed, rode down with him, all the while knowing snipers were watching them. At the base of the mountain, Matt shook hands with the miners and continued on alone across the valley.

Glad to reach Mountain Springs late that evening, Matt secured his buckskin at the livery and headed for some rest at the boardinghouse. He saw no sign of Mrs. Ledbetter.

The next morning, Matt had breakfast with the other male boarders. Mrs. Ledbetter, cheerful as she served them, showed little interest in Matt.

Later, Matt walked in the sunlight through the alley to the boardwalk, just as Jennifer came out of her office. Pretty as a picture in dark calico and a navy cape, she looked worried and glad to see him.

Her green eyes got to him, a little more every time.

"How about some coffee?" Matt offered.

"Please, come with me to the sheriff's office."

"What's happened?"

"After they let Lucifer go, he was found dead at the livery, later that night. Right alongside his horse and a pack mule. Stabbed in the back. Just like Hancock."

Matt frowned. "Does Ralph know?"

"He's at the courthouse with the judge and McComb right now. And Marshal Brady."

Jennifer, upset, walked fast, Matt at her side. He could see that it was all getting to her. He wanted to put his arm around her, to comfort her.

"Lucifer's pockets were empty," she said, "but I'm sure he was leaving with some kind of payoff."

"You're probably right."

"I'm so weary of this."

Suddenly, she stopped in front of the drugstore and turned to look up at him.

"Is Grant safe, Matt?"

"It's being taken care of."

"Are you going to bring him to Mountain Springs?"

"It'll be Grant's decision."

"So now what happens?"

"You pack a picnic for tomorrow."

She smiled, realizing what he meant.

That night at the Horton ranch, Grant stuffed himself with apple pie. Reis couldn't move. They had arrived with appetites and now were content and sleepy, as they settled in chairs near the hearth. The fire crackled and spit.

The room, smelling of food and incense and lamp fumes, felt warm as toast against the cold night air that tried to seep through the walls.

Emma Horton fussed over them like a mother hen.

"More coffee, General?"

Grant blew out some air. "Madam, I'm not sure I have any more room."

"You can try."

He smiled at her. "Yes, I can."

She refilled their cups and smiled down at Grant.

"General, you have such soft blue eyes. Just like my late husband. He was a sergeant in the Union army. We came out here to raise horses. I'm sure he'd want you to have your choice of any animal on the premises."

"I'd be glad to pay for any I choose. But of all the horses you have on the place, none can possibly match that buckskin stallion that Matt is riding. I'm still hopeful he'll sell."

"He'll be here tomorrow," she said.

Grant leaned back as she sliced the pie once more.

The next morning, with the sun shining bright, Matt drove a buggy out of Mountain Springs and into the valley. Jennifer sat at his side. She kept her soft blue cape tight over her yellow dress. In the backseat, a picnic basket bounced.

His buckskin stallion trailed. Sheriff Hicks rode ahead of them. They enjoyed the gorgeous day and now a rising, restless wind. The grass had never looked greener.

When they were out of sight of town, Matt turned the black buggy horse west toward the Horton ranch. He hated all these complications. He would rather have been going on a picnic, where he could lie on the green grass and stare up at the blue of the sky with Jennifer fussing over him.

Except that's how a man got into trouble.

When they arrived at the ranch and went inside, they found Grant and Reis sitting on chairs, looking overly stuffed. Jennifer hugged Emma Horton and shook the two men's hands.

Matt and Hicks came inside, both glad to see the general and Reis had safely arrived.

Emma Horton turned to the sheriff and smiled up at him with twinkling eyes. Hicks melted. She easily rattled him.

As they sat around the hearth with coffee, Reis told them about Grant's wild ride through the funnel. Matt enjoyed the dancing lights in Grant's eyes. It felt good to see the general come to life.

Grant smiled as he leaned back. "So what's next, Matt?"

"Do you want to come to Mountain Springs and let the town celebrate?"

Grant frowned. "I want to see your office, but I'm very uncomfortable at public speaking. I've answered the same questions over and over so many times, I don't see how I can go through that again."

"We'll make new rules," Jennifer said. "No questions. No speeches, just a lot of hand-shaking. Music. Dancing."

"And safety?" Reis asked.

"I don't know," she said. "But most of the people in Mountain Springs were for the Union. The few that were not, they want to see money in their pockets. They know if the general comes to town, we may end up with the railroad spur. You'd be putting us on the map. It would be so grand."

Reis looked grim and not ready to agree.

Hicks shrugged. "The Southerners from Silver Gulch are bound to show up."

"But," Grant said, "it is unlikely they would try anything in town."

"Eberley's offered you his house," Matt said. "There will be a reception at Mrs. Frost's, if you agree."

Grant fondled his cup, thoughtful. "If I was to ride into Mountain Springs, I'd sure like to be riding that buckskin."

Grant smiled at Matt, waiting.

Matt stiffened, his face damp.

"Matt," Emma said, impatient. "Will you please sell him the buckskin so we can get on with this? You can have your pick of any other animal on the place."

Matt looked at Grant, his hero, a man he would have followed anywhere. He knew he had been put on the spot.

Worse, it struck his fancy that general should ride into town on the handsome stallion. What a sight that would be for the town.

Before daylight, a small procession headed for Mountain Springs. In the lead on the buckskin stallion, Grant sat erect with a big grin on his face. It was a magnificent sight.

Reis rode a respectful distance behind Grant.

Jennifer drove the buggy with Emma at her side.

Sheriff Hicks rode on one side of the buggy. Matt, astride his new bay gelding, stayed on the other side, his gaze fixed on the buckskin.

Behind them rode a dozen of Emma's ranch hands, all heavily armed.

The sun rose in the east, above the shining mountains.

They entered the nearly empty main street. Taken by surprise, the town didn't suspect until the druggist came running out on the sidewalk.

"It's Grant!"

Windows opened, faces appeared in doorways. Half-dressed men came outside into the cold morning. Everyone shouted and waved.

The procession moved up the street to the courthouse and stopped.

Eberley, who had been opening his law office, came hurrying into the crowd with a big grin. He approached Matt and his party, reached for Grant's hand.

"Welcome, General!"

The mayor, half-dressed, ran around ecstatic and promising a great celebration. The street filled with smiling women and grinning men, all waving and cheering.

Gentry came hobbling up the street. Marshal Brady and Judge Waller came out of the courthouse with big smiles.

Nothing settled down until Grant and Reis reached Eberley's mansion up on the hill. Emma and Jennifer, Matt and Hicks and Gentry, along with Marshal Brady, crowded the parlor. It had been difficult to shut the others out of the house.

Outside, Emma's dozen men were scattered and on duty. One played with Eberley's little black dog.

Inside, Eberley fussed to make everyone comfortable.

Eberley's housekeeper, an elderly woman with a big smile, served fine wine, cider, ham and bread, and hot coffee. Eberley could hardly contain his joy and reassured Reis.

"Matt will be staying here with us for added safety."

"The reception's tonight at Mrs. Frost's," Sheriff Hicks said. "And the town celebration is set for tomorrow. But you've got to know, General, a sniper could be anywhere."

"And the Southerners from Silver Gulch are bound to show," Matt said.

Grant smiled. "My only regret is that we have none of that fine apple pie."

"Except what's in the picnic basket," Jennifer said.

While Grant settled in at Eberley's that afternoon, a rider hurried on his way to Silver Gulch. When he reached Ferman's office, his horse covered with sweat, he could hardly wait to give the news.

Grant had arrived in Mountain Springs.

Ferman and Bittner, alone later, shook their heads in surprise.

"Drat," Bittner said, "this is another phony?"

"No," Ferman replied, convinced. "And you know what's interesting?"

"Yeah, the reception's at Morna's."

"Not so much that," Ferman said. "It's the street celebration the next day. Anything can happen."

That chilly evening, Grant, escorted by Horton men, rode down to the Frost mansion. He dismounted and entered via the front door with Judge Waller and the mayor.

Morna, in a yellow silk gown, beamed. Town dignitaries crowded the well-lit ballroom as a great feast spread in a grand buffet. Wine and champagne and punch glistened on tables.

Ladies looked grand in their finest gowns. Men looked starched and handsome. A few veterans wore their old army uniforms, some a tight fit.

A young redheaded woman played the piano. Two old fiddlers added sweet music.

Reis, wearing his dress uniform as a major, arrived late at the reception. He had spent his time checking the grounds where the Horton men were stationed. He came to the back door of the ballroom.

As he stood just outside in the sweet-smelling garden, he gazed through the open door at the crowd. Grand as he looked in uniform, he would not be comfortable in there.

His gaze scanned the room. There she stood with Grant.

Morna, a golden goddess in a yellow silk dress, her hair up in shining waves. A glittering jeweled necklace graced her throat and spread down to the edge of her low-cut gown.

Reis had never seen such a woman. He fought for his breath.

She had to be the hostess, the way she moved among the others and greeting and smiling like an enchantress. Morna Frost, the widow. He couldn't take his gaze from her.

Fiddlers played a waltz. Reis moved into the doorway. He stared, heart pounding.

She was chatting with Grant, who now led her over to Reis.

"Mrs. Frost, may I present Major Williams?"

She smiled at Grant and turned slowly to look up at Reis.

When she saw him, she caught her breath. Frozen, her color fading and hands twisting her dress lace, she felt like she and Reis were alone, floating in some kind of soft wind.

Her dark-blue eyes held his gaze so long, others stared.

"The major has always been a good friend," Grant said, watching them.

Morna and Reis did not hear him. They only saw each other. They didn't hear others talking nearby and didn't care. They spun in a dreamworld, just the two of them.

Reis held out his hands. She moved toward him.

Grant stared after them and then smiled.

Reis and Morna started dancing without so much as a word. They whirled slowly and gracefully in a waltz, as if they had been dance partners for years. They gazed at each other in wonder, for neither had felt such sudden and strange attraction. Neither spoke.

They had entered another world alone, away from the crowd, floating in some outer space. Magic held them. The magic of sudden love.

Morna forgot to flirt. Transfixed by his soft but dark-brown eyes, she was lost. No longer a coquette, she felt like a princess looking for her knight in shining armor and, finding him so suddenly, it took her breath away.

Reis could not take his gaze from her lovely face. He saw deep, so deep, she flushed. He moved closer. She responded without the practiced seduction, frozen by his gaze and his soft voice.

"Once the general is safe in Denver, I will return."

"Major, you know nothing about me."

Reis didn't care. He only knew what he saw in her face and wide blue eyes. On the battlefield, he had had no one waiting for him. No letters. No woman in his life. He had never thought his nightmares about the war would ever leave him, but with her, he knew it could be set aside once and for all.

"You'll be my wife," he said.

Tears brimmed in her eyes.

They continued dancing, dance after dance, staring at each other in awed silence, ignoring anyone who tried to cut in to their world, sometimes still dancing after the music had stopped.

Meanwhile, Jennifer, wearing a light-blue dress of fine silk and white lace, moved around the guests to take in their comments. Jewels adorned her shining chestnut hair. Her green eyes glistened.

Ralph and the other lawyers enjoyed the reception, as did the judge and every guest.

McComb claimed Jennifer for more than one dance. She smiled up at him as he whirled her about the floor.

"Mr. McComb, I never knew how well you danced."

"That's from the old days, Jennifer."

"From the Old South?"

"Like many who remember, yes."

"What do you think of Grant?"

"A fine gentleman."

"Even though he was not on the same side?"

"Jennifer, I think very highly of him."

"Tell me, Mr. McComb, were you an officer?"

"Are you interviewing me again?"

"Shouldn't I be?"

"Not unless you are asking my intentions, and you know what they are." He smiled, dancing closer. "They're very serious, Jennifer."

"You're very good at changing the subject."

He smiled, leaning his face to a few inches from hers. "You are fascinating."

When the dance was over, the judge appeared and began a conversation with McComb.

Jennifer slipped away and walked to the back door to peer into the colorful garden. Matt came quickly into view. He had been out in the darkness.

"What were you looking at?" she asked.

"Emma's men out there."

"Did you see the major and Morna?"

Matt nodded. "He's done for."

"So is she. They're in some kind of dreamworld."

"Want to walk in the moonlight?"

She flushed, gazing up at him. "It might be cold out there."

"I'd give you my coat."

Jennifer hesitated. "I'm not sure I want to be alone with you."

"Why not?"

"Because you're far too attractive."

"So we're both in danger."

"From the first time I saw you. You came walking in like a little rooster. You were so lovable, I wanted to pet you."

Matt grinned. "You can do that now, if you like."

"You forget our agreement. To be friends."

"That's right. Neither one of us wants to marry."

"I'm holding out just fine."

"So am I."

Eberley came walking from the crowd to join them. "How about a walk in the garden? It's stuffy in here, and too much smoke."

Matt and Jennifer, unhappy to break their teasing argument, accommodated Eberley. The three walked into the lush garden where red and white caught the moonlight as it came and went between clouds.

They had hardly ventured into the night when Ralph came charging after them.

"Jennifer, this is our dance, remember?"

"Of course, I remember. We just wanted some air."

Ralph took one of her arms. Matt took the other. Eberley, amused, followed them back from the cold night. Inside, Ralph spun Jennifer into a dance.

Matt turned to see Grant, in the doorway, gazing out at the garden. Matt hurried over to him.

"General, the light's right behind you."

Matt marched Grant back out of the exposure. Grant had to laugh at him. "You haven't changed, Matt. Always looking after me."

"I think you have to dance with Mrs. Frost."

"That will be a pleasure," Grant said.

"If you can get her away from the major."

"He's a lonely man, Matt. I hope this turns into something good."

The mayor's wife came to lead Grant over to other dignitaries. Grant, surrounded, looked uncomfortable.

Matt, jealous, watched Ralph swing Jennifer around the dance floor.

Eberley came over to Matt.

"If you don't act pretty soon, you could lose her."

"She doesn't want to marry. Neither do I."

Eberley laughed. "You don't know much about women, I can see that."

"What I know, I learned the hard way," Matt said.

Matt couldn't stop watching Jennifer, who had the next dance with Grant.

Reis and Morna had stopped long enough for Reis to go for punch.

Matt walked over to Morna, who had taken a seat near the garden door. When she saw him, she smiled.

She seemed so different to him. He studied her with new admiration.

"Matt, I'm so glad to see you."

"I saw you dancing with Major Williams."

"Yes," she said softly. "Do you know very much about him?"

"He's a good man."

"Would I be bad for him?"

"From what I see in your face right now? No."

"Thank you, Matt."

"In fact, it's what I don't see that matters."

She smiled her thanks.

Matt studied her a long moment. What he had to say might upset her, but maybe it would open the way for her life with the major. Free her from Red Ferman.

He spoke in a low voice.

"I guess you know that Ferman and Bittner plan to murder the general."

Sobering, she stared up at him. "Matt, I hope you're wrong."

"Maybe tomorrow, at the celebration."

Morna, distressed, couldn't respond.

Morna stood as Reis returned with the punch. Matt, ignored, watched them leave to walk in the garden.

Maybe Matt didn't understand women, but he felt genuine joy for Morna. Her transformation, a miracle in itself, came from instant love.

Matt reflected on how he had felt when he had first met Jennifer: overwhelmed.

When Matt danced again with Jennifer, he told her what he had said to Morna about the conspiracy, and how Red Ferman could be involved.

"Why did you do that, Matt?"

"Because I want her to tell Ferman."

CHAPTER 32

THE RECEPTION FOR GENERAL GRANT ended at the Frost mansion late in the night.

Grant, escorted by hands from the Horton ranch, walked off through the garden to the horses at the Frost corrals.

Matt turned to see Jennifer, alone, way over in the sweet-smelling red roses. He walked to her side, then glanced over his shoulder to be sure that no one noticed them.

He put his hand on her arm.

She turned slowly, gazing up at him with her green eyes glistening. He put his right fingers at her left cheek, stroking the soft skin. He touched her chestnut hair so firmly held back with a ribbon.

"Someday, I want to untie that," he said.

"As a friend?"

"As a friendly gesture."

Lips parted, she faced him slowly. "Matt, someone will see us."

"See us what?"

He bent his head. Their lips met with warm passion. She moved into his arms, clinging to him, her hands at his back. He held her tight.

Still against him, she rested her face on his shoulder. He stroked her hair, and they stood wrapped together in a long silence.

Then finally, she moved free of him. She wrapped her arms about herself, gazing at him with affection. "As friends?" she asked.

Matt nodded and swallowed hard.

A man called to them. "There you are."

They saw Ralph, hurrying over to them with a frown.

Long after midnight when the Frost mansion stood empty except for Morna, Red Ferman came slipping into a back door. It had been left open. He found Morna seated at the table in the parlor, fully dressed, framed in the lamplight.

The night air smelled of sweet scents from the garden, through the open front door.

She had been expecting him but not with romance in mind.

"Hello, Red."

He tried to approach her but she rose and moved around the table.

Red frowned. "I wasn't invited to the reception."

"I didn't have anything to do with the guest list."

He could see she was upset. "Morna, what's going on?"

"You can meet Grant tomorrow. There'll be a barbecue and music. The celebration's taking place in front of the courthouse at noon. We're hoping it will bring enough attention to get us that railroad spur."

"Yeah, so?"

He moved around the table, but she kept pace, away from him.

She spoke calmly. "Matt Tyler told me something I can't quite believe."

"What was that?"

"That you and Bittner are trying to assassinate Grant."

Ferman drew himself up. "He's lying."

"Red, there were two sides to the War between the States, but I don't want anything to happen to Grant. He was a hero to me and my family."

"I told you, I admired Grant."

"Promise me nothing will happen to him."

"If it does, I will have no part of it."

Morna did not believe him. Not for a minute.

"Thank you, Red. And now please leave."

"No, I have to get your head straight."

"It is, for the first time," she said.

"I've waited too long for this. We're going upstairs, right now."

"If someone finds out, they'll know you shot Jared."

He caught up with her, gripped her arms, causing her pain.

He snarled. "Not unless you tell them. And I'm tired of waiting. Come on."

"Not until Grant is safe."

"To heck with Grant. Get up those stairs."

"No, Red. Never again."

She tried to get free. He slapped her hard across the right cheek. She went spinning in a whirl of skirts, crashing against the wall with a gasp.

He rushed over and grabbed her arm before she fell. He threw her against the wall again. Morna, breath knocked out of her, winced in fear.

He had never struck her until now.

"Listen to me, Morna. The only reason you're still alive is because of me. Everybody else wanted you dead to shut you up. And I ain't forgot you could get me hanged for killing your old man. Now make it worth my while."

Morna shivered, staggered away from him. He grabbed her arm.

"Go on upstairs," Ferman said, shaking her.

"No, Red. We're finished. For good."

"Why, you little—"

A man's grim, quiet voice startled them.

"Pardon me."

Ferman spun around, his hand on his holster.

Walking in from the garden through the open door, Reis Williams, still in uniform, had his hat in hand. "I beg your pardon, Mrs. Frost, but I forgot my tobacco pouch."

Ferman grimaced so hard, his face turned dark as he snarled.

"Get out of here, Mister."

"Major Williams is my guest," Morna said, catching her breath.

Ferman glared at her, then at Reis. He didn't want anyone to know the truth about Frost's death, nor did he want shots fired with Grant just up the hill.

He let her go and backed away. "We'll finish this later."

"No, we won't," she said, catching her breath.

Ferman glared at Reis. Fury red in his face, he turned and stormed to the back door, exiting and slamming it behind him.

Morna hurried over to lock it.

She clasped a hand to her breast as she tried to recover.

She slowly turned. "Major, you don't smoke."

He smiled, held out his hand. She put her cold hand in his warm grasp.

He led her to a chair, where she settled down, so weak she feared she would faint. She gazed up at him as her face turned from white to pink. Her dark-blue eyes brimmed.

"Are you hurt?" he asked.

She shook her head, almost afraid to ask. "You heard?"

"I heard your loyalty to Grant."

"Red's been lying to me."

"Can you secure all doors so he can't get in?"

"Yes."

"I'll send a man to watch the garden."

"You're very kind."

"I told you, I want to marry you. I raise horses in Kentucky. Have you ever stood in a field of bluegrass?"

"Major, you're making a mistake."

"I want children. I was hoping you would also."

She stared at him. "After all you heard?"

"Especially after what I heard."

"Red Ferman will kill you."

"It would be worth it."

She wiped her eyes with the back of her hand.

She managed a smile he would treasure all of his life.

"I'm glad," she whispered. "And yes, I want children. With you."

She stood up slowly. They gazed at each other with longing.

Lamplights flickered. The room, its furniture, the whole world around them, no longer existed. Their dreamworld encircled them. Floating. Misty. Warm.

She took a step toward him. He held out his arms.

With a deep breath, she took another step.

He slowly drew her into his warm embrace. His arms, strong and protective, held her against him like holding a child. No, like holding a dream, a wish.

Her lips, soft like rose petals, parted.

He bent his head, hesitant, almost afraid.

Then his lips pressed to her soft ones. For just a moment.

In near collapse from the joy of it, they held tight with her face to his chest.

Morna felt the years tumble back in time.

A young girl again, ready to start anew, she knew that her prayers of thanks would be endless this night.

Reis, a lonely man all his life, could hardly believe his good fortune.

When he drew back, his eyes wet, he kissed her cheek.

At noon the next day with the sun bright, the whole town of Mountain Springs turned out with picnic tables in rows along the main street. Flags and banners waved from every pole and roof. Three elderly fiddlers played and tapped their feet on a hastily constructed bandstand. It lay centered in the street, halfway between the courthouse and the jail.

Grant rode proud on the buckskin stallion with its black mane and tail.

Grant's escort, all Horton men, led him to the celebration.

Cheers burst from the crowd.

Down the street to the west, some hundred or more Southerners reined up behind the gambling hall and saloons. Well armed but silent, they left their horses and spread out among the buildings to work their way unnoticed into the celebration. Most were unkempt miners in contrast to the dressed-up citizens of Mountain Springs.

One large group, older and more settled, gathered around Hennesy, who had led them into many a battle during the war. They trusted him.

Burly, clean-shaven with big hands, Hennesy honored that trust.

"So what do we do?" a short man asked Hennesy.

"Nothing." Hennesy frowned, his mouth bone dry. "It took me all these years to get myself together. Same as you. We've worked too hard to throw it all away."

"What if some Yank starts trouble with us?"

"Defend yourselves. With your fists."

The short man grinned. "That would be a pleasure."

"No weapons," Hennesy said.

"We won't need 'em," a hefty bearded miner said.

Up the street where Grant stood as the center of attention, a noisy crowd cheered him.

At Jennifer's insistence, no one could question Grant.

The only speeches were from the mayor and some veterans of the war, all praising the Union, Lincoln, and Grant.

Jennifer squirmed as she listened, afraid of offending the Southerners.

"And we have with us," the mayor said, "General and former president of this United States, Ulysses Simpson Grant. He honors us with this visit."

The townspeople cheered.

Hennesy's group lounged back down the street. The other Southerners began to appear around the courthouse, mixing with the townspeople, who didn't notice them at first.

Near the crowd around Grant, Morna moved about in a dark cape over her yellow silk dress. She had never been so happy. Her blue eyes shone like a mountain lake in the sun. Whenever she caught Reis's glance, she beamed and blossomed. She dared to believe her life could change overnight because of this wonderful man.

Matt nervously moved among the crowd. He could not let anything happen to Grant in the middle of the celebration. He would have eternal guilt because he had helped to bring Grant here. He watched everyone's moves, listened well, and kept his hand on his holster.

"A great day," said Moose, poking Matt as he headed over to join Grizzly.

Marshal Brady, Sheriff Hicks, and Deputy Lacey, ever alert, moved about.

Gentry, keeping back from the crowd, had his Winchester, his mouth dry as his gaze scanned the crowd. He saw Emma's men on the fringes, watching.

A young blond girl stood on the bandstand, singing the "Star-Spangled Banner."

Boys played with fire, even as their mothers chased them furiously.

A woman recited excerpts from the *Rime of the Ancient Mariner.* Another sang of the gold rush in the "Dreary Black Hills." The fiddlers continued to play tunes acceptable to any political view.

Some couples danced and whirled about the platform.

Matt gazed around at the busy tables, set with food and punch. Cakes and pies and cookies, gobbled up as fast as refilled, lined a center table.

The fiddles played neutral songs at Jennifer's direction. She had managed to arrange one for Matt, a lively, traditional tune sung by one of the old fiddlers.

"Well, come along boys and listen to my tale,

I'll tell you my troubles on the old Chisholm Trail—"

Matt found himself grinning and humming along with the song, but his gaze watched the faces in the crowd. He saw Ferman and Bittner way off on the boardwalk beyond the courthouse with Mrs. Ledbetter.

He turned to gaze at the bandstand as the last verse was sung.

"With my feet in the stirrup and my seat in the sky,

I'll quit punchin' cows in the sweet bye and bye."

The crowd roared their approval even as the chorus ended.

Now another woman, gray but lovely, stood up there, singing the traditional "Barbara Allen" in a sweet soprano.

"In Scarlet town, where I was born,

There was a fair maid dwellin'—"

The singer followed with "Green Grow the Lilacs." With each love song, there was cheering. The fiddlers paused for punch. Noise filled the air.

Matt looked around for Jennifer. He didn't see her, but he saw Grant well surrounded by the Horton men, Reis, and the lawmen. The general stood near the bandstand, enjoying every minute of the entertainment.

The fiddlers, alone on the stand, began to play the "Battle Hymn of the Republic."

Matt stiffened, even as most of the townspeople began to sing, voices loud and in unison.

"Mine eyes have seen the glory of the coming of the Lord..."

While Matt headed for the bandstand to stop the music, Jennifer hurriedly pushed her way through the crowd with the same intention.

The Southerners, stirred up in a hurry, looked angry.

Standing near the courthouse with Mrs. Ledbetter, Ferman and Bittner listened to the song. She held a basket of bread and looked surprised.

"I heard Jennifer tell them not to play anything to start a riot."

"All three fiddlers are from Georgia," Ferman said. "We have our men spread all around, just waiting for the next song. The town will explode."

"I want him dead just as much as you," Mrs. Ledbetter said, "but I thought a sniper would do it. Why take chances now? A lot of us could get hurt."

"That's the idea," Bittner said. "When there's a big fight going on, we finish Grant."

Ferman tugged at his hat brim. "We can't keep the colonel waiting."

They moved to the edge of the crowd. Ferman nodded to the Southerners who were furious at the song being played. The Yanks continued to sing.

"I have seen Him in the watch fires of a hundred circling camps—"

But suddenly, with Jennifer shouting at them, the fiddlers switched to "Turkey in the Straw," "Buffalo Gals," and other lively tunes.

Things seemed to calm down for a while.

Matt joined Jennifer near Gentry, but he remained nervous. That song had stirred up the Southerners for certain.

The street filled with dancing and shouting and singing. Grant, well guarded by Horton men and the lawmen, stood deep in the middle of the activities, feasting on barbecued beef, downing lemonade, and enjoying the attention.

Everyone in town had to come and speak to Grant—farmers, ranchers, cowboys, merchants, and their families. At least two thousand people crowded the street, not including the watching Southerners.

True to Jennifer's promise, no one questioned Grant. They were just glad to see him, and he was having the time of his life. Reis stood around with Grant, watching every nearby movement anxiously. Morna took their arms and stood between then with a happy smile.

Sheriff Hicks made his patrols with Lacey. Gentry remained watchful.

Marshal Brady moved about and paused by Matt, who spoke quietly.

"I saw Ferman and Bittner a moment ago."

Brady nodded. "I wonder where they are now."

"I don't know," Matt said, "but half of Silver Gulch is out there circling the crowd right now. A lot of mean faces out there."

"There's Mrs. Ledbetter. She may be our only chance to learn the truth with Lucifer gone."

All of a sudden, the fiddlers began to play "Dixie."

Brady stiffened. "Stop it."

"So that's their plan," Matt said, his hand on his holster.

The crowd reacted. Roughhewn Southerners began moving in from the fringes, singing loudly.

"In Dixieland, I'll take my stand, to live and die in Dixie—"

Men began to shove one another.

Yanks shouted at the Southerners to shut up. Some tried to pull the fiddlers off the makeshift stand. The music stopped. The fiddlers jumped off the back and fought their way out of the crowd.

Women from both sides tried to calm everyone down.

The struggle expanded. Men hit one another. One man dived into another's gut, and they went rolling. Others started kicking and shoving.

Now the entire street erupted into a brawl that surrounded the guest of honor. Hundreds pushed, yelled, and kicked, fists flying.

Confusion reigned as some attacked their own side by mistake.

Soon, no one cared who he pounded.

Moose picked up a miner and tossed him into the watering trough with a splash. Grizzly grabbed the burly blacksmith, struggled, pounded him, then sent him skidding across a table of food, carrying it with him into a group of women who scattered.

Another miner jumped on the tables and shouted and waved his fists. A woman swatted his legs with her parasol. Another woman threw a pie at him. He skidded around and sailed off the table, landing on his rear as another man attacked him.

"Look out," Grizzly shouted, too late.

An iron frypan landed on Moose's head, a woman clinging to the handle. Moose staggered, his eyes rolled. He recovered. The woman looked up at him, hands on hips.

"Stop this foolishness."

"Yes, ma'am."

She suddenly smiled. "My, you're a big one."

"Yes, ma'am."

Moose hurried away from her.

A Southerner and a big Yank crashed against the barbecue spit, throwing half the beef into the dirt, both men landing on top of it and the hot coals.

Women from both sides shrieked at the men to stop. One hit a man with her shoe. Children ran to hide and watch, so excited they giggled.

Men getting dirty, drenched with sweat, panted for breath.

The more they fought, the less they cared who they hit.

"It's a ruse," Reis said, moving in front of Grant.

Morna quickly threw her arms around Grant from behind and shoved him against Reis, just as a bullet from another direction sliced down across her back at her left shoulder blade.

She cried out. Reis fired over the crowd, scattering it.

Reis grabbed Morna as she collapsed, and he lifted her in his arms. He handed her quickly to a Horton man, who ran for the boardwalk on the north side.

Matt and Hicks joined Marshal Brady and Reis to surround Grant with the help of Horton men.

Gentry saw Carruth cocking his Winchester on the courthouse roof and aiming for another shot. Gentry drew his army Colt and fired.

The slave enforcer jerked crazily, then came rolling off the roof like a sack of flour, crashing into the alley in a heap. Carruth rolled over, dead.

Gentry's mouth twisted into a grim victory.

"That's justice," he said.

But the noisy brawl exploded even more.

Mrs. Ledbetter, jostled about in the crowd, neared Grant and his protectors. She reached under the bread in her basket and drew a Colt revolver, pulling back the hammer as she dropped the basket. She held it both hands and aimed.

A frantic Emma Horton knocked it out of her hands and shoved her to the ground, then pounced on her. The two women rolled in the dirt, struggling for control. Two merchants came to help and separate them.

Emma got to her feet, shaken.

"He killed my husband," Mrs. Ledbetter, still on the ground, sobbed.

The riot continued as people scattered. Men crashing against posts brought down an overhanging roof onto the boardwalk. The noise rattled in the air.

"Get to the jail," Reis said.

Hicks and Lacey, surrounded by Horton ranch hands, marshaled the protesting Grant over to the sheriff's office and barricaded themselves inside.

The brawling crowd ignored anything but this chance to vent their fury.

Men smashed one another, yet neither side used a gun, club or knife. They fought with their hands and feet and teeth, taking great pleasure in hand-to-hand combat.

Soon Yanks hit Yanks, and Southerners fought among themselves as if it was suddenly sport. Some were being thrown into windows, crashing inside the stores.

Pop stood guard outside his restaurant with a shotgun. After a while, he couldn't stand it. He set the shotgun inside and charged into the Southerners with a yell.

Matt and his friends tried to maintain order, but nothing could stop the fighting as hundreds of men scrambled to best one another.

No weapons were pulled. It no longer represented the war. Just men having a great old time.

Watching safely from the boardwalk in front of the café, Ferman and Bittner looked furious.

"Where'd Grant go?" Bittner demanded.

"I don't know. But they shot Carruth. And they took Mrs. Ledbetter. The colonel's going to have a fit."

Bittner nodded. "Let's get out of here."

Matt came out of the brawling crowd.

He saw Ferman and Bittner on the boardwalk. He came over to them with his face dark, his hands at his sides.

"This is your doing, Ferman."

Red Ferman pushed his hat back. "Prove it."

Ferman and Bittner went inside the café.

Up the street near the courthouse, the fighting spread in all directions and spilled into the alleys. Matt turned to watch as he shook his head in dismay. People didn't care who they were hitting.

At the same time, Jennifer had slipped behind the buildings, terrified it would expand to her office and the prized Washington Press. She made it back to her building and discovered the front door unlocked. She hesitated, then decided she had just forgotten in the excitement.

She remembered the Winchester rifle behind her desk. She didn't have her handbag with the revolver with her because of the celebration.

Once inside, she stared out the window, up the street at the brawl, with tears brimming. A terrible way to greet Grant. She wiped at her eyes.

"I've been waiting," a man said from behind her.

She spun around in terror and saw Raddigan.

He came from behind the rail with that sleazy smile.

She fell back against the window, horrified.

He came so close, she could smell his tobacco breath.

She inched closer to the door, her heart in her throat and face burning.

"What do you want?" she whispered.

"You, of course."

"You touch me, and Matt will kill you."

"That's what I'm counting on."

Realizing his plan, she flattened against the wall, trying to take back her words, her heart racing.

"Matt will never draw on you."

"He'll draw when I'm finished with you."

She inched toward the door a little farther.

He leaned the Winchester on the wall as he crowded her. Her heart rose to her throat. The evil in his nearly white eyes seared her flesh. His mouth curled into a hungry smile.

"First, we're going to have a little fun."

"Get away from me."

He grabbed her by the arms and jerked her against him, his mouth covering hers in a harsh mauling. She bit his lip. He drew back, slapping her. Her head snapped back, leaving her dazed.

He pulled her up against him. Terrified, she gasped for breath.

She struggled. His mouth covered hers as he pawed her. Strong and overpowering, he had her crushed and nearly helpless. No one would hear her scream.

Raddigan sneered, holding her with her arms pinned down.

He kissed her hard, grabbed her collar, tore it open, and bared her right shoulder. She gasped and hit at him. He tore the other half of her blouse at the left shoulder, until the lace top of her bodice was exposed.

She clawed at Raddigan's face. He slapped her so hard, her head jerked back. She was dazed and about to fall. He grabbed her brutally by the arms, keeping her against the wall.

"We'll finish this out of town."

"Why are you doing this?" she gasped.

"Let's just say certain men want Tyler dead because he saved Grant's life."

He dragged her out the door and onto the boardwalk, his hand in her hair. She swayed and fought and kicked. He slammed her against a buggy, startling the horse.

Up the street and unaware of her plight, Matt turned from the boardwalk in front of the café. He shook his head at the brawl as it expanded, breaking windows, scattering horses.

Weary men on both sides could hardly stand, as they fought for breath and continued to beat one another, faces and noses bloody. Yet no one pulled a weapon.

Matt backed away as Bittner and Ferman came out of the café, not having been served, as Pop had dived into the brawl long ago.

Bittner sneered. "Raddigan's looking for you, Tyler. He has something you want."

"Which is?"

"Witherspoon's gold watch."

Matt's eyes narrowed. "And where is he?"

"Just down the street."

Matt rested his hand on his revolver. Slowly, he turned his head and looked west along the cluttered street, down to the newspaper office.

Matt froze.

Raddigan and Jennifer, her dress torn from her shoulders, stood in front of the newspaper office, still fighting.

Raddigan struck her hard on the jaw.

She collapsed like a rag doll. He tossed her inside the backseat of the buggy as the horse in harness jerked its head and nervously moved about at the end of the tether.

Matt Tyler had never known such fury as crawled through him at this moment.

"Go get him, Tyler," said Ferman.

Matt stayed on the boardwalk, moving toward Raddigan, knowing this is what Ferman wanted. Hot as Matt was, he yet iced over down to his boots.

Raddigan, a cold-blooded killer, would be faster.

Matt had no choice but to move toward him.

Jennifer lay crumpled in the back of the buggy, hurt and struggling to sit up, her hands on the sideboards as the horse continued to shuffle about.

Raddigan, sneering with delight, moved to the middle of the street.

Matt walked slowly on the south side, still on the boardwalk.

Raddigan looked calm as death, white eyes gleaming under heavy brows.

Matt paused on the boardwalk.

They were sixty feet apart, out of reliable range.

Raddigan moved to cut the distance.

Matt knew Ferman and Bittner were behind him, waiting for the kill.

Matt couldn't watch all three. He stood a long moment, his breath so short, it hurt, his heart thumping faster by the second.

The brawl, back up the street and behind him, sounded broken and dissipating.

Matt grimaced. He knew Morna had been hit, and Grant had been rushed to the jail. The assassin and former slave enforcer, Carruth, lay dead, shot from a roof by Gentry, but all other information escaped in the whirl of the riot.

Matt moved by a buggy and a nervous black gelding, then past a sorrel mare tossing its head with its ears back. Farther along, several geldings pawed the dirt.

Matt moved to the edge of the boardwalk when he passed the geldings.

His right hand hung near his holster.

Sweating but cold, he knew he could die any moment.

He had to take Raddigan with him. He had to save Jennifer.

Raddigan, in the middle of the street, stopped within range. His face calm, his hands loose at his sides, his confidence radiated.

They were out of earshot of all but Jennifer.

"Miss White is going with me," Raddigan said.

"Not a chance."

"You think you can stop me?"

"I can try," Matt said.

"You're going to die just like Little and Witherspoon."

"Is this a confession?"

Raddigan smiled. "For your ears only. Because I want you to know you're going to die the same way. I'm going to get you right between the eyes."

"Drop your gun belt."

"I'm going to kill you, Tyler."

"You got a reason?"

"A lot of money."

"Who paid you?"

Raddigan worked his fingers. "Ferman and Bittner."

"What about Mrs. Ledbetter?"

"She was in it, all the way. So were Frost and Hancock."

Raddigan figured Matt would not live to tell it. Matt knew he could be right.

"And the colonel?"

Raddigan snickered. "That you have to figure out for yourself."

"Who shot Frost?"

"Red Ferman, and that's all you need to know."

Matt, his whole body stiff as a board, knew he had to loosen up, had to be able to move, to draw his sidearm, to somehow stay alive with Raddigan's confession. Sweat all over his body, drenching his clothes, he felt hot all over.

He saw Jennifer trying to rise up in the buggy.

Matt prayed she would just get out of there, but she collapsed out of sight.

Raddigan, his back to her, concentrated on Matt.

"You'd better draw and defend yourself," Raddigan sneered.

Raddigan's pale eyes gleamed like ice, sunlight dancing on the silver conches of his hatband.

Matt wet his lips, his mouth and throat dry as bone. He moved slowly into the street to be sure that Jennifer would not be in his line of fire. Sweat tricked down his neck.

Suddenly, Raddigan went for his gun.

Matt drew and jumped aside as he fired.

Raddigan missed as Matt hit the dirt, fanned the hammer, and fired again.

Still on his feet but shot, Raddigan spun away.

Matt rolled and quickly rose on one knee.

Raddigan charged him like a wild man and fired again, even as Matt pulled the trigger.

Raddigan's bullet struck Matt on the left side of his forehead, stunning him as he rolled aside.

CHAPTER 33

As the riot in Mountain Springs dissipated up the street, with Grant sequestered in the jail, Ferman and Bittner waited in front of the café, hoping for Matt to die.

Down the street, Raddigan and Matt continued to try to kill each other.

Dazed, with his head bleeding as he lay in the dirt, Matt fired again.

His last bullet hit Raddigan square between the eyes.

The startled gunman staggered forward with his mouth wide open, firing into the dirt as he dropped to his knees.

A bullet whistled past Matt's head. It came from behind him.

Matt rolled over, his vision blurred by his sudden movement. He could make out Bittner running toward him with weapon drawn and firing.

Ferman, a distance behind Bittner, began dragging his feet.

Bittner kept coming toward Matt, his bullet spitting the dirt as Matt rolled away.

Matt squinted, desperate to keep his vision in a wave of darkness. He rolled over again.

He could make out Bittner's portly shape.

"Blast you, Tyler."

Matt fired. He saw the shadowy figure stagger to a halt, then spin crazily around. When Bittner dropped to his knees, Matt rolled on his side as he slowly lost consciousness.

As he faded away, Matt thought of Jennifer.

Bittner, dying and still on his knees, went pale as blood streamed down his neck. He crashed facedown into the dirt, jerking about and then lying still in his own blood.

Hicks came running, Gentry hobbling behind him. They had the drop on Ferman, who stopped at Hicks's command.

Jennifer managed to climb out of the wagon and stagger forward. She hurt from Raddigan's beating, but nothing mattered except Matt.

Moving to where Matt lay unconscious in the dirt, she dropped beside him and grasped his shoulder. Tears dribbled down her hot, bruised face.

Just up the street, Gentry and Hicks had their guns on Ferman, who slowly dropped his gun belt. Marshal Brady joined them with cuffs ready.

Hicks steamed. "That's attempted murder, Ferman. And a conspiracy. And maybe you killed Frost."

"He did," Jennifer said, looking up. "I heard Raddigan tell everything."

Ferman glanced over at the prone Matt, hoping the lawyer had died. The man who had saved Grant had no right to live. Ferman felt great satisfaction.

Ferman turned to sneer at Hicks and Brady. "You can't prove anything."

Brady gestured. "We'll see which of you turns state's evidence first. You or Mrs. Ledbetter."

Hicks handcuffed the furious Ferman. Gentry and Brady marched the prisoner up the street.

Hicks hurried past the dead Bittner to Matt's side where Jennifer held him.

After Matt's fight with Raddigan, the town settled down in the bright sun.

The Southerners, seeing Bittner and Carruth dead, and Ferman arrested, decided to fight another day and dispersed. With them, they were taking something they had not expected, a feeling of peace for the first time since the War between the States.

They felt somehow vindicated and were not thinking of Grant, only of the men they had now fought hand to hand.

Both sides, however, suffered pounded guts, fractured jaws and ribs, broken teeth, and torn ears. The miracle had been the lack of gunfire and knives. Every one of them had pride in that fact. Sweaty and torn and bruised, they grinned, all spent.

The town women remained furious, the children excited.

Hennesy wiped his bloody face with a big hand as he spit out a tooth. He turned to growl at Moose, who was getting to his knees and trying to fish a tooth from his own mouth.

"You hit me when I wasn't looking," Moose said.

"That was the idea."

"Yeah, well, next time, we'll do a little bare-knuckle fighting under the rules, and we'll see how you come out of it."

"You're on," Hennesy said.

"Next Saturday, noon, in front of the Red Light."

"You'd better rest up, Yank."

"We need a couple more fighters. Makes for better bets."

Hennesy grinned, holding his jaw. "I got some mean ones."

"Not the sissies I saw today."

"We got grizzlies down in the mines."

"Chain 'em good."

"Hey, Hennesy," one of his men called to him. "We ain't had no grub."

Hennesy spit out another tooth, as Moose gestured up the street.

They could see the women fussing over the tables of food and drink.

"My treat," Moose said, "but watch out for the women. They're real mad at all of us."

With the weary men from Silver Gulch stuffing themselves with the townspeople, and all of them repairing their aches and pains, the celebration struggled to continue but with more enthusiasm.

Ferman and Mrs. Ledbetter remained in custody at the jail.

The undertaker had Raddigan, Bittner, and Carruth.

The fiddlers had disappeared. Young Henry picked up his own fiddle and played as best he could. The frustrated women still scolded the men from both sides as they tried to keep the food on the tables.

Reis stayed with Morna at the elderly doctor's office.

Jennifer, wearing a different jacket, salve on her face and left hand bandaged, fussed over the unconscious Matt on another table. Worried, she could do nothing but hold his hand.

Morna, already bandaged, smiled up at Reis. "You're missing the party."

Reis smiled affectionately. "You saved Grant's life."

"Doctor," Morna said, "I want to go to the celebration."

"You must be in pain," the doctor said.

"I never felt better in my life."

The doctor grunted. "Well, the bullet bounced off the bone, so you'll be all right. I'd take it real easy." He looked at Reis, then her. "And try to stay off your feet."

"No problem, Doc," Reis said. He lifted Morna, blankets and all, into his arms. "I'm going to take good care of her from now on."

Morna settled in his embrace and gazed up at him as her new life began to surround and caress her. She would pray with thanks the rest of her life.

Reis carried her out to the street and down to where the party continued without the music. He set her down on a bench in front of the law firm's office, then sat beside her, her hand in his. Like youngsters, they cozied to each other, his arm around her.

"I feel blessed, Morna."

She rested her head against him. "So do I, Reis."

Her prayers had been answered. She would give thanks by being a good wife to the major and giving him wonderful children.

The crowd rocked full of battered men on both sides, but they all cheered as Grant came back, the Horton men escorting him. To their joy, Grant had decided to make a short speech and stood on the bandstand, surrounded by Marshal Brady, Horton men, and Sheriff Hicks.

The crowd fell silent as Grant spoke clearly.

"God has blessed me twice. Matt Tyler saved my life at Pittsburgh Landing. Mrs. Frost saved me again today. And I find a spirit in this town that I shall never forget. I also saw good men on both sides fighting with their hands instead of their weapons, and I saw no malice when it stopped. With God's blessing, maybe the war is finally over."

Loudly cheered, he came down from the bandstand with Brady and Hicks on his heels. The Horton men closed in for protection.

Emma came to take Hicks's arm, her smile rosy.

"So then, Willoughby, it seems it's all over and done with."

He grinned down at her. "You'd better start calling me Will, I mean in case we ever, you know..."

She smiled as she took his arm. "Yes, Will."

"Wait," he said. "Does that mean a yes?"

"Willoughby, it's always been yes."

Hicks had a silly look on his face as his knees caved.

As the happy crowd milled in the streets below, Matt's life appeared to hang by a thread.

Up in the doctor's office, Matt, fully clothed with his head bandaged, lay unconscious, while Jennifer watched over him. Tears trickled down her face, as the doctor shook his head.

"Not much of a wound, but I've seen these things in the war. Some never woke up."

"Can't you do anything?"

"Sorry. Call me if there's any change. I want to see Grant."

The doctor left, closing the door behind him.

She pulled up a chair next to the table.

She rested her right hand on Matt's. He lay still but breathing steadily. She bowed her head and whispered a prayer. She wiped away her tears.

She looked up as Ralph Smythe came charging inside, hat in hand, his round face pink. He paused in dismay as he saw the way she hovered over Matt.

"Is he dead?"

"No."

"Are you all right?"

"I will be. What's going on out there?"

"Blanket federal immunity came through for Lucifer, so the judge has transferred it to Mrs. Ledbetter. She says Ferman killed my brother."

"I'm so sorry."

"She's already naming names, including McComb, who apparently planned the whole operation, except they can't find him now."

"McComb was the colonel?"

"Sure was. Mrs. Ledbetter's spilling everything."

"But McComb is a lawyer."

Ralph nodded. "So were Hancock and Frost."

"But McComb wanted to be governor. I mean, he was really sincere."

"Apparently that's not all he was sincere about. Except he made sure he never dirtied his own hands."

Jennifer felt sad. "I'm sorry to hear it."

"Mrs. Ledbetter will also be testifying how Crazy Albert did their bidding. Choper was killed just to scare you off. And she's also going to give evidence about the claims Ferman was jumping, and how he not only falsified evidence but had some witnesses murdered."

"And the land grant?"

"Ferman obtained it by fraud, all right. She's going to blow it all wide open."

"But she's just as guilty."

"She has full immunity. Besides, she was sick and driven by unresolved grief, not pure revenge like the others. She needs help, not prison."

"What about the men and that woman at Irwin?"

"She doesn't know, except about Shockley over in South Arkansas. There's a warrant out for him."

"And the men from Silver Gulch?"

"Carruth is dead. So are Raddigan and Bittner. The judge isn't worried about the rest. He figures the war is over once and for all, and he wants to keep it that way. He just wants Ferman."

"So it's peace at last."

"Yes, so why don't you come along to the celebration?"

"I have to stay with Matt."

"He may never wake up. Look at him."

"I'm not leaving."

Ralph frowned at her. "What about me? I stood aside for my brother, but I won't stand aside for Matt Tyler."

"I'm sorry, Ralph. I'm in love with Matt."

"He's a reckless fool. You're out of your mind."

"Maybe I am," she said, "but I fell for him on first sight. He was so cocky and lovable."

"That's woman's talk."

"But, Ralph, I am a woman."

"You don't have to tell me that."

"Before I came to Colorado, I was in love with a man who turned tail when my father was in trouble. Maybe he couldn't have saved my father's life, but he didn't even try. I thought I'd never meet anyone I could trust, ever again. But now I trust Matt Tyler with my life."

He spun around and left, slamming the door behind him so hard the wall shook and the windows rattled.

Jennifer stared at the closed door, sniffing back her tears. She had liked both Ralph and his brother, but neither one had made her heart sing. Only one man had made her forget the press and her crusades.

She leaned forward and put her head down on the bed while still holding Matt's left hand. All of a sudden, she felt fingers on her hair. Before she could raise her head, the ribbon had been untied. Matt's right hand spread her thick, chestnut hair about her face.

She looked up and saw him gazing at her with a dazed smile. Excited, she straightened, her heart dancing.

"Oh, Matt, can you see me?"

He nodded, still dazed.

She stood up and leaned over to kiss him while his fingers worked her hair. He kissed her back and held her down across his chest with both hands, even as he winced in pain. But he smiled as she drew back.

"I am lovable, aren't I?" he asked.

She flushed. "You were listening."

"I liked what I heard."

Before she could answer, they were interrupted by a hard voice from the now open door.

"Matt Tyler."

Matt turned his head slowly to see McComb, wearing a dark suit and hat, standing in the doorway. Matt tried to rise, but failed.

McComb had a strange look on his face, his deep-set eyes dark and gleaming. He had a revolver in his right hand. He looked fierce.

Jennifer straightened, her heart racing.

Matt's revolver hung in his gun belt on a bedpost at the foot of the bed. She slowly stood up, backing away from Matt.

"Don't move," McComb said to her. "You're going with me, Jennifer, as soon as I kill Tyler."

"But why?" she asked, taking another step back.

"Because he saved Grant's life."

"And this is his reward?"

"I lost half my men at Shiloh because Grant was still alive and calling the shots."

"You were an officer?"

"Colonel Travis McCandles."

"And you're the one who planned all this?"

"It was a long time coming, and I had to work with fools and lowlifes to get this far. Now Ferman and Mrs. Ledbetter are over there throwing me into the fire, so I have to leave, as soon as I finish Tyler."

"Please, Travis, things will go better for you if you put that gun down."

Matt rose on his left elbow, still dazed. "Let her go."

McComb smiled, glad to see Matt alert and ready to die.

"She's my safe ride out of town. Now get away from him, Jennifer."

She kept backing up, praying he had not noticed the gun belt. "Please, Travis. You can't change anything by doing this."

"Come over here by the door."

Jennifer froze, her mouth so dry it hurt. "Only if you leave Matt alone."

Matt blinked. "She's not going with you."

McComb raised his revolver, aiming at Matt. "Say your prayers, Tyler."

Jennifer gasped, frantic. "Travis, I can't let you do this."

"I missed Grant, but Tyler goes."

"You're blaming Grant," Matt said, "but it was you who kept throwing those boys into our fire. They were slaughtered. Even our men threw up at the sight, but you kept sending them to their death. It's a wonder you had any left. You should have been court-martialed."

McComb lost his concentration, his face red with anger.

Jennifer spun around and grabbed at the gun belt on the bedpost.

McComb fired, the bullet crashing into the holster. She gasped and backed away from it.

Her movement had sent Matt's legs swinging off the bed. He charged right into McComb's weapon.

They crashed against the door as Matt fought for the gun. They spun around.

The weakened Matt struggled against a man of great strength.

Jennifer grabbed the revolver from the gun belt, pulling back the hammer, but she didn't have a clear shot.

McComb, furious, slammed his fist into Matt's face.

Matt kept fighting and pounding at the man's gut with his right hand while gripping the man's gun arm with his left.

They spun around again. Matt threw his weight against McComb. They fell back to the wall, knocking bandages off a shelf, then whirled and dropped to the floor, rolling in a furious grip.

Matt, weak and spent, couldn't stop McComb from cocking his pistol.

Suddenly, McComb turned it toward Matt's middle.

"Stop!" Jennifer said.

McComb turned to see her holding Matt's pistol on him.

McComb laughed shortly, releasing Matt, who collapsed.

On his feet, McComb started toward her.

"You won't shoot me, Jennifer. I'm in love with you."

Staring at him, she knew he was right. Any minute, he would take the weapon from her.

She ran around behind the bed and released the hammer. As McComb came at her, she threw the weapon to Matt, who knelt on the floor.

Catching it in his right hand, Matt sat up and fanned the hammer, just as McComb turned to fire. Both men pulled the trigger at the same time.

McComb missed as Matt rolled aside.

Matt's bullet went dead center.

As McComb grabbed his bloody chest, Jennifer cried out in horror, her hands to her face.

Matt sat up away from the dead man, who fell toward him, then rolled aside as Matt pushed at the body.

Jennifer scurried around the bed, her hands on the railing, tears in her eyes.

The door swung open wide.

Sheriff Hicks came charging inside, followed by a wide-eyed Gentry. Both men had weapons drawn. They paused to stare at the dead McComb.

Hicks holstered his Colt and knelt to check the body.

Then Hicks stood and turned to help the dazed Matt to his feet.

"There's your colonel," Matt said.

"What a waste," Gentry said, shaking his head.

"Now," Matt said, "I can make my report to President Hayes."

"Yeah." Hicks grinned. "Want me to write it for you? I'd give him an earful."

"No, thanks," Matt said. "He won't believe half of what happened, as it is."

Hicks helped Matt sit on the bed.

Deputy Lacey came rushing inside with gun drawn, then drew a deep breath and holstered his weapon. Hicks ordered him to dispose of the body. Lacey dragged the man outside.

Gentry went to shake Matt's hand. "It's all over, Matt."

Then Gentry left to help Lacey outside on the steps.

Matt told the sheriff how Jennifer had thrown the gun to him just in time.

"Well," Hicks said, "she's a real fighter."

Matt held out his hand to Jennifer. She came slowly to his side, her legs weak from the excitement. Gazing down at him, she smiled with tears in her eyes, then bent over to kiss him, her hair flowing about her face and his.

"Well, isn't this a sight?" Grant asked.

She drew back to see Grant standing in the doorway with Eberley and Marshal Brady as Hicks moved aside. The sheriff told them about McComb's identity.

Grant recognized the name at once. "Travis McCandles? Yes, at Pittsburg Landing, near Shiloh. He sacrificed his men to make a name for himself."

"Well, he's paid for it," Matt said.

Grant walked over to smile down at the exhausted Matt, who now lay on his back with his hand on his brow.

"A strange thing happened out there, Matt. I saw some of those Southerners with smiles on their faces. I suspect Silver Gulch and Mountain Springs will be a lot friendlier in the future."

"You could be right," Matt said.

Grant cleared his throat. "I have Witherspoon's watch. It was in Raddigan's pocket. And something else. Mrs. Frost saved my life. She took a bullet in the shoulder. Right now, Major Williams is out there fussing over her like a mother hen."

"A real sight," Marshal Brady said, grinning. "They'll be getting married in Kentucky. He's a goner for sure."

"Mrs. Horton stopped Mrs. Ledbetter from taking a shot at the general," Hicks said. "Landed right on her."

Matt grinned at Hicks. "You'd better marry that woman."

"Yeah, I surprised her and popped the question. She said yes."

Jennifer smiled at the word "surprised."

Grant turned to Matt. "I suppose you'll be back to work soon."

Matt nodded without much enthusiasm.

"You'll be in charge at the office, Matt," said Eberley. "As partner. I plan to take it easy from now on, but we can hire Ted Loring. He just got his ticket. And a couple lawyers I know in Denver. We can dump all the Ferman mess on them."

"Good idea," Matt said.

Grant came closer. "Matt, I have a favor to ask."

"Anything," Matt said.

"I can't take the buckskin on my travels. Maybe you could keep him for me."

"Yes, sir." Matt grinned with delight. "And General Grant, if you could be around to see us married, that would sure make me happy."

"Make it Sunday," Grant said, "and I'll be there."

"Hold on," Jennifer said. "Nobody's asked me."

Matt grabbed her hand. "Will you?"

"Will I what?"

"Will you marry me?"

"I thought we were going to just be friends."

"We can stay friends and still marry, providing you can cook."

"Of course I can cook."

"And no more of those hot editorials."

She made a face. "Don't order me around, Matt Tyler."

"Will you marry me or not?"

"Of course."

"I want ten children."

As she smiled at him, Jennifer already knew she would much rather make a home with Matt and their children than try to make ends meet at the paper and fight for advertising. She'd proven she could do it. She knew her father would rest in peace. Besides, she'd rather hold a baby in her arms than an ink roller.

The paper had killed her father. She didn't want it to kill her.

Somehow, she had to find a new owner.

It took only seconds for Jennifer to find her answer.

She smiled. "I'd like very much if Mr. Eberley would buy my newspaper."

Eberley stared at her. The thought had never occurred to him.

Everyone waited for his response. Eberley pondered the offer.

Abruptly, Eberley smiled. "Great idea."

"Yeah," Matt said. "Jennifer's going to be busy with the kids."

"It's going to keep us both busy," she said. "It's time you men shared the chores."

Matt grinned. "We're kind of useless, you know."

"I'll train you."

Matt gazed at her lovely face and glistening green eyes. Getting older, he had to be flexible. Especially if it meant she would be in his arms every night.

"Well," Grant said, "now that that's settled, let's get on with the celebration. I'm having the time of my life, and I know there's more apple pie out there."

Matt slowly sat up, but he was dizzy. "I'll be right along. Save some pie for me."

Grant reached over and put his hand on Matt's shoulder.

"I'm right proud of you, Matt."

"Thank you, sir."

Grant, emotional, drew back.

"One thing," Hicks said to Eberley. "Make sure when you're writing your editorials, you write so common folks can understand what the heck you're saying."

Eberley nodded, as they all laughed.

"Yeah," Matt said, "don't be quoting the Constitution word for word."

Again they laughed. Eberley smiled and shook Matt's hand.

"Hold on," Matt said, sobering. "Mr. Eberley, with Loring and those two Denver lawyers, you don't need me."

Eberley, startled, shrugged and waited with a smile.

"I've just decided I want to buy some land and raise horses. I got my hands on a real stud." Matt turned to Grant. "OK, General?"

Grant laughed. "Yes, just save me a colt."

"Wait," Jennifer said to Matt. "I'm giving up the newspaper, and you're quitting law, so we can have kids and raise horses?"

They all held their breath, including Matt, who nodded.

Jennifer frowned. "You know what I think?"

Matt couldn't find his voice. He waited.

She smiled with her green eyes shining. "It's a wonderful idea."

All were relieved. Hicks reached over to shake Matt's hand. As did Eberley and Marshal Brady. They left ahead of Grant, who lingered a moment.

Grant raised his right hand in a salute to Matt.

Matt sat as straight as he could. He returned the salute.

"Get your rest," Grant said. "You're going to need it."

Jennifer blushed as the general turned to leave with the others. The door closed behind them.

Matt fought the sudden wet in his eyes. His hero, alive and well, could live forever.

Jennifer helped Matt sit up more comfortably, his legs dangling.

She settled down at his side.

His left arm around her, he drew her up against him.

Her cheeks reddened as he leaned over to kiss her with passion.

Finally, she pulled back, her face so red her freckles looked white.

"Calm down, Matt, and have a little patience."

"Since I met you, I lost every bit of it."

They smiled at each other. They laughed. She reached up and twirled his cowlick back from his face, something she had wanted to do from the first time they met.

He kissed the tip of her turned-up nose.

She cuddled against him. He held her gently.

Together, they could take on the whole world.

THE END

Made in the USA
Charleston, SC
03 November 2015